Acclaim for the novels
of award-winning Anita Mills

Bittersweet

"A sensitive, poignantly written story from
one of the masters of the genre."
—*Romantic Times*

"A wonderful love story."
—*Rendezvous*

Dangerous

"Delightfully funny and heart-warming,
Dangerous is fast-paced and filled with witty
dialogue and laugh-out-loud episodes . . . a
gem of a book from this versatile storyteller."
—*Romantic Times*

Continued on next page . . .

The Duke's Double

Anita Mills

A SIGNET BOOK

SIGNET
Published by New American Library, a division of
Penguin Putnam Inc., 375 Hudson Street,
New York, New York 10014, U.S.A.
Penguin Books Ltd, 27 Wrights Lane,
London W8 5TZ, England
Penguin Books Australia Ltd, Ringwood,
Victoria, Australia
Penguin Books Canada Ltd, 10 Alcorn Avenue,
Toronto, Ontario, Canada M4V 3B2
Penguin Books (N.Z.) Ltd, 182–190 Wairau Road,
Auckland 10, New Zealand

Penguin Books Ltd, Registered Offices:
Harmondsworth, Middlesex, England

First published by Signet, an imprint of New American Library,
a division of Penguin Putnam Inc.

First Printing, February 2000
10 9 8 7 6 5 4 3 2 1

Capri: April, 1816

Joanna Sherwood stared absently, oblivious to the bright sunlight, to the brilliant sky reflected in the deep blue water of the bay below. She and Gary had fled a hostile world to live in exile here, and despite the acute loneliness she felt now, she didn't want to return to England. Gary would have understood. Gary would never have asked her to go back. But dear, sweet, kind Gary was gone. Forever.

"Really, my dear," the sprightly dowager Countess of Carew insisted behind her, "it is of little import *where* you mourn my son, and surely you as a lone gentlewoman with two small boys cannot wish to remain here. It is time you took them back the Haven."

Joanna could feel the lump rising in her throat again. Swallowing it, she closed her eyes. "I cannot—I just cannot."

Her mother-in-law's black silk skirts rustled as she moved about the small drawing room, reasoning gently, "Joanna, nothing can bring Gareth back, and we both know it. As painful as it is to accept that, you have to do so—your concern now must be for your sons, and Justin must grow to manhood conscious of his responsibilities as my son's heir. He is, after all, Earl of Carew now."

"He's only five," Joanna protested.

"My love, he must know that he is English! You cannot rear him in Italy and expect him to learn what it means to be Carew." As her daughter-in-law turned away again, Anne Sherwood lowered her voice to plead, "Please, Joanna, for the love of Gareth—for the love he bore you—don't make exiles of his sons. I beg of you—think of *them*, dearest." When she received no answer, Anne sighed heavily. "Joanna, it is what Gareth would have wanted—I know it. It was different when he was here to support you, but now—well, you know he wouldn't want you alone in this place. And I want my grandsons—both of them—to grow up in England where they belong."

Joanna swung around to face her. "And would you have them learn of the other also, Maman?" she asked bitterly. "Would you have my sons hear that their mother was adjudged guilty of adultery and divorced? Do you really think Gary would have wanted that?"

"Of course not, but at the Haven—"

"If I go back to England, there will be no haven for me—surely you cannot have forgotten how it was."

"*Was*, dearest. But nearly six years have passed since then, and who can say how it will be now?" Reaching out, Anne laid a gentle hand on Joanna's shoulder. "Indeed, but in his letters Gareth often expressed the hope that one day he could bring you home. Now it is up to you to fulfill that hope—I'm asking you to bring him home to lie with his ancestors at the Haven, my dear. For four centuries every Sherwood to hold that land has been laid to rest in the chapel there. I cannot bear the thought that he will spend eternity among strangers."

"I'd like to think he's spending it in heaven," Joanna replied, betraying asperity. "If ever any deserved that, it was Gary." Taking a deep breath, she exhaled slowly.

"But I expect you are right about taking his body home."

"And you will come also?" Anne persisted.

"In time, but not just yet—I'm not ready to face that again."

"But there is nothing to hold you here! As Gareth's widow, you belong at the Haven—as his heirs, Justin and Robin belong there!" Catching herself again, Anne asked softly, "Can you not do this for Gareth? My dear, it is so little to ask when one considers that he gave up everything for you—everything."

"None knows that more than I. But he's gone, Maman."

"And you and the boys are all I have left to love, my dear."

As she looked into Anne's eyes, Joanna couldn't help feeling guilty. As much as Gary's exile had pained her, his mother had never held it against the daughter-in-law she could not have wanted. Not even in the darkest days had Anne Sherwood ever uttered one word of reproach. "But the scandal," she said desperately. "I'd not bring it down on you or my sons."

"All the more reason to make the move *now*, dearest. The sooner you return to the Haven—the sooner the scandal is faced—then the sooner 'twill be lived down. Listen to me—new *on-dits* replace old ones all the time, Joanna. Oh, I daresay the unpleasant gossip may be revived for the moment, but circumspection on your part will surely cause it to die down. The *ton* will forget the tale in time."

"Will they?" Joanna looked away. "I very much doubt that," she said low. "How could they? Adrian brought public charges against me—he saw to it that I shall never be received anywhere in England again. And what of Justin? Would you have him know?"

"Right now he's too young to understand."

"And later?"

"It will be forgotten long before then," Anne predicted. "And who is to say that you will not wed again? With your looks and Gareth's fortune, I am sure—"

"And who, pray tell, is to have me—some gazetted fortune hunter whose need for money outweighs his sense of propriety? No. That will not happen, Maman—Adrian has seen to that. The day that Parliament passed the bill of divorcement, I was branded for life. And it won't be forgotten, for the Haven is too close to the Armitage."

"He's never there. He won't even know you've come home."

"Never there?" Betraying her disbelief with a lifted eyebrow, Joanna declared, "The Armitage was the great love of his life, I assure you. As seat of the Roxbury dukes, it was the symbol of his consequence, and he lavished attention on the place."

"Well, whether from shame or pride, he's not been back since the divorce. I expect the scandal may have had something to do with his absence."

"Roxbury *caused* the scandal. And of all the things one can say of Adrian Delacourt, one cannot say he suffers from the least sensibility."

"Well, I never believed he meant to create such a dust. I blame his mother for that."

"Helen?" Again the disbelieving eyebrow. "While she told the tale, he did not have to credit it, did he? I was his wife—he could have at least asked me if it was true, which he did not. If he'd ever loved me, he would have asked," Joanna declared, betraying her bitterness again. "Instead, he chose to disgrace me before the world."

Afraid she'd bungled the matter by mentioning Roxbury, Anne said soothingly, "And I'm telling you he's not shown his face in the neighborhood since. Besides,

I'm sure I have as much credit as he does, and I mean to make it plain to every gossiping biddy in the parish that I never believed the tale in the first place. I watched you grow up, Jo—all three of you—Gareth, Adrian, and you—all of you ran tame in my house. I saw my son fall in love with you—I know there was no dishonor there, and if I must shout it from the rooftops, I shall."

"You're very much like Gary—you've always been very kind to me." Turning away, Joanna looked out the window again, this time to the courtyard directly beneath her. Everything was so green, so vibrant, so very bright in contrast to the gloom in her heart. It was as though the world either didn't understand or didn't care that her life was in shambles. Again.

Holding her tongue, Anne waited, watching, thinking what a fool Roxbury had been. Joanna Milford had been a Diamond of the First Water in her Season, and a dozen men, including Gareth, had come up to scratch despite her lack of fortune. A mere baron's daughter, Joanna had chosen Roxbury, and they had married before the end of the Season, only to be divorced within the year. The charge against her had been adultery with Gareth, who'd been Adrian's best friend, and as the scandal broke, Gareth'd lent credence to the tale by standing with her. Indeed, within days after the bill of divorcement had passed, Gareth had taken her to Italy, where he'd married her, writing to Anne after the wedding, saying, "Today I must surely be the happiest man on this Earth," a sentiment echoed in nearly every letter since then. And when it had been Joanna's turn to write of the terrible boating accident that had taken his life, she'd said, "Gary was without doubt the best friend, husband, and father that anyone could have asked, and I will miss him to the end of my life."

Surprisingly, scandal and tragedy had failed to mar

Joanna's incredible beauty. She still had that thick wheat-gold hair, expressive cerulean blue eyes, delicate, perfectly sculptured nose and chin, and the same exquisite figure that had made her the toast of London in her Season. Despite the fact she was still in mourning, there'd been no dearth of hopeful Italian noblemen eager to take Gareth's place, making it even more imperative to Anne that she return home.

In the small, gated courtyard below, the Italian governess sat watching Justin and Robin Sherwood sail paper boats in the fountain pool. The older boy blew his across the water, while his three-year-old brother shouted encouragement at the bobbing craft. Both boys were extremely handsome in different ways—Justin tall for his five years, with nearly black hair and dark, dark brown eyes, Robin stockier with a mass of red-gold curls and beautiful blue eyes. Even as Joanna studied her sons, the little boat capsized, and Justin snatched it from the water. Flinging it to the ground, he burst into tears and buried his head in the governess's skirt. Her heart aching for him, Joanna fought the urge to run down and scoop him up in her arms In another two months, Gary would have been gone a year, and yet her elder son still grieved intensely for him. It seemed as though every day something reminded him of his loss, and the tiny size of the island made such memories impossible to escape.

She sighed, thinking how this small place had sheltered her from the unpleasantness not only of a condemning *ton* but also of a world gone mad with war. She'd shared this villa with Gary, and her sons had been born here in the shadow of Mount Solaro. Nearly a thousand evenings had been spent walking the narrow beach bordering the bay with the kindest husband any woman could ever hope to have, but now that same bright seawater had come to hold naught but anguish to a boy too young to understand why it had taken his father from him. And time had been exceedingly slow to ease his pain. As she watched him from the window, she had to concede it was probably her own selfishness that had kept her and her sons here. The choice between Justin's anguish here and hers in England was not an easy one, but despite all her protests to the contrary, she knew in her heart that Anne was right.

"He is certain to be remarked," she murmured, thinking aloud.

"I am sure he will," Anne agreed mildly.

"You are quite certain that Adrian never goes home to the Armitage?"

"Not once in these past six years."

"Well, I suppose I should not be required to go about much," Joanna mused finally. "Indeed, I doubt I should be asked anywhere."

Sensing victory, Anne smiled. "My dear, if I have any say in the matter, you'll never regret this."

As the young governess consoled her son with soft Italian words, Joanna felt as though her own heart would break again. "All right," she decided reluctantly, "I'll take them back to England. Perhaps Justin will not miss Gary so much there." Turning to face Anne Sherwood, she forced her own twisted smile. "I just hope you are right about Roxbury, for I don't think I could bear to see him again—not now, not ever."

The Armitage: Early June, 1816

As her son paced the breadth of his library, his hands held loosely at his back, Helen Delacourt folded the paper she had been reading and looked up in exasperation. "Adrian, I wish you would sit down," she remarked irritably. "You remind me of one of those caged animals in the Royal Menagerie."

"I still fail to see the need to entertain Almeria here," he snapped back.

"It is only fitting that she should visit your principal seat," the dowager answered in a more reasonable tone. " 'Tis past time you came up to scratch and offered for her, and you know it. Unlike that other creature, dear Almeria is everything I could wish for in your duchess."

"So you have said a hundred times," he reminded her. "Nonetheless, madam, it was not your place to invite her here with neither my knowledge nor my approval. Had I known of your little ploy, I should have stayed in London."

"With your Cyprians?" she asked archly. "Don't you think it time you looked to your nursery?"

"That is my business, Mother—not yours."

"Adrian, the Armitage needs your attention," she argued, sighing. "Every Roxbury duke for the past two hundred years has lived here—and nine Roxbury earls before them, not to mention every Delacourt since Henry VII rewarded Lord Richard with the Esmonde heiress after he distinguished himself at Bosworth. You have a duty to your line. You surely cannot mean to let your bloodline die out."

"No, of course not. But I'm not interested in tending to that matter just now."

"Nor to anything else, it would seem. You've not bought so much as one new drapery since that woman left."

"I've not lived here since—nor do I ever intend to do so again," he reminded her bitterly, biting off each word. "I've come to hate every inch of the place."

"Because of the Milford witch, which is pure silliness on your part, I say—as if she ever cared for this house or anything in it," Helen said, sniffing. "No, all she wanted was your consequence, Adrian, and even that was not enough to—"

"I thought I'd made it plain that I would not discuss Joanna—not then . . . not now . . . not *ever*," he declared, interrupting her.

Undeterred, his mother persisted with, "Well, I knew it was a mistake when you married her, after all. All looks and no breeding, and so I told you at the time. But no—'twas little Joanna Milford or none—a nobody, Adrian—daughter of a mere baron!"

"I said I've no wish to discuss her."

"No, of course you wouldn't. Not after the way she and Carew carried on their little affair right under your nose," she reminded him nastily. "I cannot think you would wish to remember how they cuckolded you. But then I am sure I never understood what you *or* Gareth Sherwood saw in the scheming little minx."

"I think," he managed stiffly, "that the discussion

was why I must needs entertain Almeria Bennington here. I am by no means certain that I—"

"Adrian," she cut in purposefully, "you are nigh thirty. If I may repeat myself, 'tis time you took a suitable wife and looked to your succession. Surely I have made myself plain on that head."

"In every way possible." He stopped pacing in front of her and fixed her with very dark eyes. "You are set on this marriage, aren't you?"

"I am. The girl has looks, money, and breeding. I'm sure you could have no complaint of her."

"I've no need to hang out for a rich wife," he reminded her. "I believe I've been able to keep everything Papa left me—all seventy thousand pounds of it. In fact, I've even been fortunate enough to improve on the sum."

"One cannot have too much money, Adrian."

"I don't care a snap of my fingers for Almeria Bennington. I'm not even certain there is an intellect behind that perfectly controlled facade of hers."

"Well, you cannot be said to favor any other, can you? And she would certainly show to advantage, you cannot deny that. You once wished a career in politics, did you not?"

"That was a long time ago."

"Almeria would make an exquisite hostess."

"She's an ice maiden," he muttered.

"She certainly has more breeding than that shameless jade you wed the first time," she shot back. "Unlike Joanna Milford, I'm certain that she will understand her responsibility to the name you give her."

"I'm not giving Miss Bennington my name," he managed through clenched teeth. "And for the last time, I've *no* wish to discuss my wife!"

"Your *former wife*," Helen corrected him. "I believe she is a Sherwood now—though I'm sure Anne was no happier to see Gareth throw himself away on Joanna Milford than I was when you offered for her. First a duchess, then a countess—what an overreaching creature your dear Joanna was, wasn't she?"

His face darkened, and his fists clenched. Too furious for words, he turned on his heels and strode out of the room as she called after him, "Wait! Adrian, where are you going? We've got to plan for Almeria!"

"Riding!" he shouted, flinging the word over his shoulder.

The dowager sank back in her chair and shook her head. She'd probed the old wound and found that it still festered beneath a scab of denial. Well, a more suitable wife would cure that, she told herself. And in the coldly beautiful Almeria, she recognized a determined ally, for beneath that imperturbable facade was a girl whose desire to be a duchess was paramount. Yes, this time she'd have a daughter-in-law worthy of the Delacourt name.

Her gaze traveled to the blank place over the mantel where Joanna's portrait had once hung. It was time to put another there, and the sooner the better, for she'd been uneasy ever since word had come that Gareth Sherwood had drowned last year off the coast of Italy. And now an unsettling rumor had it that Anne's man of business was busying himself refurbishing the Haven. Well, if Joanna did dare to show herself in England again, she was going to find Adrian safely leg-shackled, Helen promised herself.

She turned her head to the fireplace positioned exactly opposite the first one and stared for a long moment at the full-length portrait of her son. It did not do him justice, of course, but then, nothing could quite capture Adrian as he was, certainly not canvas, anyway. Oh, it was easy to see from the painting that he was a handsome man—tall, well-shouldered, and muscular with-

out being ungentlemanly in appearance, with black
hair that curled just enough to give him naturally what
many a Corinthian spent hours to achieve, and dark
eyes that seemed to pierce one when he stared. He was
the sort of man that women universally found attractive, and yet, with the exception of the muslin company, he'd shown no interest in any of them since his
divorce from Joanna Milford.

Four years younger than Adrian, that scheming little
minx had nonetheless managed to gain his notice when
she could not have been above thirteen or fourteen,
and once he'd thrown his hat over the windmill for her,
there'd been no other. She should have seen it, Helen
supposed, but it had never occurred to her that Adrian
could be so lost to what he owed his blood that he
could see the Milford chit in her place.

Joanna. Helen stared absently for a moment, pursing
her lips in disapproval, then she sighed. She'd thought
she'd cured him of his reckless passion once and for
all, but now she was not so sure. Despite the terrible
wound to his pride, he still couldn't even bear the mention of the woman's name, making it even more imperative that he come up to scratch for Almeria. And soon.

The Haven: June 22, 1816

Servants bustled about removing holland covers from the furniture, and the place abounded with the sounds and smells of extensive refurbishing. Carpenters hammered, new plaster moldings dried, and the odor of fresh paint permeated the air. Joanna inspected work begun before her arrival and then repaired to the small study that had been Gary's to take stock of her new life by poring over the estate's books. While money had never been a consideration, only now did she realize the enormity of the fortune he'd left her. She was, by any account, a very wealthy widow.

"Mama! Mama!"

She looked up to see her elder son barreling into the room with his new governess, Miss Finchley, in pursuit. By the harried look of the young woman, Joanna could tell that the young earl was in the suds. Amused, she nonetheless schooled her voice to ask sternly, "And just what is it that you've done this time, young man?"

Justin Sherwood stopped short and his face colored guiltily. Not waiting for him to answer, the governess caught him by the hand while apologizing, "Your pardon, my lady, for the intrusion. I assure you that the matter is quite in hand."

"Yes, I can see it is," Joanna responded with a hint of a smile. "I collect you meant to give him a scold and he ran away." Fixing the boy with her best parental stare, she demanded, "Well, Justin?"

When he murmured something totally unintelligible in a low voice, Miss Finchley felt it incumbent to blurt out, " 'Tis nothing, madam, except that he mixed all the watercolors together, and now they are quite ruined. But I daresay I can send to town for another set."

"All the colors, Justin?" Joanna asked. "Why?"

"Merely boyish mischief," the governess answered for him.

He looked up and his dark eyes flashed briefly. "Fustian, Finch!" he retorted stoutly. "I did it 'cause I wanted to see what color they'd be." He faced his mother and squared his shoulders. "She told us that blue and yellow would make green, Mama, so I wanted to see what all of them would do."

"I see." Joanna nodded gravely. "And what did you get?"

"Ugly."

"Perhaps you ought to have asked first, don't you think? Then Miss Finchley could have advised you not to do it." She leaned closer and brushed back an errant lock of dark hair from his forehead. "You knew to ask, did you not?"

"Yes," came the sullen reply.

"What do you think I should do about it?" she asked gently. "If you were me, what would you do?"

"Birch me," he answered without hesitation.

She appeared to consider the matter for a moment and then shook her head. "No. If you had asked and then deliberately disobeyed Miss Finchley, I should birch you, of course, but as that is not the case, I shall not. Instead, I think you should apologize to Miss

Finchley for not asking, and to your brother for destroying his paints."

Relief flooded over the small boy's face. "Your pardon, Finch. I did not mean to ruin them, I promise."

"And I accept your apology, Justin," the governess responded with a smile. "If you will but ask when you want to know something I have not said, we shall get on very well."

"Now, my son, you need to find Robin and the matter is settled," Joanna prompted. "Go on—do it and you will feel better, I promise. Then you may come back and we shall do something together, just you and I."

Both women watched him go and shook their heads. "I've taught a number of young boys, Lady Carew," the governess observed slowly, "but none like his lordship. He's so . . ." She groped for a word to describe her meaning. "Well, he's so . . . sober. Well, perhaps not that precisely, but . . ."

"I know," Joanna agreed, sighing.

"Of course one cannot blame him," Miss Finchley added judiciously, "for it is no small thing to lose a parent. Yet one would think that at his age he would recover soon. It has been some time, hasn't it?"

"Nearly a year." Joanna stared absently at the open door for a moment and then collected herself. "It's not an easy task to see that he does not forget Gareth and yet ease the pain at the same time." Turning back to the governess, she added, "They adored each other from his birth, you see, and Gary was forever amusing him with stories and taking him places." Her face clouded with memories of her own still too painful to recall, and she found herself wiping her eyes. "My husband was an exceedingly good man."

"I am sorry, madam," the governess sympathized. "I should not have broached the subject."

"No—I am quite all right, I assure you. 'Tis just that no one can ever know just how truly wonderful he was—I was so very fortunate to have known him." Joanna gulped and sniffed as she took a handkerchief from the pocket of her plain blue day gown and blew her nose. " 'Tis I who should apologize to you, my dear, for being so blue-deviled." Turning the subject back to her son, she smiled tremulously. "He is doing well otherwise, is he not?"

"I have never seen his like, Lady Carew—truly I have not. For one so very young, he has an exceptional understanding of things. He knows all the names of his watercolors, can work with simple sums, and can read far better than many several years older than he. Indeed, he does prodigiously well. Now, Master Robert is not nearly so bright and inquisitive, but at three years, he is still little more than a babe."

"Master Robin will be a shameless scapegrace, I fear—much more like me than Justin is."

"Oh, I did not mean—"

"Of course you did not, but 'tis true nonetheless. Justin will be a brilliant scholar and probably have a career in Parliament, while Robin will get into one scrape after another. I was a hopeless hoyden myself until—"

"Mama!" Justin Sherwood stopped short when he realized that Miss Finchley was still with his mother. "Your pardon for running in the house, Mama," he finished lamely.

Joanna stuffed her handkerchief back in her pocket and forced herself to smile brightly. "So long as you know better and will work on the problem, my love, you are forgiven. And if Miss Finchley can be persuaded to give you leave from your tasks today, I thought that you and I might walk where I played when I was but a few years older than you are. We had a fort, you see, and when I was very good, the boys would let me stand sentry for them."

"A fort! Did they have guns?" he demanded enthusiastically.

"Alas, they had the same guns you have, but sticks worked remarkably well for them too." She reached to ruffle his dark hair affectionately. "As I recall, your papa and—and his friend—stood off armies all the time."

"When? When can we go, Mama?" His dark eyes shone with more life than she'd seen in months.

Joanna looked over his head to the governess. "Well, Miss Finchley, what do you think?" she asked conspiratorially. "Can he be spared from his studies today?"

"Oh, I should think it would not be harmful in the least, madam. I shall merely take the opportunity to practice counting with Master Robert."

"Capital! I say, Finch, but you are a great gun, too!"

"Then 'tis settled," Joanna declared. "I shall have Cook pack a small nuncheon for us, and we'll be on our way. Three manors march together where I used to play, so you can see from the river where I grew up."

"Can we go there too, Mama?"

Her smile fading, she hesitated before answering, "No, Justin—not today." Changing the subject abruptly, she said, "You'd best go put on a sturdy pair of shoes, for it is quite a walk."

"I'll be right back," he promised.

As he and his governess left it, Anne came into the room. "Well, you've certainly brightened his spirits," she observed.

"We're going on a picnic—just the two of us. And once Justin lets that cat out of the bag, I daresay Miss Finchley will have her hands full with Robin."

"She seems quite competent for one so young, doesn't she? Though I must say I find it sad that such a pretty girl must spend her days trying to drum sums into my grandsons. She *is* quite pretty, you know, but if I had those riotous auburn curls, I should have them fashionably cropped rather than bundled into that ugly knot. The effect that would have on those lovely hazel eyes must surely be devastating, don't you think?"

"Yes, but no doubt she's already discovered her looks to be a detriment to respectable employment. I daresay she thinks she must make herself as plain as possible to keep her position."

"But she had such a good character from Lady Rivington, did she not?"

"Indeed. But judging by the excessive praise, I'd say there was a decided overeagerness to see her situated elsewhere," Joanna observed, smiling. "However, having met Lord Rivington once myself, I expect the poor girl had to duck and dodge him at every turn. So their loss is my gain, don't you think?"

"Indubitably, my dear. I've not the least complaint, though I can quite see if one has a husband with a roving eye, Miss Finchley must surely be counted a rival. In your case, however, that observation need not apply, for you are a Diamond of the First Water yourself."

"Not anymore, I'm afraid."

"Nonsense, my dear. Your mirror ought to tell you differently. You could still cast all the girls on the Marriage Mart into the shade."

"You are very kind, but I'm afraid that part of my life is over, Maman. And therefore I don't happen to begrudge Miss Finchley her looks in the least," Joanna added lightly. "Well, I had best see to the packing of our nuncheon, else Justin will be peckish before we even set off."

A brief stop in the kitchen yielded the promised food, and soon mother and son were on their way to explore the familiar paths of Joanna's childhood. The sun had dried the last vestiges of an early-morning shower, and the air was fresh and sweet with the smell of meadow grass and wildflowers. They walked slowly to allow for the child's shorter steps and rested frequently while he plied her with a spate of questions ranging from what each flower was to whether his father had climbed this tree or that one. After a rest at the crest of a grassy hill and the consumption of most of the bread, cheese, and fruit they carried, they abandoned the hamper under a tree and trudged on, hand in hand.

A rabbit broke from a thicket and crossed the clearing in front of them to the delight of the boy, who wanted to chase after it. But Joanna drew up suddenly at the sound of gunshots somewhere in the distance.

"It must be the warden," she decided aloud.

"Where, Mama? What's over there, Mama? Do you think they're hunting for that rabbit? I hope not, 'cause he's a pretty fellow."

"No, of course not," she reassured him. " 'Tis too far, for one thing, and besides, I don't think anyone hunts over there anymore."

"Over where?"

"The Armitage. It's a place across the river."

"I want to see, 'cause I heard it, too." He tugged on her hand, pulling her. "Come on, Mama—let's go there."

"There's nothing to see, Justin—I promise you there's not. Besides, it's time we were getting back."

"You said you'd show me where there's three manors," he reminded her mutinously. "You did—you promised it."

"Justin—"

"Please, Mama—please. I don't want to go back—I don't. I want to see it, Mama."

Her enthusiasm dampened by the reminder of how close she was to the place she most wished to forget, she hesitated. She'd thought the years would have erased the bitterness and the pain, but they hadn't. A pang of loss stabbed her between her breasts. "No, I don't think so, dearest—not today, anyway," she answered evasively.

"But Papa would have shown me—I know he would. You said you would," he persisted plaintively. "You promised to show me your fort."

She stared down at her son and felt guilty at his disappointment. It was, after all, to cheer him up that she'd undertaken this little expedition, and now she was stopping short of her promise. Besides, she was a twenty-five-year-old woman and not some silly romantic girl, she chided herself, and her response to the old familiar places was unreasonable. She'd chosen to come back, and the sooner she faced her own losses, the sooner she could deal with his. She squeezed his hand and managed a quick smile.

"So I did, dearest, and I think I can still find it. If I remember it aright, 'tis but over the next hill and above a spring-fed river that divides the properties there. When you reach the place we had our castle, Justin, you can see the chimneys of Winton Abbey, where I was born, and then if you follow the river to the south, there is the Armitage."

"Can I see where you were borned?" he asked innocently.

"Born," she corrected him. "And, no—not today, I'm afraid."

"But why? If you was born there—"

Unwilling to tell him that she'd been disowned by her own father, Joanna just shook her head. "Because we cannot."

"But—"

"Would you like to race me to the top of the hill?" she asked, hoping to change the subject.

For answer, he dropped her hand and ran pell-mell ahead of her, zigging and zagging up the path as fast as his young legs could carry him. She lifted her skirts indecorously and ran after him, taking care not to outdistance him before he reached the top. At the crest, he turned around triumphantly.

"I won!"

"Well, ladies do not generally run, you know."

"I know, but Papa said you was a great gun for a lady."

"He did?"

"Uh-huh—said you was the best ever."

"That sounds like your papa."

His dark eyes sparkled suddenly and his chin quivered dangerously. She dropped to her knees and enveloped him against her as his face crumpled piteously. "I want my papa!" he cried out. "I hate the sea—I hate it!"

"Shhhhh, dearest," she soothed helplessly. "I miss Gary too, but we cannot cry forever, you know. Indeed, but Papa would not wish you to, Justin." She rubbed the thick dark hair, caressing it with her fingers and smoothing it back from his face. "Listen to me, my son—Gary would want you to be strong for me and for your brother. Robin hurts too, but he is too little to even know exactly why he hurts."

"Papa loved me best!"

"No, he did not, Justin, and you must never say that to Robin. It will be difficult enough for him to even remember Gary, so you must not make him think he was not loved, too. Gary loved both of you."

"But he did more things with me."

"Of course he did, but that was because you were older. Now, come on, and I will show you where your papa manned the ramparts against Viking invaders." She set him back and dabbed at his tear-streaked face with her well-crumpled kerchief. "You'll have to pretend you see them."

The place was much as she'd remembered it—the old logs still lay at angles, forming what she and Gareth and Adrian had dubbed variously their fort and their castle, depending on whether they were fending off pirates, Vikings, or knightly besiegers. Even the tall, spreading tree that sheltered their childhood treasures was still there. Her eyes traveled over the familiar things, and memories of a far happier time flooded over her.

"Did you know Papa when he was as old as I am?"

"Huh?" Reluctantly she returned to the present to answer, "When your papa was your age, Justin, I'm afraid I was just learning to walk. I was even younger than Robin. It was not until I was a little older than you that I really came to know either of the boys, and then it was because my governess married the Delacourt tutor. When they were courting, they'd come here to talk, and we were left to our own devices, with none of our parents the wiser."

"That was stoopid."

"Oh, I don't know—they had a very real regard for each other, Justin. And it gave me a chance to know your Papa and the duke, which probably wouldn't have happened otherwise. In the ordinary way of things, I would have had to wait until I was old enough to be properly introduced to them, probably at some dance. As it was, I think the boys let me trail after them just to get out of their lessons," she reminisced. Pointing, she told him, "Miss Satterly and Mr. Bates used to meet over there and send us off to play while he read poetry to her and talked a great deal of nonsense. They courted for years, of course, because neither had enough expectations to marry at the time. Finally an old uncle of his left him a small sum and they ran off together to Scotland."

"It still sounds stoopid."

"It was very touching, I assure you, and it gave me the opportunity to play exciting games with Gary and Adrian rather than sitting primly at home learning watercolors and needlework like other girls did. And my papa did not even notice, for he was far too busy trying to find an heiress to fix his rackety fortunes after my mama died. He was seldom home, of course, because all the ladies around this neighborhood knew he hadn't a feather to fly with."

The explanation was too much for a five-year-old boy. He broke away and clambered over the logs, exhibiting an imagination that rivaled Gary's and Adrian's. Brandishing a stick like a sword, he shouted challenges to imaginary foes, daring them to attack. Watching him, Joanna's thoughts turned to another, nearly forgotten time when it was she and Adrian and Gary taunting imaginary invaders. Of course, Adrian always had the ordering of their defenses because he was a duke and Gary was an earl. Even then, rank had its privilege, as she recalled. But they made an exception for her, forgetting she was a mere baron's daughter by making her a princess they had to defend from the marauders. Gary had even made her a paper crown.

She looked over to where they'd once eaten many a small nuncheon away from the courting teachers. The old fallen tree trunk was still there, barkless and bleached gray by years of exposure. Drawn to it, she made her way over to sit once again where she'd spent so many happy days in her youth. Pulling her legs up on the log, she clasped her knees and stared absently, listening to echoes of a forgotten past.

Adrian had been so tall for his age, towering over both Gary and her, so he was always Robin Hood or King Richard or King Arthur. And the irony wasn't lost on her that she'd once played Guinevere and Gary had pretended to be Sir Lancelot, an ill omen of things to come. No, none of that bore thinking now, she reminded herself as the old bitterness welled within. She'd rather remember happier times, times when all three of them had been friends.

Still, as she sat there, she recalled that last day before the boys had gone away to school. Running to escape an imaginary Hun, she'd tripped over this log and scraped her leg badly, tearing her stocking and bloodying her dress. Gary had washed the wound for her matter-of-factly, soothing her tears while Adrian had stood there looking down on the forbidden sight of her bared leg with that odd expression on his face. She'd been thirteen then, she remembered. And it had been another several years before she came to recognize that look as desire.

Resolutely Joanna tore herself away from those memories and turned her attention toward their secret hiding place, a hollowed-out pit at the base of a huge spreading tree. There they had once kept the treasures of childhood, the silly things that appealed to them then. The tree still stood, but the dead grass and twigs that once covered the place had long since decayed and returned to the earth. She slid off the log and walked to dig curiously in the damp forest earth with the toe of her sturdy walking shoe.

The box was still there—she could feel it. Dropping to kneel in the sparse grass, she picked up a stick and began unearthing it. When a corner of the rusted tin showed, she eagerly dug beneath it and then levered it out. An earthworm dwelling in the soft ground under the box slithered to disappear into a moist clump of dirt. At once curious and eager, she worked the hasp open to stare in fascination at the long-forgotten keepsakes they'd once buried as pirate treasure.

The enamel on Gary's father's snuffbox was still bright in contrast to the heavily tarnished silver surrounding it. She lifted it out and turned it over in her hand, remembering how proud Gary had been when his father, the seemingly distant Earl of Carew, had given it to him rather than merely discarding it. And there was Adrian's broken watch chain gleaming against scraps of faded paper laid over a yellowed envelope.

And there was her own contribution—the locket her mother'd given her shortly before she'd died was mottled from changes in temperature, but it was still intact. Laying aside the snuffbox, Joanna picked up the locket and carefully opened it, revealing the painted miniature inside. Staring at her mother's beautiful face, she had to swallow the lump rising in her throat. How could she have ever buried this? She supposed now she'd done it to deny the pain and the anger of that terrible, unbearable loss. Closing the locket, she slipped it into her pocket. She was ready to cherish it now.

Deliberately ignoring the faded envelope, she turned

her attention to the papers. There was their compact, the agreement they'd signed among the three of them when they'd promised to be friends forever and meet again on her eighteenth birthday. It had been drawn up to stop her tears when she'd found out they were going off to Eton. In it, they'd both agreed to write every week. A faint smile crossed her face as she remembered that Gary had kept his promise while Adrian had failed her in that, too. Indeed, after the first month or so, his letters had grown so scarce that she'd been certain he'd forgotten her.

Until her come-out. Closing her eyes, she allowed herself to remember that starry May night in London. When her Aunt Kate had sent out the invitations, it'd been so long since she'd seen him that Joanna had been certain Adrian Delacourt wouldn't bother to attend such a small, shabby party. But when he'd come through the receiving line that night, she'd been instantly struck by how strikingly handsome he was, how sophisticated he'd become, and she'd heard the gasps of her envious cousins, their whispers that "Roxbury's heir makes our little nobody into somebody with his presence here."

And what a triumph it had been. Adrian Delacourt had danced with her not once but *four* times, demonstrating a particularity that had shocked everyone in attendance, and before the night was over, he'd drawn her into her aunt's garden, where he'd stunned her by offering for her. She could still smell the fragrance of the flowers when he'd first kissed her and told her that he'd been waiting for her to grow up. That kiss had ignited a passion that she'd never even suspected existed, and from that moment, she'd been utterly, completely in love with him.

Poor Gary. He'd had the misfortune to offer that same night, and while he'd taken her declaration of love for Adrian quite calmly, he hadn't been able to hide the pain, the disappointment she saw in those beautiful hazel eyes. He'd wished her happy, of course, saying that if he couldn't be her husband, he hoped he could still be her friend. And he'd been Adrian's chief supporter at her wedding.

Ah, how could she not have known that good, kind, gentle Gary was to prove himself the better of the two? She'd just been blinded, utterly mesmerized by Adrian at the time. Not that Gary was not a handsome man himself, for the young Earl of Carew cut quite a dashing figure, and at least a dozen beauties had cast out lures to him that Season, she recalled wryly. But Adrian—well, Adrian was exciting—darkly handsome and volatile. In the end, it had been that volatility that had broken her heart.

She'd lost them both in very different ways, and the pain of each loss was too acute to bear. As she thought of them, the ache in her chest cut like a knife against her breastbone still. Tears coursed unnoticed and unchecked down her cheeks as she silently refolded the paper and put it back with the watch chain and the snuffbox. Laying the tin where she'd found it, she stood and pushed the clods of earth over it with her foot. Brushing the dirt from her hands on the skirt of her gown, she turned around.

"It's—it's getting late, Justin," she managed to choke out. After taking a deep breath, she mastered herself. "We'd best be getting back before Robin gets worried."

There was no answer and no sign of the boy who'd been so bravely swinging his stick sword a few moments before. He was hiding to jump out at her, she supposed, and she was in no mood for games. "Come on, Justin—we've got to go," she called out. She waited expectantly, but there was no answer. "Justin, where are you?" It was not really like him to tease her, and certainly not like him to ignore her. She walked back to the log fort. "Do not be playing with Mama, Justin— come on, 'tis late."

There was no sound at all, and Joanna realized she was alone. Alarmed, she climbed up on the logs and called out, "Justin! Justin!" The cry echoed ominously without answer. "Justin!"

He must have wandered off while she'd sat too absorbed in her own reverie to notice or to hear him. A frantic survey of the area gave not a clue to his direction and left her frightened. He would not have gone back without her, and yet he was unfamiliar with the area. The little clearing where she stood was bounded by woods, and beyond that lay the river that divided the Haven from Winton Abbey and the Armitage. He'd been curious about Winton Abbey, but surely he would not have ventured that direction after she'd told him that they could not go there.

Her heart pounding now, Joanna listened for him, hearing nothing. Suddenly, the silence was broken by more shots, and it sounded as though they came from the Armitage side. Dear God, but a boy could not wander where men hunted! Gathering her skirt above her ankles, she ran toward the sound, her only thoughts that she had to stop them before Justin got hurt, that no matter what Roxbury thought of her, his bailiff or warden couldn't refuse to help a little boy. She emerged from the woods above where the river was shallow and a ford had been filled in to facilitate travel between the estates in friendlier times. Another shot rang out close by. Too close.

"Wait! Help! Do not fire!" she screamed as she ran tripping across the ford, heedless of the muddy water seeping through her shoes.

Brush crackled as booted feet cut through it, and then two men emerged in response to her cries. She drew up suddenly and her hands flew to her face in dismay.

"*You!*" she gasped. "Oh, no!"

"Jo." The word formed silently on Adrian Delacourt's lips as he stared, too stunned to speak.

His companion looked from one to the other, puzzled by the shocked disbelief on both faces. Remembering that she'd called for help, he stepped forward. "Er—perhaps I can be of assistance," he ventured, breaking the awkward silence.

Unwilling to look at Adrian, Joanna turned gratefully to the other man. "You have not seen a small boy, have you, sir? My son wandered off somewhere, and when I heard shots, I was afraid he might be mistaken for game before he could be seen." Her gaze dropped to the hunting piece he carried, and she added with visible relief, "I see it was you I heard."

"We've been in the area only a short while," Johnny answered. God, but the woman was beautiful, too beautiful to be wandering in the woods alone. Recalling himself, he assured her quickly, "However, you find us ready to aid in the search, ma'am."

Joanna gazed up into a very fine pair of gray eyes situated in a strong, well-defined, and quite handsome face. Too distracted to take in the excellent cut of his shooting jacket, the perfect fit of his breeches, or the unmistakable fit of Hoby's boots, she failed to be impressed, piquing his interest even further. The Corinthian flashed her a winning smile.

"Barrasford—John Barrasford at your service, ma'am. If you will but describe the boy, Roxbury and I will comb these woods for him while you wait here. I cannot think he has wandered far, given the lay of the land."

"No!" Adrian spat out. "I won't have her here!"

"I say, Roxbury!" Barrasford protested. "Surely you

cannot wish a child to wander alone in a place like this, after all. But if you won't go, I will." Turning again to Joanna, he said, "I apologize for the duke's sad want of manners," adding, "I'll get my horse and ride along the bank first and then cut back through the woods. It would be helpful, however, if you could give me some idea of his direction as this is a deuced big place."

She shook her head. "He wandered off while I was preoccupied with something else. But if you can take this side, I'll go back and retrace the way I came, sir. Perhaps he will have returned to where we were."

"Done," Barrasford agreed. He started to leave, then turned back to ask, "The name—what should I call him?"

"Justin—Justin Sherwood. He is but a small boy, sir, not yet six—but he's unafraid of strangers."

Out of the corner of her eye she could see Adrian Delacourt stiffen and then turn away. Without a word, he stalked back into the thicket. Lord Barrasford shook his head.

"I don't know what maggot's got into his brain today, Lady Sherwood," he murmured apologetically. "Usually Roxbury's not given to such queer starts."

She sucked in her breath and prepared for the worst. "I am not Lady Sherwood precisely, sir—I am Lady Carew. my husband was Gareth Sherwood, the late earl. I was widowed last summer."

The name appeared to mean nothing to him. "I am sorry—I'm afraid I didn't have the pleasure of his acquaintance. I'm afraid I spent a great deal of my time in Ireland—Irish title, you know," he explained somewhat wryly. Returning to the matter at hand, he told her, "If I don't find the boy, I'll cross over when I've covered this side. If I do see him, I'll fire my gun twice into the air to let you know of it."

"Thank you, sir."

Johnny walked back to his horse and swung up into the saddle. There was no sign of his hunting companion. Odd, but he'd never thought Roxbury such a dolt when it came to beautiful women, he mused, turning the horse toward the river's bank. Well, it was just as well, he supposed, for Lady Carew had piqued his interest, and he'd hate to have the duke for a rival in that quarter. When he'd come here, it'd been to acquaint himself with a new piece of property he'd acquired at the gaming tables, a respite from the Season's matchmaking mamas and their insipid daughters. But this surprise encounter with the young countess suddenly made his summer look quite promising. Now all he had to do was find the boy.

Dispirited over Justin's disappearance and very disturbed by her chance encounter with Adrian, Joanna walked back across the ford to follow the course of the river toward Winton Abbey. Stopping frequently to call out for her son, she prayed that she would find him quickly.

Adrian could hear both of them yelling for the boy as he rode away from them. Conflicting emotions warred within him, igniting the terrible fury, yet filling him with longing. Damn her. Damn her to hell for doing this to him. She had no right to be here. She had no right to come back to England.

It had been more than six years since last he'd seen her, but the few memories of her he'd allowed himself hadn't done her justice. He'd wanted to believe that those years had taken a toll on her, but they hadn't. He'd always thought her the loveliest creature he'd ever seen, and time hadn't changed that.

Closing his eyes to shut out her image, he was haunted again by the vision of how she'd stood, white-faced and incredulous, when he'd confronted her the day he'd accused her. He'd known she'd played him false with his best friend, but a part of him had wanted to keep her anyway. Yet he'd wanted her to deny it, to make him believe differently. Instead, she'd left him standing there, shouting after her. And in the end, his pride had ruled his heart.

He saw her as she'd once been, those lovely eyes lit with passion, that unusual wheat-colored hair hanging between them like a silken scarf, shimmering in candlelight. He'd been with others before and dozens since, but none had compared to Joanna. He'd loved her to distraction in his salad days, and she'd betrayed him. Bitterness rose like bile within him, fueling the old anger yet again. He'd been a fool, an utter fool—he'd made her a duchess over the objections of his family, and she'd been unfaithful to him, robbing him not only of his honor but also of Gary. Hell was too little punishment for what she'd done to him.

"Mama . . . Mama?"

It was a small voice, coming from somewhere over the hedgerow, and it quavered with uncertainty. Adrian started to spur his horse on and found he couldn't. No matter what Joanna had done, the child couldn't be blamed for the sin. Sighing, he nudged his horse with his knee, guiding it to the edge of the field, and then he dismounted to walk along the row. He could hear the boy sobbing.

"Here—over here! Come out—you are found!" he yelled.

There was a pause in the crying that sounded like a hiccup, and then a rustling as the thick bushes parted. A small fellow barreled out and collided with him, clutching his leg.

"I want my mama!" the boy cried. "I didn't mean to come over—I didn't!"

Impulsively Adrian swung the boy up. As the child's face neared his own, the duke gave a violent start.

Stunned, he stared numbly at the thick black hair, the dark, almost black eyes, and the high cheekbones that mirrored his own. His breath caught painfully in his chest and his heart paused, holding time in abeyance for a moment. The boy stopped crying to stare at the strange expression on the face of the man who held him. For a long moment they contemplated one another.

"You must be Justin," Adrian said simply when at last he found his voice.

The boy nodded and rubbed his eyes with now grubby fists. "I want my mama," he repeated more calmly. "Please, sir—I want to see my mama."

"So do I," Adrian said grimly. A dozen unanswered questions crowded his mind as he settled the child against his shoulder and walked back to his horse.

His terror over, Justin Sherwood clung to Adrian trustingly. "I wanted to see where my mama was borned, but she wouldn't take me," he offered in explanation at first. When the man who held him did not respond, he continued, "My mama's Lady Carew, you know, and my papa . . ." The childish voice trailed off for a moment and then finished, ". . . my papa was an earl, but he died." He turned his head up to look at Adrian. "Did you know my papa? I m-miss him, but Mama says I have to get over it, and I c-can't—I just want God to give him back."

"Of course you cannot," Adrian murmured soothingly.

"But did you know him?" Justin persisted. "He lived at Haven when he was little like me."

"Yes." The answer was too short, but Adrian was still shocked by the astounding discovery that he had a son. Finally, he managed, "Of course I knew him—we were boys together from the time we were out of leading strings."

"And did you know my mama?"

It was an innocent question, but a painful one. "Yes, I knew her then too."

"Was she always pretty like she is now? Papa said she was the prettiest female in the whole world."

"She truly was."

"Papa said she was the best ever."

Desperate to change the subject without hurting the child's feelings, Adrian asked him, "Did you like Italy?"

"Uh-huh, but Grandmama did not. She made my mama come back so I could be an earl, but I didn't want to come," Justin confided. "I don't want to be an earl."

"Why not?" Adrian stopped to put the boy up in the saddle and then mounted the bay behind him.

" 'Cause everybody calls me 'my lord' instead of my name."

"Now, that *is* a problem," Adrian agreed.

"You're funning with me!"

"I assure you I am not."

"Well, would you like to be called 'my lord' all the time?"

"I never thought about it, I suppose, but then, I've lived with the problem all of my life. Only now it's 'Your Grace.' "

"You have?" Justin twisted his head to look at him. "Are you an earl too?"

"No, I am a duke, and a duke is supposed to be puffed up with his own consequence, or so *my* mama tells me."

"You've got a mama?"

"Most people do at one time or another."

"Well, I hope she is as good as mine—mine's a great gun, you know. Except when she's unhappy—then she cries. Like today."

"Oh?"

Justin nodded. "We went to look for her fort, and it

was capital. But then she started reading something, and she was sad. So I went 'sploring, and I got lost."

"Someday you'll have to visit the Armitage and see where I live."

"No. My mama don't want to visit anywhere—I heard her tell Grandmama," Justin confessed. "But" he added, brightening, "I can tell Robin I crossed a river all by myself."

"Robin?"

"My brother. He's little."

Somehow the thought that Joanna had borne another son to Gary was almost more than Adrian cared to hear. He lapsed into a preoccupied silence that the boy did not notice.

Justin chattered incessantly, telling of the trials of having a younger brother, and boasting finally, "Papa loved me best—I know he did, but Mama does not want Robin to know it, 'cause he's little and wouldn't understand."

"Huh?"

"Look! There's the river!"

At almost the same time that the child cried out, Johnny Barrasford hailed them with, "I see you found the boy! Good show, Roxbury!" Adrian reined in and waited for his hunting companion to catch up. "Lady Carew! Lady Carew!" Barrasford shouted across the ford. "Roxbury's found the boy!"

Joanna's rush of gratitude faded as she realized Adrian Delacourt held her son. Steeling herself, she walked through the shallow water again to face the man she'd once loved beyond everything. "My thanks, my lord," she told him abruptly, reaching for Justin.

"Jo—"

"Mama, he's a duke, and he wants me to visit him!"

"No." She pulled the boy down and inspected him. "You are unhurt?" she asked quickly.

"Uh-huh—but I was scared. Mama, I did not mean—"

Joanna dropped to her knees and enveloped him in her arms. "Of course you did not, dearest, but you were not the only one frightened. I was half out of my mind with worry for you."

"Are you going to birch me?"

"Yes."

"For God's sake, Jo! He's but—"

Adrian's words were cut short as she straightened and whirled around. "Stay out of it, my lord! 'Tis not your affair!"

Perplexed by something he did not quite understand, Lord Barrasford looked from one to the other and literally felt the tension between the two of them. Then he looked at the boy and at the Duke of Roxbury. Newcomer or not, he was no fool. "My God," he said softly.

Joanna's face colored as she took Justin's hand. "Well, now that he is found, we really must be getting back. I daresay Maman will have a search party out soon if we do not return. Justin, say farewell to Lord Barrasford and to the duke, if you please."

As she literally pulled the boy after her across the shallow ford, Adrian watched helplessly. Lord Barrasford, his interest in the lovely Joanna written on his face, called out to her, "Lady Carew, perhaps when you are settled . . . that is, I should like to pay you a morning call." She paused for a moment, hesitated, and then nodded as her eyes met Adrian's defiantly. "Yes, of course—if you wish."

Roxbury's face darkened, but rather than make a fool of himself in front of Johnny Barrasford, he said nothing. Yet a single thought reverberated through his mind, repeating itself over and over. *He had a son, and his son bore another man's name.*

The famed Delacourt temper, punctuated by black moods and self-doubts, strained the atmosphere at the Armitage until dowager duchess and servants alike left the duke in solitude to contemplate his awful discovery. A feeble reminder that Almeria Bennington and her parents were due to arrive momentarily netted his lordship's mother such a forbidding scowl that, for once, she forbore quarreling with him and retreated.

Alone, Adrian fumed first over the brazen audacity of Joanna in coming back, then he brooded over the small but troubling doubt that somehow he could have been wrong six long years ago. And that latter possibility was more than he could bear. As his rage abated, he sank into an equally ill-tempered bout of sullen self-pity, until finally, over his tenth bottle of Madeira in three days, he forgot his bitterness long enough to admit his sorrow over Gareth Sherwood's death.

Gary. There had been a time when he would have wagered all he had on Gary's loyalty and friendship. God, how many times in these six years past had he wanted to share some deep thought or discuss some complex problem with him? And then he'd have to remember it had been Gary who'd betrayed him with Joanna, and he'd want to kill both of them. But now . . .

now what he felt most was the loss, the emptiness beneath his breastbone.

As for Joanna ... every time her image rose in his mind, he tried to blot it out with another glass of wine. The sight of her had been enough to tear his very being asunder, to evoke anew the terrible pain he'd felt when she'd played him false with his best friend. For six years his pride had denied that pain, had smothered it with a cold, hard anger, and now in one brief, stunning encounter, she was haunting his dreams and destroying his peace all over again. Damn her. How could she dare to come back, to show her face in England again? And yet as he closed his eyes, reliving that awful moment of realization, it was the boy's face floating before him, his own image frozen in time. It was a mistake. A cruel jest played on him by a twisted fate.

He drained the last of his bottle as the clock struck an hour behind him, breaking into his melancholic reverie and bringing him suddenly into the present. With a start, he realized that the sun was not only up, but it waxed high in the sky. A quick pass of his hand over his face revealed a good three days' growth of dark stubble. He could still taste the wine, but it failed to obscure the brackish, odoriferous taste of all that had gone before it. Then came the realization that his head ached like the very devil.

He rose, weaved, and squeezed his eyes shut, trying to dull the pain. The boy's face, framed by black hair and enlivened by dark eyes so like his own, was still there. With a groan, he lurched for the door.

"Well," his mother reproved him without looking up as he entered her sitting room, " 'tis certainly time you came to your senses. Dear Almeria will be here this—"

"Hang Almeria!" he spat out with such vehemence that she recoiled.

A sense of foreboding clutched at her stomach as she

took in his disheveled appearance and the wild expression in his eyes. He moved slowly, unsteadily, to tower over her. "You're foxed," she decided aloud.

"I want the truth, Mother, and I want it now!"

"You are foxed," she repeated, obviously disgusted.

"Aye, but I am not so disguised that I do not know what I am doing," he retorted. He leaned forward, placing his hands on her chair back. "Tell me again how she played me false—how you were so very sure, Mother."

"What on earth—? Really, Adrian, but I'm sure I've not the least notion—"

"Joanna—I want to hear it all again."

She was taken aback by his bringing up the old scandal, but managed to hide the sudden fear she felt. "I cannot think why—it does you no credit, you know."

"She's back."

"Yes, and I could not believe my ears when I heard it— of all the effrontery— well, it does not bear thinking, does it? As if anyone could have forgotten what she was— well, I for one haven't, I can assure you. Why, there's no one foolish enough to receive her, and I'm sure—"

"No," he cut in harshly. "I won't be put off by rattling on, Mother. I would hear the story you told again. Tell me what you saw and what you heard between Jo and Gary."

"Really, Adrian, can you not sit down?" she demanded peevishly. "Surely after all this time, you cannot wish to be reminded of how she made a fool of you before the world."

"Mother—" he said, warning her. "I tell you I'm in no mood for dissembling."

"Well, I refuse to say anything if you insist on hovering like a hawk about to swoop down on me."

"Very well." He straightened up and stepped back.

"*Now*, Mother, I'd like to hear you repeat what you told me then."

"Adrian, you cannot expect me to remember exactly after all these years—I mean, I cannot even recall everything. Besides, with Almeria due to arrive momentarily, this is scarcely the time or the place just now. Almeria—"

"Did you not hear me? I said hang Almeria!"

"I wish you would not use that tone with me," his mother muttered, aggrieved. Looking up, she noted the set of his jaw. "Oh, all right, then, though—"

"Go on."

"Adrian, I saw them with my own eyes! I saw that . . . that little strumpet flaunt herself before Gareth Sherwood every time you were gone from this house. Oh, you were too besotted to see, but I watched how she comported herself with him and let him run tame here in your absence. They were a pretty pair, I tell you—fairly showering each other with their little love tokens, panting after each other beneath my very nose as though I must surely be blind and deaf. That's how it was, Adrian—she wed you for your money, for your consequence, and nothing more. She was wearing your jewels, calling herself Duchess of Roxbury, while she entertained Carew in this house as though she were a common whore! There—I have said it!"

"She was my duchess," he reminded her curtly.

"Humph! She was never anything but little Joanna Milford, as far as I was concerned. And it was not just me—your father Roxbury was aghast when he discovered you'd thrown yourself away on John Milford's daughter, believe me."

"You poisoned his mind against her. He didn't even know her until you convinced him she was unworthy of the Delacourt name. If anything can be said of my father, it was that as long as you left him alone to pursue his lightskirts, he'd dance to your tune when he came home," he reminded her brutally. "The two of you didn't even get on well enough to provide any more heirs to his name, as I recall."

"We had a civilized marriage, the sort common to our class. And had you done the same, you wouldn't have found yourself in need of a divorce."

"I wanted passion—I didn't want your damned civilized marriage, as you call it. I wanted someone I could give a damn about, Mother."

"Marriage is an alliance of wealth and breeding, Adrian. Passion in marriage is for the lower classes, for they've not the money to buy it elsewhere. You owed your name, you owed your blood far more than Joanna Milford, and you know it. No, you chose unwisely, I'm afraid, and she made you pay dearly for the mistake."

"We're not speaking of me. I asked about Joanna, and thus far you've not been able to convict her of anything more than entertaining a childhood friend."

"He sent her gifts! She wrote him love letters! You were blind!"

"I saw no letters."

"Well, I did, and when she discovered I was on to her, she destroyed them. Her maid watched her consign them to the fire. Adrian, listen to me—she gave him a lock of her hair! Have you forgotten what her maid said?"

"No, but I would hear it again."

"You heard it—she gave him the hair to put into a watch case. She said to the maid it was to be a reminder of her love when they were apart."

"How did she know it was Gary that Joanna spoke of?"

"Oh, for heaven's sake! 'Twas to Gary that she gave it!"

"He loved her, Mama. Even when we were children,

he loved her, but that does not mean that he seduced her."

"He didn't have to, Adrian—she seduced him!"

"How do you know? Tell me again!"

"I saw them! I saw them walk into the forest together. I followed them, Adrian, and they were trysting! *I* caught them there!" Helen Delacourt rose and walked behind her son. "Would you have me forget that I am a gently bred female and tell you how she lay in his arms—how she comported herself with wanton abandon beneath my very eyes?" she demanded. "Indeed, there was enough evidence to convict her three times over, as you will recall. In England, a man cannot shed his wife without proof, and I provided you with enough proof that even Parliament passed the bill of divorcement. So you've no right to ask me to repeat myself yet again—indeed, I will not do it."

"No—no," he responded wearily. He felt empty. "But I'd have you send word to the Benningtons that I am unable to entertain them just now."

"Adrian, you would not—you cannot! They expect—"

"They expect me to make Almeria an offer, Mama, but I cannot."

"But *why*? Adrian, she is everything a man in your position could ask for! And Lord Bennington is willing to overlook the divorce!"

"I told you—Joanna aside, I'll not wed where there is no passion. You cannot ask a man who has known fire to be content with ice."

"Fire?" Helen Delacourt's lip curved disdainfully. "Joanna Milford was fire like Harriette Wilson. If you ask me, they were cut of the same cloth, only the Wilson woman became a Cyprian while you made the Milford chit a duchess!"

"I loved her."

"You were a fool."

"Was I? I wonder still," he admitted more to himself than to her. "I wonder if I ever shall truly know the whole truth of what happened here."

It was too much for his mother. She reached to grasp his shirtsleeve and sputtered indignantly, "Not know? 'Tis a great piece of ignorance if you do not! If you would doubt your own mother, then consider that she married Carew the instant Parliament passed the bill! 'Twas as plain as may be that they legitimatized the liaison because of his child! They say she was showing before he even got her out of England!"

"His child?" Adrian half turned to look down at her, and his mouth twisted bitterly. "What a cruel jest that is, Mother. That is the final wound, you know. Gary's heir is my son."

"No!"

"I have seen the boy, and even a fool could not deny he's mine." For a long moment mother and son stared at each other, then he nodded. "It was like looking into my own face."

"But—Adrian, this changes nothing! Almeria—"

"It changes everything for me! I have a son, Mother. Now, if you'll pardon me, I need time to think." With that, he wrenched open the door.

"Wait—you cannot mean to leave! Not now—not with Almeria coming!"

"She's your guest, not mine!" he flung back at her before he escaped the house.

Helen Delacourt sank back in the nearest chair, her chagrin written on her face. How very ironic, she murmured to herself, that Joanna had managed to bring a child who resembled Adrian into the world. Not that it would make much difference in the end, she reflected smugly. The boy had been born a Sherwood, after all.

With that comforting thought, Helen turned her

thoughts to Almeria. It was time she had a very candid conversation with that young lady. Yes, Joanna's arrival at Haven would complicate matters, but between them, she and Almeria could put the conniving little upstart in her place. A few carefully dropped reminders among the neighbors and Joanna Sherwood would find herself an utter outcast again. Glancing once again to the empty place on the wall, Helen envisioned a portrait of Adrian's second duchess there.

Returning from his long, solitary ride, Adrian was on the landing above the main foyer when he heard the rattle of the carriage coming up the long drive. The Benningtons. With an inward groan, he headed for the servants' stairs, and when he reached the back of the house, he escaped through a passage that in Elizabethan times had led to the old kitchen. He heard the carriage roll to a halt, the exchange between his servants and Lord Bennington's coachman. A quick glance provided the unwelcome notion that Almeria and her parents meant to make it a protracted visit—a second coach had stopped behind it, and as the doors opened, he could see it was full of trunks.

"I cannot think where Roxbury is," he heard his mother say. "I'm quite sure he will be devastated when he realizes he's missed greeting dear Almeria," she added smoothly. "He's spoken of little else these last several days, I can assure you."

"I daresay he's a busy man," Bennington allowed, looking around. "Pretty place he's got here."

"Well, I own I am disappointed," Almeria admitted. "One would have thought—well, it isn't as though he did not know of our intended arrival, is it?"

"Hush, Puss," her father warned her. "Best be cream, not vinegar about it."

Having heard enough to know he lacked the civility

to endure the haughty Almeria or her matchmaking parents at the moment, Adrian headed back to the stables. The Benningtons could damn well cool their collective heels for a while, he decided grimly.

His head still ached like the very devil, and his mind was in too much turmoil for sleep or company. As he walked, he took a deep breath and looked skyward. The sun shone despite a bank of clouds on the horizon, and the wind was warm and moist enough to smell of rain. It looked now as though a storm could be rolling in, providing a wildness, an exhilaration, a certain gamble to this second ride.

He waited while an ostler resaddled Ajax, the big bay he favored, and then he swung into the saddle. The horse was restless, but Adrian held the reins in check until they cleared the paddock, then he gave the animal its head. Ajax took the fence in smooth stride and cut across the field into the wind.

They ran along the brake as far as it stretched, until they reached the hedgerows that bordered the Armitage. Below a gentle slope lay the river and the ford. Adrian reined in to survey the place where boundaries of the Haven and Winton Abbey joined the Armitage, and as he looked across that river, he felt his throat tighten, felt the ache of loss. There'd been a time when those lands had been as familiar as his own. But that had been a long time ago, he reminded himself. Before Joanna had betrayed him with Gary. And still as he stared through that damp summer haze, he could almost see her coming down that path, he could almost see that glorious mane of wheat-gold hair, those lovely eyes, the once-familiar smile on her nearly perfect face. His gaze traveled to where she'd walked across the ford the other day, but now the whole place was almost eerily silent. God, what a shock that had been. Even now, he had to fight the anger, the bitterness he'd felt then. It wasn't supposed to happen that way, he told himself. He should have felt nothing.

What had the boy told him? That they'd come to see where she'd played as a child. Again the poignant pain of loss gripped him. Those weren't her memories alone—they'd belonged to him, too. And to Gary. Impulsively he nudged the bay through a break in the hedgerow and down onto the flat rockbed of the ford. The shallow water splashed up, wetting Ajax's forelegs as they crossed onto Haven land.

It was strange how little nature reflected the changes in a man's life, Adrian thought soberly as he scanned once-familiar places. He could see the old logs he and Gary had used as a fortress. He closed his eyes, straining to hear the shouts, the boyish challenges again. It was folly—utter folly—to have crossed the river. There was no way to go back in time. And yet he edged closer to the small clearing, spying the fresh-dug earth beneath the old tree, and he was inexorably drawn to it. Dismounting there, he explored the soft, mossy ground with the toe of Hoby's finest boot until he struck the solid edge of something metal, and he knew instantly what he'd found. The childhood treasure chest of three youthful friends. Heedless of his fine buff kerseymere pants, he knelt, eagerly digging for the box.

His hands shook as he pried it open, then he stared at the things they'd buried—Gary's snuffbox, his own watch chain. But Joanna's locket was missing. No doubt she'd found that and reclaimed it. Mesmerized by his discovery, he unfolded the papers and reread the youthful promises they'd made to each other. *To meet again in five years. To dance attendance on Joanna at her come-out. To be friends forever.*

As he turned the snuffbox over in his hand, he couldn't help thinking of Gary, of what a capital fellow he'd been, so very full of life. Always laughing, always viewing everything with that wry, dry sense of humor. He hadn't thought of Gary like that in a long time, he realized sadly. As Gary's face came to his mind, it wasn't that of the boy he remembered—it was the pale, angry face of the man calling him an utter fool. Stung by the bitterness of that memory, Adrian refolded the papers and reached for the envelope.

Odd, but he hadn't seen that before. Turning it over in his hand, he felt a hard bulge in it. Curious now, he slipped his fingers inside to retrieve the small object, and as the filtered sun touched it, diamonds and sapphires winked. It was Joanna's betrothal ring. As his palm weighed it, he stared, studying it. He'd paid a king's ransom for it, he recalled, reliving the moment he'd presented it to her.

It was as though the ring released a floodtide of old memories. God, he'd never forget the elation he'd felt when she'd accepted him instead of Gary. "Dree, I think I've loved you my entire life," she'd said simply. "No, I know I have." He'd almost felt sorry for Gary, for the poor fellow had come up to scratch just a few minutes later.

Adrian was only twenty-three, barely into his salad days, when they'd married, but he'd known he wanted her above any other, and he'd refused to listen when his parents had urged him to reconsider. Every word of censure they'd flung at him still rang in his mind. She was a mere baron's daughter, his father had said; she was a hopeless flirt bent on his destruction, a grasping adventuress, his mother had added spitefully. But with the confidence of youth, he'd expected them to accept what they could not change, and it had not happened. On his deathbed, Adrian's father had rebuffed Joanna's attempt to comfort him. And his mother had been little more than a spy, reporting every small error as a cardinal sin, sniffing that "dear Joanna allows the servants to call her Lady Jo, when she knows a baron's daughter has not that right." But none of that could excuse Joanna's infidelity.

It was too painful to go on, this reverie of times best forgotten. Adrian pocketed the ring and laid the rest back in its earthen grave. Straightening up, he wiped his hands on the buff breeches and walked to the waiting horse.

Damn Joanna anyway, he thought savagely—why did she have to come back and punish him with the boy? The boy. She'd borne him a son without telling him, a son that carried the Sherwood name and now held Gary's title. What a blow that must have been to Gary's pride. How he must have felt when he looked at the boy, for only a blind man could have denied those Delacourt eyes, that thick black hair. But even as he thought it, Adrian could hear the child's small voice. *Papa loved me best . . .* In that at least, Gary was a better man than Adrian would have been.

Remounting, he started back across the ford and halted at the edge. No, he had to know—he had to hear from her lips that the boy was his. Wheeling savagely, he turned toward Haven. As much as he hated her, as much as he hated seeing her, he wanted to hear her say it.

He was so preoccupied with the questions in his mind that he barely realized he'd reached Haven until he saw the familiar tile-roofed gables, the sprawling stone manor house. Seat of every Sherwood baron and earl since old Henry Tudor had bestowed it on a Lancastrian loyalist after he'd deposed Richard III at Bosworth, he recalled. The Sherwoods had been neighbors of the Delacourts for more than three hundred years. And outranked by them, too, his mother would remind him. Turning up the carriage lane, he felt almost at home, as if Gary would be waiting for him. He even recognized the faces of those who stopped to watch him approach the house.

Before he could dismount, Perkins, Gary's old bailiff, was in front of him, and there was no welcome in the man's hostile face.

"Hallo, Perkins."

"You are trespassing, my lord," the older man reminded him coldly. "I'd thank you to leave ere there's trouble."

"I came to see Lady Carew." Somehow, the name almost stuck in Adrian's throat.

"She don't want to see you, Your Grace."

"You mistake the matter—I've come to return something of hers."

"Then you'd best leave it with me."

It was like a slap in the face to hear such coldness from a man who'd often taken two small boys hunting in the days when Adrian had run tame at Haven. Looking around him, Adrian realized he was surrounded by grim-faced ostlers. "Perkins—"

"Duke or no, you're not welcome here, my lord."

Just then, Adrian saw the children chasing around the corner of the house. "Never mind," he muttered. "Justin! Justin!"

The elder boy stopped and turned around. "Duke! 'Tis the duke!" he shouted to the smaller child as he trotted on sturdy legs toward Adrian. "Robin, 'tis the duke I told you about!" It struck Adrian that the younger boy had red-gold hair like Gary's. And those bright, bright blue eyes.

"Justin! Justin, come here on the instant!" Joanna shouted as she emerged from the house. Both boys halted midstep.

"But, Mama, 'tis—"

His words were cut off as she swooped down on them and ruffled each child's hair. "Go on inside—Miss

Finchley is looking for both of you," she said with a calmness she did not feel. "You mustn't keep her waiting, my dears."

"But—"

"Justin—" There was no mistaking the warning of her voice.

"Oh, all right," Justin capitulated gracelessly, "but—"

"No—go with Robin."

For a moment Adrian thought she meant to speak to him, but instead she ignored his very presence by hurriedly following her sons toward the house.

"Wait, Jo! Jo, I have to talk to you—I have to know!" He swung down and strode after her.

She paused briefly and straightened her already regal carriage. With her back still to him, she answered, "I have nothing to say to you, my lord—'twas all said at the time."

He caught her arm and spun her around to face him. "The boy's mine, isn't he, Jo?"

Almost immediately they were ringed by Haven servants. "Let her go, Your Grace, else you'll be shot for trespassing," Perkins told him matter-of-factly.

"It's all right, Mr. Perkins. There is no need for violence as I'm quite certain His Grace is leaving." Turning cold eyes back to Adrian, she shook her head. "No," she answered, " 'twas Gary's name he was born with and it was Gary's hand that rocked his cradle."

"But he's not Gary's, Jo—any fool can see that."

"Gary was proud to claim him." Her eyes dropped to where his hand held her elbow. "Now, you will pardon me, of course, but I do not intend to ask you in."

"Let her go, Your Grace," the bailiff warned again.

"Why did you not tell me?" Adrian demanded.

She jerked away, betraying the anger she felt. "Because you would have believed nothing I said! There, does that satisfy you?"

"It does not!"

Fighting to master herself, she forced herself to tell him evenly, "I have already told you I have nothing to say to you—not now, not ever. Good day, my lord." Turning on her heel, she marched for the house.

Two men reached for Adrian, but he shook them off and ran after her. She walked faster, but he caught her again as she reached the lowest step of the portico. This time, he could see the bitterness in her face as she turned on him. "Haven't you done quite enough?" she demanded angrily. "You have no right to come here— no right at all! And you certainly have no right to ask anything of *me*!" Her voice dropped. "How dare you— how dare you show your face on Gary's land?"

"I have to know, Jo—the boy is mine, isn't he?"

"No—he is mine."

"I don't have to ask, Jo—I can tell. You had no right to keep him from me."

Her eyes met his squarely then, and her lips curved scornfully as she took in the man she'd once loved beyond everything. A derisive little laugh escaped her. "I'm afraid you've mistaken the matter," she said, biting off the words. "You lost any right to me or mine when you so publicly dragged my name and my honor through every gutter in England in your quest for divorce. I am an adulteress, you will remember—and Gary—sweet, loyal Gary, you branded my lover. You hounded him out of this country, and I'll never forgive you for that, Dree. Never."

"He's my son, Jo—admit it."

She sucked in her breath, then let it out slowly before she bit off her answer. "He's Justin Anthony David Sherwood, Earl of Carew, Your Grace. And I'm sure if Gary were here, he'd tell you that Justin is every inch a Sherwood. Now, if you'll unhand me, I really must attend to business inside."

"This is your revenge, isn't it?"

"You know, Gary was right—you were and are a bloody fool, Dree. And if you do not take your hands off my person and your person off my property, I shall have you forcibly removed. Regardless of what you seem to think, I did not return to England to be harassed by you—or by anyone else, for that matter. I came back to rear my sons in peace."

"Jo, you cannot do this to me."

"To you?" Her eyebrow arched in disbelief. "After what you did to me? No, Dree, you did this to yourself. Now, you really must excuse me, but I've better things to do than this."

He fumbled in his pocket and drew out the ring. "Here—" he said, pressing it into her palm. "I found something you lost."

She barely looked down before she dropped her hand, letting the ring fall to the ground. "It wasn't lost—'twas buried with the rest of my childish things. Now, for the *last* time, good day, my lord," she declared with utter finality.

This time, he let her go, then he watched helplessly as she ran up the steps and into the house. Behind him, John Perkins touched his shoulder. "I'd say her ladyship made herself pretty plain on that head, Your Grace, and now you'd best mount up and be on your way, else I'll be sending Will into the village for the constable. I'd hate to be doing that, ye know, what with Lady Carew wanting her privacy here, but there's not a man jack on this place as wouldn't say you didn't have a comeuppance due you. And if you wasn't a duke, I'd be tempted to try my fives on you mesself."

"You'd lose," Adrian retorted.

"Mebbe," the older man conceded, "but it'd make me feel good to try."

Inside the house, Joanna clung to the newel post at

the bottom of the stairs as she tried to control her fear and her anger. How dare he? How *dare* he? Hadn't he done enough to hurt her six years ago?

"Mama, why—why couldn't I show him to Robin?"

She looked to her older son, and his bewilderment tore at her. "I'm afraid you're too young to understand, dearest."

"Papa wouldn't say so—he wouldn't."

"Papa's gone." As soon as she said the words, she saw his face crumple, and she wished them back. "I'm sorry, Justin," she managed. "I—I miss him too, you know."

"But he loved me best—he loved me more'n Robin— more'n anyone!" he cried. "I didn't want him to leave me!" Clutching her skirt, he buried his face in it. His shoulders shook as he wept uncontrollably.

Her heart aching for him, for Gary, and for herself, Joanna caressed the thick, dark waves of his hair as she fought her own tears. "Dearest, he didn't want to leave us," she whispered. "God took him to heaven."

"But he went without me, Mama, I—why couldn't I go, too?"

"Because God wants you to grow up. He wants you to be a man like Papa."

"But I want Papa!" he choked out. "Mama, I want my papa! God didn't need him as much as me!"

She wanted to tell him that someday he'd understand things like loss and death, but she couldn't. At twenty-five, she still didn't understand why someone as good as Gary had to die. "I know," she said simply. Unable to stand her son's pain, she gently disengaged him, then she knelt down to wipe his wet face with her handkerchief. "Come on—you are my big boy, darling. I need you to help me with Robin. He needs you to help him grow up, too." Forcing a smile, she chided him lightly. "I see both of you managed to escape Miss Finchley again."

"We wasn't escaping her, Mama. We was going to paint trees, but Robin forgot the brushes, and I was s'posed to watch him while she got 'em."

"Oh, I see—and where is he now?"

"He was going to tell Finch about the duke." Embarrassed now by his unmanly display of tears, he looked at his feet. "I—uh—I'd best find him."

At that moment, the young governess came down the stairs with the three-year-old boy. "There you are, Master Justin. Your pardon, my lady, but I was going to take them out to do watercolors this morning as it looks very much as though it means to rain later. I'm hoping I can teach them to see the beauty in the world about them, even in those gray clouds. I want them to know that without the rain, there'd be no lovely trees or flowers for us to draw."

"Then you've not much time, for it looks as though the sky could pour."

"Yes." The young woman hesitated, then added, "I hope you do not think I'm neglecting their lessons, my lady."

"No, of course not."

"I thought while Master Robin napped this afternoon, Justin and I should work on his letters. He's doing quite well with them, really. They are both quite exceptional children, each in his own way."

"Thank you."

"I'll draw you a big tree, Mama," Justin promised. "A pretty one."

"I'd like that."

"Why don't you both find the best-looking tree on the front lawn? I'll be along directly with the paints and brushes," Miss Finchley told them.

"And the paper," the older boy reminded her.

"And the paper." As soon as they'd raced out the door, the governess turned back to Joanna, her hazel eyes mirroring her concern. "Forgive me for saying so, my lady, but you look a trifle unwell. Do you wish me to summon someone?"

"No." Joanna sighed heavily. "I'm just a bit blue-deviled, I'm afraid. We'd been sharing a little cry before you discovered us."

"I do try to keep his spirits up, you know."

"Yes. It just takes time for both of us."

It wasn't until after Miss Finchley was gone that Joanna realized she still shook as though she'd taken a chill. And she felt very alone and terribly afraid. Bitter experience had taught her that Adrian Delacourt could be a powerful enemy.

"You cannot run away from this, my dear," Lady Anne said patiently. "To take the boys back to Italy now would merely postpone the unpleasantness."

"But, Maman, Adrian was here! He wanted to know about Justin—no, he *demanded* to know about him!"

The dowager countess looked to where Joanna's clothes were being sorted for packing and shook her head. While she'd never denied that Justin's parentage would cause comment, she'd also truly believed that once Joanna had the chance to reestablish herself, it eventually wouldn't matter. But Adrian Delacourt's unfortunate presence in the neighborhood had been utterly unforeseen, and the timing of Justin's chance encounter with him couldn't have been worse. And his precipitous visit to Haven had unnerved the usually plucky Joanna.

"All right—he knows," she conceded. "But surely he won't behave foolishly in the matter."

"Not behave foolishly?" Joanna's voice rose in incredulity. "Not behave foolishly? Maman, he already has! He came here and fairly shouted it out in front of Mr. Perkins and everyone! By tomorrow, 'twill be the *on-dit* of the neighborhood!"

"Well, the tale certainly does you more credit than him," the older woman reasoned. "Indeed, perhaps it is

better to have it out in the open now rather than have
it hanging over your head like—"

"Like the sword of Damocles?" Joanna supplied.
"And that is just what it is. Only it affects not only me,
but also my sons. Just what is Justin to think when he
hears?" she demanded, pacing. "He loved Gary,
Maman."

"And Gary loved him," Anne acknowledged mildly.
"My love, Justin's still too young to understand any of
this. And I scarce think anyone would repeat such gossip to a child, anyway."

"Adrian is capable of anything. Any doubt I ever had
on that head was dispelled when I was presented with
a summons to answer his petition to divorce me,"
Joanna reminded her bitterly. "I could not believe his
effrontery when I saw him here this morning—how
dare he come here—how *dare* he set foot on Haven?
Had it not spread the tale faster, I wish Mr. Perkins
would have sent for the constable. I should have liked
to see Adrian's face when I had him arrested for trespassing on our land."

"My dear, he has overset you needlessly," the older
woman murmured sympathetically. "Come, let us reason this out," she soothed. "So he knows, and perhaps
so will everyone else in time, but what difference will
that make in the end? Given Justin's marked resemblance to him, it was a certainty to happen, and we
both knew it."

"He was supposed to stay in London! I was led to believe he couldn't cut up my peace here, and yet the first
day I took Justin out walking, there he was, as arrogant
as ever!"

"But what can he really do about anything? No matter who Justin favors in looks, he is legally a Sherwood.
And as for spreading the tale, I'm sure once Adrian
comes to his senses, he'll realize all he can do is make

himself look ridiculous. No, his pride will tell him to hold his tongue."

"His pride caused the divorce."

"Ah, but he was very young then. No, if he cuts up a dust, he'll look like the veriest fool, and the sympathy will all come to you."

"I don't want sympathy—I just wish to be left alone. I should never have left Capri, Maman."

"Justin was unhappy there."

"You cannot say he is any happier here," Joanna countered tiredly. "If anything, he misses Gary even more now than he did before we came home. And if Adrian insists on his knowing this, he will be more confused than ever."

"I daresay once Roxbury considers—well, it will look more than peculiar that he accused you of committing adultery with my son when you were obviously carrying his child."

"He never knew. Gary wanted me to tell him, but I couldn't. Even if it had been possible, I couldn't have gone back to Adrian after what he'd believed of me. Then, when Gary heard the charges read at the bishop's hearing, I think he finally understood why I didn't want Adrian to know."

"I know he did," Anne agreed, moving to lay a comforting hand on Joanna's shoulder. "You must not think I have ever reproached you for what happened, dearest. Once Gary decided his course of action, I could see there was no turning back. It was enough for me to know that you made him very happy and that he loved the boy. Indeed, his sense of honor made me very proud."

Tears welled in Joanna's eyes and she brushed at them, murmuring apologetically, "I do not know how 'tis that I've turned into such a watering pot. But life is so very unfair, Maman. It is as though even God punishes me for something I could never have done."

"You must not say that, my dear. Gary—"

"Gary's dead!" Jo's face crumpled piteously. "He's gone, and I cannot face everyone without him!"

Anne Sherwood's grip tightened on her daughter-in-law's shoulder and she gave her a slight shake. "You can—and you will!" she declared forcefully. "You are made of sterner stuff than this—you'll hold your head up and face the world for your sons!"

"I cannot!"

"Joanna, collect yourself! Time will heal the hurt and you will wed again, I am certain. Indeed, that is the very answer."

"Never!" Joanna fought for control and succeeded in hiccuping a stifled sob. Blowing her nose on her handkerchief, she shook her head. "I would not even wish such a thing, Maman, because the losing pains too much."

"You would not rear two boys in a houseful of petticoats, would you?" Anne asked reasonably. When Joanna did not answer, she said more kindly, "Oh, I would not have you rush into another match, of course, but I think there will come a time when you ought to consider it." Dropping her hand, she turned to where the maids still packed, and she sought the words to convince her wounded daughter-in-law. "Jo, you are English, and your sons are English. I ask you, from the bottom of an old woman's heart, not to take your sons away from the land of my son's birth. Don't let Adrian make exiles of them also."

"They will be shunned because I am their mother," Joanna countered bitterly.

"I cannot believe that. Once Justin's resemblance to Adrian is seen 'twill be said you were the innocent victim of Roxbury's jealousy."

"His mother's, you mean. No matter how I tried to please her, she hated me. I think she would have destroyed Adrian to rid herself of his unworthy duchess."

"And she very nearly did." Feeling as though she were winning, Anne pressed her advantage. "Please, dearest—I would not see you hurt further for the world—but at least attempt to go about and try the waters. What harm can there be in that, I ask you? Then, if you see that 'tis indeed hopeless, I shall go back to Italy with you."

"Do you mean that?"

"You and the boys are all that I have to love in this world."

"And you are more than my own mother to me."

"Don't let Roxbury drive you from the country again." Her expression sober, Anne looked into her daughter-in-law's eyes. "Don't let Helen win again. Go out and hold your head high for Justin's sake."

It was a hard thing that Gary's mother asked of her, but the woman's words touched her pride. Looking away, Joanna took a deep breath, then exhaled it fully before she answered. "All right. I suppose I am not so poor-spirited that I cannot face the unpleasantness for a time," she conceded. "But regardless of how I go on, I doubt I shall be invited anywhere."

"Good. Now, as a first step, we shall take our pew in church this Sunday. And I should like to have Justin seated on my side, for I mean to show the world that he is as much my grandson as Robin."

A discreet knock at the door interrupted them, and Anne nodded to a maid, who promptly opened it. James, the footman, apologized for the intrusion as he presented an elegantly engraved white card. "There's a gentleman below asking to see you, madam," he addressed Joanna. "I told him I did not believe you were receiving, but he insisted I ask before he leaves."

Jo took the card and turned it around to read, "J.T.E. Barrasford."

"Who is it, love?" Anne asked curiously, looking over her shoulder.

"Adrian's hunting companion—I met him at the ford when I was looking for Justin." Jo stared at the card in puzzlement for a moment, musing aloud, "I suppose he is come to see how Justin does. He helped in the search, you know."

Anne took in Joanna's lovely face and slim figure and doubted very much that was the case. "Then, by all means, you must see him. Esther, fetch a cloth soaked in cold water for Lady Joanna's eyes and, Kate, do not be hanging up the gray twilled silk, after all."

"Maman, 'tis too fine for at-home wear," Jo protested. "The brown gown I have on will do fine."

"Nonsense," the dowager dismissed briskly. "When one is still in mourning, elegance of fabric and design will have to do what color cannot. Besides, brown becomes no one. Indeed, I will be glad enough when we are out of widow's weeds next week. There's too much dreariness in this house."

"Maman!"

"Well, there is," Anne declared firmly. "But do hurry. James, you will inform Lord Barrasford that her ladyship will be down directly."

Had her spirits not been so cast down, Joanna would have been amused by the concerted efforts of Anne and the two maids to make her presentable. As it was, she was dressed in the gray gown, her blond hair was brushed and coiled neatly atop her head with only the barest wisps allowed to soften the severity of the style, and lavender water was dabbed to erase the tearstains on her cheeks, all within fifteen minutes.

"You could invite him to dine," Anne suggested as Kate held the door.

"And have him think me as fast as my shocking rep?" Jo asked, lifting an eyebrow. "I don't think that would be wise."

John Barrasford turned around as she entered the blue saloon, and his breath caught in his throat. Ever since he'd first seen her, he'd been telling himself that she could not be as lovely as he remembered her, and yet there she stood in the flesh. Speechless, he again took in the perfection of her fine-boned features and her narrow-waisted figure. She waited, a question in those cerulean eyes of hers, as his gaze returned to her face. There was a sadness about those eyes, he decided, a sadness that was out of place amid such beauty. With an effort, he collected himself and managed to move forward to greet her.

"Lady Carew. Your pardon for intruding on such brief acquaintance, but I would know how the boy does."

A faint smile curved the corners of her mouth but did not reach her eyes. "If one does not count ten switches with the birch, sir, he suffered no ill from his adventure." She gestured toward the settee that faced an empty fireplace. "Would you care to sit down? I should be happy to ring for some tea."

"I should like it above all things," he admitted, flashing an engaging smile. "I am parched from the ride in the sun."

"Yes, it is rather hot, isn't it? Perhaps lemonade would be preferable."

"I am quite easy to please, Lady Carew. I shall just take whatever you are having."

She felt ill-at-ease in the presence of the handsome stranger, wondering if perhaps he'd come for a closer inspection of an infamous woman. His next words dispelled that notion.

"Actually, Lady Carew, I came because I am new to

the neighborhood myself and know almost no one beyond Roxbury. Lady Sheffield is giving a small party for the purpose of introducing me to the local gentry." He paused to take in the gray gown and then blurted out, "Are you still in mourning for Lord Carew, ma'am?"

"My husband died a year ago this week," she answered quietly.

"Oh." He cleared his throat and pressed on manfully, feeling for the world like a callow youth rather than a thirty-three-year-old buck of the *ton*. "Then you would not be expected to be in black gloves next week, would you?"

"No." She eyed him curiously and waited.

"Well—that is to say, shall I expect to see you at the Sheffields'?"

"I'm afraid I was not invited."

"I'll ask her to send a card around, Lady Carew, for I doubt she even realizes you are in residence. I know I did not. Indeed, I should be happy to take you up with me."

Joanna sucked in her breath and turned away to compose her words. "Do not think me ungrateful, my lord, but I cannot impose on your kindness." Resolutely she turned back to face him. "You cannot have heard the story, else you'd not be here, I am sure."

"I beg your pardon?"

"My lord, plain speaking will serve us best, I think." Having said that, she searched his face and wondered if he would recoil when he heard of her scandalous past. He was a handsome, well-favored man, and his eyes, although gray rather than hazel, reminded her somehow of Gareth. "Perhaps then you will not even wish to stay for lemonade." She drew in another deep breath and then plunged ahead baldly. "My first husband was Adrian Delacourt," she said simply. As she saw the surprise in those gray eyes, she looked away, giving him time to adjust to the shocking news. In the ensuing silence, she managed to add, "We were divorced six years ago."

"I see," he said finally. "Of course—that explains the child."

"The charge was adultery, my lord," she admitted quietly, sparing herself nothing.

"My God."

"If you would rather not stay for the lemonade, I quite understand."

"And then you married Carew," he observed slowly.

Her mouth twisted, betraying the bitterness she still felt. "Lord Carew, a childhood friend—my dearest friend—stood with me and married me as soon as we heard Parliament had approved the bill of divorcement that Adrian brought against me. We went to Italy— Capri actually—and lived there in relative peace despite the war that raged around us. Then, last summer, Gary went fishing with one of the villagers, and a storm came up before they could get in. Two days later, his body washed up across the bay." She paused to swallow the lump in her throat, then went on. "We brought my husband's body home to be buried in Haven's chapel a few weeks ago. My mother-in-law could not bear not having him here."

"Lady Carew, please accept my condolences," Barrasford said softly.

"Thank you." Her voice dropped to a near whisper. "Justin believes Gary was his father—he loved him so. I never thought Adrian would see him so soon. I was told he never came home to the Armitage anymore."

"I understand he opened the house to entertain—" Realizing the awkwardness of the situation, he caught himself. "Well, there's no sense in repeating idle gossip, is there?"

"No. I don't care *why* he's here—I just wish he'd never seen Justin. I just wish we'd stayed in Italy." Recalling herself, she added a trifle defiantly, "So, my lord, if you cannot bring yourself to further your acquaintance with a woman of my reputation, I shall quite understand. After all, my own father does not speak to me, so why should you?"

"I am determined to have that lemonade," he declared, smiling. "Dear lady, I have seen a number of free-favored women in my time, and I can tell you truthfully that I do not think you are one of them. Indeed, I should be honored to know you and proud to be seen in your company." Possessing himself of both of her hands, he looked into her eyes. "Just tell me one thing—if I am able to procure you an invitation to Lady Sheffield's little affair, would you consider attending?"

She'd just told him she was a divorced female, and she found it hard to believe that it hadn't mattered. And yet as she met his gaze, she saw only kindness in his face. "I don't know," she answered faintly. " 'Tis rather sudden—"

"Unless you have some serious objection, Lady Carew, I mean to pursue your acquaintance," he assured her. His smile fading, he told her seriously, "If you'd give me the chance, I'd stand your friend."

"I'm sure Lady Sheffield would rather invite a viper."

"And forgo the opportunity to introduce an eligible bachelor into the neighborhood?" he countered lightly. Aware that he risked pushing too quickly, Johnny favored her with another, more boyish smile. "You don't have to answer now, dear lady."

"Yes, well, I'd have to receive the invitation first, wouldn't I?" she murmured. And yet as she said those words, she couldn't help thinking he reminded her of Gareth Sherwood. It was the kindness, she told herself.

As her coach rattled down the rough country lanes, Joanna leaned back against the squabs and closed her eyes, trying to hide the panic she felt. She had to be the greatest goose on earth for allowing Lord Barrasford to plant such an impossible notion in her head. At the moment, she felt as though Gary's mother and Barrasford had connived together in the matter, he by procuring the invitation and Anne by insisting it would do her good to get out and about. But at least she'd come in her own carriage, so she could leave quietly if the situation became too unpleasant, she consoled herself.

"Buck up, my love," the dowager countess murmured. "You must consider this a new beginning."

"Or another chapter of the same nightmare," Joanna muttered. "I cannot think what possessed me when I said I'd come."

"You are too young to shut yourself up at Haven, dearest."

"Yes, well, just now I feel a hundred years old."

"Nonsense. You are in looks tonight."

Conversation lapsed then, and it wasn't until the Carew coach drew up to the Sheffield portico that either of them spoke again. As the vehicle halted and a coachman jumped down to open the door, Anne told

Joanna, "Remember that you received a card just like everyone else."

"Only because of Lord Barrasford's kindness. Lud, but I wonder what Annabelle thought when he suggested it, don't you?" Once she was handed down, Joanna smoothed the soft blue silk gown with her damp hands in an attempt to erase wrinkles from the carriage ride, but otherwise there was nothing in her face to betray the inner turmoil she felt.

Heads turned as her soft kid sandals trod the steps behind her mother-in-law, and more than one buck was heard to whisper, "Who's the fair beauty?" Joanna schooled herself not to listen for the answer.

Even though it was well past nine o'clock, the night was still quite warm outside and the air inside stifling. As she entered the ballroom, Joanna could see servants opening the French doors at either end of the long room to create a breeze from the formal gardens. The fresh air that rushed in was fragrant with the scent of Lady Sheffield's roses, giving Joanna pause. It had been just such a night in London when she'd made her come-out.

"So kind of you to come, my love," their hostess murmured as she leaned to plant a genteel kiss on Anne Sherwood's softly powdered cheek. "It has been such an age that we'd despaired of your ever coming back."

"Italy *was* lovely, of course," Anne admitted, "but there is nothing quite like one's own home, I vow." With a slight inclination of her head toward Joanna, she added, "And I am certain that you remember my daughter-in-law."

For the briefest moment Joanna thought her heart would stop. To her relief, Annabelle Sheffield merely nodded and extended her hand. "Lady Carew," she acknowledged, her voice quite neutral.

"So you decided to come, after all," a decidedly masculine voice whispered behind her ear. "Dear lady, you have quite made my evening."

She turned and nearly collided with Lord Barrasford. His eyes betrayed an interest that she recognized on the instant, but unlike so many others of his sex, there was that unmistakable kindness also. Indeed, in the several morning calls he'd paid her since that first visit, his behavior had been exemplary. "Thank you, my lord," she murmured gratefully.

"Shocking squeeze already, isn't it? Perhaps you would like a chair near a breeze and a glass of lemonade," he suggested. "I should be happy to procure both for you and your mother-in-law." The corners of his mouth lifted into a smile and his eyes warmed appreciably as he took in her blue silk dress with its high waist, wide neck, and slim skirt. It was the epitome of simplicity and it suited her perfectly. "Your beauty makes the gown, my dear," he said softly. "Too often, one finds it the other way around."

"Spanish coin, my lord," she replied with an answering smile as he offered his arm. She hesitated before taking it. "You are quite sure you wish to acknowledge the acquaintance so publicly?"

"I shall be the envy of every man here," he replied gallantly.

"Do go on, love," Anne urged. "I see Margaret Thayer, and we have not conversed in an age."

Before Joanna could demur, Barrasford had her arm tucked into the crook of his elbow, and they were headed for a quieter place. "Would you mind terribly if I took the liberty of calling you Joanna?" he dared to ask. " 'Tis so confusing when there are two Lady Carews in attendance."

"Lord Barrasford—"

There was a wariness in her eyes that told him he pushed too fast. "All right—Lady Carew it is."

She relented. "Joanna will be fine, my lord."

"John—or Johnny. My given name is John, and my friends call me Johnny."

As if on cue, a young man caught up with them. "Johnny, pray present me to your fair goddess. " 'Tis not fair for you to steal such a march on the rest of us, dear fellow."

Barrasford stopped. "Ah, Symington, is it? Very well—Lady Carew, may I make Charles Symington known to you? Charles, this fair lady is Joanna, the younger dowager Countess of Carew."

There was a perceptible change in the young man's attitude, a sudden boldness as he stared at her with new interest. She met his gaze coolly, hiding her irritation. "Mr. Symington."

"Didn't know you was back in—"

The young buck's words were cut short by a lean-faced woman who pushed her way to clutch at his sleeve. "Charles!" she uttered sharply. Without so much as an acknowledgment of Joanna, she addressed Symington, telling him, "Mrs. Corville is here with the Misses Corville, Charles, and I have assured her that you mean to be all that is polite to them, if you take my meaning. Miss Emily is Lord Wemble's goddaughter, you know, and as he is a bachelor . . ." She let her voice trail off significantly, then she turned to Joanna's companion. "Your pardon for the intrusion, Lord Barrasford, but I'm certain you can understand a mother's concern for her only son." Without waiting for a reply, she firmly propelled Symington away from Joanna.

"An ambitious mama," Barrasford observed.

"So I collected." Joanna sighed. "I fear you have witnessed my first cut direct tonight."

"She is not worth knowing, anyway, so I would not

repine." Dismissing Mrs. Symington, he changed the subject abruptly. "Tell me, my dear—do you waltz?"

"Yes, but I hardly—that is, I don't think it would be wise to put myself forward on my first foray out."

"Nonsense. Beard the old biddies in their dens," he advised. "Otherwise, they'll think they can put you on the run. Besides, I am expecting at least two dances this evening—that is, if you do not object, of course."

Across the room, matchmaking mamas watched in chagrin as Lord Barrasford found Joanna a seat and joined her for an obviously friendly conversation. His recent arrival in the neighborhood had raised a number of hopes, particularly when it was observed that he not only was a singularly handsome bachelor, but he was rumored to have enough money in the funds to provide him an income of nearly twenty thousand a year. Not nearly as much as Roxbury, of course, but the consensus was he was much more likely to make an amiable husband. That, and the fact that the duke was said to be ready to come up to scratch for the incomparable Miss Bennington, made Lord Barrasford a singularly attractive prospect. And yet there he sat entertaining a female whose proven immorality made her a totally ineligible connection. He silently noted the number of speaking looks cast his way with satisfaction. It was the same everywhere from London to the smallest hamlet in England—encroaching, ever hopeful mothers circled him like birds of prey, waiting for an opportunity to advance the fortunes of their daughters. He'd once found the exercise amusing, but now it had become a deuced nuisance.

"One would think," observed Mrs. Chatsworth with a sniff, "that dear Lady Sheffield would be nicer in her tastes, don't you agree? Surely she cannot think we wish to renew that acquaintance."

"I daresay Anne Sherwood had a hand in this," her

companion decided, "for she never could see Joanna
Milford for what she was—a scheming, heartless minx
bent on poor Gareth's destruction."

"Well, I for one do not intend to acknowledge her
presence, and I note that Lavinia Symington has already given her the cut direct."

"I don't know—Anne is a dear creature, after all—
perhaps I shall merely do the indirect."

"Pooh. I say 'tis time we stand together and make it
plain that Joanna Milford is not welcome in polite society. If we do nothing, she will be everywhere, and
every man in the county will be dangling after her."

"Well," breathed Ancilla Carleton as she joined the
group, " 'twill be interesting to see what happens now.
Unless I am very much mistaken, that is Roxbury coming in with a Miss Bennington, who visits the Armitage, I'm told, and we all know what that means.
And there is Lady Helen and the Benningtons directly
behind them."

"Miss Bennington?" Mrs. Chatsworth was momentarily diverted. Staring toward the doorway where
Adrian and his party had paused greeting the hostess,
she nodded her head. "I believe Annabelle had it from
the dowager duchess herself that Roxbury means to
make her an offer," she confided. "A pity he had to go
to London to find another wife, but I daresay she's an
unexceptionable girl."

"The reigning Incomparable, I'm told—but a trifle
haughty, if my dear Bevis can be believed. When I men-
tioned Roxbury's interest to him, he said he could not
fathom why the duke would wish for such an ice
maiden when he has no need to go fortune-hunting."

The object of this buzz of gossip, Miss Almeria, laid
a proprietary hand on the duke's arm as they swept
into the room, turning heads as they passed. She was
slightly taller than was fashionable and her hair was as

dark as Adrian's, and her breeding was unmistakable. Her rose pink muslin was of demure cut, but it showed her slender figure to advantage, and tiny pink rosebuds were twined through the crown of black curls atop her head. A single strand of perfectly matched pearls encircled her slender neck and nestled in the hollow of her white throat. And with every move, every step, she carried herself with the assurance of one who believed herself born to the purple. Just the sort of female Roxbury should have married the first time, Mrs. Chatsworth decided. So very unlike Joanna Milford.

Ancilla Carleton was the first to find her voice once the Incomparable was identified for certain. "That dress alone must have cost a hundred pounds," she managed faintly.

"Oh, I doubt that would pay for it. I'm told Lord Bennington spares no expense where his daughter is concerned, and full half of her clothes are said to be made by Madame Cecile herself. Not that the gentlemen in the room will even note the gown," Mrs. Chatsworth pronounced grimly. "While my own dear Charlotte is a most agreeable girl, I cannot think she will be even noted tonight. First the Carew hussy, and now this—I vow my heart is breaking for our girls."

"Well, I for one am utterly outraged," Lady Carleton declared. "My Emily is quite cast down, for she was wishful of making Lord Barrasford's acquaintance, and it is utterly obvious he has eyes only for Roxbury's castoff wife."

Behind them, Mrs. Symington, who had hopes of a match between her son and dear Emily, drew her lips into a thin line of disapproval. " 'Tis all of a piece, if you ask me—Annabelle Sheffield planned this for her own diversion without a thought to the effect on our own young people. Our girls will all be cast in the shade, and our young men will make cakes of themselves."

Lord Barrasford watched as Joanna became aware of Adrian Delacourt's arrival. Aside from a certain rigidity to her already perfectly straight posture and a whiteness at the corners of her mouth, she betrayed none of her inner feelings at seeing him again. Instead, she turned to Johnny and flashed him a smile designed to show the world that the Duke of Roxbury lacked the power to injure her further.

"I find I am thirsty after all, my lord."

He responded with alacrity. "Punch or lemonade?"

"Lemonade, I think."

Settling back in her chair, she cooled herself with an exquisite oriental fan and waited for him to come back. For one uncomfortable moment, she looked up to find Adrian Delacourt staring at her, and she fought the urge to flee from that black-visaged gaze. Rather than dropping her eyes, she merely turned her head to study a row of rather plain young ladies along the far wall, wondering how it was that they should always collect together rather than mix among the company.

Two matrons drifted past her, their voices low in conversation. A third joined them and nodded in Joanna's direction, prompting a sudden silence and frosty looks. She wished she had not sent Barrasford away.

"Lady Carew?"

"Yes."

An aging roué with creaking corsets lowered himself into the seat beside her and leaned closer in an altogether too-familiar manner. His eyes traveled from her face to linger on her breasts, and his full lips pursed appreciatively. His manner, rather than being friendly, bordered on the insulting. She drew herself up haughtily and fixed him with a frozen stare.

"You have the advantage of me, sir, but I do not believe I care to further the acquaintance."

"Well, now, a bit nice in your tastes, ain't you?" he asked, sneering. "There's those around here as ain't forgotten you was Roxbury's cast-off, you know."

"You're disguised, Falburton," Lord Barrasford spoke coldly behind them. Handing Joanna a glass of lemonade, he moved around in front of the older man. "And decidedly *de trop*, too," he added pointedly.

"Now, see here—"

"No," Johnny said firmly. "And I believe you are in my chair, now that I think of it, and I am afraid I wish for it back, sir."

The old rake flashed him a malevolent look, but lumbered out of the chair, grumbling, "It ain't like you to interfere in a man's sport, Johnny."

"I am sorry, my dear—I should not have left you alone to fend off the likes of him," Lord Barrasford murmured in a low undervoice.

"Perhaps I should not have come."

"Nonsense."

Helen Delacourt observed the little contretemps between Falburton and Barrasford with a certain degree of satisfaction and proceeded to make the most of it. It was outside of enough that Adrian must needs stand there like a moon-calf, ignoring a seething Almeria to stare at Joanna. No, he mustn't be allowed to whistle the Bennington fortune down the wind over some renewed passion for that encroaching upstart. With grim determination, the dowager duchess moved to drive Joanna from the field.

"Ah, Sally," she said, approaching the vicar's wife, "one must always wonder at the wisdom of a squeeze, don't you think? That is to say, a smaller party is preferable to me. Then one can be certain one will not encounter just anyone there."

Sally Greenlea followed her line of reasoning perfectly. "Just so. I cannot think what Annabelle was about, but then, one supposes she did not wish to offend Anne Sherwood."

"Well, Anne is a peagoose if she does not know what that woman is up to—poor Gareth scarce dead a year and already she has Barrasford in her clutches," Helen declared disdainfully.

"*Poor* Gareth?"

"Oh, I never blamed him—'twas her casting lures that ruined him. No, Joanna Milford was naught but a siren, my dear. And now the scheming adventuress has marked a new victim. If I knew him better, I should warn him, for she is like a spider, destroying every man who wanders into her web."

It was a conversation that Joanna and Lord Barrasford could not avoid hearing. "A siren, an adventuress, and a spider," Joanna murmured wryly. "You cannot say you have not been warned, can you?"

He set aside his glass abruptly. "I believe they are striking up a waltz, my dear. You do have room on your card for me, do you not?" he asked, keeping his voice light.

"I expect I could find a place, but—"

He leaned closer, murmuring for her ears alone, "Now is not the time for a faint heart, my dear—keep your chin up and follow my lead."

"But—"

Taking the glass from her hand, Johnny placed it on the chair. "Outface 'em—it's the only way, I assure you." Before she could protest further, he'd pulled her from her seat and propelled her toward the dance floor. She closed her eyes briefly as his arm encircled her waist, and she counted out the steps silently in an effort to maintain her composure.

"That's the ticket," he encouraged. "Now, if you can

but contrive to appear to be enjoying this, we'll put the tabbies on the run."

Adrian, having overheard his mother's concerted efforts to discredit Joanna, moved to silence her. "Speaking of peagooses, Mama," he hissed under his breath when he caught up to her, "I cannot credit that you are determined to bring up an old scandal that does no credit to any of us. If I so much as hear you utter her name again here tonight, I'll leave you to entertain the Benningtons alone, and you can make whatever excuse you choose."

"Well, I can scarce credit that you, of all people, would condone her flaunting herself among polite society after what she did to you," Helen countered spitefully.

"I would not call sitting quietly 'flaunting' herself."

"And just what do you call that?" the dowager demanded as Joanna and Barrasford waltzed in full view of everyone. "The little schemer would even sink to an Irish title, but then I daresay she has no hopes of an English one this time. At least, 'twill be a comedown, I suppose."

"There's nothing wrong with Johnny," Adrian retorted. "The title may be newer than mine, but the money's old." A pang of envy cut at his breastbone as he watched them waltz. It seemed that she was more beautiful every time he saw her. He stood transfixed, his memory harking back to a time when she'd floated in his arms. She'd been the green girl then, and he was the accomplished flirt, but when he'd held her, he'd been overwhelmed by what he felt for her. He'd stolen a march on Gary on just such a night as this. He'd won Joanna Milford in the teeth of Gary and a dozen other suitors on a warm summer evening seven years ago.

"Ah, Roxbury." Almeria, her face still flushed from the last country dance with a local buck, cut into his thoughts by placing a hand on his arm. When he said nothing, she followed his gaze, and her eyes hardened momentarily. Then, secure in her own worthiness, she smiled coquettishly. "I believe we are promised to waltz, my lord," she reminded him, showing him her filled card. "Ah, yes—here you are."

"Huh?" Reluctantly he tore his eyes away from Joanna to look down at her. There was no question about it, Almeria Bennington was an Incomparable, and he ought to feel something, but he didn't. A quick, surreptitious glance to where Joanna moved gracefully to Barrasford's lead decided him. "So we are, Miss Bennington," he agreed with a determined smile of his own.

For Almeria, the triumph was brief. Whatever status she obtained by standing up with the Duke of Roxbury was mitigated by his maneuvering on the floor. She found herself being expertly led in time with the music until they were but a few feet from his former wife. And although he never missed a step, it was obvious to all who watched that he had eyes only for Joanna, following her and Barrasford as they whirled and floated to the lovely, lilting music. When the last notes mercifully ended, Almeria pleaded thirst and was rewarded by an offer from a nearby gentleman to procure her something from one of the refreshment tables. As if she had not endured enough, she realized Adrian still only had eyes for Lady Carew. Indeed, he scarce noted it when she and Mr. Chiddington left him.

When he finally collected himself from his near trance, Adrian saw Miss Bennington standing in a small group, surrounded by half a dozen admirers, her smile brittle and her eyes burning with a sense of ill-usage. His mother plucked peevishly at his coat sleeve, hissing, "Adrian, how could you? 'Tis outside of enough that you make a fool of yourself yet again over

that trollop, but must you insult your intended as well?
What must Lord Bennington think, I ask you?"

"Hang Bennington!" he muttered with feeling.
Nonetheless, his sense of duty prompted him to attempt amends to the lovely Almeria. It was not her
fault, after all, that he could not forget Jo. Resolutely he
made his way to the refreshment table, only to be
brought up short by Miss Bennington's spiteful tongue.

"Well, I for one would not associate with the creature, of course, but I cannot but pity her—it must be a
blow to have lost a husband like dear Roxbury through
her own folly. But then I daresay she has only herself to
blame for it."

Damn her! Adrian fumed to himself. La Belle Bennington was making certain that everyone within hearing recalled the old scandal yet again. Abruptly he
turned on his heel and crossed the room to where
Joanna stood conversing with her mother-in-law. He
could tell by the expression on Anne Sherwood's face
that she was aware of the unpleasant gossip, but she
was gamely trying to ignore it. He saw no sign of
Johnny Barrasford. Without thinking, he grasped
Joanna's elbow firmly and muttered, "If you would
save face, come with me."

"I beg—"

"Don't be a fool, Jo!" he snapped with unwarranted
temper. "I'm about to restore your lost credit."

"I beg your pardon?"

His grip on her elbow was almost painful, but she
knew that to pull away would be to create a humiliat-
ing scene. She blinked back angry tears and forced a
stiff smile as he pushed her onto the dance floor.

He pulled her tense body into his arms and swung
her to the music. She stiffened in shock, missing a step,
and then exhaled sharply. "You can do it, Jo—pretend I

am Gary, if you must," he whispered harshly above her ear.

"Really, but I don't think—Dree, I don't wish to do this."

"Just smile, for God's sake," he ordered. His arm tightened around her waist, pulling her closer. "And it would help if you'd smile at me."

"You've taken complete leave of your senses," she decided. "And you are making me look utterly foolish, as if I should willingly—" She caught the outraged expression on Helen Delacourt's face as they passed her, and for the briefest moment felt some small satisfaction. A sudden hush had rolled through the crowd, making her acutely aware of their silent, stunned scrutiny. She closed her eyes to avoid the stares and tried to concentrate on the music, praying that the dance would soon end.

The musicians, caught up in something they did not understand, repeated every note, playing the whole piece again. For Adrian, it was as though time had stood still, as though he were at Joanna's come-out again. The soft, fragrant breeze, redolent with the mingled perfumes of exotic flowers, wafted through the ballroom. Her flesh was warm and alive through the silk of her gown, and the crown of her hair was like satin against his cheek. This was the way he'd remembered her, and every fiber of his being was aware of the intense longing he felt even now.

"I've never forgotten you, Jo," he murmured into her wheat-gold hair. "I've missed you so."

She had been almost seduced by the beauty of the music and the gentleness of that breeze as she'd leaned into the warmth of his embrace, but his words brought her up short, and the old bitterness flooded over her.

"Really, Dree?" She stiffened and pushed him away.

"And what of Gary? Do you miss him, too? 'Twas you who threw us both away," she reminded him coldly.

His arm slackened as she brought him back to reality. She pushed him away and started off the floor before he realized her intent. "Jo!"

She half turned back, and her mouth twisted as she asked, "Did you think I'd let you make a public spectacle of me twice, Dree?"

He'd gone white at her words, but she didn't care. She had to get out of the suddenly oppressive room. Stumbling blindly, she managed to call for her shawl.

"No!" Adrian said harshly. "Wait! Jo!" He pushed past the shocked crowd and caught her in the doorway. Shoving her through the center hall beneath the bemused stares of the Sheffield servants, he thrust her out onto the portico. "Do I think of Gary, Jo? Often. And I think of you!" he admitted savagely. "God, how I think of you!"

"Unhand me, Dree."

"And I think of the boy, too. You have no right to keep my son from me, no right at all. And do not deny he's my son—he's in mine own image!"

The color drained from her face, blanching it. Her stomach knotted painfully. "Leave me alone!"

Reaching out for her, he stunned himself by blurting, "I am prepared to forgive you, Jo—I want you and the boy."

The words hung between them. Her eyes widened in shock as they sank in, and then she found her voice. Her sense of ill-usage complete, she choked out, "Forgive me? How dare you? There is nothing to forgive, Dree—and 'tis I who shall never forgive you!"

"Joanna—?"

Adrian dropped his hands at the sound of Johnny Barrasford's voice and stepped back helplessly. Barrasford looked from one flushed face to the other. "Your pardon, but—"

"No." Joanna's voice was suddenly hollow. "Lord Barrasford, I should like to go home. If you will but find my mother-in-law—"

Her silk shawl still dangled from her hand. Barrasford reached out and solicitously draped it over her shoulders. "Roxbury, if you will excuse us, I mean to escort Lady Carew home. Pray be kind enough to apprise the dowager countess that she has left." To Jo, he said, "There's no sense in spoiling her evening needlessly, is there?"

"No, of course not." Looking up at him, she forced a smile. "You are exceedingly kind, my lord, but there's no sense in spoiling yours either, is there?"

"Nonsense. With you gone, there's nothing here for me, anyway."

Without a word, Adrian turned on his heel and walked back inside. As he crossed the threshold, he was met by Almeria Bennington, who pressed her hands against her lovely temples and complained of the headache. "My lord, I would that you took me home—I cannot abide it here so much as a minute longer."

"Neither can I," he told her tersely. Privately, he just wished to go home and drown himself in enough Madeira to make him forget how it had felt to hold Joanna. He closed his eyes momentarily. *Damn her. Damn her for doing this to him again.*

In Lord Barrasford's carriage, Joanna leaned her head back and stared into the darkness. The vehicle moved slowly, threading between the conveyances still parked in the Sheffield drive, until it reached the open road. Johnny silently sparked the wicks of the interior lamps and settled back into the seat across from her. It was some time before she spoke, and then her voice was low.

"It was foolish of me to think that because I'd been invited there, they would be civil. No, I did not really think it—I knew they would not. The world will never forget that I was divorced," she said wearily. "I could have had a dozen children by a dozen different men, and even if it were common knowledge, that would have been forgiven, you know."

"But you didn't, my dear. I don't think it is in you to play anyone false. And anyone who says differently must surely be a liar."

"Roxbury believed the lies. No, it was just foolish of me to attempt going about in society."

The tonelessness of her words affected him far more than tears. In his desire to be seen with her, he'd encouraged her hopes, and now he could see he'd been wrong. His heart went out to her while his mind groped for words of comfort. "Do not refine too much on the spite of a few tabbies, my dear," he offered quietly. " 'Twas jealousy and nothing more."

"Was it?"

"You were the most beautiful female there, Joanna. Perhaps if I had stayed at your side—"

"No—it would not have served, sir. I am sorry—I should not have embroiled you in my affairs." A heavy sigh escaped her as she opened her eyes to look at him. "Associating with me can do you no credit, my lord."

" 'Tis of no consequence to me, my dear," he assured her. "As a man, I could keep even the most notorious female company without causing comment."

She flinched visibly, and he wished he could bite back the ill-chosen words. Leaning across the seat, he reached to touch her hand. "And, no—I do not consider you notorious in the least, Joanna. Indeed, I would not have you think my intentions were other than honorable." His fingers closed over hers, then squeezed them.

Her gaze dropped to where his hand held hers. "My lord—"

"Pray hear me out, my dear." He'd meant to wait, to conduct his courtship of the lovely widow more slowly. Instead, he found himself saying, "I am three-and-thirty—I am no callow youth fancying himself in love for the tenth time in as many weeks, Joanna. Believe me, I know what I want." When she did not pull away, he slid over to sit beside her and fixed her with serious gray eyes. "I am head over heels for you already—if you would say the word, I would marry you and take you away from this. As my wife, you would not have to face such censure."

She stared, speechless, and then averted her head to look out into the darkness of the country lane. Her free hand knotted the silk fringe of her shawl against her lap. "You do not know me, my lord," she said finally.

"It is too soon. And it is not just me you would be getting, you know, for I have two sons. If I ever marry again, I will have to consider them as well as myself. I am not the sort of mother who can banish them to some distant estate without me."

"Don't be hasty in rejecting my suit, Joanna, for such a marriage is not without advantage. Oh, I know 'tis an Irish title, but that means we can repair to my estate in Ireland and never come back unless you wish it." His voice was gentle and reassuring. "I like children, you know, and I would be good to your sons—you'd find me a kind fellow, really." When she still did not answer, he pressed on with, "I have reached the point in my life when I am ready to set up my own nursery, so do not think I offer lightly without regard for the future." He added, "At least, I know you are not barren. I can close my eyes and see our children riding about the park in pony carts. I can see you going about the neighborhood over there in peace. I've sown my wild oats, Joanna, and I'm ready for that peace. I'm tired of being a frivolous fellow, spending my nights gaming and whoring. I'd be proud to call you my wife—I'd shout it before the world, if you didn't mind it."

She turned around at that and met the gray eyes. There was an appealing warmth in them that tempted her. A rueful smile quirked the corner of his mouth as he admitted, "And alas, I have no mother to plague you—I regret the lack, of course, but you behold my immediate family in me."

Deeply moved by the kindness of his offer, she could only manage a tremulous smile. With a catch in her voice she mused slowly, "You know, you sound so very much like Gary. Only he had to take me to Italy. He said the war could not be as cruel as the people here."

"Did you love him so very much?" he could not help asking.

She was silent for several seconds as she composed her answer. "I did not at first, I suppose—it is quite different, what one feels for a husband and what one feels for a dear friend." Her voice dropped even lower and he had to strain to hear her. "But then I came to love him for what he gave up for me. If I had not had him, I could not have gone on, sir."

Barrasford was taken aback by her confession. Given what he'd heard earlier in the evening from the gossips he'd thought Gareth Sherwood to be the great love of her life. He could not resist asking, "And Roxbury?"

"There was a time when he was everything to me," she admitted simply.

"I see." He stared out the window for a moment to collect his own thoughts. "But you both must have been very young then, my dear. People change." Abruptly he returned to his offer. "If you cannot give me an answer just now, at least tell me that you care for him no longer, and I'll not despair."

She took a deep breath, then exhaled it slowly. "How could I care for anyone who would believe such baseness of me? No, Adrian killed my feelings for him when he accused me."

"Then my offer stands. If you cannot bring yourself to accept me today, then perhaps after you have thought it over—perhaps tomorrow or next week—or next month even."

"You do not know what you ask!" she wrung out miserably. "You might think my reputation does not matter now, but later you could come to regret the cost of it. Gary didn't really wish to leave England until he realized there'd be no peace for either of us here. There was even an attempt on his life after the bill of divorcement was passed. As he left Parliament the day the decree was read, there were people shouting, 'Whoremaster!' at him. You do not know how much hatred there is in this world until something like that happens to you."

"Hush." He interrupted her with a finger to her lips. "We'll speak no more of this tonight. Believe me when I say I would not overset you for the world."

"I'm not overset, my lord. I'm just telling you how it was. Gary said it did not matter to him, either, but once we were wed, he knew it would be years, maybe even a lifetime, before we could come home to England."

"Joanna, I do not even pretend to know the whole—indeed, I've no wish to probe your wounds. But I am certain, however, of one thing: it is not in you to play the harlot. As I think I said before, I've known enough of the other sort of women to know the difference." He reached again to still the hand that worked a crease in her gown. "Whether you accept me or not, my dear, I would stand your friend."

In the carriage behind them, Adrian Delacourt shared a stony silence with his mother and Miss Bennington. Both women fairly seethed at what they perceived to be his foolish infatuation with Joanna Sherwood, and their inner rage was rendered all the more impotent by his cold indifference to their anger. Helen Delacourt spent the better part of the ride composing what she would say to him once they were alone, while Almeria considered her next move. Indifference and disdain were certainly not what she was used to, and she wondered briefly if even a duke's title could compensate for his lack of gallantry. Then she recalled herself. Nothing, not even the Sherwood woman, would keep her from being a duchess.

As for Adrian himself, there was only a deepening scowl when Barrasford's carriage turned off toward Haven. He leaned forward for a time, scanning the moonlit horizon until the other coach was out of sight.

Then he sank back gloomily, barely answering in monosyllables when Almeria went so far as to venture that the moon made for quite a lovely night, didn't he think?

The dowager, determined to have a row with her son over his foolishness, bade Almeria good night in the lower hall and then proceeded to invade the library. Shutting the door behind her, she took in the glass of Madeira in his hand and remarked acidly, "Joanna Milford made a fool of you once, Adrian, and she has done so again tonight. I vow I could have swooned when I saw you lead her out! Have you no pride? Did she not bring enough shame to your name the last time?"

"I don't want to hear this," he told her coldly.

"Well, you will. Can you not see that she means to add Lord Barrasford to the list of her conquests? Her disgraceful behavior tonight will be the *on-dit* of the neighborhood for weeks! I shudder to think what Lord Bennington must think after this—no, I *know* he surely thinks you a dashed loose screw!" she finished with uncharacteristic cant. "What on earth were you thinking of? Can you not answer me that?"

"I don't know. I don't even know what I think of anything anymore. I just know I don't want to hear you spreading your venom where Joanna is concerned ever again. Whatever she did, she's surely paid for it by now."

"You cannot mean to let that little harlot lead you about by your private parts again surely?"

"Did you not hear me?" he asked, his voice rising. "I said I didn't want to listen to you carp about Jo—not tonight, not ever."

"Well, you will! How you could ever forget what she did is beyond belief! No—I shall not hold my tongue this time! Let her go back to Italy or wherever she's been, and let her take her brats with her!"

"Her oldest brat, as you choose to call him, is my son!" he all but shouted at her. "*Your* only grandson, madam! Does that mean nothing to you?"

"It does not! Really, Adrian, I cannot credit that she has taken you in yet again with her wiles! If the boy is indeed a Delacourt, why did she not speak up at the time? I seem to recall that she did not even challenge the bill or the charges!" she reminded him spitefully. "So he does not look like Sherwood—what does that prove? Perhaps," she added nastily, "dear Joanna could not be certain just who the father was. May I remind you that there are other dark-haired men in this neighborhood?"

"Enough! You couldn't question it if you saw him, I tell you. There's more than a speaking likeness, Mother—it is like looking into a mirror and seeing myself twenty-three years ago." Refilling his glass, he gulped the Madeira again. "I have a son," he repeated evenly.

"And what is that to anything, anyway? If Gareth Sherwood was foolish enough to claim him, there's naught you can do now. Even if he is, as you say, your son, Adrian, what is to be gained by shouting it about? She was married to Carew when he was born, was she not? He is Earl of Carew and no concern of ours."

"You don't listen at all, do you? He's my flesh and blood as much as hers."

"By rights, he was Carew's! Forget him! Forget her!"

"I would that it were that simple, but it isn't. You'd have me ignore my own blood." He drained the glass, then flung it into the cold brazier, where it shattered. He raised his eyes to where Joanna's portrait had once hung. "I destroyed her, you know. It's scarce a wonder that she didn't want me to know about the boy."

"Adrian . . ." Knowing she'd gone too far again, Helen moved to lay a gentler hand on his shoulder, cajoling in a softer voice, "Do your duty to your family and marry Almeria—she will make an exemplary duchess. Come, do not let us quarrel over something best left in the past."

He felt taut as a bowstring. He'd seen Joanna again—had held her in his arms even—and he'd wanted her again. Even now, he knew if he closed his eyes again, the intensity of the passion they'd once shared would overwhelm him. And tonight he'd told her he wanted her back—he'd not meant to say it, but he knew it had been the truth. "No. I don't want Almeria Bennington in my bed, and I never will."

"Then you are a fool!" Helen Delacourt snapped.

"I told you—I want passion."

"Passion!" She spat out the word as though it had a bad taste to it. "There are opera dancers for that, but when it comes to blood—" She stopped. "If you are speaking of Joanna, look where that led you and Gareth! The two of you were after her like hounds after a bitch, weren't you? Aye, you were friends until she got her clutches in both of you, weren't you?"

"You are not content to wound, are you, Mother?" he asked bitterly. "You would kill every decent memory I have of them, wouldn't you? You always hated her."

"She was a nobody!"

"She was my duchess!"

"You were a fool over her!"

"So you have said a thousand times over." He turned to pierce her with those dark eyes. "But maybe I was a fool to believe you."

Her face went white at his expression. "And what do you mean by that?"

"You always hated her—you found fault with everything she ever did. Mayhap my greatest foolishness was to leave her here with you. Maybe I should have taken her to London with me, but I thought if you got to know her—"

"I knew her far too well, Adrian."

"You didn't know her at all." He looked up at her. "There are times now, Mother, when I wonder how she could have survived here. There are times when I almost cannot blame her for turning to Gary, for I am sure you must've made this place a living hell for her."

"She was a trollop!"

"She bore my son!"

"That changes nothing! There's nothing you can do about that now!"

An oddly arrested look on his face, he stared for a moment. "No? There you are wrong, Mother. If I have to look the veriest fool—if I have to admit to being wrong—I mean to have my son. And I am willing to take her to get him."

"*What?*" It took her a moment to find her voice. "No—I won't have it!"

The room was stifling. Rising, he loosed his cravat and flung it into a chair, then he strode for the door.

"Where are you going?" she demanded in alarm. "Adrian, have you no pride?"

"I had a surfeit of it once."

"I would not have the Benningtons hear us quarrel over that woman."

"Unless they are deaf, I'll warrant they already have heard more than they care to. Good night, Mother."

"Adrian!"

The side door slammed behind him. The dowager moved to pour herself a glass of the wine, and she stood sipping it. Her son was handsome, he was all she could have wanted for a Roxbury duke, but he had a stubbornness and a misguided sense of honor that vexed her beyond everything. Why could he not see what he owed his name?

"Your Grace?"

She turned around to face Almeria Bennington. "Come in, my dear," she said tiredly. "I daresay you could not help hearing everything."

The young woman started to deny it, then thought better of the idea. "Yes, but I could not credit my ears, ma'am. I had not supposed his depth of feeling for her."

"Humph! Do not mistake the matter, my dear—what Adrian feels for Joanna Sherwood is no different from what any buck feels for a pretty soiled dove, if he would but admit it."

"Mama thinks we should leave."

"I am not through yet, my dear." Helen Delacourt drained her glass and set it down. Her eyes were hard, her mouth drawn thin. "No. I think that between us, we may still retrieve the situation—provided you still wish to be Duchess of Roxbury. You see, I have a scheme."

"Oh, dear ma'am . . ." Almeria's interest in the title was still evident, satisfying Helen.

"Then. we are decided. I must speak with Lord Bennington, of course, before we act."

"I don't understand—"

"If there is one thing we can rely on," the older woman mused aloud, " 'tis Adrian's sense of honor. We must compromise you, that is all."

"What?" the girl gasped. "I will not—"

"You will not have to do anything but pretend an interest in the Wells. I mean to insist that Adrian accompany you there, of course, and your maid will become separated from you. Your father will insist that you have been compromised, and my son will of course do the right thing." Helen raised her eyes again to the place above the mantel. "You will make the perfect Duchess of Roxbury, my dear." Turning back to Almeria, she added smugly, "When I am gone to my maker, you will take my place here."

"I hope so, ma'am—I sincerely hope so."

"You will." And yet as she said it, Helen Delacourt felt a twinge of misgiving. Perhaps, she thought to herself, a bit of well-placed gossip about Joanna and Barrasford . . . Ah, if Mary Cummins were only here now. There was something to be said for a maid with connections to every other household in the neighborhood. Sighing silently, Helen realized that this time she'd have to take care of the matter herself. "You *will*," she repeated more forcefully. "And you and I, dearest Almeria, will deal well together, I am sure. You even remind me of myself."

Anne Sherwood climbed the magnificent staircase at Haven with a heavy heart, wondering if she'd been wrong after all to insist that Joanna and the boys come home. Certainly she'd been terribly wrong to encourage her to attend Annabelle's party, she reflected sadly. But after six years—well, she'd expected nothing like the censure she'd seen tonight. And it did not help that she knew where to lay the blame for it. No, as much as she hated to admit it, Helen Delacourt's spite had won out yet again.

It was beyond reason to think that a woman like Helen could have borne the dark-haired boy who'd once run tame here. Knowing his parents, Anne had actually felt sorry for him despite all that wealth, despite the grandness of the title he was to inherit. Indeed, she'd lavished almost as much attention on him as on Gareth, and the two boys had loved each other more than most brothers, and they'd done everything together, even falling in love with Joanna. But it hadn't been Joanna who'd come between them. it had been Helen, and the results of that woman's evil had been devastating for all three of them. While Anne considered herself to be of a charitable nature, she found herself hoping that Helen Delacourt would pay dearly for her sins, if not in this world, then in the next.

A slice of faint light shone beneath Joanna's door.

Anne hesitated as the clock in the hall below struck three, and then she tapped gently on the gleaming mahogany panels.

"Come in," came the muffled reply.

She found the younger woman abed with the curtains undrawn. Propped up amid several silk-covered pillows with her hair brushed down over her shoulders like a schoolgirl, Joanna seemed terribly young and vulnerable. But Anne realized with relief that her daughter-in-law's eyes were clear and dry.

"I had not expected to find you still awake. Perhaps you would care for some warm milk, my dear."

"No."

"Oh, dearest, I should never have insisted you go, but—"

" 'Twas not your fault, Maman. You could not have known she would be so eager to remind everyone."

"And I had not thought that anyone would credit her vicious spite." Anne sank to sit on the edge of the bed. "I am so sorry, Jo. If you find you cannot stay in England, I've come to the decision to support you whatever you choose. We still own the villa on Capri, and I am prepared to repair there with you and the boys."

"No. Oh, I admit I wanted to run earlier, but I've decided I'm not going to let her deny my sons' right to live here. As you yourself have reminded me, I have to think of them now. Besides, I realize now that I could not face my reflection in my mirror if I gave up the field to her again." Her jaw set, she turned toward her mother-in-law. "She had no cause to do that to me, and I will retreat no further from her insults. I've decided if she wishes to tell the tale again, I will see that the world knows the truth this time. I was a green girl then, Maman, but now I am five and twenty and not nearly so green."

"Perhaps if you went to Adrian even now and explained—" Anne stopped short, quelled by the outrage that stiffened Joanna and threatened her composure. "No—I quite see that you would not wish to do so."

"He did not have to believe her. No, if I choose to fight, 'twill be for the boys. I would not have them think that I—that their mother was some sort of harlot. I want them to be proud rather than ashamed of me."

"Well, I cannot say but what I am glad for this, my dear—'tis what I have always wished. I have long thought that her story would not stand scrutiny if you would but dispute it. Indeed, I wanted Gary to fight the charges in every court—in Parliament even. But there were other considerations at the time, of course," Anne allowed. "A drawn-out battle would have seen Justin born before you were out of the country. And you and Gary were determined that there be no question of bastardy. Of course, if Adrian *had* seen him then, things might have turned out differently."

"I could not live with a husband who had no faith in me. I wouldn't have wanted to live with one who kept me simply because he realized I'd borne his child."

"No, I suppose not."

"Lord Barrasford said something tonight, Maman— that he could see I was no harlot. If someone like him can believe that, then perhaps others will also."

"He said that? I own I had thought him merely another Corinthian concerned with the cut of his coat, but—"

"He has offered marriage."

"*What?*"

Joanna nodded. A rueful smile played at her lips. "That is, of course, if I can stomach an Irish title. 'Tis odd, isn't it? My shocking rep means less to him than my opinion of *him*."

"He never said that, surely."

Joanna nodded. "He did."

"But the boys—a man like Barrasford must—"

"He loves children, you see. Maman, he must certainly be the first Corinthian to admit that, don't you think?"

" 'Pon my word . . ." Anne peered closely at Joanna, uncertain as to whether she ought to take her seriously.

"Yes, and he has no interfering mama, he regrets to say." The smile deepened. "He'd heard Helen, you see, so he thought perhaps that would weigh with me."

Silent for a moment, Anne digested this new turn of Joanna's fortune. It was the first time she'd seen even a glimpse of her daughter-in-law's light humor since Gary died. A mental review of all she knew of Lord Barrasford yielded nothing against him. Indeed, another marriage was what she herself had urged only a week or so before, she reminded herself. Aloud she could only manage, " 'Tis so sudden, my love. Er—what did you answer?"

"He did not press me. I tried to tell him that my reputation is like to haunt him also, but he would not listen." The smile faded and the blue eyes were suddenly serious. "It would be so very tempting, you know. So very tempting. I think he would be exceedingly kind to the boys."

"He's a very handsome man," Anne conceded.

"But it is the kindness that reminds me of Gary."

As her shock faded, Anne gave the matter more consideration. "There is a great deal to be said for kindness, isn't there?"

"More so than for passion. Believe me, it is far more comfortable."

"Perhaps you ought to consider his suit, my dear—the name's old, the fortune quite respectable."

"And I would not have to face the *ton* unprotected," Joanna added in Barrasford's favor. "Indeed, if I chose to live in Ireland, I should not have to face them at all.

And Ireland is not so very far," she mused. "I mean, you could visit the boys often—or I am certain that Lord Barrasford would not mind it if you wished to live with us, for that matter. I could not bear it if you were not part of our lives."

"Fiddle. If he does not have an interfering mama, I'm sure he won't want one. Besides, I do have my dower properties, Jo. I probably should have taken up residence on one of them long ago, but with you and Gary out of the country, it didn't seem wise just then. And then with Gareth's death—well, I felt you and the children needed my support."

"I need your love, Maman."

"Well, you've had that since you were a little girl. I never approved of Milborn's disinterested behavior, I can tell you. But we were speaking of Barrasford, were we not? 'Pon reflection, there is much to be said for the match."

"Yes." Joanna stared absently as she admitted slowly, "Except that I do not love him. And it is too soon to know if I ever will. That, too, should be a consideration, don't you think?"

"You loved Adrian Delacourt to distraction, my dear," Anne reminded her, "and you cannot say that the result was happy."

"We were happy once." Joanna's eyes met Anne's and held steadily. "But Lord Barrasford is a great deal more like Gary."

"You made my son very happy." Anne reached to pat her hand affectionately. "But then, a marriage is something that only the principals ought to decide. Oh, I realize that is a rather modern notion, but I've seen far too many instances where the arranged sort become nothing more than a license for both parties to seek satisfaction elsewhere as soon as an heir is provided." Standing up, she smiled. "For all that has happened, my love, I still say there are those who would count you fortunate. 'Tis a rare female who could bring Roxbury, Carew, and Barrasford up to scratch in one lifetime."

"Helen wouldn't see it that way, I'm sure. She'd say I've thrice overreached myself."

"Helen will get her comeuppance one day," Anne predicted. "But for now, you'd best get your sleep."

For a long time after Anne left, Joanna made no move to douse the candles, but sat there reviewing this last encounter with Adrian and contemplating how best to defeat his mother. There was no doubt about it: he still believed the story Helen had told, and even after the passage of so many years, that still wounded far more than anything anyone else could say. The clock downstairs struck four, the candles were nearly gutted, and still she had no answers. She rose reluctantly to blow out the flickering flames and throw open the shutters. A damp breeze blew in, promising rain. Her thin lawn nightrail billowed out from her hot body, fanning and cooling it.

She stood there staring at the dark clouds shadowing the full moon, and she remembered again the feel of Adrian's arms about her, the smell of the Hungary water he always wore. The intensity of their physical union. Unable to bear the sensations such memories evoked deep within her, she took refuge from them by seeking her bed and forcing herself to think of Johnny Barrasford.

But sleep would not come. She could reach that hazy netherworld between rational, conscious thought and oblivion, but she could not cross it. Barrasford was there, urging her to take the security he offered, but behind him stood Adrian, accusing her of betraying him. And there was Gary, so good and strong, offering to protect her and the baby. And, above them all, she could hear Helen Delacourt saying, "I saw them—I saw them with my own eyes. Ask her maid—she'll tell you also."

"I want to hear it from your lips," Adrian pleaded. "For God's sake, tell me why?" But the look in his eyes stopped her—she knew he already believed the lies.

With a groan, she turned away to pound a fresh place in the other pillow, and she tried to blot all of them from her mind. The first drops of rain hit the roof tentatively, the wind gained strength, and then the sky poured rain. Above her, there was a steady staccato that gradually lulled and dulled. But as the night finally closed around her, she imagined that Adrian's arms were wrapped around her, that he was holding her as she slipped into sleep.

"Mama! Mama!"

Joanna came awake with a start as the door of her bedchamber burst open to admit her sons. Rolling over, she shaded her eyes against the brightness of day and grimaced. Her few short hours of restless sleep were not nearly enough.

"Master Justin! Master Robert!" Miss Finchley whispered loudly as she caught up to them and grasped each boy by an arm. "You mustn't wake your mama!"

"'Tis all right," Joanna muttered, sitting up sleepily and rubbing at her itching eyes. "By the looks of it, I've been here overlong."

The governess shook her head and cast a meaningful look at her charges. "But I told them not to disturb you, my lady. Indeed, Lady Anne was wishful that you get your rest." Firmly pulling both children to face Joanna, Miss Finchley ordered, "Beg your mama's pardon for the intrusion, if you please, and we shall get back to our studies."

"But I don't please!" Three-year-old Robin broke

away and scrambled up on the bed with Joanna. "Mama, look out the window!"

"Master Robert—" There was a warning note in the governess's voice that went unheeded.

In spite of the fatigue she felt, Joanna managed a smile at her younger son. "See what, dearest?"

"A rainbow!" Justin burst out. "'Tis a rainbow!"

"'Tis not fair!" Robin turned to his brother and accused him, "You just did that to steal a march on me! 'Tis not fair! Mama, I saw it first, and I wanted to tell you!"

"Boys!" Miss Finchley moved to the bed and reached for the little boy. "You mustn't fight in front of your mother. Come now—there's work to be done."

"But—"

"'Tis all right," Joanna repeated to mollify the governess. Turning her attention to Robin, she gave him a quick squeeze. "If you will but get off the covers, I'll come see your rainbow."

The boy slid obediently off the bed and tugged at her hand. "Over here—you can see it from over here!"

Heedless of her nightshift, she let him pull her toward the window, where she stood looking as he pointed. Justin jealously clung to her leg to compete with Robin from her other side. For a moment Joanna could only stare at the great arc of color that brightened the morning sky. The rain-washed air was fresh, and the garden below was ablaze with a profusion of bright colors. The storm was over, replaced with a warm, fresh peace. She ruffled each child's head in turn, hugging him to her side. Forgotten were the bitterness and turmoil that had plagued her night as she contemplated the beauty of the rainbow and the summer morn. No matter what, she reminded herself fiercely, she was the most fortunate of women—she had two bright, handsome sons to love.

"Mama," Robin asked suddenly, "you didn't mind getting up to see it, did you?"

"Of course not, dearest," she reassured him sincerely. "I should not have wanted to miss it for anything. It isn't every day that one gets to see something like this."

"What makes it?" Justin wanted to know, his inquisitive mind already searching for the cause of it.

"I don't know, but perhaps Miss Finchley will help you discover the answer."

"Papa would have known," he insisted.

"Papa knew many things, Justin, but even he did not know everything. I knew your papa quite well," Joanna responded with a twinkle in her blue eyes, "but I cannot recall ever having heard him say where rainbows come from."

"Oh. Well . . ." He brightened. "I daresay he could have found out."

"I don't care where it comes from," Robin declared mutinously. "It's pretty—and I like it!"

"And I like it too," she agreed. "Besides, one does not have to know about things precisely to enjoy them." Her fingers worked the red-gold hair that reminded her so much of Gary. The child was possessed of the same sweetness and generosity of spirit as his father, she reflected briefly, and that alone was something to be nurtured and treasured.

"Could we go look for where it touches the ground?" Justin wondered aloud.

"No—we'd never find it," she answered. "I think its touching the ground is an illusion."

"What's that?" he demanded.

"Something that just seems to be but isn't really. And do not be asking me to explain further just now, Justin, because I cannot. All I can tell you is that often things are not what you think you see, and when that happens, it is called an illusion." She caught the disbelieving lift of his dark eyebrow and for a flitting second she saw Adrian in him. Then his expression cleared and an understanding of sorts dawned on his young face. "I see—it's like when the bed curtains fly out at night and I think something's there."

"I believe you could call that an illusion if you wished," she decided. "Now, if you will but go with Miss Finchley so that I may get dressed, I'll be down directly and see the watercolors you have done. She tells me they are quite fine, you know." She gave each of them a playful push toward the governess. "And thank you for sharing your rainbow with me—I liked it very much."

She stood at the window for some time after they left, contemplating the beauty and the peace of the scene before her. The previous night, she'd struggled with the past, but it was time to put that behind her. There was nothing she could do now to change what had been done, after all. Her eyes focused on the rainbow—man's symbol of better things to come, of hope for a brighter day. There would always be those who would shun her, but there'd also be those who would stand with her. She'd run no more from the lies that had ruined her, she told herself fiercely. And even if she did not wed Johnny Barrasford, she had a friend to help her face them.

"Madam, there is a Mr. Thorpe to see you."

"Mr. Thorpe?" Joanna laid aside the book she'd been reading, a lurid gothic novel ordered from London, and tried to place the name. "I am afraid I do not know anyone—"

Anne looked up from her needlework. "I daresay 'tis but a tradesman come to take your order for something. We were expecting someone about chimney repair for the main saloon, were we not?"

"In this weather?" Joanna favored her mother-in-law with a wry smile. "I very much doubt he would wish to climb up in the rain, but then, perhaps he will be able to estimate the work without doing so." She rose, glancing toward the multipaned windows as she did so. "I certainly hope so, in any event, as 'tis pouring outside. Where did you leave him, Thomas?"

"In the main saloon, madam."

"Good." Anne nodded appreciatively. "Then he can quite see that the chimney leaks." She settled back in the big wing chair and smoothed the fabric she had been working against her lap. The rain had been steady, necessitating that they keep inside, and yet Joanna's spirits had been remarkably cheerful since the Sheffield debacle. Indeed, she reflected as she jabbed her needle into her design, their positions had almost reversed. Now she feared that Joanna would never be reestablished, while dear Jo did not appear to care. Perhaps that was the influence of Lord Barrasford, Anne conceded. Certainly he was most assiduous in his attentions and scarcely a day passed without his paying them a morning call. But then there was nothing to suggest that Joanna meant to accept him—quite the opposite, in fact. She'd come down the morning after the Sheffield party smiling, and when taxed with Barrasford's offer, she'd announced that she would very much rather depend on his friendship than his name to see her through. With a sigh, Anne knotted the center of a small flower and began working on the petals.

"Mr. Thorpe?"

Her visitor was not readily apparent when Joanna entered the saloon, but then, the darkness of the day did nothing to provide illumination through the unshuttered windows. outside, the rain came down steadily, ricocheting off the puddles that dotted the lawn.

"Mr. Thorpe?" she inquired again.

"Aye." The man moved from where he'd been observing the trickle of water that edged down from the bricks in the fireplace into a strategically placed pan. "You ought to get that repaired, ma'am, before it ruins the floor." His eyes traveled over the richly furnished room, taking in the elegant detail work on the moldings. "You've got too fine a place to risk mildew or worse, and if the floor must needs be replaced, it'll cost you a pretty penny."

"I am aware of the need, sir, and cost is but a small consideration," Joanna cut in smoothly, "but I would know how you propose to fix it. The last person to examine it insisted 'twas the roof, and it was not. I hope you can find the source of the leak."

"Me?" He appeared taken aback.

"Oh, I should not expect that you do the work yourself, of course." She noted the cut of his plain brown frock coat and trousers and decided he was more prosperous than many of the tradesmen in the area. He'd obviously taken great pains to be presentable for his foray to inspect one of the premier country houses. "You *will* be able to estimate it today, won't you? I should like the work commenced as soon as the weather clears."

"Madam, I would not know where to start, I assure you. Perhaps—"

"You are not here to inspect the chimney?"

"Lud no! That is to say—" Obviously affronted by the assumption, he hastened to dig into his coat for his card. "Perhaps this will be of some assistance," he explained as he handed it to her. "I am a solicitor representing His Grace, the Duke of Roxbury," he announced importantly. "Perhaps if we could sit down, I could discuss the nature of my call, Lady Carew."

"If Roxbury has some complaint about boundaries, he can discuss them with Mr. Perkins, Mr. Thorpe."

"No, no—nothing of the sort, madam!" He cleared his throat. "Ahem—'tis of a much more delicate matter that I am commissioned to approach you."

"I have nothing to say on any head to His Grace," she declared, turning for the door. "You will forgive my lack of manners, sir, but you must know the duke and I are not on particularly civil terms."

The solicitor's expression was pained. "You mistake the matter, Lady Carew. Pray sit down—please." When she did not move, he unbent enough to explain, "It concerns the boy Justin. Roxbury believes he has an arguable interest in that quarter, and I am inclined to agree with him."

She spun around, her blue eyes flashing. "My son was born a Sherwood, and is therefore none of his concern. Pray inform His Grace that I have nothing to say to him on that subject either. Good day, Mr. Thorpe."

"Madam, I suggest you hear me out. His Grace is prepared to be all that is reasonable, but he wants to know young Justin. Indeed, he wishes to take responsibility for the boy."

"*What?* Oh, now that is too much, sir—he has no responsibility to Justin."

"Surely you can understand a man's concern for his son."

"His son?" Her voice rose in incredulity. "*His* son? If you are indeed referring to Justin Sherwood, I take leave to inform you, Mr. Thorpe, that he was born to Gareth Sherwood and myself on the Isle of Capri nearly six years ago, and he was born in wedlock."

"Be that as it may, madam—"

"No—you may tell Adrian Delacourt that he has no claim to my son!"

"I regret to inform you that His Grace believes otherwise."

"I do not care what His Grace believes," she snapped. "Gareth Sherwood signed the church register and affirmed my marriage lines when my son was born. Justin's legitimacy cannot be questioned by Roxbury or anyone. Now, if you will pardon me—"

"We are prepared to allow the courts to determine the boy's parentage, but the duke would rather avoid further scandal—for the boy's sake, of course."

"He would not dare!"

"Alas, but we believe—"

"I told you that I do not care what you believe, sir!" Her eyes sparked dangerously, but she bit off each word precisely. "You may tell Adrian Delacourt that I let him besmirch my name and my honor once, but I'll not let him do it again. If he so much as even attempts to file a suit to get Justin, I shall tell the whole story to

the world, and he will look very much the fool. I
should have spoken out the last time, and believe me, I
shall not let the opportunity pass again. Then we shall
see who has to leave this neighborhood. Roxbury will
rue the day he came up with this nonsense."

"The resemblance between him and the boy is a
marked one," he reminded her grimly.

"It does not make any difference who he looks like,
Mr. Thorpe. My son was born to Gary and I doubt that
any court in England would set that aside without my
consent. As you must surely know," she added acidly,
"this is a country whose laws are based on all that has
gone before. I defy you to show me one place where a
child born to a marriage and acknowledged by the husband has ever been declared another man's legal flesh
and blood." Not waiting for his response, she walked
to throw open the door. "Do not be forgetting your hat,
Sir, or you'll lose it, for I can promise that you will not
be allowed again on my property."

"That is your last word on the subject, madam? His
Grace had hoped to avoid any unpleasantness for you,
but—"

"Really?" Her mouth twisted, betraying momentarily the bitterness that threatened her composure. "As
he so obligingly did in the past? I think you'd best report to him that I will fight him at every turn before I
will let him even speak to my son again. And if he
should ever come on Haven land again, I will have him
arrested for trespass."

"Madam, you have not heard me out," Mr. Thorpe
protested.

"Good day, sir." She held the door and waited.

"Very well, Lady Carew, but His Grace will not be
pleased. Indeed, you should expect to hear from him in
a less pleasant manner, and I need not remind you that
he is a wealthy and powerful man." The solicitor

picked up his hat and passed into the hall, where Thomas and Wilton, the butler, waited to let him out into the rain.

Joanna walked back into the saloon and stood staring from behind a heavy drapery as the old-fashioned coach lumbered down the drive and out into the lane. When tears of anger and bitterness threatened to well over, she shook herself resolutely and pondered her best course of action. So Adrian thought to get Justin, did he? Well, he couldn't. Or could he? That gave her momentary pause. He'd had her adjudged wrongly before, and with Gary dead, that could come back to haunt her yet again. She'd be an adulteress, a woman already found guilty in a court of law. Did he think to call her fitness to be Justin's mother into question? Did he think to have himself named the boy's guardian so he could wrest her son away from her? She sank into a chair to think.

She had another card to play—Barrasford. She would explain everything to Johnny. She would be honest with him, and then if he still wanted to wed with her—well, she could do far worse. She'd wed for passion once, then for kindness, and kindness had proven far more sustainable. If only Johnny would understand . . .

"Mama?"

She let the drapery drop and turned to force a tremulous smile at Justin. His face betrayed a petulant impatience with the continuing rain that kept him inside. "Well, Master Scholar," she said with a lightness she did not feel, "how did you manage to escape Miss Finchley this time?"

"Robin wanted to play spillikins in the nursery." He traced the pattern in the wool rug with the toe of his shoe for a moment. "I didn't."

"I see. Well then, you are welcome to join me. I suppose we could try our hands at cards or I could read to you," she offered.

"I hate rain! I want to go home!"

"This is your home, dearest," she reminded him gently. "We are English, and you are lord of Haven. You must learn to take Papa's place here."

Without warning, he burst into tears and flung himself facedown on the camelback sofa, sobbing into the rich damask fabric. "I hate it here! I want my papa back!"

"Justin . . . Justin . . ." She murmured softly as she sank down beside him and began stroking his dark hair. "You must not do this, darling, you must not. I miss Papa too, you know."

"It isn't fair! Papa loved me!"

"Of course he did. And I love you, too. But he is not coming back, Justin, and you must accept that." She settled onto the sofa and pulled him onto her lap. "Indeed, Papa would not wish for us to live in the past, you know. He would want us to go on and do as well as we can without him." He stopped crying and buried his head against her breast. "Perhaps it is time to look to a new life and a new papa," she ventured softly as she caressed the thick dark hair.

He stiffened in her arms, then struggled to escape her embrace, pushing her away. "I don't want a new papa! I want *my* papa!" he screamed at her. Tears welled anew in the dark eyes and his chin jutted mulishly. "Mama, you do not understand! I hate God!"

"Justin—"

He slipped off her lap and ran for the door, flinging over his shoulder, "I don't want another papa! I want to go with mine! I wish I was with my papa!"

"Justin! Justin!"

She started to go after him but thought better of it. Out in the hall, Thomas and James, the two footmen,

caught him, while Wilton demanded with mock severity to know just why the young master was running in
the house. For once, Justin's basic good manners as-
serted themselves and he stammered out an apology.
And then Joanna overheard Thomas allow as how the
rain was enough to blue-devil any young man, but if
Master Justin could but wait until the last of the plate
was polished, they'd play smugglers in the cellar. No,
best to let the doting footman lighten the child's spirits,
she decided. All she'd done was make a botch of the
matter.

The dimness of the room and the sheeting rain on the
windows did nothing to alleviate her own sense of loss.
"Gary, I would you were here now," she whispered. "I
have such need of you now." But as the lump in her
throat ached unbearably, she knew she could not give
herself over to such thoughts. *No*, she told herself resolutely, *the sooner we move ahead with our lives, the sooner
this new business with Adrian can be resolved.* No, despite
Justin's vehement rejection of the notion, another marriage was the only answer if she was to keep her son.
Besides, she did not doubt for one minute that the kind
and personable Lord Johnny could win over both boys.
It would just take a little time, something she didn't
have right now.

"Still here, my love? I thought I heard Wilton show
someone out some time ago." Anne Sherwood started
into the room but stopped short. "Oh, my dear—is
something the matter? You look as though you've just
seen a ghost."

"Yes, terribly." Joanna turned around and managed a
brief, bitter smile. "Mr. Thorpe had not the least interest in our chimney, I am afraid. Indeed, he is a solicitor
come to tell me that Adrian means to get Justin."

"Oh, no! Joanna, he cannot do such a thing! Indeed,

the courts—that is, how could he even think it possible?"

"I expect he means to say that an adulterous woman is unfit to rear children—or something very like that. I suppose he will apply for a guardianship of Justin—and maybe of Robin, too. I mean, it would look rather odd if he were to separate them, wouldn't it?"

"If adultery were a bar, full half the matrons of the *ton*—"

"Yes, but they were not found guilty of the crime," Joanna pointed out grimly. "But as long as there is breath in my body, he shall not do it, Maman," she declared fiercely. "I mean to keep my son—even if I have to marry Lord Barrasford to do it."

"You are actually thinking of accepting him?"

"As you said, I could do far worse."

"Lord Barrasford, my lady," Wilton announced.

"Dear Joanna, given the muddy roads, I came as speedily as my carriage would allow," Johnny declared as he crossed the room to clasp both of her hands in his. "You must forgive my mud spatters, but this damnable rain has turned everything to mire." His gray eyes met hers. "I hope you know I would have swum the river to get here."

Her eyes widened at the warmth and eagerness in his voice. Indeed, she'd been surprised that he'd arrived so soon after her own messenger had returned from Aston Glen, his nearby estate. Certainly his words gave the lie to his appearance—there was not so much as a speck of mud on his perfectly blackened Hessians or on his buff-colored doeskin breeches. Once again, he was the epitome of the Corinthian—with his fair locks arranged in a perfect Brutus, his snowy cravat tied in the nearly impossible Wyndham fall, his plain dark coat an advertisement for Weston's tailoring as it lay smoothly across broad, athletic shoulders. He created a distinct impression of understated wealth and elegance. But it was those fine gray eyes that drew one to his handsomeness. And today there was a question there that she intended to answer.

She took a deep breath to collect her disordered thoughts. John Barrasford was everything a woman could want in a man, she told herself resolutely, and surely she would come to love him as she had Gary. Outwardly she managed a welcoming smile and indicated a chair across from hers. "Would you care to sit, sir, and perhaps take some refreshment?" Her voice sounded like a stranger's to her. "Alas, my mother-in-law is abed with some small complaint, so I was about to have my tea alone."

If he perceived the strain in her voice, he gave no sign. Reluctantly he released her hands and stepped back to take the chair. His handsome face never betrayed the incongruity of being asked to travel miles in the rain for tea. "But of course." His eyes were warm with his answering smile.

She reached for the bellpull and told a promptly responding James that Lord Barrasford would take the small sponge cakes with his tea. Then almost as if by afterthought, she added that she'd like for Miss Finchley to present the children downstairs. Turning back to Lord Barrasford, she apologized, telling him, "I hope you do not mind too much, sir, but I should like for you to meet my other son. Though he is not yet four, he conducts himself quite well in company," she said proudly.

"I believe I told you that I like children," he reminded her.

"Yes . . . well . . ." She hesitated for a moment and then plunged on, "I find that while sometimes one may like children as a group, it is possible to take exception to individual members."

Amusement gleamed in his eyes. "Dear lady, are you asking me to determine if I shall like your sons?"

"Yes—and just as importantly, I should like to know if they will like you," she admitted.

"I see. Well then, that does put the burden on me, doesn't it?"

"I'd like to see if you can get on together."

"Believe me, Joanna, when I say I mean to make every push to be agreeable to them."

"Oh, I should not expect you to toadeat them, my lord—hardly that." As the humor of the situation struck her, dimples formed above the corners of her smile. "They are, I regret to say, capable of being grubby, willful, exasperating little boys, after all."

"I should think them odd otherwise."

"Oh, lud!" Joanna rose nervously from her chair and walked to lean against the fireplace mantel. "I'm making a ridiculous mull of this, aren't I? Sometimes I find that the constraints of polite discourse leave so many things unsaid, you know." A throaty chuckle escaped her as her eyes met his. "Here I am, saying all that is proper instead of what I really mean. My lord—Johnny—that is to say, I have made up my mind."

He was by her side immediately. "Then I am not mistaken—you are about to accept me. Joanna—"

"On condition, my lord," she interposed quickly. "Perhaps when you know the whole, you may not—"

They were interrupted, first by James bearing the tea tray, and then by Miss Finchley leading the two boys. The governess stopped stone-still when she saw Barrasford, and her hands flew to her mouth. "Oh!" Recovering almost immediately, she looked to Joanna. "Pardon the intrusion, my lady, but I was told you wished to see the children."

"No—'tis quite right, for I should like you and the boys to make the acquaintance of Lord Barrasford. John, this is Miss Finchley."

"Lord Barrasford." Miss Finchley inclined her head to note the introduction, but when her eyes took in his handsome face, she colored.

"Miss Finchley." He stepped closer. "Ah, but we are already acquainted, I think, are we not?"

Her color deepened. "Yes." The word was little more

than a whisper. "It was a long time ago, my lord. I did not think you could remember it."

"Nonsense. You are Miss Charlotte, the vicar's eldest daughter. I remember your father quite well, you know." Looking over his shoulder to Joanna, he explained, "Miss Finchley lived not far from my godfather at Baxter Greys, where her father led the local parish. But, my dear Miss Charlotte, how is it—? That is, I should dislike prying, but I would never have thought to find you here."

She dropped her gaze to her hands for a moment, then her chin came up. "Yes, well, circumstances sometimes change, my lord. Papa died, you see, and Mama married Mr. Wellstone."

"Wellstone? I don't believe I knew him."

"He came to Baxter Greys about seven years ago—shortly before my father died. And he cut quite a swath with his gentlemanly ways, I must admit. Alas, we learned far too late that he was living on expectations that he had already gambled away. He had quite a fondness for gambling, you see, and Mama's small portion did not last him very long."

"My dear, I had no idea."

"I don't mind my life, my lord. If anything, my lack of money has allowed me to teach, which is something I quite enjoy."

"And your sisters?"

"Meg is married to Mr. Hoopes."

"Old Hoopes? Dash it, but the man's sixty if he's a day. And how old is your sister? She cannot be above twenty surely. I mean, you—"

That elicited a smile that lit her hazel eyes. "Actually, I am four and twenty, which makes Meg twenty-two. And Lizzie is nineteen. She threw her hat over the windmill for a soldier," she added. "She is the happiest of us all, I think."

"But Hoopes?"

"Meg had no dowry, my lord. I suspect she preferred being an old man's wife to being an elderly female's companion. And, unlike me, she does not particularly like children," she explained candidly. "She thought at his age, Mr. Hoopes would not likely wish for another family."

"I see." Recovering somewhat, he murmured sympathetically, "I was in Spain when I heard of your father's death, else I should have attended the funeral. He was a good man, Miss Finchley."

"Thank you."

Turning to Joanna again, he recalled, "The Finchley girls were the toasts of Baxter Greys, for every one of them has that same red hair you behold. Though I seem to recall that Miss Charlotte was remarked for being the hoyden of the lot," he added, grinning.

"That was when I was a grubby little schoolgirl, my lord," Miss Finchley reminded him. "I'm much more prim and proper now, I assure you."

"Yes, you are." He took in her trim figure, her plain gown, and the somewhat rebellious bun of unruly auburn curls. "But you are still a very pretty girl."

"I daresay that's Spanish coin, my lord." Nonplussed and more than a little afraid for her position, the governess looked to Joanna. "My lady, I have brought the boys down as directed. Justin, make your bow to Lord Barrasford," she added, nudging the older boy forward. As soon as the child had obediently bobbed his head, she gently pushed the other one toward his lordship. "Lord Barrasford, may I present Master Robert Sherwood?"

Lord Johnny looked from one boy to the other and was struck by their dissimilarity. While the older one bore the obvious resemblance to Roxbury, the younger one was quite fair, but in a different way from Joanna. Watching him, she nodded.

"Alas, they got very little from me, I fear."

Barrasford took in Robin's warm, apple-cheeked fairness and the red-gold ringlets before turning to compare him to his mother. "He has some look of you, anyway," he decided.

"Does he? My mother-in-law assures me that he is just as Gary was."

The sturdy, slightly chubby child, restive under the stranger's scrutiny, blurted out, "I don't like being Robert, sir—I'd rather be Robin."

"Then Robin it is." Turning his attention to the darker boy, he asked, "And what about you? What would you be called?"

"Well, I hate being 'my lord,'" Justin confided. "Do you like it?"

"I never thought much about the matter. But then I daresay since my parents died when I was young, I got used to it quite early. Indeed, I cannot remember when I was not 'my lord.'"

"The duke did not mind it either, but I do. I wish my papa was still here so I could just be Justin."

"I see."

"Did you know my papa?"

"No, but I wish I had. I'm afraid I wasn't in the neighborhood when your father lived here."

"The duke knew him."

"Justin—" Joanna was not prepared to endure another tearful outburst, particularly not in Barrasford's presence.

"No—'tis quite all right," Johnny reassured her as he bent down to speak to the boy. "I know I would have liked your papa, though," he added, "because if he had you and your mother, he must've been bang up to the mark." Changing the subject gently, he asked, "Do you ride yet?"

"A little."

"Well, if you come to visit me in Ireland, I have a big stable with more horses than you can count, and I'll wager that I can find a pony just your size. We'll have you racing him in no time."

"I want one!" Robin chimed in. "I want a horse! Mama, can I have one, too?"

"A pony," Barrasford answered, correcting him with a smile. "And I daresay I can find a pony and a cart for you until you are old enough to ride alone."

"A pony and a cart!" the boy said with awe. "Hear that, Jus?"

"It's a good one, too. 'Tis painted all green and white, and it has a seat for a driver and a place to take someone along. I used to put a foxhound in it and give him rides when I was little."

"When? When can we go? When?" Robin demanded eagerly.

"Now, *that* is up to your mother," Barrasford admitted.

"Mama?"

"Soon, dearest—quite soon, I think." She smiled over Robin at Johnny. "Indeed, I think it can be arranged."

Justin, who had turned around when Robin asked her, saw the look that passed between Joanna and the visitor, and he didn't like it. A sense of unease stole over him. "Well, I don't want to go!" he announced suddenly. "And I won't! And I don't want a horse, either!"

"Justin!" Miss Finchley reproved him sharply. "Mind your manners and apologize for speaking so to his lordship."

"And I don't like him!"

"Justin." Joanna's tone was calm but firm. "You will

apologize this instant to Lord Barrasford, and then you will return to the nursery while Robin remains for tea."

Tears brimmed in his dark eyes and his chin quivered dangerously as he faced his mother, but the expression on her face told Justin that she would brook no further insolence. He looked up at Barrasford for a moment, and then he nodded. Mumbling a quick, "Your pardon, my lord," he turned and ran from the room.

"Well, I want to go, anyway," Robin decided.

"Of course you do," Joanna soothed, "and you shall. And I'm sure Justin will come around when he thinks about it."

For Barrasford, the twenty or so minutes spent making mundane conversation over tea and small cakes was interminable. The elder boy's sudden departure had dampened Joanna's enthusiasm, and she sat quietly while Miss Finchley shyly tried to maintain polite conversation. From time to time, Robin managed to inject himself into the discourse by asking more about the pony and cart promised him. Given his young age, the child's manners were quite good, and Johnny found himself actively trying to engage the little boy. Then, when the cups had been removed, Robin ventured close enough to examine his lordship's watch chain, and he was instantly rewarded with a lift onto his Barrasford's lap.

"Robin, you must not spoil Lord Barrasford's breeches," Joanna protested.

"Nonsense—they are wrinkled from the rain, anyway. And I think I told you I like children, didn't I? I always regretted not having brothers and sisters, you know." Returning his attention to the little boy, he asked, "Here—would you like to see the inside of the case?" He opened his watch. "See this picture?"

"Uh-huh."

"Reynolds painted this for my father before I was born."

"Who is it?"

"My mother as a young girl. I keep it to remind myself how she looked."

"My papa's dead, you know."

"Mine, too. He died when I was little like you."

"My papa's boat turned upside down." Robin eyed the watch case again. "She's not as pretty as my mama."

"Robin!"

"Well, I'm not sure anyone could be," Johnny conceded, smiling.

Curious, both Joanna and Miss Finchley moved to look over his shoulder at the picture of a very lovely girl, her hair powdered and piled high atop her head, her slender neck adorned with a cameo on a ribbon.

"Why, she's beautiful, my lord," Jo insisted.

"I'm told this is exactly how she looked at her court presentation. She was seventeen then, I believe."

"What's this?" Robin asked, patting his pocket.

"A snuffbox."

"Can I see it?"

As Johnny obligingly dug it out, Joanna stopped him. "My lord, he'll have your breeches wrinkled and your pocket full of snuff. Robin, you've imposed on his lordship's kindness long enough for today." She held out a hand to the boy, who took it and slid off Barrasford's lap. "Now, if you will but go with Miss Finchley and find your brother—"

"But, Mama, I like Lord Barrasford! Cannot I—"

"Not today, I'm afraid." As the child's face fell, she ruffled his hair. "I daresay you will see him again, dearest—indeed, I am sure of it. Now, go on with you."

"Don't forget the pony!" Robin called out as the governess propelled him firmly through the door.

"I won't," Johnny promised. "When I get home, I'll order the cart painted so it'll be ready for you. And you can tell Justin I'll have a saddle made up just for him."

"Gor!"

Charlotte Finchley turned back for one last look at Barrasford. "Good day, my lord. It was kind of you to remember me."

After she and the boy had left, he shook his head. "She was Reverend Finchley's pride, you know. He said she had more brains that half the fellows he'd tutored before they were sent off to school. As pretty as she is, I would have expected her to marry well. I know there was a time when my cousin Ned was dangling after her."

"Well, apparently he didn't wish for a penniless wife."

"A pity. He was plump enough in the pocket that her change in circumstance shouldn't have mattered."

"Unfortunately, not very many men look at it that way, my lord."

"Still—a governess? What a comedown that must seem to her," he said, shaking his head.

"The poor girl had to do something respectable. In any event, she came with excellent characters for one so young, and I cannot say I've been disappointed in the least. She has quite a way with both boys. Indeed, I should like to take her to Ireland with us."

"My dear, you may bring anyone you wish," Johnny assured her. He looked to the door. "It is a shame when the Almeria Benningtons of this world are cosseted and admired while a female like Miss Finchley must earn her own bread, isn't it?"

"Yes, it is—it truly is. For want of a dowry, she'll spend her life teaching other people's children instead of her own," Joanna murmured. "But I didn't know you knew Miss Bennington."

"The Ice Maiden? We all called her that, you know. Oh, she was much admired for her beauty, but I found her far too cold and expensive for my taste—definitely not what a man ought to wish for in a wife." His eyes took on a wicked gleam as he added, "Now, don't misunderstand my meaning, dear lady—expensive is all right, provided there's a little fire for recompense."

"Oh."

"Did I offend you by saying that, my dear?" Instantly contrite, he reassured her, "'Twas not my intent, believe me."

"No, of course not."

"However, if you were accepting my suit, I do think we should be able to speak plainly to one another."

"Yes."

"Joanna, I think I've been head over heels since my first sight of you."

"Surely not."

Coming up behind her, he laid his hands on her shoulders, turning her to face him. "I'd just like to say that I've no wish for one of those bloodless marriages so common to our class. I want fire, Joanna. You do understand that, don't you?" As her eyes widened, he nodded. "And I am prepared to give as good as I get, I'll promise you that."

"My lord—"

"Johnny."

"You may not want me when I tell you that Adrian means to rake up the old scandal yet again."

"It doesn't matter to me, but if you wish, I'll call him to book for it."

"No, of course not." As he bent his head closer, she admitted baldly, "I need your help, Johnny, for he wants to take Justin from me." Acutely aware that he was but inches from her face, she blinked to focus. "Do not think I have turned to you lightly, my lord. I believe you are my only hope if I am to fight Adrian in this."

"Joanna." His voice was soft now and his warm breath caressed her face. "Do you not know that I would struggle against the devil himself to hold you in my arms? I don't care what Roxbury says—I don't care what anybody says. I'll even fight him in Parliament if it comes to that." His arms closed around her, enveloping her in the warmth of his embrace. Her lips parted to receive his gentle kiss, and her arms twined about his neck as that kiss deepened. She closed her eyes and felt again the strength of a man's body against hers. A year's abstinence kindled, then fueled the surge of desire that coursed through her as she clung to him, demanding more.

"Joanna." It was scarce more than a croak when at last he released her bruised lips. "My God," he whispered, searching her face. When at last she opened her eyes, he was elated by the mirrored desire there. Crushing her to him again, he savored the very feel of her body against his as he murmured into her wheat-gold hair, "I'll make you happy, I swear. As soon as we are wed, I'll take you and the boys to Ireland. If you don't mind, I'll puff off the announcement immediately, then we can be married by Special License whenever you wish, Jo."

Jo. That was what Adrian had always called her, she realized with a start. And at that moment, she felt the heat ebb from her body. Dear God, after all these years, how could she still feel the pain, the loss of that grand passion? It was something that even six years with Gary couldn't cure. And now, in Johnny Barrasford's arms, she felt guilty, as though she were deceiving him, too.

He felt her body stiffen, and he mistook the reason. Releasing her, he favored her with a twisted smile. "I rushed my fences, didn't I?" he murmured ruefully. "I should have known it would take you a little time to get used to the notion."

"I just hope I can make you happy," she managed.

"You already have."

She searched his handsome face, thinking how fortunate she was and forcing her misgivings aside. "Well, there's so much to do—the packing—everything."

"How long do you need?"

"Two weeks—perhaps three. I've got to prepare Justin and Robin, you know."

"What about Roxbury?"

"Surely it will take him longer than that to begin any proceedings, don't you think?"

"At least. And maybe the announcement will give him some pause." He stepped back and exhaled. "Well, the matter's settled, then. I'll send word to open the house. Once you see it, I expect you'll wish to refurbish it to your tastes, of course. It's quite a comfortable place, but there's not been a mistress there since I was in leading strings."

"I'm sure I'll like it."

"The castle itself dates back some five hundred years, but the manor house was built late in Queen Elizabeth's reign. The park and gardens were redone by Capability Brown and his son-in-law, Henry Holland, at my great-grandmother's insistence, and they are truly beautiful still. And since we raise thoroughbreds, there are plenty of bridle paths for Justin and Robin to explore. It's a wonderful place to rear children, Jo—yours and ours. They'll have horses, dogs, geese—even cats, if they want them. And I've hopes we'll have a grand time there, too."

"Yes."

"I'll get the announcement sent off this afternoon."

"And I'll tell the boys. You are in a fair way to be-

coming friendly with Robin, but he does not really remember Gary. Justin, as you already have seen, is another matter. I don't expect him to be happy at first."

"Would it be easier if I told him?" Johnny asked.

"No."

"He's young, Jo. It may take him time, but he'll come
'round, I promise you. Tell you what—I'll bring him a
pony the next time I come to visit, and I'll make a push
to get better acquainted with him."

The storm, which had abated for a while, appeared
ready to regain its intensity. Lightning struck close by
and a rumble of thunder shook the house. Johnny
glanced out the window at the darkening clouds. "By
the looks of it," he observed, frowning, "we're in for
quite a storm. The river was already coming up when I
crossed it earlier, and unless you wish to scandalize the
neighborhood by harboring your betrothed overnight,
I'd best be getting on the road."

Turning back to her, he lifted her hand to kiss each
finger gallantly. A wicked light danced in those gray
eyes of his as he told her, "I'd kiss your lips again, my
dear, but I fear I'd never be able to leave." Squeezing
her fingers lightly, he released them. "You've made me
very happy, you know. No, no—do not be seeing me
out. I want to fix you in my mind as you are now—
waiting for me rather than waving good-bye."

With those parting words, he let himself out of the
saloon and was crossing the entry hall when he noticed
movement behind a hall table. Impulsively he walked
back around the wide landing of the magnificent staircase and found Justin Sherwood crouched there, his
nankeen pants wet and caked with mud, his shoes ruined. Muddy tracks came from the back of the house.

Barrasford dropped on his haunches next to the boy.
"Been outside?" he asked casually.

"Yes," was the sullen reply.

"I daresay Miss Finchley will be worried about you."

"I don't care."

"Justin . . ." Johnny eyed the mutinous set of the child's chin. "I cannot even pretend to know why you have taken me in such dislike, but I think fairness would demand that we at least be allowed to get acquainted before you make such a judgment." The boy stared straight ahead in stony silence. Barrasford sighed and tried again. "Is it perhaps that you think I mean to take your mama away from you? If so, I can assure you that such is not the case. I mean to marry your mama, you know, but that will not change things between the two of you."

"I don't want you for my papa!" the child burst out. "I want my own papa back! You cannot be my papa!"

"It won't happen overnight, Justin," Johnny continued gently, "but in time, we will learn to love each other simply because we both love your mama, because we both wish her to be happy. Can you understand that?"

"I'd rather die and be with my father," the boy answered evenly.

"Perhaps you think you would now, but do you truly think your papa would have wanted you to feel that way? Do you think he would want you to go away forever and make your mother sad again?"

"She'd forget about me like she forgets about Papa."

"I don't think so. But then, I don't think she's forgotten him either, Justin. You know, it *is* possible to go ahead and do other things without forgetting someone you loved."

"I won't go to Ireland—I won't go! And I don't want a pony!"

Johnny sighed. "I collect you were listening at the door."

"Yes." The boy looked up with tear-reddened eyes.

"I climbed out the nursery window and came back through the servants' door."

"And what else did you hear?" Barrasford asked quietly.

"Nothing—you were leaving."

"Then perhaps I ought to tell you that your mother needs my assistance in a matter of great importance to her. And I will have to marry her to give her that assistance. So you must not fault her for what she does, Justin." Another huge thunderclap shook the house. "I've got to go home now, but we'll discuss this again. As it stands now, I may just barely be able to cross the river." Johnny pulled himself up with the edge of the table and stood over the boy, holding out his hand. "If you do not want me for your papa, then perhaps you will consider me for a friend."

"I'd rather have the duke—at least he knew Papa."

Barrasford sighed again. The wooing of the boy was far more difficult than the wooing of the mother. "I'm afraid that's not possible, Justin, because the duke makes your mama unhappy. Perhaps someday she will be able to explain just why, but I would not press her just now." Reaching out, he ruffled the thick, dark hair on Justin's head. The boy ducked away angrily. "Things will seem better later, I promise you, little one."

Justin waited until Lord Barrasford left, then he dropped his head onto his knees, wailing, "I don't want a new papa—I don't!"

"Justin, where have you been?" Miss Finchley asked, coming down the stairs. Then, seeing that he was obviously upset, she quickly knelt beside him. "Oh, dear, and what is the matter now?" she clucked sympathetically, drawing him close.

"Mama's going to make us live in Ireland with Barrasford, and I don't want to go! I won't go!"

"I see," the governess said faintly. "Are you quite certain of this?"

"Finch, I heard it with m'ears!" he wailed, turning his face into her chest. "I don't want a new papa, Finch!"

"Justin, whatever—?"

Miss Finchley looked over his shoulder to Joanna, who stood in the saloon doorway. "He's overset again, my lady." Standing up, she smoothed her skirt. "I'll take him upstairs."

"He seems to have taken Lord Barrasford in dislike."

"I expect he'll get over that, my lady. Lord Barrasford is quite easy to like when one gets to know him. And he does have a way with children," the young woman added. "I once saw him take off his coat and play spillikins on the floor with some little boys. Not the sort of thing one would expect from a Corinthian, is it?"

"No. You should have said you knew him, and I would have invited you down to renew the acquaintance before today."

Miss Finchley smiled. "I didn't even expect him to remember me," she admitted wryly.

"I cannot think why not."

"After Mr. Wellstone died and it became known he'd left us penniless, nobody seemed to care about us anymore. Indeed, when Mama passed on, only the vicar who replaced Papa and his family came to her funeral. The rest of her so-called friends had already turned away from her, and no doubt they knew they wouldn't have been welcomed, anyway."

"How terrible for you."

"Oh, I've reconciled myself to my circumstances, my lady. But I shall have to write Meg and Lizzie that Lord Barrasford asked of them—Meg had such a tendresse for him, you know. But then I think every female in Baxter Greys did. I know I used to think him the handsomest man I'd ever seen." She hesitated, then blurted out, "If it isn't too forward of me to say it, I think you are quite fortunate, for his lordship must be everything a female could wish in a husband."

"I do count myself exceedingly lucky. I find him extraordinarily kind."

"Yes, he is that, isn't he?" Reaching for Justin's hand, the governess said a trifle quickly, "We'd best get back to the nursery before your brother makes a shambles of it. And once he is down for his nap, I will tell you some stories."

"What sort of stories?"

"Oh, I don't know—you like Robin Hood, don't you?"

"And Friar Tuck—and Will Scarlet?" he asked excitedly.

"Most definitely. Now, come on, or we won't have enough time for all of them," Miss Finchley murmured, leading him away.

Telling herself that Justin was too young to know his own mind, Joanna went back into the saloon. In time, she was sure he and Robin would come to love Johnny. Moving to a window, she stood staring out into the steady drizzle, hoping she could also. She already had enough guilt for what she'd done to Gary without adding Johnny to that burden.

Adrian sat at his desk examining his bailiff's report and the stack of tradesmen's bills, while Lord Bennington occupied himself with the newspapers posted from London. For both men, it was a respite from the frenetic activities imposed on them by the ladies, who on this day had elected to pay morning calls in the village.

Adrian muttered a curse under his breath as he sorted the slips of paper his mother had crammed into the nooks of the desk. Lord Bennington looked up from his paper sympathetically.

"Deuced nuisance, if you was to ask me—paying the damned tradesmen, I mean. Bad enough settling a gentleman's gaming debts on quarter day, if you ask me. I mean, ten to one, a man's got his eye on a piece of horseflesh or a prime article, only to find out the females in his family have spent the blunt for him. Of course, men of substance like you and I—well, at least we got the blunt to do it."

Adrian broke the seal on an envelope and retrieved Thorpe's bill. "'Tis the damned solicitors I fault, for they expect to be paid whether they are successful or not." He crumpled the paper in his hand, muttering tersely, "Thirty pounds for botching the business. I should have paid that call myself."

"Must cost a pretty penny to run an establishment

like the Armitage, eh? And that don't begin to count the duchess's expenses, I'll warrant. Aye, and if you was to ask me, I'd guess that little party she put on t'other night set you back a penny or two. Bringing the Mantini from London to sing was a nice touch, though." When Adrian didn't respond, the older man rattled on. "Can't say you haven't been all that is proper to my Almeria, my lord—not but what I didn't have my doubts at first, mind you. Bluntly speaking, we was about to leave after that little contretemps at Lady Sheffield's, but we've naught to complain of since then." Still no comment. To gain his host's attention, Bennington paused and coughed apologetically before touching on the delicate matter. "Daresay it was the shock of it—seeing that woman again, I mean." Unable to see Adrian's jaw tighten, he was emboldened to continue. "Bad business, that. I know it must've been deuced uncomfortable for you to see the woman flaunting herself right there in front of you. Thought Lady Bennington was going to faint when you led the creature out, mind you. Bad business, but you managed to drive her from the field, so I daresay you knew what you was doing."

Adrian clenched his hands and gritted his teeth as he sought to control his temper. While he had alternately been forgiving and condemning Joanna in much the same vein, he had no wish to hear the overweening Lord Bennington discuss her. Resolutely he reached for the butcher's bill and stared determinedly at it.

"Now, you take my Almeria—there's a girl that'd be a credit to a man, if you know what I mean. Girl's a beauty, if I do say so myself, but she ain't showy like some of 'em—keeps herself aloof like a lady ought. Knows her worth, too. You won't find her throwing herself at a man's head."

"No," Adrian muttered succinctly.

Mistaking this terse comment for agreement, Bennington considered it an opening for a more auspicious conversation. "I mean to do handsomely by my daughter, you understand. If a man with the right title was to offer for her, there's no saying what I might settle on her." He eyed the back of Adrian's head and waited, but there was only silence. "Well, that is, I've been thinking it won't do to be a pinchfarthing, you know—got to do handsomely by her." Clearing his throat, he declared baldly, "Now, if she was to be a duchess, I'd dower her with twenty thousand at the least—what do you say to that, Your Grace?"

But Adrian did not rise to the bait as expected. "I'd say her dowry is your business rather than mine." Carefully piling the bills into a neat stack, he began listing them aloud. "Seven pounds, six shillings," he noted as his pen scratched across the vellum. "Fifty-two pounds. Twelve pounds, three shillings. One hundred four pounds, eight shillings, nine pence." When he felt he'd sufficiently mastered his irritation, he held up a bill from a greengrocer. "The price of peas this year is outrageous," he observed pointedly. "The only thing worse seems to be that of apricots."

The message was not lost on Lord Bennington. He sank back and readjusted his newspaper to hide his chagrin. The Duke of Roxbury'd made it quite plain—he'd no wish to discuss a marriage with Almeria. Not yet, anyway. But it didn't matter, Bennington decided, for it was already determined that if the duke did not come up to scratch on his own, he'd find himself outfaced. It was a havey-cavey business, to be sure, and one that Bennington had not wanted to push, but Adrian Delacourt was leaving him little choice, he reflected resentfully. It was time to approve the outing to wells if Almeria was to become the duchess she wished herself.

Adrian finished totaling the household expenditures and set them aside. After three weeks of entertaining Almeria and her parents with rigid politeness, he was heartily sick of the whole encroaching family. Nothing seemed to depress their pretensions to his title, and they insisted on going on with plans for this little party, that little outing, until it was the gossip of the neighborhood that he was certain to make Miss Bennington an offer. He rose and stretched before turning to Lord Bennington.

"I find that I shall be going to London on business later in the week," he announced casually, "and I cannot say when I shall be returning. You are welcome, of course, to remain with my mother."

"So soon?" Bennington's florid face betrayed his alarm. "But—but I say—that is, Almeria has expressed such an interest in Wells, sir!"

It was a sore point, one that Adrian and his mother had had more than a few words about, but he'd resigned himself to doing his duty one last time to his unwanted guests. After that, they could damned well entertain themselves or leave. No, they'd be leaving, all right, probably within hours of his own departure. On that happier thought, he answered pleasantly, "Oh, I mean to take Miss Bennington to Wells the day before I leave."

"Kind of you to do so." The older man relaxed visibly and turned his attention back to the latest copy of the *Gazette*. "Egad!" He reread a small notice unobtrusively placed among several others, then declared, "Well, of all things! I'd not thought Barrasford such a fool!" He looked up, but the duke was not attending. "Your Grace!" he said, waving the page in Adrian's direction. "You will not credit it, but La Carew has found herself a suitor! Man's got to be a damned fool to take her, but here it is for the world to see it—right here in the paper."

By the triumphant tone of Bennington's voice, Adrian knew he was speaking of Joanna. Rising, he strode across the room to jerk the newspaper from the older man's hands. Perusing the page quickly, he found the offending notice, read it several times. In unalterable black and white, it stated quite simply, "John Arlen Barrasford, Lord Barrasford of Kinshannon, announces his betrothal to Joanna Milford Sherwood, widowed Countess of Carew. After private nuptials at the bride's home, the couple will travel abroad before taking up residence at Kinshannon."

"Whatever can Barrasford be thinking of?" Bennington demanded, recoiling as Roxbury stared at the words. "Surely a man of his social standing must know the consequences! Deuced silly, if you was to ask me, for him to marry her—ought to mount that little fancy piece for a mistress instead! Countess indeed! And I say she's not fit for a barmaid!"

"Shut your mouth! Shut your foul mouth!" Adrian exploded as the color returned to his face. "Lud, what can she be thinking? She cannot love him—not yet surely," he muttered distractedly. Bennington forgotten, Adrian began to pace and muse aloud, "Got to think this out. Why? Why would she remarry yet again to a man she barely knows? Gary was one thing, but Barrasford!"

"It is as plain as day, my lord," Bennington sniffed. "He's rich."

A derisive snort escaped the duke. "My dear sir, with what Gary would have provided her, Joanna is an extremely wealthy woman in her own right. No, it's not money, for she never cared for that."

"Then perhaps it was his willingness to overlook the hussy's shameful past, or he's played too deep at the tables and needs her money," the older man offered. "Besides, it is of no moment now, is it?"

"Johnny doesn't need her money, I'm sure of that. Besides, he's never been a gazetted fortune hunter."

"My dear sir, I fail to see what—" Bennington was cut short by the look Adrian gave him. "Well, 'tis done, in any event, isn't it? He will take her to those Irish estates of his and 'twill be the last you have to hear of her."

Kinshannon. Ireland. As it sank in, it explained everything. "Well, I won't let it happen—I won't let her leave England without a fight!" Adrian declared, slamming his fist into his hand. "No, before I pay Thorpe, he can call on her again and make her another offer. By God, he bungled the matter the last time, but he'll not do so again," he muttered to himself. "And if he cannot resolve the matter, I'll find someone who will."

"Surely you cannot care where the woman lives, Your Grace. After all she's done, you must wish her at Jericho, I'd think."

"I'm afraid I cannot allow her to leave."

"Well, as she is to marry Barrasford, I don't see as you can prevent that, sir," Bennington told him stiffly.

Adrian's face was grim. "I intend to find a way. She's not leaving England with the boy."

"What boy?"

"I've no wish to discuss my private affairs with anyone, sir."

There was no mistaking the coldness in Roxbury's voice. Rebuffed, Almeria's father picked up the *Gazette* and gazed malevolently at the offending notice, wishing for all the world that he'd held his tongue and quietly destroyed the whole damned paper.

Although it was yet early in the day, the weather was unbearable with unshed rain, high temperature, and no wind, causing Haven's servants to throw open windows, shutters, and doors in the hope of catching even the slightest breeze. For once, Joanna longed for the interminable rains that usually plagued the English summer. The unusually hot weather was making her clothes stick to her body and her temper short. Fanning the high-waisted skirt of her muslin gown against her damp skin, she thought of those fashionable ladies who resorted to dampening their dresses to make them cling, and she was sorely tempted to try it for a very different reason.

It was all of a piece, she decided wearily—even nature conspired to make her miserable. Her spirits at low ebb and her head aching abominably, she considered just going back to bed, but it was futile to think she'd get any relief there. No, as soon as she lay down and closed her eyes, her thoughts would start to tumble, and there'd be no peace. She'd try to think of Johnny, but as soon as rational thought gave way to that netherworld that came before sleep, Adrian would be there to plague her.

Shortly after she'd accepted Johnny, shortly after that storm had passed and the roads became dry enough for travel, Adrian had again dispatched his solicitor to

see her. A sense of anger and bitterness flooded over
her every time she relived that interview over and over
in her mind. She'd wanted to refuse to see Thorpe, but
Anne had prevailed, and she'd gone down to hear him
out. The duke was willing, he'd said, to allow Justin to
stay with her for the time being on two conditions—
one, he must be told that Adrian Delacourt was his
father, and two, Joanna must not remarry during the
boy's minority. And as an afterthought, he'd added
that the duke expected the right to visit his son without
interference.

His son. She could not even think of Justin as such,
and it was compounding injustice for Adrian to expect
any rights when he'd merely been there at the child's
conception. No, it was Gary who'd loved the boy and
Gary that Justin had adored in return. Indeed, if she'd
even tried to tell Roxbury she'd carried his child at the
time, he wouldn't have believed her, she was sure of
that. And now, just because he'd seen himself in Justin,
he wanted her to forget the hurt, the terrible pain he'd
inflicted on her, and give over her son. Well, she could
not and would not give in to Adrian's demands. Let
him get his own heir of Almeria Bennington and leave
Justin where he belonged. Gary would have wanted it
that way. Gary had never made any difference between
the two boys.

At least Johnny was prepared to fight for his soon-to-
be stepson. And with no encouragement from Justin,
she conceded wearily. No matter what Johnny did, no
matter how many attempts to win the boy over he
made, it had made very little difference. Johnny had
been rebuffed with such hostility that Joanna was beginning to think the situation hopeless. Even worse,
her impending marriage to Barrasford was straining
her own relationship with her son. Just yesterday he'd
shouted that she might forget his papa, but he never

would. Finally, when reason had utterly failed, Anne and Miss Finchley had birched him and put him to bed. Now even the servants seemed to be taking sides in the matter.

The whole house was at sixes and sevens, it seemed. Anne had been quietly supportive, of course, and Robin had tried in his small, childish way to comfort her, but several members of the household, while not daring to be openly hostile, covertly displayed an unbecoming coldness toward Barrasford. And the irony of it was that it obviously had less to do with Johnny than with several old retainers' loyalty to the memory of Gareth Sherwood and their fear that his heirs would be reared in Ireland. Had they known about Adrian's attempt to interfere in Justin's life, they would surely have understood, Joanna reflected wryly, but then, unlike Adrian, she'd never been one to air her dirty linen.

If there had been any comfort in her life, it was Johnny himself. While she knew she did not love him, she was gaining more respect and admiration for him with each passing day. Snubs and barbs rolled off his back like so much water, or so it seemed. But he'd gone to London for the Special License as well as to take care of some property matters, so he'd not been apprised of Roxbury's latest offer. And the worst of it was that she didn't expect him back for several days.

Picking up the brush from her dressing table, she began pulling her damp hair back from her moist temples. She'd never quite been able to crop her hair in the current mode, and for once she regretted it. But the men in her life had all admired her thick hair—Adrian had called it a silk curtain, Gary had likened it to shimmering satin, and now Johnny pronounced it the most beautiful he'd ever seen.

Her disjointed musings were interrupted by her maid.

"Madam—" The girl sketched a hasty bob and reported, "Thomas says to tell you that Wilton has admitted that Thorpe person again."

"I gave orders that I am not at home to Mr. Thorpe."

"Yes, ma'am, but Wilton told Thomas it was important."

Joanna turned around, her irritation evident. "Ask Thomas to inform Wilton that he is to tell Mr. Thorpe he was mistaken—I am *not* at home." These last few words she bit off individually and precisely.

"Shall I ask Lady Anne?"

"Lady Anne is not at home to him either. There is no purpose to be served by oversetting either one of us on a day like this."

"Yes, madam."

"And, Maggie—"

"Yes, madam?"

"See if there is any chilled rose water in the cellar, if you please. I have the headache, and perhaps if I dampened a cloth and put it over my eyes—"

"I'll get you some," the girl promised.

Joanna waited until she'd left, and then she removed her dress to lie down in her thin lawn underchemise. In a matter of minutes the girl returned with the soaked cloth and placed it over Joanna's closed eyes. In the drive below, they could hear the sound of Mr. Thorpe's coach departing.

Joanna lay very quietly, willing herself not to dwell on the past or to puzzle over the future. She'd accepted Johnny Barrasford, and she'd just have to accept her life as it continued to unfold. With that fatalistic decision, she concentrated instead on the clothes she'd ordered from the dressmaker. After more than a year of mourning, she was ready for pretty dresses again. Idly, she wondered if she would be considered fashionable in Ireland—or if she would be snubbed there also.

Finally, she managed to drowse despite the headache, until Miss Finchley knocked and called through the door, "Your pardon, Lady Carew, but is Justin with you?"

"No." Joanna sat up groggily and collected her surroundings. It was even hotter and more sultry than when she'd lain down. "What time is it?" she called back.

"'Tis almost eleven, my lady, and Justin's not been seen since he left his lessons unfinished this morning."

There was something about Miss Finchley's voice that betrayed her concern. And since she was usually an uncommonly levelheaded woman, Joanna rose and pulled on her dress. "Come in," she said loudly.

"I would not have disturbed you for the world, Lady Carew," the governess apologized again on entering, "but 'tis not like him to disappear. And I have asked the countess, Wilton, James, Thomas, the cook, Mrs. Beech, the maids—the ostlers even. No one can remember seeing him for some time."

"Perhaps he told Robin."

"Master Robin and he quarreled, I am afraid." The young woman hesitated as though uncertain how best to explain her fears. "I ought to have gone after him at the time, I can see that now, but he was so overset and—"

"What was it this time?"

"He still weeps for his father, and he thinks Robin exceedingly disloyal for liking Lord Barrasford."

Joanna sighed. "I've done everything I know to reassure him, but I am at a loss as to how—while I don't want him to ever forget my late husband, I want him to understand he must continue to live, that he must grow up into the sort of man Gary would have wished."

"Master Robin was telling me about his cart and pony in Ireland when Justin began crying that he was not going to Ireland—that he wanted to go where his own papa was. Since he has done this before, I let him go in the hope that he would come back ready to work on his sums. Then Robin and I were cutting and gluing pasteboard pictures, so I did not note the time until about an hour ago."

"I wouldn't worry just yet, Miss Finchley," Joanna said soothingly. "As you say, this is not the first time that he's threatened this." Sighing again, she added, "He cannot quite understand what death is, you know—indeed, it is difficult for a grown person to accept such loss. I expect he's hiding somewhere, trying to punish me for what he perceives to be my disloyalty, too."

"But Thomas and James and the ostlers have spent this past hour looking everywhere, my lady—he is not *anywhere*."

Joanna sat on the edge of the bed and reached for her stockings. "I'll find him," she promised grimly, "and this time, I mean to put an end to this. Too long he's used his sadness to do what he wants to do." Drawing on the stockings and tying the garters, she stood and felt under the edge of the bed for her slippers. Dragging them out with her toes, she slid her feet into them. "You see to Robin, and I shall take care of Justin."

But when she got downstairs, Joanna found that Miss Finchley had not overstated the case. Mrs. Beech, the housekeeper, could not remember seeing the boy after an early breakfast. Thomas and James had seen him when he came down from the nursery, because James had tried to convince the sniffling child to go back, but Thomas had suggested that perhaps Master Justin simply needed some time alone. Then Wilton remembered that he was outside when Mr. Thorpe had come, but there was no sign of him later.

A dreadful suspicion took root in Joanna's mind.

"You are certain that you did not see him after Mr. Thorpe left?"

"I did not."

"What was he doing when you did see him?"

"As I told Miss Finchley, madam, Master Justin was sitting on the portico side steps when Mr. Thorpe arrived. The gentleman stopped to speak with him about his spaniel, as I recall."

"I'd scarce call Mr. Thorpe a gentleman," she muttered. Returning to the matter at hand, she asked, "Wilton, did Mr. Thorpe say anything else to Justin? Can you recall anything else he might have said?"

The butler considered for a moment and then nodded. "He said that Justin must visit the duke soon—that the duke remembered him and would like to further the acquaintance."

"Adrian. Maman, Adrian is behind this."

Lady Anne, who had been listening to each of the servants describe his search for the boy, shook her head. "Joanna, Roxbury would not behave so shabbily."

"Maman, he would do anything to punish me," Joanna said with feeling. "Have you forgotten the last time Mr. Thorpe called? Adrian would have the ordering of my life, and he would have my son."

"You cannot know that."

"His solicitor was here this morning and my son is now missing!" Joanna cried. "Well, he will find that I will fight this time!" Turning on her heels, she went toward the stairs. "Have my horse saddled, if you please," she said, flinging the words crisply over her shoulder.

"Joanna!"

"No, my mind is made up—he won't succeed in this!"

Anne Sherwood did not believe she meant to do it

until Joanna actually came down in her Italian riding habit. "Where do you think you are going?" she asked in alarm. "My love, you cannot just—"

"I am riding to the Armitage, Maman, and I mean to have this out with Adrian. He knows he cannot win in the courts, so he's simply taken my son, and I'll not stand for it."

"Joanna, think! I mean, why would he do such a thing? How can he hope to accomplish anything by such a rash move? Please, let us send out a search party. If Justin is not found, Barrasford can—"

"Barrasford is in London, Maman!" Joanna snapped. "And if I waited for him, Adrian could have Justin hidden or spirited out of the country."

"But Adrian has no reason—he's always been a kind person—"

"Kind?" Joanna's temper flared. "*Kind?* Would you call my divorce kind? Would you call what he did to Gary kind? No—he's done this to spite me, I tell you!" Brushing past her mother-in-law, she strode angrily outside to where an ostler held two saddled horses. She eyed the sidesaddle on one contemptuously, put her foot in the stirrup of the other one, and swung up. As she sat astride, her riding skirt revealed the tops of her smart boots and gave a glimpse of her leg below the knee.

"Joanna!" Anne came out on the long Georgian portico and stood beneath the Corinthian column. "You cannot go alone! And you cannot ride like that without scandalizing the neighborhood!"

"As if they are not already! Besides, I've not the time to bother with a sidesaddle!" Jo shot back as she laid a spur against the horse's flank.

"Oh, dear! Someone has to go with her!"

The men all looked at the sidesaddle and shook their heads. "Eh? Naw," the ostlers decided in unison. "'Er's got good bottom," one of them reassured the dowager countess.

"Joanna!" Anne, forgetting her own gentility for a moment, stood on tiptoe and cupped her hands to call out, "Be careful!"

The air clung to her like a thick, wet blanket, hot and heavy. A heavy, roiling bank of black clouds rolled ominously along the horizon in sharp contrast to the bright, still sky overhead. Joanna spurred her horse across the ford, crossing the river over the slippery, algae-covered rocks, and onto Roxbury's land. Reining in briefly, she noted the stillness, uncommon for a place where river meets woods. Overhead, a bird circled, cawing twice, and then it swooped down somewhere beyond the hedgerows, and all was still again. The heat was oppressive, the calm that comes before a storm.

She gave the animal its head when they reached the road to the Armitage and was rewarded by the feel of air blowing against her face. Damp tendrils escaped the ribbon she'd used to tie her hair up off her neck and whipped around her forehead and temples. The familiar huge trees, hedgerows, and meadows spread out from the road, looking for all the world exactly as she remembered them. In more than six years, nothing appeared to have changed.

The Armitage loomed ahead, a magnificent crown placed on the crest of the hill. Before it lay the park, a broad expanse of emerald grassland as smooth and lush as a carpet divided neatly by a narrow brick-paved road. In the house itself, old architecture blended with new to create an immense structural mix from Elizabethan to Georgian. Joanna's breath caught painfully as she looked at the grand house she'd once called home. Resolutely, she turned her horse up the long drive.

It was not until she reached the rail and dismounted that it even occurred to her that Adrian might not be there. Taking a deep breath, she smoothed her skirts against her damp legs and climbed the low steps to lift the knocker, telling herself that if he was not home, she'd wait for him. She wasn't going to be fobbed off by anyone—and she certainly wasn't going to leave this place without Justin.

She didn't even care if Helen Delacourt was here. If the woman wished to repeat her ridiculous lies, Joanna would take great pleasure in telling Adrian the truth this time. She was no wounded girl anymore, but a woman grown, so if His Grace of Roxbury meant to make trouble for her now, he'd find himself in a battle royal. Her heart racing, her palms moist, she waited for someone to come to the door.

"My lady!" Adrian's aging butler goggled a moment, and then he recovered. "Is anything amiss, madam?" he asked politely.

Fearful he'd try to bar her way, she tried to peer over his shoulder for a glimpse inside the house, and she answered loudly, "You may inform Roxbury that I have come for my son."

"Your son? Madam, I am certain there's some mistake. His Grace—"

"And do not be telling me he is not in, for I shall demand to wait upon him."

"No . . . no. That is to say he is at home." Standing aside, he allowed her to enter. "Indeed, I shall be most happy to inform His Grace that you are here. I am not precisely sure where he is just now, but I know he is somewhere within the house." Casting a furtive glance toward where voices could be heard in the blue saloon, he gestured to the open library door. "If you will but wait there, my lady, I'll have him found for you."

She walked into the library and paused as she looked around. It was as though she'd taken another step back in time. It too was exactly as she remembered it—with one obvious exception. The full-length portrait of her that Adrian had commissioned the great Lawrence to paint on their betrothal was gone. Its companion piece, the one he'd done of Adrian, still hung above the opposing fireplace. There was no question about one thing—Lawrence had certainly managed to capture Adrian's piercing gaze. It was as though those nearly black eyes bore into her. Even now, with all that had passed between them, she was again drawn by the magnetism of those dark depths. As she stared back, she remembered how those eyes could warm with their intensity, or they could chill with their coldness. Today it seemed they merely mocked.

Perhaps it was the faint smile that lingered at the corners of that all-too-sensuous mouth. For an instant, the old familiar longing flooded every fiber of her being. Closing her eyes, she neither saw nor heard the person come up behind her.

"How dare you—how *dare* you come here?"

The words were low and malignant. Joanna spun to face Helen Delacourt's fury. Had it not been for her own anger, she would have recoiled from the hatred in Adrian's mother's face.

"My business is with Dree, I believe," she answered coldly.

"You will leave my house this instant!"

For answer, Joanna casually laid her riding crop on Adrian's writing desk. "I think not—not until I have collected my son from him."

"So that's your little ploy this time, is it?" the dowager spat out spitefully. "You think to use your brat to entrap my son again. Well, Joanna, you are quite out. You waste your time, for Almeria Bennington is to be his duchess."

"It is no concern of mine what Dree does in that quarter, I assure you," Jo responded dryly. "'Tis only when he demands I give him Justin that I care." Her eyes met Helen's and held. "Justin is mine, madam, and as long as there is breath in this body, I will fight to keep him."

"Get out of here," the older woman said hoarsely.

"If you truly wish to be rid of me, I suggest you persuade Dree to give him back," Joanna countered reasonably. "Otherwise, Lord Barrasford and I will file suit for his return. And this time, my dear duchess, Adrian just might learn the truth."

The dowager paled. "Get out of my house!" she hissed. "Get out before I have you put out!"

"You do not dare."

Helen reached for the bellpull, then hesitated. "For the last time, I am ordering you out of my house!"

"Give me my son."

"I believe the house is mine, Mother."

Both women stood stock-still at the sound of his voice. Joanna brushed past his mother to face him and demand furiously, "What have you done with my son? I warn you—I am not leaving until he comes with me!"

"Here . . . here, what's going on?" Lord Bennington demanded at Adrian's elbow. "I say, Roxbury, but—"

"Papa—" Almeria caught at her father's sleeve, then stood on tiptoe to peer past him. "Lady Carew!" she gasped. "Oh, of all the insufferable—"

"Be quiet!" Adrian ordered without taking his eyes from Joanna.

"Now, see here, Your Grace," Bennington protested.

"You will send that hussy packing on the instant," Helen declared forcefully.

"Get out of here—all of you." Adrian's voice was calm, but his pulse raced as he looked at Joanna. His hungry gaze took in the windblown hair, the plain white cotton waist that clung damply to the swell of her breasts, the blue riding skirt that flared over the gentle curve of her hips, and his mouth was suddenly too dry for words. "Leave us."

"I think not!" Helen Delacourt tried to push Joanna aside. "I'll not stand by and watch you make a fool of yourself again!"

"You made him the fool, not I!" Joanna snapped. "But that is not to the point just now, anyway." Raising her gaze to his, she said evenly, "I've come for Justin, Dree, and I will not leave without him."

"I say, Lady Carew," Bennington expostulated, "but why would you think—"

"Leave us," Adrian repeated curtly. "I would hear from my wife how it is that she thinks I have my son."

"Your son?" Joanna's lip curved disdainfully. "*Your* son? That's rich, isn't it, Dree? You threw me away like a cast-off mistress without so much as a thought that you could have been wrong, and—and now you would have the child I carried! Not while I have breath in my body, Adrian Delacourt!"

"For God's sake, Jo! Have you taken complete leave of your senses?"

"No—have you?" she shot back.

"You are making no sense!"

"I'm telling you Justin is mine! Mine—do you hear me? And before I'll let you have him, I'll refute your slanderous lies in court! In Parliament, too, if need be!"

"We do not have to listen to this!" Helen declared, shoving Joanna toward the door. "You are not welcome in this house, you conniving little witch, and if you think to come back, I shall call the constable!"

"Oh, you shameless—you—" Almeria caught the fury in the duke's eyes and snapped her mouth shut.

Grasping his mother firmly from behind, Adrian pulled her away from Joanna. Then, with an unceremonious jerk, he thrust her through the door. "Don't you ever speak to her again like that! She was every bit the duchess you are!" Turning back to the Benningtons, he demanded of them, "Now, do you go—or must I put you out also?"

"Really, my lord, there is no need for this. Indeed—" Noting Roxbury's thunderous expression, Lord Bennington paused, fearing violence. Firmly grasping his daughter's arm, he dragged her forcefully from the room. "Come, my dear—we are de trop just now," he said in obvious understatement.

Adrian kicked the door shut behind them, then he turned back to Joanna. "Now—what the devil is this all about, Jo?"

"You know quite well!" she snapped back.

"No, I don't, but if you will cease behaving like a veritable harridan, I am willing to listen."

"I want my son, Dree. You cannot hide him from me, you know. I am his mother, and even your political connections cannot change that."

"Jo, what nonsense is this?"

"Surely you don't deny you have Justin? That Mr. Thorpe abducted him this morning?"

"Yes, I deny it! Did you speak with Thorpe?" he asked. "Did you hear my last offer?"

"If you are meaning that fustian that I may keep Justin so long as I do not remarry—well, I can tell you you are very wide of the mark there! You have no right to make conditions on my life, my lord. Pray let me remind you we are divorced—and by *your* express wish, I might add."

"No, no—that was not my last offer."

"Dree," she cut in impatiently, "where is Justin?"

"I do not know—believe me, I do not know."

"Liar!" she spat at him.

"Jo, look at me!" He caught her by the shoulders and gave her a shake. "I may be a fool, but I am not a liar. You cannot truthfully say that I ever lied to you, and you know it." His fingers cut into the thin cotton as he searched her face. "Admit that, at least."

She was white-faced, her blue eyes enormous. "Yes, Dree, you have," she answered finally, her voice even. "You once promised to love me forever."

His hands slipped from her shoulders around to her back, pulling her taut body against his. Her nerves were like drawn bowstrings, tensed to the point of breaking.

Her breasts pressed against his chest as his fingers splayed across her hips. "Jo—Jo . . ." he whispered above her ear, his breath coming in loud rushes that sent shivers down her spine. He bent his head to lightly brush along the bony ridge of her shoulder where the soft cotton waist exposed her warm skin.

As his lips traced fire, a shudder of desire sliced downward, robbing her of breath. Using anger to hide the intense physical need she felt, she pushed him away. "Stop it!" she cried. "I will not be put off, Dree! My son is missing—Justin is missing! Where is he?"

"I don't know, Jo."

"Where is he?" she persisted.

He dropped his hands wearily and shook his head. "I'm telling you I don't know."

A clap of thunder sounded, its rumble muted by distance, but the breeze had stirred, it carried the scent of rain through an open window. Although it was barely past noon, the sky was darkening. "You swear, then, you have no knowledge of Justin's whereabouts? You do not think that Mr. Thorpe—?"

"No. He'd have no reason."

"Perhaps Helen—" Even as she said it, she felt foolish. She knew she was grasping at straws now.

"Hardly. Jo, my mother would know that you'd come after the boy. Think on it—do you truly believe she'd do anything that would bring you here?"

"No, of course not," she conceded wearily. She turned her back to stare unseeing at the empty fireplace. She'd been so certain that she'd find Justin here—that Adrian had somehow abducted him. Now she was at a loss. Hooking her thumbs in the pockets of her riding skirt, she tried to focus on other possibilities. "But he's not home, Dree—we've searched the whole place for him. He's a little boy—he couldn't go far on his own."

He moved behind her and laid a consoling hand on her shoulder. "Believe me, Jo, when I say that 'twas never my intent to take the boy away from you. But you cannot deny he *is* my son—you know you cannot. All I am asking of you is the chance to know him."

"You have no right there, Dree. You have no right to ask that of me," she answered finally in a low voice. "Gary was his father in more ways than mere blood."

"Gary's gone." He twisted a strand of wheat hair where it lay against her neck. "Let me help the boy with his grief."

"You would destroy his memory of Gary." Unwilling to let him know what he could do to her still, she pulled away. "I am sorry, Dree, but I cannot allow what you ask. Now, if you will excuse me, I must be getting home. It's going to storm, and I've got to look for him. Once it begins thundering, he'll be afraid." Her mouth twisted. "It was a storm that caused Gary's boat to capsize, you know." Turning around, she managed to meet his eyes briefly. "But you are right in one thing: he cannot seem to recover from Gary's death. He's taken Johnny in unreasonable dislike, because he does not want another papa, and he's threatened to join Gary."

"My God."

"Yes, but I am quite sure that he does not know what death is. I don't think he has any notion as to what it is to drown."

"You don't think he could have gone to the river?" he asked quickly.

"I don't know where he is."

"How did you get here?"

"I rode a horse."

"Alone?"

"Alone. I had neither the time nor the patience to wait for anyone. I expect I've scandalized full half of Haven today," she admitted.

"You always had good bottom, Jo—I've ridden into battle with men who couldn't sit a horse as well as you." Looking into the roiling clouds outside, he returned to the matter at hand. "I can smell the rain already," he said, frowning. "Tell you what—I'll send you home in my carriage, and I'll raise a search party on this side of the river. One of the grooms can ride to Winton Abbey and ask them to join in the search."

"My father would not care if my son drowned," she reminded him bitterly. "That's something else I lay at your door."

Ignoring the barb, he went on, telling her quickly, "Trust me, Jo—I'll see the boy is found. You go on home and I'll send word as soon as I know anything." When he could see he hadn't convinced her, he added, "Look—it's just possible he's already at Haven and you'll be sending word to me. I know—I know—

you've looked there already, but he's a small boy. He could be hiding in some cranny somewhere."

A discreet knock sounded on the door, interrupting them. Adrian looked up impatiently and barked, "Yes?"

"Your pardon, Your Grace, but there's a man here from Haven," the butler answered as he opened the door.

Adrian flashed Joanna a triumphant smile. "See—what did I tell you? You've worried yourself for naught."

The Haven man came in diffidently. "Beggin' yer pardon, ma'am, but 'er la'ship sent me t' 'elp bring th' little master 'ome. Said ye wouldn't be carryin' 'im on th', horse, ye unnerstan'."

"Then he's still not been found?" Adrian demanded.

"No, Yer Grace."

"Damn. But you *are* still searching over there?"

"Aye, m'lor'—been fr'm t'ouse t' th' river, and 'e ain't there. 'E ain't nowheres. Ain't a body as is seen 'im since afore noon." The man shook his head. "'E's just disappeared."

"Don't worry, Jo." Already in the hall and headed for the door, Adrian told her over his shoulder, "My mother will order the carriage for you. Since your horse is already saddled, I'll take it, and when I find the boy, I'll bring him over to Haven to you."

"No!"

He paused momentarily. "I give you my word, Jo."

"I'm going with you."

"Don't be a goose," he snapped. "It's going to rain—you'll get soaked."

"No.!" She shook her head stubbornly. "I am going with you, Dree. As you said, my horse is already saddled."

"The devil you are! If we are to find him, we cannot keep a lady's pace! No, you'll go on home."

"And I ride as well as most men—you just said so yourself. No, Dree, he's *my* son! I can't go home without him—and I won't!"

"You always were a stubborn female," he muttered under his breath. Uncertain of what he might find, he did not want her there. Exhaling slowly to calm his own fears, he shook his head. "No, Jo—not this time. I'll either bring him to you, or I'll send word if I don't find him." Before she could prolong the argument, he hurriedly exited the house.

She waited only until he'd disappeared in the direction of the stable before she let herself out the door. Lightning flickered constantly along the horizon now, making her horse skittish as she swung up into the saddle. She could hear him shouting for a search party to form. Twisting her reins around her hand, she waited for him to come out, telling herself that Adrian Delacourt was going to find that he couldn't bully her as easily as he'd once done. He was going to discover she wasn't the wide-eyed nineteen-year-old girl he'd once left at the mercy of his mother. These six years just passed had tempered her, making her a far stronger woman than he remembered.

"You go with Tompkins and Burk. I'll take Sims. Collins and Ellis will take the road to Winton Abbey, Sims and I will stay along the river, and you can keep to the road between here and Haven."

"No." Joanna shook her head with determination. "I am going with you, Dree. I want to search along the river myself."

They were reined in at the trifork in the main road from the Armitage. Exasperated, Adrian snapped, "Jo, it's wet and muddy along the bank—I cannot be responsible for you."

"I didn't ask you to be." To demonstrate her stubbornness, she nudged her horse next to Sims's. "We're wasting time arguing when we ought to be looking. I'm not a milk and water miss, Dree. In fact, I'm not a miss anymore at all."

"You always were a hopeless hoyden—I hope you know that."

"Yes. But I daresay dear Almeria will prove much more to your taste," she answered sweetly.

He looked over at her, taking in her heat-flushed cheeks, the wisps of damp hair that clung to her temples, the trickle of sweat that disappeared beneath the neck of her cotton waist, and then the outline of her leg where it straddled the horse. "Somehow," he drawled lazily, "I cannot quite think you would wish Barrasford to see you like this."

"Johnny?"

"The impeccable Lord Johnny," he reminded her.

"I shouldn't mind, actually. And if this heat continues, I expect he will." Nonetheless, she took out a handkerchief and mopped at her face and neck. "There—am I fit to be seen with Your Grace now?"

"I never said you weren't." He leaned forward in his saddle and looked toward the riverbank. "Are you quite certain you wish to chance that? It could be slippery."

For answer, she spurred her horse forward. "You forget—I've every bit as good a bottom as you," she retorted.

They picked their way slowly along the muddy bank, with Sims scanning the opposite side, Adrian looking for tracks, and Joanna keeping her eyes intent on the brush and woods that separated the riverbed from the fields beyond. The starch from her waist felt sticky against her skin. "I almost wish it *would* rain," she muttered under her breath.

"You won't when it does," he answered. "And by the looks of it, it's going to right now."

A strong breeze blew across the river and rattled the leaves beside her even as the first drops hit the water like a blast of bird shot. Then the sky poured, drenching them. Sims leaned over his pommel and plodded on. "You never did know when you were well off, did you?" Adrian shouted at her over the sound of water ricocheting off water.

"Never!" she shouted back.

"Can you see?"

"Not very well!"

He rose in his stirrups and cupped his hands around his mouth. "Justin! Justin! Justin Sherwood—

can you hear me?" he yelled at the top of his lungs. "Justinnnnn—!" It was as if the rain drowned the words the moment they escaped him.

"Your Grace," Sims shouted, turning around to call out, "d'ye think we ought to go back?"

"No! It'll slacken soon!"

Joanna took up the call, standing high in her saddle to yell over and over again, "Justin! Justin—over here! Justin, it's Mama!"

After several minutes, the storm slowed to a steady staccato on the water. Rain washed over their faces, dripped off their hair, and soaked them thoroughly. The skirt of Joanna's habit hung heavily down over her elegant riding boots, but she didn't care. Her eyes anxiously scanned both sides of the river, the muddy banks, and the thick brush as they plodded soddenly along for nearly a mile.

"He cannot have walked this far," Adrian decided aloud. "We'll have to go back and cross the ford while it's still passable."

Already the runoff from higher ground was turning the river a milky brown, frightening her. She dared not think what the rain-swollen branches upstream would do to the ford. "All right."

"Y'r Grace, 'tis hopeless," Sims spoke up finally. "We'll have to come back when the rain stops."

"No! If he's out here, he could drown!" Joanna shrieked. "Dree, you cannot stop now! Justin cannot swim!"

"No," Adrian decided, shaking his head grimly. "We'll press on."

"But, Y'r Grace—"

"Sims, if it—were your son lost, would you quit?"

"But the rain'll wash away any sign—"

"Would you, Sims?" the duke persisted.

"No. Aye," the man said, sighing. "We've a ways to go before we've seen everything."

Hampered by the mud and rain, they took well over an hour to reach the ford, which had become submerged beneath swirling, muddy water. When the groom hesitated, Adrian spurred his horse forward to cross the slippery rocks. The current rushed against the animal's knees, pushing it sideways, sending it twenty yards downstream. "Wait over there!" he yelled back at Joanna, but she was already in the water. "I'll give you one thing," he muttered as he leaned to catch her skittery horse's reins. "You always were pluck to the bone."

Not to be bested by a female, Sims plunged across and emerged unscathed, grumbling, "If we'd but waited for the rain to stop, the water'd be gone down in a couple of hours."

"Dree—no!" Joanna leaned to clutch at his sleeve, her voice anguished.

Adrian followed her line of vision and saw the brim of a child's straw hat wedged in the branches of a submerged tree trunk. His heart thudded painfully and the fingers of his free hand covered hers on his arm. "There's no body, Jo—'tis just a hat," he tried to reassure her. "You wait here and I'll get it."

Dismounting, he walked slowly along the muddy bank, heedless now of Hoby's boots or anything else save the fear that the son he'd just discovered was dead. Edging down through the mire, he managed to grasp a tree branch and wade into the swirling water to reach the hat and dislodge it. Then he felt gingerly down in the water, sweeping his hands all the way to the mud beneath the tangled roots in search of the child's body. Mercifully, he came up empty-handed. Slogging back up the bank, he carried the hat to her.

"Justin's?"

Already the steady rain was washing the silt and leaves from the blue ribbon. She nodded, then her face crumpled. "Oh, Dree, it cannot be! He is but a little boy! No! Justin!" she screamed. "Justin, where are you?"

He lifted her from her horse and enveloped her in his arms. She struggled, then sagged against him and buried her face in his shoulder to weep uncontrollably. He stood there, one arm tightly supporting her, the other smoothing the wet, tangled mass of hair, while tears of his own coursed silently to mingle with the rain. Sims observed them helplessly for a while and then bent to pick up the hat where Adrian had dropped it. Straightening up, he touched his master's shoulder gently.

"There's nothing more to do here, Y'r Grace, but we ought to get her ladyship inside somewheres. I can ride to Haven for help."

"No." Joanna's voice was muffled against Adrian's wet coat. "No, Dree, I cannot leave him out here alone—I cannot—he's such a little boy."

"Shhhhh," he murmured. "We'll find him, Jo—he'll be all right—we'll keep looking," he assured her. Meeting Sims's eyes over her head, he told the man, "I'll cross back and go downstream to look." To Joanna he said, "Sims will take you back to Haven, and I'll continue the search."

"No—I'm going with you. I have to know, Dree—I have to." She clutched at his arms and pleaded, "Let me go with you—please. Please, Dree—I was there when he was born, I can be there when . . ." Her voice trailed off, choked by a suppressed sob.

"All right."

The water was still rising, but they managed to cross back to the Armitage side, where the bank was flatter and wider going downstream. After painstakingly covering some three-quarters of a mile of the river, Adrian reined in again. "'Tis no use—I don't think he would have floated farther than this, Jo. But Sims is right: we've got to get you in somewhere before you take ill."

"I can't stop looking, Dree—I cannot," she said hollowly. "I've got to find him."

"I said I'd find him, and I meant it. But you've got to look after yourself. No matter what happens, you've got another boy to consider," he reminded her. "Justin is my only son."

"Ain't nothing over here but the old crofter cottage," the groom observed, "and the water's too high now to take her back to Haven. Mebbe we ought to head for the Armitage. I mean—" The man eyed Joanna. "Ye'd best be gettin' into something dry, ma'am."

"I'm all right," she insisted.

"No." Somehow Adrian could not bear the thought of taking her to his mother—not after all the bitterness between them, not in her emotional state. "We'll take her to the cottage," he decided.

"Dree, my son's out here! Listen to me—I won't leave him!"

He reached to take her reins. "You have to, Jo—he's not here. Come on," he coaxed, "you must have a care for yourself, you know. If you take ill, who's to look after Gary's son?" Resolutely, he nudged his horse with his knee and led her toward shelter. The rain was still steady, but the sky was lightening to the west. "I promise you that when the rain stops, there'll not be an inch of Roxbury, Carew, or Milford lands unsearched," he declared grimly. "I'll not rest until we have Justin."

"Be a body ye'll be looking for, Yer Grace," Sims offered.

"I won't hear that—not yet," Adrian answered coldly.

The cottage stood as it had for more than two hundred years, a stone-and-thatch affair, now abandoned since the land had been let to another farmer, who'd chosen to ride over to work it rather than live there. Sims dismounted, picked the lock, and threw open the door to the small two-room dwelling while Adrian lifted Joanna down. A faintly musty odor, the product of old thatch, greeted them, but the rooms inside were dry.

The windows were shuttered, making the cottage dark. Sims threw them open to admit both light and rain, then he went back out to tend the horses. As the horror was beginning to sink in, Joanna stared almost unseeing around the small room and walked absently to the now empty stone fireplace that took most of the wall. She did not think she could bear her loss.

"I remember this place in happier times, Jo—do you?" Adrian asked softly behind her.

She closed her eyes to fight the lump in her throat and nodded. For the briefest of moments, she allowed herself to think of that other time, a time when they'd loved each other wrapped only in his greatcoat on that bare floor. But then, the Armitage was full of such places, she recalled. In the early days of their marriage, it had seemed impossible for either of them to ever have enough of the other. If she dared to think of such things, she could remember dozens of times when they'd succumbed to such passion. Now she sighed heavily to blot out such memories. She had other, more painful thoughts to deal with just now. Turning around, she faced the man she'd once loved so intensely.

"He is such a good child really, Dree," she nearly whispered. "So very inquisitive for his age."

"I saw that."

"Gary did love him, you know."

He nodded. "Tell me about him, Jo."

"He was born just past Christmas in Capri—we'd

gone there to escape the French on the mainland. He
was . . . that is, he will be six this next winter, Dree. He
came late, you know, and the physicians despaired of
my having him, but after a labor of two days, I finally
had him." A wry smile quirked the corners of her
mouth. "Quite odd what one remembers, isn't it? I remember Gary washing my face afterward and telling
me we had a son. I had hoped for a daughter, of course,
so that 'twould be Gary's own flesh that inherited, but
I guess God had other plans. And then I saw him, Dree,
and he had that black, black hair just like yours. My
first thought was that we could never bring him back
to England without resurrecting the scandal all over
again. I felt terrible at first, thinking how Gary had
been cheated in his heir, but he never minded in the
least. He loved me rather blindly, you see, and because
Justin was my flesh as much as yours, he loved him,
too."

"Why didn't you tell me?"

"Tell you what? That I carried your child? To what
end?" Bitterness crept into her voice, betraying the old
hurt. "And what would that have served, I ask you?
Would you have dropped your petition of divorce?"

"I don't know—I would have waited, I suppose."

"And what if Justin had looked like me? You would
have accused me anew, wouldn't you? And your ever-
so-aristocratic mama—" Joanna gave a derisive little
snort. "Well, even if he'd resembled you, she would
have said I was sleeping with you both. No, there was
nothing to be gained by telling you anything then."

"Were you? Sleeping with both of us, I mean?"

"'Tis odd that you would ask that question now,
Dree, isn't it? Once I would have given anything to be
asked rather than accused, but now it doesn't matter
that much. I don't feel I owe you the answer anymore."

"Gary called me a blind fool at the time."

"Did he now? I never knew what he said to you except that I asked him not to defend me. I told him he owed you no answer to such vile charges." Her eyes met his steadily now. "And what do you think? Were you a fool, Dree?"

"I don't know. I know I paid a bitter price for my pride, so maybe I was. Perhaps I should have been like Caro Lamb's husband and ignored the whole thing."

"You paid a bitter price." She shook her head in disbelief. "*You* paid a bitter price, you say. Well, my lord duke, 'twas a pittance to the price we paid. You ruined me, and you ruined Gary. We could not even stay in the land of our birth because of you. My father disowned me—my children will never know their Milford heritage because of you. You cast off the two people you claimed to love the most with no regard for the truth—indeed, I don't think you would have believed either of us, anyway."

"Jo—" He took a step toward her.

"Don't touch me! Don't you dare touch me, Adrian Delacourt! I should have never come back!"

"You're overset."

"Of course I am!" she snapped. "One look at Justin and you were willing to do anything to get him, weren't you? And you still would, wouldn't you? You would even turn me up sweet if you could! Well, you cannot! Take your Miss Bennington and get your own perfectly correct little heirs from your perfectly correct duchess, Dree! And do not be worrying about Joanna Milford or her sons either! We are going to Ireland!" Turning away, she covered her face with her hands. "Oh, Dree—whatever will I do if he's dead?"

"Jo . . . Jo . . ." he said gently, laying his hand on her shoulder.

"Please . . . I'll come about—just leave me be." She

fumbled in her soaked skirt for her handkerchief and wrung it out before blowing her nose.

"Jo, I'm sorry." He dropped his hand. "There was a time when I would have died rather than hurt you or Gary."

"Looks like the storm's breakin'," Sims observed from the door. "Just a little mistin' now." He looked from the duke to Joanna. "She all right?"

"No."

She blew her nose again and then sniffed before turning to Sims. "I am fine, thank you."

"Well, the river'll be down by nightfall, and we can take you home, my lady," the groom said diffidently.

"I want to find my son first."

"Mebbe you ought to go home and let His Grace take care of that."

"I want to be there."

The insistent bark of a hunting dog sounded not too far away. Sims listened for a moment and then went to the window. "Now I know there ain't anyone huntin' in this weather," he observed to himself. "Somebody's lost a dog."

"It'll find its way home—they always do," Adrian answered absently. "Did you find a place for the horses?"

"Got 'em in one of the plow sheds."

They stared at each other, the three of them. Without so much as a place to sit down, they were in an awkward position. Joanna moved restlessly about the small room, keeping her back to Adrian. He walked over to the empty fireplace and began scraping the mud from an irreparably damaged pair of Hoby's boots. He could have wrung water out of every garment on his body if he'd tried, he decided. His coat alone weighed an extra five to ten pounds. Peeling it off, he twisted it over the hearth, wringing the rainwater from it. Joanna turned around at the sound of the water hitting the stones, and for the first time, both of them became aware of her soaked cotton waist. She looked down where her breasts were outlined against the wet cloth and she crossed her arms in front of her, covering herself. Sims, always conscious of the barriers between himself and his betters, murmured something about seeing to the horses again.

After the floodtide of emotions before, the silence hung between Adrian and Joanna like a curtain. Finally he flung his wet coat on the floor impatiently. "Are you really going to marry Johnny?"

"Yes."

"You cannot pretend to love him. I mean, you haven't even had enough time to know him."

"I see much of Gareth Sherwood in him."

"Really? I never thought Gary much of a Corinthian."

"I meant his kindness and his concern, Dree."

"I thought perhaps 'twas his handsome face."

"He's no more handsome than you are—'tis his disposition that makes the difference." She gave him a faint smile. "As I am sure that Almeria's disposition is quite different from mine. I understand I am to congratulate you in that quarter also. But then, somehow I cannot see that you will suit." She looked pointedly at the floor in front of the hearth. "I'm afraid I cannot see her there, after all. But no doubt she will countenance a mistress for that sort of thing."

"Who told you I am to marry Almeria?"

"Your mother." She raised an eyebrow at his expression. "Dear me, did you not know it is as good as an accomplished fact? I daresay she is as determined to get you a proper duchess as she was to get rid of your last one."

"Well, I am not hanging out for a wife just now, and

if I were, it wouldn't be Miss Bennington, I can assure you."

"More's the pity. Then you could have had two females to rule the roost for you."

"Jo . . ." He took a warning step toward her. "Sometimes I do not know whether to laugh or wring your neck, but I suspect a good wringing is in order. My mother does not rule my roost, as you call it. Oh, I admit she tends to bully, but most of what she says falls on my deaf ears. You just never learned to stand up to her."

"I shouldn't have had to, Dree. I'll always blame you for that."

"I had hopes she would come to tolerate you."

"You had to know she hated me—she certainly made no pretense otherwise. She made my life so miserable that before you were to come home that last time, I'd already informed her that I was going to ask you to pack her off to her dower estate. At the time, she laughed in my face, telling me if anyone left her house, it would be me. *Her* house, Dree—not mine. And foolish me, I thought I'd be the one to win. I was your duchess, but I could not even have the ordering of anything about the Armitage."

"You should have come to me. I could have settled that for you."

"Oh, but you did. And with utter finality, too." Moving away from him, she sighed. "Let us hope that she and Almeria will be happy together."

"I told you I'm not offering for the chit. I'm not interested in any eighteen-year-old girl, no matter what her accomplishments."

"She'll be a credit to you, I'm sure."

"Jo, what the hell is this? You're making no sense."

"Helen wants her for you, Dree. What you want won't matter."

"If my mother was making your life hell, you should have come to me instead of cuckolding me with Gary."

She opened her mouth to speak, then shut it, shaking her head. "I don't have to say anything to you anymore, Dree," she managed finally. "You will never understand, will you?"

"Y'r Grace! Y'r Grace!" Sims called through the window, interrupting them. "Ye'd best come—I've found the boy!"

"'Twas the dog's barkin', Y'r Grace," Sims explained over the abandoned well. "I came to get the dog, and while I was callin' it, I heard the boy."

Joanna's heart sank when she saw the abandoned well. Justin's spotted spaniel lay quiet now, its nose between two of the rotted boards that had covered the hole. Coming from somewhere in the depths below, she could hear her son's frightened cries. Adrian kicked aside one of the boards and knelt in the boggy grass.

"Justin! Can you hear me, Justin?" he called loudly.

The crying stopped with a hiccup, then resumed with loud wails of "Mama! I want my mama!"

"She's here!" Adrian moved over to give her room. "Be careful—'tis deep and the grass slippery," he murmured as he helped her kneel at the edge of the old well. "Talk to him until I can determine what's best done."

"Justin! Justin!" Frantic when she could not see into the dark hole and knowing that the sun would be going down too soon to fetch help from either Haven or the Armitage, she counted several deep breaths to master her own terror. "Are you all right?" she demanded foolishly, knowing that he could not be.

For answer, there was a splash as he tried to move, and he began crying more loudly. Adrian pulled her back slightly and leaned farther over the hole. "Justin, we are going to get you out! Be a brave fellow for your mama and talk to her so she will know you are all right! I'm going to find a rope and hang it down for you to hold—do you understand me?"

"Justin, it's the duke!" Joanna shouted.

"Duke?" There was a brief break in the loud weeping. "I want out, sir—please," the boy pleaded, his voice quavering. "I-I'm cold—and my leg—my leg hurts!"

"I'm going to get you out!" Adrian shouted again. "Can you see light?"

"Way up." Again the child splashed.

"Dree, there's water in there!" Joanna cried. "'Twill fill up from the groundwater!"

"I know," he acknowledged grimly. "Sims, see if you can find anything that we can use—the old bucket rope may be stored somewhere—anything. Jo, keep talking to him, and for God's sake, don't make him any more frightened than he already is."

She nodded. Lying on the wet grass, she hung her head over the hole. "'Tis Mama, Justin—everything's all right. The duke will get you out if you can have a little patience. You must not cry, dearest, or I cannot understand you—do you understand me?"

"Y-yes!"

"Now, how much water is down there with you?"

"I don't know!" he wailed.

"Listen to me," she told him firmly. "Is it to your knees? Your waist? Your shoulders? How deep is the water?"

"'Bove my middle!"

Adrian muttered an oath at her side.

"Are you standing up?" she asked.

"No!"

"Stand up then!"

"I—I cannot!" He began to cry again. "Mama, my leg hurts! I cannot stand it! I cannot stand up!"

"You must try, Justin. You've got to, dearest—you've just got to do it!"

"I cannot!"

"Justin!"

"I—I'm trying, Mama, but I cannot!"

"Justin—please!"

There was another splash of activity below, followed by loud sobbing. "I'm standing, Mama, but it hurts—it hurts so badly I c-cannot s-stand it!"

"Justin, listen to me," Adrian called down the hole. "This is the duke speaking, Justin! You will be all right if you can but keep your head above water. There's going to be more water, but you're going to be all right. Where is the water now?"

"'Bove my middle!"

"That's what you said when you were not standing!" Joanna reminded him.

"Then it was way 'bove my middle! Mama, I want out!"

"Found the rope, Y'r Grace! 'Tis old, but it ought to hold the boy." Sims came at a lope, carrying a thick gray coil from which frayed ends dangled.

"My thanks, old fellow." Adrian unrolled it and judged its length. "Justin," he shouted, "I am dropping the end of this rope down to you. If you can but tie it around your waist tightly enough to hold you, I'm going to pull you out." Turning to Joanna, he added, "You and Sims both hold this end so that it does not slip."

He recoiled the rope and threw it against the side, where it thudded and unrolled before splashing into the water below. "Can you see it, Justin?"

"I can't see anything down here!"

"Feel for it!"

"I got it!"

"Tie it around your waist!"

"I cannot!"

"Justin!" Joanna took over. "Put it around your middle and make a knot—please!" She waited several seconds, then asked anxiously, "Did you tie it?"

"Y-yes!"

"Good boy! We are going to pull you up!" Adrian shouted. He began slowly tightening the rope, testing the tension. For a brief moment it was taut, then it slackened.

"Mama, it came loose—"

"Dree, he cannot tie very well. Perhaps if he just tried to hold on and balance himself against the sides—"

"No—the rope's slick from the mud now, and the rocks are loose already. I'm going to have to go down after him."

"It'll cave in, my lord—ye can hear 'em fallin' in as the water's coming up," the ostler warned. "Perhaps if I rode to Winton Abbey for help—"

"There's not time!" Adrian snapped, and caught himself. "Your pardon, Sims, but there isn't."

Joanna eyed his tall frame with misgiving. "If there's a danger it will cave in, I am smaller than either of you—let me go, Dree."

"No."

"He's my son!" she all but shouted at him. "I don't want him—"

He clamped a hand over her mouth and hissed, "Don't say it—don't even say it, Jo! Do you want to frighten him further?"

"He's my son," she repeated through his fingers.

"And mine. I hate to say it again, but you've got the other boy to think of, Jo. I, on the other hand, have no one." He released her and nodded to Sims. "I don't think both of you can risk trying to hold me—get Ajax."

Joanna stared numbly at him and then back into the dark, narrow hole. Justin was crying still, but there was nothing she could do. Already it was beginning to rain again, and great drops of water hit the sodden ground like hard pebbles, adding to her sense of desperation.

When she said nothing, Adrian reached to push a heavy strand of wet hair away from her face. "I've got to do this—for you, for him—for myself even. I owe you this."

Sims led the big bay up behind them. "He don't like all this rain," he observed laconically as the horse shied back from the hole.

Adrian dropped his hand from Joanna's hair and reached to pick up the rope. Straightening up, he walked to check the girth of his saddle, then he eyed the saddlehorn with grim satisfaction. The Spanish cavalry saddle was one memento he was glad he'd thought to bring back from the Peninsula, for it was about to prove far more useful than its English counterpart. Looping an end of the rope, he tied it around the horn, then he pulled it tight, testing its hold. Satisfied, he ordered, "You come over here and hold him, Jo."

"But Sims—"

"You've always had a way with horses, and you speak more softly than Sims," he reminded her. "I think Ajax less likely to be skittish for you than for him."

"Dree—"

"Besides, I want you away from the side—if it starts to cave in, I don't want three of us down there. I want you able to go home to Gary's son." As Ajax side-stepped away from the little spaniel, which kept yipping excitedly between its legs, Adrian cursed under his breath. "Put the dog in the shed, Sims—I don't want the horse to bolt."

"Dree, I wish you would let me—"

He looked unbearably tired as he waved her off. "Just do as I ask for once." Walking back to the well opening, he began knotting the other end of the rope under his arms. "Check the knot, old fellow," he told Sims.

"Aye, Y'r Grace."

"Mama! Mama!" The child cried frantically now. "The water—it's getting deeper!"

"Justin, I am coming down to get you!" Adrian shouted over his screams. "I am coming down now! You just have to be a brave boy for your mama a little longer, and then we'll have you out." As he said those words, he moved closer to the edge.

"Dree!" He turned back at the sound of her voice. There was nothing more she could say, but she couldn't just stand there. She didn't want him to go down, but she wanted desperately to save her son. "Be careful," she managed, forcing a crooked smile as tears welled in her eyes. Her lower lip quivered and her voice dropped to a painful whisper. "Please be careful, Dree. I love him so much—so very much. And I'd not have anything happen to you either."

They stood barely five feet apart, separated by the chasm of six bitter years. He sucked in his breath and nodded. "I'll be fine, Jo, and so will the boy. But if anything untoward should happen, I want you to know something: even when I hated you for betraying me with Gary, I never stopped loving you. My pain was unbearable, too."

"Mama! Mama, help me!"

Adrian took a deep breath, then nodded. "Ready, Sims? Jo, don't let the horse move."

She dropped the reins and caught the bridle bit to

steady the animal. Pulling its head close, she closed her eyes and leaned her forehead against its long, hard nose. The horse half sidestepped once when the rope on the horn went taut with Adrian's weight, but then it dug in and stood wide-stanced, its hooves firmly planted in the slippery mud. Time stood still for her— there were no jumbled thoughts, no frantic prayers now, only a desperate hope.

"Watch out! There's rocks falling! The side's giving way, my lord!"

She could hear Sims's voice, but it did not really penetrate her consciousness. Her mind was blank, but her hand was steady on the horse's bit. She could not have said how long it took before Adrian called out, "I've got him—walk the horse!"

When she did not move, Sims yelled at her, "You've got to walk the horse about twenty feet, ma'am!"

Relief flooded over her. Tugging at the bit, she pulled the big bay farther from the well. She could hear rocks hitting the water inside the shaft, but she knew if the rope held, Adrian and Justin would make it out.

"Steady . . . steady . . ." Then came the triumphant shout, "I've got him, Y'r Grace."

She turned back to see Sims lifting Justin's inert body from her former husband's arms. As for Adrian himself, he was half in and half out of the opening, his boots braced on either side between rock and mud. "Another few feet, Jo!" he called out. Ajax took three more steps, then Roxbury wriggled out, belly down onto the slick, muddy grass. He lay there for a moment, breathless.

Releasing the horse, Joanna ran back to where Sims held her son. "Is he—that is, he's all right, isn't he?"

"He's alive, Jo," Adrian managed, panting. "Leg's broken badly—rocks hit him on the head—but he's breathing."

"Got a nasty lump and some cuts, ma'am," the groom added as he examined the boy, "but nothing that won't heal." He looked closer and grinned. "Comin' around already, he is."

She dropped to her knees and cradled her son. "Justin . . . Justin . . ." she murmured soothingly. "You are all right, dearest—Mama's here."

"No, I ain't," he answered feebly as his dark eyes blinked open. "Mama, it hurts—it hurts bad."

She stroked the wet black hair back from his face and examined the bruise that was already forming. "Oh, Justin—you gave me such a fright!"

He tried to wriggle upright and fell back into her lap. "My leg hurts, Mama!" And then, as if by afterthought, "I s'pose you're going to birch me."

"I ought to," she admitted as she picked the debris from his hair, "but I daresay you have already been punished enough. The duke saved your life, you know." She turned to where Adrian now sat cross-legged in the wet grass. His expensive clothes were torn, his face cut, and his hands bleeding. "You are fortunate to be alive yourself, Dree. Thank you—thank you from the bottom of my heart."

He looked away. "I told you—I owed you this at least."

"Boy's got to have a doctor, my lord, and it's going to get dark." Sims pulled at his soaked clothes. "Be a wonder if we all don't get carried off with something from this."

Adrian stood up, his rent clothes bagging from the water. "Well, there's no crossing the river now—we'll have to head for the Armitage."

"No!"

"Would you rather go to Winton Abbey?" he asked quietly.

"You know I cannot."

"Then it will have to be the Armitage, won't it?" he asked reasonably. "We'll get you both dry, put the boy to bed, and send for the doctor. I don't know about you, Jo, but I am ready for a warm bath and a bed."

"I cannot go home with you."

"Don't be a fool, Jo!" he snapped. "You can scarce do anything else, can you? Are you afraid of what Johnny will say? If he's any man at all, when he hears the story, he'll know that you had no choice in the matter."

"No."

"For God's sake, Jo! You always were a stubborn female!"

"I will not subject my son to your mother's gibes!" she said, her own temper flaring briefly. "God only knows what awful thing she might say to him."

"Is that it? Let me assure you, my dear, that my mother need not be a consideration."

"Since when?"

"Since today."

"Beggin' your pardon, my lady, but I don't see as where there's much to argue about. This boy's got to have a doctor." He rolled Justin's breeches up higher and exposed the place where a bloody piece of bone jutted sharply through the skin above an ugly lump. "This has got to be cleaned and set, else he's apt t'be losin' his leg."

"I'll take him up with me," Adrian decided. "Sims, you ride for the doctor—tell him we need him immediately."

Joanna looked down at her son's leg, and the sight made her utterly ill. As a wave of nausea threatened what was left of her dignity, she said faintly, "I had no idea—that is, I didn't know—" Telling herself she had to be strong, that she couldn't lose her composure now, she swallowed hard. Adrian had already risked his life for Justin, earning him a considerable measure of her trust, but she still didn't want her son exposed to Helen Delacourt's hatred of her.

As if he understood her silence, Adrian placed a bleeding hand on her shoulder. "My mother need not be a consideration," he repeated quietly. "There's no excuse sufficient for what she said to you today. For what it's worth to you, I won't let her say anything like that to you ever again."

"You don't need to tell me this now."

"Jo, whatever happened six years ago was between me, you, and Gary, and I don't mean to let it touch Justin. My only concern now is that he gets well, that he can run and play again like any other little boy. He needs that leg treated, and he needs his mother, and if that means going to the Armitage with me, then I'm asking you to do it."

Swallowing the lump of fear in her throat, she finally nodded. "All right—we'll go there," she managed, her voice scarce above a whisper. "Dree, I'm so afraid."

His hand squeezed her shoulder, then released it. "I've hopes the worst is over, Jo."

A drian carried the boy past his mother, the Ben-ningtons, and the astonished servants. Joanna, heedless of her thoroughly bedraggled appearance, trailed them up the stairs and into his bedchamber, while an aggrieved valet, two maids, and the house-keeper followed.

"Egad, Your Grace! Your coat—'tis ruined—utterly ruined! And what on earth—? That is, who—? Really, sir, but you surely cannot mean to put him here! I mean, he's filthy!" Catching up to him, Blake plucked at his sleeve. "My lord, we've got to get you out of this coat!"

"Hang the coat, Blake!" Adrian barked. "What we've got to do is clean up this child!"

At that, the valet peered at the boy, then gasped, "My word, but he's—"

"We've already sent for the doctor," Adrian said curtly. "Now, fetch one of my shirts from the drawer. Martha, I'd have a basin of hot water, if you please. Bess, turn back the sheets." With Justin still in his arms, he turned to the housekeeper to explain. "Mrs. John-son, he's been in an accident, and we shall require some laudanum."

"Yes, Your Grace," the woman responded, her eyes on Joanna, her lips tight with disapproval.

"And Lady Carew will require dry clothes and a

bath. Pray inform my mother that I shall be down after we've got the boy settled into bed."

"My lord, you are dripping mud on the carpets," Blake reminded him. "Perhaps the nursery would be more suited—"

"The nursery's been closed for twenty years. No, we'll put him here. Just fold a blanket to protect the coverlet until we get these clothes off him."

Before the valet could move, one of the maids had the blanket laid out on the bed. Adrian placed Justin on it and began stripping the wet clothes off him. The child's face was pale and bruised, and he was barely conscious, but his breathing was even. When he reached the breeches, Adrian looked up. "I need scissors—they've got to be cut off."

"Dree, I don't know if you—"

"I've seen this bad and worse on the battlefield," he told her tersely.

The housekeeper hovered behind him, peering curiously at the boy. Then she looked at Joanna, and comprehension spread across her lined face. "'Pon my word! Oh, dear—I had not the least notion!"

Someone handed Adrian a pair of scissors, and he began cutting the wet nankeen just below the pockets, exposing the ugly break. Even Blake had to look away. "It's going to hurt like the devil when he wakes again, but we can be grateful he's out of it now. Jo, did anyone fetch the basin?"

She took the bowl of warm water and the cloth from the maid and carried it to the bed. "I'll wash him."

"No—I do not mind doing it, and it's not a pretty sight for a mother's eyes." Wringing out the cloth, he began wiping mud and debris away from the wound. "Sit on the other side," he advised her, "and hold his hand in case he wakes."

"You'll get the bed wet and muddy, my lady," the

housekeeper reminded her, this time not unkindly. "You'd best let me get you those dry clothes before you sit down."

"There's not time." Adrian didn't look up. "Order her a bath and have it put behind the screen once we are done here."

"Here, my lord?" Mrs. Johnson asked, clearly scandalized again.

"Here. Blake—"

"Yes, Your Grace?"

"Help me get the rest of this off his leg, but don't pull too hard. Cut it some more if you need to do so."

Between them, Adrian and his valet managed to get Justin undressed, washed, and clothed in a lawn shirt that seemed to swallow him. Blake stood back and viewed his handiwork with a rare smile on his thin face. "Fits like a tent, my lord. But that break—'tis a terrible sight. A terrible sight," he repeated, shaking his head.

Tossing in the great four-poster bed, Justin cried out, "My leg hurts, Mama—it hurts bad! Mama, where are you?"

"Here, dearest." Joanna moved closer with the bottle of laudanum. "Dree, I do not know how much—I was never ill a day in my life."

"I don't know. Mrs. Johnson?"

"He's not very big, is he?" the woman said, peering at the boy again. "No more than six drops to the cup, I'd think."

"I'm not thirsty! My leg hurts!" Justin wailed.

Adrian took the bottle and the cup of water one of the maids held out. Counting drops of the opiate into the water, he swirled it around. "Come on," he encouraged the boy as he lifted him, "drink it down—'twill ease the leg."

Justin took a small sip and choked. "No—I won't!"

"Please, love," Joanna urged.

He turned his head away from the cup and shook his head. "No."

"You know," Adrian remarked conversationally, "I can remember when your papa was as little as you are, Justin. He fell out of a tree right by this house and broke his arm. I thought he was very brave at the time, too. Even though it tasted horrible, he drank every bit of this very same medicine." He held the cup to the boy's lips. "Yes, every bit of it, as I recall." Tipping the cup, he waited. "It did make him feel better," Adrian prodded. For a moment, the child's pain-dulled eyes looked up at him, then the boy nodded and put his hands on the cup to drink. When he finally pushed it away, the cup was empty.

"Your papa would be proud of you if he could see you now," Adrian said softly.

"He can," Justin said, closing his eyes. "He watches me from heaven, Duke."

"Lady Carew—" Roxbury's housekeeper touched Jo's shoulder. "You'd best be getting dry things on."

"As soon as he goes to sleep," she promised. "'Tis Dree that needs something done for him. I'll be all right—I will."

The doctor arrived before the laudanum took effect and the ensuing examination had everyone in tears. Justin screamed as the leg was manipulated, but there was no help for it. "Aye, 'tis a nasty break," Dr. Goode observed with a shake of his white head, "and I am not certain that 'twill heal completely."

"What do you mean?" Adrian demanded. "He's young—it has to heal."

"Your pardon, Your Grace. 'Twas a poor choice of words on my part." The physician traced the outline of Justin's already swollen and discolored thigh, stopping where the jagged edge of bone still protruded just above the knee. "See this—'tis the longest bone in the body, and it bears most of the weight. I can set it straight, but there's no promise that it will be the same length as the other when 'tis healed." He shook his head again. "I've seen some where the leg is as good as ever and others where there is a pronounced limp." He glanced over to where Joanna stood, white-faced, and sighed. "I wish I could wrap it in clean linen and say he'll be the same as he was, my lady, but I cannot." Turning back to look at Justin, he noted the deepening breathing. "The laudanum's taking effect, I believe, but he's still going to feel it when I snap the bone into place. Lady Carew, I would suggest that you leave us while 'tis done."

"I'll be all right."

"Just the same, you may wish to bathe and change your clothes and eat—'twill make you feel more the thing and I can promise you that you'll be needed more during the night."

"No."

"I'll stay, Jo—you'd best get dry before you take an inflammation or something," Adrian offered quietly.

"In this heat?" she retorted. "No, I mean to stay— he's my son, Dree."

"Lady Carew—" The doctor's expression was pained. "I cannot concern myself with more than one patient just now, and this is not going to be pleasant."

"Let her remain if she wishes," Adrian cut in impatiently. "Jo"—his eyes met Joanna's for a moment— "you never were the queasy sort of female, were you? Very well, then you get on one side and I'll get on the other. Between the two of us, perhaps we can soothe him and hold him still."

For answer, Joanna half knelt at the side of the bed and brushed back her son's thick, dark hair from his forehead. He was clammy despite the heat, and his eyes were closed. At almost the same time, she and Adrian reached for his hands and clasped them while Dr. Goode prepared to set his leg.

Justin's eyes flew open and he stiffened, his hands clutching wildly when the doctor probed along the broken bone. "Mama!" he screamed hysterically.

"'Tis all right, love," she crooned as she and Adrian pinned him back against the bedclothes. "'Twill soon be over."

"You are all right, Justin." Adrian sank to sit on the edge of the bed. "Just hold your mama's hand, and perhaps it will not hurt quite so much."

Dr. Goode, having taken measure of the break, grasped Justin's leg at the knee and jerked it downward. "Mamaaaaaaa!" The child's terrified scream cut through the steamy air, then died abruptly as he fell back limply.

"Mercifully, he's fainted," the doctor observed under his breath. Working deftly now, he cut the skin back from the wound, washed the blood away, and forced the bones together. The smell of wet hair, wet clothes, and blood permeated the room as he probed, fitted, sewed, and splinted. Straightening up at last, he surveyed the leg as it lay straight and closed. "The next several weeks will be the test of how it heals, Your Grace," he told Adrian. "He must not be allowed to move about, and he must put no weight on it." Turning to Joanna, he asked, "How old is the boy?"

"He will be six years old after Christmas."

"Then you will have your hands full, I fear. He'll feel better long before he'll be able to walk on that leg."

"How long will it be before I can take him back to Haven?"

"I'd not chance it for several weeks—perhaps not for a month."

"A month?" she gasped. "But we cannot—that is, I

cannot . . . well, I just cannot. I mean—" Her voice trailed off, but her face betrayed her consternation.

"He can stay here, Jo."

"No! Not without me, and I refuse—"

"He cannot be moved, Jo. You heard Dr. Goode—he cannot be moved," Adrian repeated for emphasis. "But we can speak of what is to be done later when you've bathed and eaten." He looked to where Justin lay quietly now, his black hair rumpled against the white pillows, his face ashen, his breathing slow and deep. "He'll sleep for some time, so I suggest we prepare ourselves for when he does wake. Mrs. Johnson will order up a warm bath, dry clothes, and some food for you so you won't have to leave the room.

She glanced about the bedchamber. "But you—"

"I'll repair to the apartment that was yours. I just don't think we ought to move him from here just yet."

"But—"

"In the meantime, I'm in sore need of a bath also. I'll inform my mother as to what has happened, so you need not concern yourself on that head." He could see that she remained unconvinced, so he added, "My mother will be all that is civil, I promise you."

Dr. Goode, despite a certain curiosity as to the peculiar civility between the duke and his former duchess, managed to cough apologetically to interrupt them. "Ahem. I believe I have done all that is possible for today, Your Grace. As you have said, the boy will sleep for several hours now, and the problem tonight will most likely be restlessness. You may give him eight drops of the laudanum in half a glass of water to keep him still, but I should not recommend doing so more than twice during the night. I cannot, however, emphasize sufficiently the necessity of his not moving the leg much. It was a particularly nasty break, and there is the danger of infection." He cast a furtive glance at Joanna, who had moved to straighten the covers over her son, and lowered his voice perceptibly. "If the leg becomes infected, I should not like to think of the consequences, Your Grace."

"No, of course not," Adrian responded grimly. "I must ask you not to repeat that where she can hear you."

"We are agreed, I believe," Goode said, nodding. "I shall come again in the morning to see how the boy does." Then, without thinking, he added, "There is a speaking likeness between you and the boy, Your Grace."

"Yes—there is."

There was a sudden flatness, a despair almost, in the duke's voice that gave Dr. Goode pause. For the first time since he'd arrived at the Armitage, he turned his attention to Roxbury and was suddenly aware of the cuts and bruises. "Your pardon, Your Grace—in my concern for the boy, I did not realize you were hurt. If you will but sit down and let me—"

"No—a few scratches merely," Adrian murmured, brushing him aside. "And by the looks of it, there's another break in the storm, so you'd best be getting home while you can." Turning his attention to his valet, he announced, "I shall be staying in the rose bedchamber, Blake. Pray have my bath drawn and have my things removed to there. Lady Carew will, of course, remain with her son."

While Mrs. Johnson ushered out the doctor and Blake gathered his basic necessities from the chamber, Adrian moved to where Joanna hovered over the little boy. Involuntarily his hand crept to stroke the wet hair that lay in strings against the back of her soaked waist. "Don't worry, Jo," he comforted her. "We'll see this through."

"Dree—" Her voice sounded hollow in her throat.

"Dree, I heard what he said about the danger of infection. Surely he does not think . . . I mean, he does not think it likely . . ." Unable to voice her fears, she half turned to face him. "Oh, Dree!" she wailed. "I could not bear it—not after all he has been through already!"

"No, he is not going to lose that leg, Jo—we won't let that happen." His arms closed around her even as her shoulders began to shake. "It's all right, Jo—I don't mind it if you cry."

Blake, seeing this unlikely occurrence, hastily picked up an armful of clothes and motioned the bemused maids to follow him. Shutting the door behind them, he indicated the next bedchamber. "You heard His Grace—prepare the rose chamber for his lordship, if you please."

"But, Mr. Blake," Martha protested, "it used to be hers!"

"Her Grace is going to be in a taking over this," the other promised direly. "She'll be readin' a peal the likes o' which we've never heard before."

"Humph!" Blake sniffed. "His Grace is older than he was the last time—I for one shall enjoy seeing her brought up short. And, mark my words, short is just where she's going to be!"

"Mr. Blake, did you note the little earl?"

"Aye, that I did."

"'Tis in His Grace's own likeness, he is," Martha breathed.

"Aye—what do you make of that, Mr. Blake?" Bess asked curiously. "You do not think—"

"'Tis plain as can be," Blake replied. "Her Grace lied."

"But Mary said—"

"Mary! Mary indeed! Silly little strumpet she was! Always casting sheep's eyes at His Grace—right jealous of Lady Jo, wasn't she?" The valet leaned closer and lowered his voice "Did you never wonder how it was that she was able to leave service here and set up a milliner's shop in that village?"

It was several minutes before Joanna mastered her tears and stepped back shakily from Adrian's embrace. "You must think me a veritable watering pot today, Dree," she said shakily, wiping her wet cheeks with the back of her hand.

"I'd think you an unnatural mother if you weren't," he responded gently. "God knows you've had enough today to overset ten females, haven't you?" He caught her elbow and steered her toward a chair placed by an open window. "What you need, my dear, is a bath and some rest." He nodded significantly to the four-poster bed where Justin lay. "If we are to keep him quiet, we'll have to rest when he does." He straightened his shoulders, his own fatigue evident, and managed a rueful smile. "I've never been much good at entertaining anyone but myself, you know, but I mean to try now." Moving toward the door, he stopped momentarily. "I know you've no wish to spend even a minute in this house, but it cannot be helped, believe me. I'll do what I can to ease things for you with Johnny," he said, reaching for the door.

"Dree?"

Hesitating, he turned around. "Yes?"

"He will be all right, won't he?"

Not trusting himself to speak, he nodded. His fingers closed around the doorknob.

"Dree?"

"What?"

"Thank you again. You saved his life."

"I told you—I owed you that much at least."

"Is that why you went down that well?"

"I did it for you—and for him. I couldn't have lived

with myself if I hadn't tried to get him out of there." He stared across at her for a long moment, his dark eyes bleak. She was wet and bedraggled, looking like some street urchin caught in a storm. Her hair hung in tangled disarray, and her clothing was torn and mudstained, but she was still the most beautiful woman in the world to him. "I'll send Bess back to help you with your bath," he said, his voice strained. Opening the door with a jerk, he escaped into the hall.

After dispatching Sims to Haven to apprise the dowager countess as to what had happened and to obtain clothing for Joanna and Justin, Adrian sat on a damask-covered bench and pulled off his ruined boots. His hands were sore and scraped from having rubbed against the rough, uneven rocks in the well, and every muscle in his arms, back, and legs ached. The physical and emotional resources that had served him earlier had deserted him, and now he felt unbearably drained. As though he had not the strength left to heave his aching body into his bath.

Blake hovered nearby, testing the water temperature in the copper tub and adding scent. "You ought to let me do that, Your Grace," he remarked peevishly as the second boot thudded on the floor.

"They were dirty," Adrian offered reasonably. "Why should we both look as though we rolled in the mud?" Looking down at his raw hands, he shook his head. "Truth to tell, I look as though I've been in a mill."

"Well, whichever it is, 'tis unseemly," the valet sniffed.

"Blake, if you think me some sort of man-milliner unable to undress myself, you are wide of the mark. The day I require undressing is the day I enter my dotage."

A quick, determined rap sounded at the door,

prompting Adrian to stop mid-button on his shirt.
"The devil!" he muttered succinctly. "Get that, will
you, Blake? And unless it concerns Lady Carew or her
son, I've no wish to be disturbed."

The valet barely had time to reach the door before
Helen Delacourt brushed past him into the room.
"Leave us," she ordered imperiously. "I should like to
have words with my son."

Casting a quick look at the duke, Blake hesitated.
Adrian shrugged tiredly and nodded. "When I need
you, I'll ring the bellpull."

Without waiting for the door to shut behind the retreating valet, the dowager duchess rounded on her
son. "Adrian, how could you?" she demanded furiously. "I vow I cannot credit you are such a fool! Whatever is Lord Bennington to think? And what of
Almeria? You surely cannot pretend that—that woman
is fit company for a gently bred female! I won't have it,
I tell you!"

"Mother . . ." Adrian's voice was low in warning, his
dark eyes dangerous, but the duchess was too angry to
notice.

"Either you send Joanna and her brat packing, or I
shall be forced to remove myself from this house."

"I would that you did."

"Adrian!"

"Surprised, Mother?" Despite the awful fatigue he
felt, he rose to face her. "I am not three and twenty this
time, you know."

"Adrian, listen to me!"

"No." He shook his head decisively. "The last time I
listened to you, I lost my wife and the best friend a man
ever had. I think you've done quite enough already."

"She's a common trollop!"

"Is she?" he demanded almost brutally. "Or did you

twist the truth into lies? I wonder, you know—I cannot help that."

"I had proof! Proof enough to stand before a court of law!"

"It doesn't matter anymore."

"Doesn't matter! Adrian, what ails you? Have you taken leave of your senses where she is concerned?"

"I said it doesn't matter," he repeated.

"Surely you cannot forgive what she did!"

"Forgive?" The black eyebrow lifted. "Do you not think we both paid a bitter price? I drove her into his arms, Mother! And then I drove them both out of the country!" he shouted at her. "She bore my son in exile! *Forgive?* No, Mother, it is she who cannot forgive me, and I cannot blame her for that. But I can make amends for the boy—and so help me God, I will."

"You do not even know he's yours! All you have is her word for it, and I scarce think—" The murderous look in his eyes gave her pause. "Well, that changes nothing, does it? He certainly could have been Gareth Sherwood's."

"Perhaps after you've finished packing your trunks, you should look at him, Mother. Then I defy you to tell anyone he isn't mine." Deliberately turning his back on her, he finished unbuttoning his shirt and drew it off. Discarding it on a chair beside the bathtub, he bent his attention to removing his stockings. "Now, if you will pardon me, I mean to bathe before this mud turns to concrete. And then I mean to tell Joanna she has nothing to fear from you anymore. Not that it will help me in that quarter, for there is Johnny," he admitted. "But at least I've hopes she will let me know the boy, even if the role I must play is an avuncular one."

Alarmed, Helen came up behind him and clutched at his arm. "You cannot mean it—Adrian, I am your mother! And what about the Benningtons? You are engaged to take Almeria to Wells in the morning."

"I don't give a damn about any of them."

"Adrian, be reasonable! Surely—"

He looked down to where her fingers curled into the flesh of his bare arm. Carefully reaching with his free hand to disengage hers, he stepped aside. "I suspect that when you are gone, the Benningtons will find it incumbent to leave also. As you have pointed out, Almeria cannot wish to be exposed to Joanna's company," he answered evenly. I, for one, don't mind it in the least."

"But the plans . . . Wells . . . Adrian, you cannot do this to me!"

"*Your* plans, I believe, but if you think she will be that disappointed, perhaps you can arrange to accompany her there on your way. Quite frankly, it is of no moment to me, one way or the other."

"You cannot turn your own mother out—think what the *ton* will say," she tried desperately. "You cannot think to survive the gossip."

"I expect the *ton* to express a certain curiosity," he admitted, "but being a duke, as you so often have pointed out, has its advantages. I daresay that my title and my fortune will still gain me entree anywhere I wish to go. If not, I won't repine, I assure you." He sat again on the bench and finished removing his stockings.

"Adrian, you *need* me," she cajoled. "If Joanna is to remain here even tonight, you will have to have me in residence."

"Why?" he demanded bluntly. "We have seen to it that she has no reputation, haven't we?"

"Adrian, I am your mother—I care about you."

"Do you now?" The black eyebrow lifted again in mock surprise. "No, Mother, I think not. If you cared about anything, you would have expressed some small measure of concern for your only grandson. He nearly

died today, and it is no certain thing that he will survive whole yet. He cannot even be moved for some
time, you know."

"Well, I daresay there can be no harm in the boy," she
allowed. "Indeed, I can arrange for someone to care for
him."

"No. He has his mother for that."

"But she cannot stay here! Adrian, think of the scandal!"

"We'll muddle through." He stood and unbuttoned
his torn and tattered pantaloons. "Now, unless you
wish to view me buck naked, I suggest you leave me to
the peace of my bath." His eyes were cold as they met
hers. "And I forbid you to even speak to Jo, for I know
you cannot be civil where she is concerned. If I hear
you've said anything to her, I'll turn you out tonight—
now, have I made myself plain on that head?"

"It is all of a piece, isn't it?" she said nastily. "Joanna—
'twas always Joanna! Well, I can promise you this,
Adrian Delacourt: I will not go tamely off to my fate. The
world will know she stays here like the common trollop
she is!"

For answer, he disappeared behind the bathing
screen, finished removing his clothes, and eased into
the fragrant water. "You will do no such thing, I think,"
he pointed out reasonably. "Indeed, were I you, I
should do as much as possible to keep the scandal
down. Otherwise, you might be suspected of promot-
ing the story, and in that instant, you would find me
unwilling to continue your allowance."

"You would not *dare*."

He lathered a cloth and began washing his face.
"Well, I should be loath to do so, of course," he admitted, "but you would have left me no choice. And you
would not be precisely destitute, for there is still that
small portion from your own mother to support you,

though not quite in the grand style you favor. You do have a dower property in Northumbria."

"Northumbria! Adrian, I will not!"

"Alas, all the other houses are mine."

"I cannot stop the gossip—you know I cannot," she said desperately.

"The house in Kent and a modest allowance—or Northumbria. Think carefully before you decide."

"I bore you, Adrian!"

"If you had any feeling for me at all, you would have accepted Joanna."

"She was a nobody! She was but a Milford!"

"No, she was Joanna Milford Delacourt, Duchess of Roxbury. But to return to the matter at hand, I shall depend on you to refrain from any unflattering gossip about her. Otherwise, you'll find yourself in Northumbria, and I'm not given to idle threats. You have my word on that."

"But there will be talk—there is certain to be!" she protested in alarm. "Adrian, think! She is betrothed to Lord Barrasford—she cannot stay here scandal-free. Be reasonable—you know not what you ask."

"Ah, but if I ever hear that a word of censure comes from you . . ." He let his voice trail off, certain that she understood his meaning.

Helen knew when she was defeated. She'd never quite understood the intensity of his feelings for little Joanna Milford, and she never would. A woman to whom aristocratic status was everything, she could not fathom the attraction of an impecunious baron's daughter. She stood there uncertainly, listening as her only son rinsed the soap from his face and upper body. Unable to completely restrain her pique, she declared spitefully, "I do not know what you expect to accomplish by having her here. She is, after all, Barrasford's betrothed!"

"She's the mother of my son."

He could hear the angry swish of her skirt against her petticoat as she crossed the room, then the door slammed behind her, leaving him alone with his thoughts. He'd not meant to handle it quite that way, but then, neither would he send Joanna back to Haven. Somehow he'd known it would come down to this, that there simply was not room for both women at the Armitage. He should have come to that conclusion seven years ago, he reflected regretfully.

Easing his sore body deeper into the warmth of the water to soak his bruises, he thought of his son. His son. A fierce pride washed over him with the memory of how the child had clung to him. When he'd descended into that well, he'd been prepared to die for young Justin Sherwood. But it hadn't happened that way—knowing nothing of the bitterness that had passed between Adrian and Joanna, the boy had clung to him with such innocent trust. Even now, as he thought of his son, Adrian was overwhelmed by the tenderness he felt.

His thoughts turned to Joanna. How many females of his acquaintance would have swooned at the sight of that bone coming out of the leg? But not Jo—she'd been too intent on comforting her son. Their son, he reminded himself again. By the right of it, he should have been there all those days she carried the child, those hours when she brought him into the world, and all those years since. But instead it had been Gary who'd stayed through it all, Gary who'd comforted Joanna, and Gary who'd shared the boy's life those first years.

Gareth Sherwood. The best friend a man could have, he'd told his mother. Now the awful suspicion that she'd lied to him lay like a heavy burden, weighing on his conscience, torturing his soul. But there'd been evidence—and Joanna'd never refuted any of it.

"Does Your Grace need anything?"

He'd been so absorbed in his doubts that he'd not heard the valet come in. Resolutely he squared his shoulders and returned to the present. He picked up the soap and began washing where the skin had been nearly scraped off his hands. "I'm going to need some salve, Blake."

"I have already brought it, my lord." Blake's thin face was creased with concern. "Nasty-looking cuts and bruises there—perhaps the doctor should have looked at them."

"No—they'll heal fine. Any word from next door?"

"Lady Carew? No, but Mrs. Johnson had a bath drawn for her. Dreadful thing to happen to that little boy, sir—dreadful—but I daresay he'll come about. And poor Lady Carew, after all she has endured—well, it doesn't bear thinking, does it?"

"She nearly lost her son."

"Just so. My lord, I wish you would at least let me rinse the hair for you—I can get it ever so much better. Here—" Blake picked up the pitcher of clear water and began washing the soap out of the thick black hair. "'Tis a blessing that powder has gone out of fashion, don't you think, sir? We'd never have covered this with a pound of powder."

"I've never thought much about it."

"Well, I have. Being a gentleman's gentleman, one thinks of such things, you know. There. Would your lordship be wishful of the dressing gown or would you dress for dinner?"

"Dinner?" He'd forgotten about eating. "What time is it, Blake?"

"Barely seven, Your Grace, and Cook is not at all upset at the delay—said we kept country hours far too much, anyway, and this time we would dine civilized. I believe eight-thirty was what she told Mrs. Johnson."

Adrian grimaced as he pulled himself up from the tub. "Well, since we took our other meals at country hours, I suspect Bennington will be most unhappy to hear we have changed times on him."

"Mrs. Johnson has already informed him, Your Grace."

"And—?" A hint of a smile formed at the corners of Adrian's mouth.

"Well, I cannot say that he was pleased, my lord," the valet admitted as he handed over a towel. "Indeed, I understand he complained that he would not stay where he was not fed."

"A pity we did not think of it sooner then."

"Er—" Blake hesitated to change the subject, but he'd been asked to inquire. "Lady Carew, Your Grace— will she be going down to dinner?"

"No."

The valet carefully laid his master's clothes over the bathside stand while Adrian dried himself. "Perhaps someone should tell Cook to prepare a tray—I think Mrs. Johnson was of the opinion that Lady Carew would join the company."

"I hardly think tonight would be the night," Adrian observed dryly. "Have Bess bring her dinner up to her room."

Still vigorously toweling himself, he glanced over at the connecting door, and the reality of where he was flooded over him. This had been her chamber when she was his duchess, and it was still much as she'd left it. In his fatigue, he'd not spared a thought to that, but he was thinking about it now. His eyes traveled around the room, taking in details, reliving memories. She'd liked to dry her hair before the fire. In his mind's eye, he could see her there still, her head bent, that tawny mane hanging forward close to the heat. Her bare arms were gilded with gold from the flames, and her breasts

strained against the bodice of her shift as she brushed
that glorious hair with long, determined strokes. He
could almost hear it crackle as the brush lifted it.

Tearing himself away from that memory, he looked
across the room, seeing her four-poster bed with its
brocaded canopy. How many nights had he spent there
with her? Nearly as many as she'd spent in his. It had
been a jest between them that the carpet in the doorway would wear out before they'd been married a year.
They'd been the best nights of his life, too, for of the
half dozen or so mistresses he'd had since, not one of
them had even come close to giving him what he'd had
with Joanna.

"Is aught amiss, Your Grace?"

"No—why?"

"You look quite stricken, sir."

"I'm just tired," Adrian lied. "Why don't you go on
down and inform Mrs. Johnson to send up a tray?" he
suggested casually. "I am capable of dressing myself,
after all, and you have become used to taking your own
meals at country hours. You might as well go on and
eat with the rest of the household staff."

"Oh, I did not mean—"

"Go on. The house is at sixes and sevens, anyway, so
I doubt anyone will note it if my cravat is less than perfection."

"You are quite certain, Your Grace? I would not have
it said that I—"

"No—go on."

As soon as the door closed behind Blake, Adrian
dressed hastily, leaving his snowy shirt open. Impulsively he walked to the connecting door and tried the
knob. The latch gave way beneath his hand, swinging
the door open and admitting him to his bedchamber.
His gaze traveled to where Justin lay sleeping still, his
small form propped on Adrian's pillows, his splinted

leg elevated on a rolled blanket. At first, Adrian thought Joanna sat in the chair near the bed, but then, as he drew nearer, soundless in his stocking feet, he could see that the skirt of her riding habit was merely lying in the seat. His pulse raced.

"Jo?"

There was a stirring of water from behind the Oriental screen as she grabbed for a towel. "Don't come back here, Dree," she warned.

She was too late. When she looked up, he was already standing there, his face betraying the hunger he felt. A shiver of excitement coursed down her spine, and she felt her own mouth go dry. Heedless of the fact that she was getting it wet, she clutched the towel against her breasts. Her face flushed beneath his gaze.

"Get out of here," she managed evenly.

"I came to see how the boy does."

"He's asleep—as surely you must have seen when you came skulking in here."

"I wasn't skulking. I was looking for my onyx studs." To demonstrate, he held open his shirt. "Apparently, Blake forgot them."

"Skulking," she repeated. "I may be grateful for what you did for Justin, but I have scarce given you leave to stand there staring at me."

"I've seen you before." A smile flirted with the corners of his mouth and lit his dark eyes. "In fact, lest you've forgotten it, I've seen considerably more of you than this."

"I remember a lot of things, Dree. Now—are you leaving or not?"

"No."

"I see." Her lips drew into a thin line of disapproval to hide her own pounding heart. She could not bring herself to meet those eyes, and instead she focused on the curling hairs exposed by his unbuttoned shirt. Exhaling slowly for control of the thoughts that sprang to mind, she tried to keep her voice calm. "There are no shirt studs here, Dree."

"Jo—" He took a step closer.

"Stay where you are," she ordered, alarmed. "If you think you can just walk in and touch me, you are mistaken."

"I've sent my mother away."

"That scarce concerns me now, my lord."

"She forced me to choose between the two of you."

"How very affecting, I am sure," she observed sarcastically. "A pity you could not have made the choice while we were wed." Fueled by the memory of Helen Delacourt's awful accusations, her anger allowed her to look up at him. "You are too late now."

"Am I?" he asked softly as he walked behind her. She clutched the towel more tightly and ducked forward when he reached into the water to pick up the cloth she'd been using. "Do you remember when I used to wash you, Jo? Have you forgotten how I used to soap your hair for you?" Picking up the cake of soap, he lathered the cloth before leaning over to wash her back. His touch was light, almost impersonal, but his voice was intimate as he leaned farther to whisper, "Remember this, Jo?"

"No," she lied. She had to close her eyes for a moment to master her reeling senses. Grasping the sides of the tub, she rose abruptly, sending a spray of water that splashed his shirt and pants. Opening her eyes deliberately now, she gibed, "Is this what you wished to see?" She dropped the wet towel into the water and stood straight. "Look long, Dree—this is the body you believed I shared with Gary while you and I were wed. If you want to relive your memories, I would that you remembered that."

Her breasts were fuller, but her waist was still narrow, and her stomach flat. He sucked in his breath harshly at the sight of her wet, glistening body. His mouth suddenly felt too dry for speech. Watching him warily, she stepped out of the tub on the other side and reached for another towel. Leaning her head sideways, she blotted her blond hair before she wrapped herself. He could not force himself to look away.

She brushed past him so close that he could smell her fragrant, freshly washed hair. He reached to twine his fingers in the wet strands, stopping her. She jerked angrily, pulling away with such force that the pain brought tears to her eyes. "Don't do that!" she cried.

For answer, his hand slid down to trace where the damp towel lay against the smooth skin of her back. A shiver followed his fingers. She closed her eyes and swallowed hard. "Please, Dree. I'm not yours anymore."

"Shhhhh." Slowly, deliberately, he turned her around. She stood still as a statue, every muscle frozen to deny the need she felt. Only the faint beat of the pulse in her neck betrayed her inner turmoil. He circled her shoulder with his arm and drew her closer, savoring the fresh, sweet smell of her. As his mouth met hers in hunger, she made a feeble attempt to turn her head, to deny the rush of emotion she felt. The kiss deepened and his hands explored her back, molding, holding her against him, eliciting a desire to match his own. Her arms slid around him, clasping him for support. The towel came loose, held now only by the closeness of their locked bodies.

"You know you want this as much as I, Jo," he whispered hotly against her bruised lips.

It was as though the years, the anger, the bitterness, were consumed by the intense heat between them, and they were in the throes of that same white-hot passion. Forgetting everything but the man who held her,

Joanna dug her nails into his back and pressed her body into his as her legs went weak with answering desire.

"Mama!"

Justin's fretful cry cut into her consciousness, bringing her back to the reality of where she was and with whom. She stiffened and began to struggle frantically. "Let me go—Justin—"

"Mama! Mama!"

She broke away and the towel fell between them. Adrian dropped his hands. "Damn!" he muttered in disappointment.

"Mama, where are you?" the child demanded querulously. "Mama, my leg hurts! And I'm so thirsty!"

"I—I'm coming, dearest!" She cast about frantically for her dressing gown.

"Here." Mastering himself, Adrian handed her the robe. "You get dressed while I try to soothe him." Still breathing in rapid, shallow gulps, he forced himself to count slow, deep breaths as he crossed to the bed where the boy lay.

"Mama?" Justin's eyes fluttered in confusion while he thrashed restlessly, hampered by the bedsheet and the splint. Adrian caught his hand and held it. For a moment the small body was still. "Papa—?" The eyes strained to focus in the dimness of evening and then recognition set in. "Duke," he said simply.

"Not feeling quite the thing, are you?" Adrian murmured sympathetically. "Here—let me lift you higher on the pillows so you can drink."

"Mama?"

"Your mama just took a bath, Justin, but she'll be here as soon as she gets dressed." Lifting the boy, he reached for the water glass. "Take a sip of this." He held the drink to prevent a spill. "That's good—capital," he said, encouraging the child to take more.

Still clutching Adrian's free hand, Justin sank back among the pillows. "Duke," he pronounced solemnly, "I was scared."

"I know. So was I."

Joanna came up then, her body safely covered in the borrowed wrapper. She'd pulled a comb through her hair and it lay smooth and wet against her head and down over her shoulders. "Is he feverish?" she asked anxiously.

Adrian brushed back the boy's dark hair and laid his free hand across his brow. "No—not yet, anyway."

"Mama, my leg hurts like the very devil!" Justin opened an eye to see the effect of this pronouncement.

"Don't say 'devil,' dearest. And I know it hurts, but that cannot be helped just yet. Your leg is broken, and it will take some time to mend." She sank down on the other side of the bed and caressed the thick hair. "What we can do, however, is to give you some more laudanum so it will not hurt quite so much."

"Ugh!"

"Just so," Adrian agreed, "but it *will* help, I promise you." Turning loose of the child's hand, he reached for the laudanum. bottle. "Hand me the pitcher, Jo, and we'll mix some of this up."

Between them, they managed to get the full dose of medicine down the boy, and then in the ensuing time between dosage and relief, they bent their full attention to distracting him from his pain. Joanna sang softly until her voice, already strained from the day's shouting, gave out. The child fitfully demanded more, until Adrian, with the rueful comment that they'd have to put up with some of the milder ditties from his Oxford days, launched into a recital of tunes thankfully unknown to her. By the fifth song, the boy's head turned into the pillow, and his eyes blinked as he fought sleep. For good measure, Adrian managed a few more bars of an old drinking round, then certain Justin slept, he reached across the bed to stroke the back of Joanna's hand.

"We could repair to the rose chamber," he ventured softly.

She jerked her hand away. "No, I don't think so," she managed stiffly. She slid off the bed and moved to stare out into the twilight.

"Your lips cannot deny what your body felt," he murmured behind her.

"If you touch me again, I shall scream." Spinning around to face him, she told him, "Don't do this to me, Dree—please. Let us be civil for Justin's sake, but do not try to deceive me again."

"Jo—" His hand grasped her shoulder.

"Don't touch me!" She broke away and stepped back. "Just because I am under your roof now does not mean that you can use me like some Cyprian, Dree. You forget I am betrothed to Lord Barrasford."

"Cry off and come back to me."

"I suppose I should have expected that of you, shouldn't I?" she observed bitterly. "Well, I won't do it—I couldn't. John Barrasford is a decent, kind man, Dree, and I have given my word. And whether you choose to believe it or not, I *keep* my promises."

"Did you keep them to me?"

"I swore I'd never answer that—it does not signify now, anyway, does it? I am afraid you'll have to look to yourself for the answer. Gary tried to tell you once, but you would not listen." She gestured to the door between the two chambers. "It grows late, Your Grace, and you've not finished dressing for your dinner, so I suggest you do so now. But before you go down, I must ask you to give me the key."

"Jo—"

"This may be your bedchamber, my lord, but the

next time you wish to invade it, I shall expect you to knock. And pray do not come in until you are invited, for I've no wish to repeat this scene again."

She waited until he'd retreated, then she carefully closed the door. But it wasn't until she'd sunk into a chair that she realized how close her body had come to betraying her.

Dinner was a strained affair from beginning to end. Upon Adrian's tardy arrival, the already hushed conversation abruptly ceased as everyone stared with some degree of chagrin at him. A quick glance around the table told the tale—the dowager duchess's face barely concealed her outrage beneath a facade of chill civility, Lord Bennington's chins quivered with the perceived effrontery, Lady Bennington's mouth froze in a determined smile, and even Almeria's carefully schooled countenance could not help betraying her bitter disappointment. As he took his seat at the head of the long table, only Lady Bennington made a feeble attempt at a cheery greeting, and the look he gave her quickly quelled any further attempt to lighten the collective mood. She mumbled something inane, then retreated into a resigned silence.

It was not until they were halfway through the third course that Lord Bennington could bring himself to inquire if "that woman" was indeed taking up residence at the Armitage. Adrian stiffened at the censorious tone of the question.

"'That woman,' as you choose to refer to Lady Carew, was once my duchess," Adrian reminded him coldly. "And, yes, I expect her to stay here as long as the boy's recovery requires." Taking another spoon of peas onto his plate, he glanced up to where a footman stood woodenly waiting to serve the next course. "You may inform Cook that her fears were misplaced—these are excellent," he said, pointedly changing the subject.

"Your Grace, I must protest this—this outrageous circumstance you would—"

"George!" Lady Bennington caught her husband's elbow to gain his attention and hissed in an under-voice, "Not now." With a furtive nod to where her daughter sat stiffly pushing her food around her plate, she added significantly, "Lady Carew is scarce a fit sub-ject for dear Almeria's ears."

"As if I did not know such women existed," the young woman retorted disdainfully. Nonetheless, she kept her eyes averted.

A knot formed in Adrian's stomach, and his food turned tasteless in his mouth. He wanted to lash out, to tell them that they were wrong about Joanna, that she didn't deserve the awful reputation he'd given her, but his defense of her now would only fuel more gossip once they returned to London. Instead, he looked down the table to Almeria, his dark eyes cold. "Joanna Sherwood is as much a gently bred lady as you are," he told her evenly. "And there is a warmth in her that few of your class can even aspire to equal."

Two spots of color brightened the girl's pale cheeks. His coldness, coupled with Lady Helen's earlier terse comment that the Wells expedition had been elimi-nated, goaded her. "If you have invited me here to in-sult me, Your Grace, you have succeeded. I do not belong in the same house or even in the same conver-sation with a divorced female," she declared stiffly.

"Puss, you were to let me do the talking," Benning-ton reminded her.

"No, Papa. I'd be heard, if you do not mind it." Turn-ing again to Adrian, she said, "It is outside of enough that you have asked me here under decidedly false pretenses, then flaunted your preference for her. For some utterly unfathomable reason you have chosen to make me the laughingstock of the *ton*, my lord, and I have done nothing to deserve such treatment." Rising regally from the table, she stared at him, her lovely face twisted into a bitter smile. "Nothing could induce me to remain in this house so long as Lady Carew continues to be welcomed here." Looking to her father, she added, "Pray excuse me, Papa, but I find I have the headache."

There was a heavy silence after she left the room. Wholly dissatisfied with this turn of events, Lord Bennington finally tried to recoup the situation he'd caused. "You must forgive her, Your Grace—female freak of distemper, that's all—be over it in the morning. And I daresay once Lady Carew is gone—well, what's to say you won't be making a little visit to Upton Grove later this summer, eh? I expect Almeria will be glad to receive you there."

"You'd put up with anything for my title, wouldn't you?" Adrian observed with disgust.

"Here now, sirrah—no way to talk to a gentleman, is it?" Bennington protested.

"Perhaps I ought to go to her," Lady Bennington ventured doubtfully.

Adrian threw his napkin down on the table and rose. "No, I believe the fault was mine, and I think it is time for some plain speaking. I'll go."

He found her pacing angrily in the garden behind the house. "Miss Bennington—" He came up behind her and waited.

"What do you want?" There was a hint of hope in her voice.

"I came to apologize for my lamentable manners. Even though I disagree with your opinion of Lady Carew, I was a poor host to speak so." When she made no acknowledgment of his apology, he plunged ahead. "I believe you came here under a misapprehension of my true feelings. My mother invited you—I did not. I admire you—you are a very lovely young woman—but it was never my intention to make you an offer. I should never have allowed you to come here, for I've not the least interest in marrying again."

"Not even your precious Joanna?" she inquired spitefully.

"Lady Carew is betrothed to Lord Barrasford," he answered flatly. "And she has made it quite plain that she would not have me again, anyway."

"I see. That leaves me quite out, does it not?"

"Joanna is Duchess of Roxbury in my heart, and there is room for no other." His voice was gentle as he reached for her hand. "Come, walk apace with me and I'll try to explain." Tucking her hand in the crook of his elbow, he led her among a fragrant display of roses. "I cannot expect you to understand, but I fell in love with her when we were yet children, and there's been no other for me." Noting her incredulous expression, he nodded. "Oh, there have been the usual opera dancers and that sort of thing since the divorce, but none to take her place."

"But she betrayed you. She—"

"I thought so once, but now I am not nearly so certain. Of all that could be said of Joanna when she was a girl, she was as honest as they came. Gary too. No, I am not sure she did." He stopped walking abruptly. "But that is a story I've no wish to tell."

Tears sparkled for effect on her lashes as she contemplated quite the handsomest man of her acquaintance. Somehow it was beyond bearing that he could be saying he did not want her. "But if you cannot wed Lady Carew—"

"You have not listened to anything I've said, have you?" he asked, exasperated.

"But you must have an heir. Surely—"

"Miss Bennington, I'm telling you that I will go all the days of my life wanting her back, and knowing that I cannot in conscience offer my name to anyone else. I'm not the sort of man who can wed just to get myself an heir, and I'm not the sort of man to be satisfied with some bloodless marriage of convenience."

She dropped her hand and turned to face him, her chagrin evident. "And you followed me out here to tell me this, Your Grace?" she demanded furiously. "And you think telling me you prefer her to me is going to make me feel more the thing? Well, it does not! I came here to be a duchess, my lord—not to be preached at!"

"I am afraid you'll have to find yourself another duke."

"As if they were everywhere!" she snapped. "I would have married you, Your Grace, and turned a blind eye to your opera dancers and your Cyprians and—and to Lady Carew even!"

"Is that the life you would wish on yourself?" he asked incredulously. "A title means that much to you?"

"Hardly any title, for you are a duke. And if it meant I should be a duchess, yes, I would. Does that surprise you, my lord?"

"It disgusts me." He turned to go back to the house. "But with that notion, I've no doubt that you'll easily find a husband when you get back to London. Good night, my dear."

Lord Bennington, still daring to hope, looked up from his dessert as Adrian reentered the room. "Nothing like a misunderstanding between lovers to liven a courtship, eh, my lord?"

"I wouldn't know," Adrian muttered as he sat down to eat.

The meal ended without any further contretemps and the men withdrew to Adrian's library for the customary after-dinner port. The dowager duchess, faced with the prospect of answering still more questions about her departure, pleaded a headache also, leaving poor Lady Bennington with nothing to do but retire for the night.

"Well, now that we are out from under the cat's-paws, so to speak," Lord Bennington began, "perhaps we ought to discuss how best to retrieve the situation. I daresay that with the boy being hurt and all, you could not quite turn your back on Lady Carew, but there'll be a devil of a scandal if the story gets out. But if you was to marry Almeria, it'd spike the gossips' guns and—" He stopped, momentarily quelled by the look Adrian gave him. But he was also a gambler, so he persisted, this time more carefully. "That is to say, if your *wife* were present, it could be said that her kind disposition made it impossible for her to turn the child away, and therefore she felt it necessary to tolerate Lady Carew's presence."

"By God, you never give up, do you?"

"That is—well, sir, you was wishful of making her an offer anyway, wasn't you? And under the circumstances, a Special License—"

"No," Adrian cut in curtly.

"But—" Nonplussed, his lordship cast about for the means to recover. "I mean—well, she's a very agreeable girl, my lord—be a credit to you."

"I am sorry that you consider yourself deceived, Bennington, but I have made it plain to your daughter that we should not suit. I believe she understands perfectly."

"But Her Grace—"

"Her Grace does not have the ordering of my life, no matter what she may have led you to believe. I expect she has already informed you of her intentions to depart in the morning."

"Yes, but I counted it all a hum. That is to say, you cannot be serious—not with Lady Carew here—I mean, it just is not done, sir! Besides, what is Barrasford to think?"

"He's an honorable man, and I expect that he will accept the innocence of the situation."

Even Bennington knew when to accept defeat. He drained the rest of his port and fixed Adrian with a look that bordered on pure dislike. "I see—that's the lay of the land, is it?" he asked heavily. "Well then, sir, if you are determined on this course, and if Her Grace will not be in residence, I see no alternative to removing my wife and daughter from this house. You may be able to benefit from the association with Lady Carew, but they cannot. I regret it, of course, but we shall be leaving in the morning."

"My mother stands ready to accompany you as far as Wells so that Miss Bennington may view the place."

"I regret we shall not be going that way. Without you, sir, Almeria has not the least interest there," Bennington admitted sourly. "Good night, Your Grace."

After Almeria's father left him, Adrian poured himself another glass and stood contemplating the empty place over the mantel. Joanna's picture, too valuable to be destroyed, lay wrapped somewhere in the cellar. And since he had no intention of seeking another wife, he just might have it brought back up and rehung as a fitting companion piece to his own portrait opposite. They were a pair, after all, in more ways than one.

His thoughts turned to those few moments in his bedchamber. God, how he'd wanted her—and he still wanted her. She was beginning to crowd rational thought from his mind to the point where he could not bear it. He'd told himself when he'd first seen Justin that it was the boy he wanted, but now he had come to admit to himself that he wanted far more than that. Without Joanna, having his son would be a meaningless victory.

Oddly enough, he no longer even cared if his mother had told the truth—it had been more than six years ago, and all of them—he, Jo, and Gary—had been very young.

Well, he was older now, had experienced his salad days and known his share of females. And it was still Joanna he wanted.

What had she said about her betrothal to Barrasford? Something like whether he believed her or not, she kept her word. He sipped pensively and pondered her meaning—was it that she'd kept her word to him also? Or was he searching for more than she'd said? He stared hard at the empty wall, trying to envision her portrait again. She'd worn a blue dress with a dark red sash tied high beneath her breasts and dainty red kid slippers peeping beneath the hem. Slowly the picture took form in his mind as he remembered more details. A large straw hat had dangled from her fingers by its red ribbon. Her hair had streamed unfashionably about her shoulders in glorious disarray. And around that slender, perfect white neck of hers there'd been a jeweled locket, a trinket she'd worn for years. She'd chosen it instead of any of the expensive jewels he'd given her, explaining, "The heart symbolizes my love for you."

He stopped short in his mental review. That had been the locket she'd ultimately given to Gareth Sherwood. What could he have done—what could have happened to have changed her so much in the space of one short year? Had it been his desire for a political career? He'd been gone from home too much, he knew, but she'd greeted him passionately upon each return.

He hadn't wanted to believe she'd betrayed him, yet

even her own maid had corroborated his mother's story. What was that girl's name again? Mary. Mary Cummings. The saucy young girl who'd always had some transparent excuse or other for waylaying him on the stairs. As he recalled, Joanna'd not been at all amused by her maid's silliness.

Reluctantly he allowed his thoughts to wander to his mother's charges against Jo. Once his wounded pride had been satisfied, once he'd punished Joanna for her perfidy in court, he'd wanted to forget the whole mess. But when it was all over, when the two people he'd loved most had fled, he'd found himself left with a small corner of lingering doubt that could only be dispelled by the fact that Joanna herself had never denied the truth of his mother's accusations. Now, a part of him wanted to seek out Mary Cummings and have her repeat her story, while another part warned him to let it lie. He both wanted to know and didn't. If the charges were true, Joanna and Gary had wronged him; if they were false, he'd wronged them terribly.

A glance at the mantel clock told him that it was nearly midnight. The boy'd be getting restless again soon, he decided, and Joanna could not be anything but exhausted. His own earlier fatigue had passed, replaced with a mind that could not rest. He'd see how the boy fared before he retired, he decided.

They were both fast asleep when he let himself in the door of his bedchamber. It did not look as though Justin had moved since before dinner, and Jo sat curled in a wing chair, her head leaned at an awkward angle against one of the sides. When he tried to shake her awake, she merely shifted slightly and continued sleeping, her breathing so light that it was almost imperceptible, her lips parted just enough to expose the edges of perfect teeth.

"Jo." He tried shaking her again, only to have her

slump farther down in the chair. "Poor Jo," he murmured sympathetically. With a sigh, he lifted her to stand. "Come on, Jo—you'll sleep better lying down. Come on—'tis but a few feet to the couch—that's the girl," he encouraged her as she half walked and half sagged against him. With one arm encircling her waist, he reached to clear off the fainting couch, and then he lowered her gently onto it. Picking up her feet, he straightened them on the cushions. Despite the warmth of the night, he picked up a folded shawl from a nearby chest and spread it over her. He'd never known her to sleep uncovered.

Walking back to the bed, he removed his shoes and lay down next to his son. If Justin wakened, Adrian would be there, allowing Joanna to sleep. He reached to touch the slightly moist brow. There was no sign of a fever—at least not yet, and that gave him hope. Turning onto his side, he wrapped his arms about the small body, and for a time, he lay there, holding his son, wishing he'd known him from the beginning, overwhelmed by the tenderness he felt for him.

The light streaming through the casements awakened her slowly, and then as she became increasingly aware of her surroundings, Joanna sat up with a start. Pushing back her tangled hair, she tried to make order of her thoughts. Her feet touched the thick wool Aubusson rug, and for the briefest moment she wondered where she was. Then the memory of the accident brought her fully awake.

"Justin?"

There was no sound in the room except for a steady, even chorus of breathing. Brushing aside the shawl that covered her, she rose and padded silently to the bed to stare in surprise. There lay her son, his body twisted away from his splinted leg, his small shoulders wrapped securely in Adrian's arms, his head cradled against Adrian's shoulder. The two dark heads lying in such close proximity were as like as two peas in a pod, and for a moment, she felt an overwhelming tenderness for both of them.

"What a fool you were, Dree," she whispered softly. Then, recalling herself, she sighed. No, the fool was she, for she had no business feeling anything but anger for him. And gratitude. There'd always be that now, for without his willingness to risk his life, she would have lost Justin, too. Leaning over them, she reached to touch her son's forehead and found it slightly warm beneath her fingertips. It was her imagination, she told herself.

As the soft cotton of her borrowed gown brushed across him, Adrian's eyes flew open, blinked several times, and then he managed a rueful smile that tugged painfully at her memory. "I must've fallen asleep," he murmured apologetically as he gently disengaged his arms from Justin's small body. Sitting up, he ran his fingers through his disordered hair and rubbed the dark stubble on his face. "Lud, what time is it?"

"I have no idea," she admitted, "but you shouldn't be here. Your mother will have the tale spread through half the neighborhood that we—" She paused and her face flushed.

"That we disported ourselves in the same bed without son?" he cut in with a grin. "No, not even Mama could do that, I think."

"Dree!"

"He'll know soon enough, anyway, Jo. You cannot keep him away from a mirror."

"No," she said, shaking her head. "He's too young to understand."

"Would you have him hear it from someone else?"

"Johnny and I are taking him to Ireland, so I doubt anyone will say anything. Duke or not, you are probably not nearly so well known there." Looking down, she picked at a piece of lint on the coverlet. "I mean to tell him in my own time, you know—I think as his mother I have that right." She touched Justin's head again, then abruptly changed the subject. "I think he feels hot," she said, frowning.

He reached over and laid the back of his hand against the boy's temple. There was no question in his mind that Justin ran a fever. "Well, it'd be a miracle if he didn't, don't you think? The skin was broken and the water was dirty—and God knows how long he was down there before we found him."

"I was hoping for that miracle."

He reached out, covering her hand with his. "But we'll see him through this—he's a sturdy little fellow."

"I didn't hear him all night."

"You were exhausted. I don't think you even knew when I tucked you up on the couch, did you?"

"No, but you should have awakened me—I should have given him his laudanum."

"He was restless, so I gave it to him about three hours ago. I guess I must've fallen asleep after that." He drew out his watch and squinted at it for a moment. "I've got to get up and make myself presentable enough to say a few farewells this morning."

"I wondered how long Almeria would stay under the same roof with me."

"It was a very near thing, I can tell you," he admitted, grinning. "For a while I thought the chance of becoming a duchess was going to outweigh anything else. Dukes, you see, are deuced difficult to come by, even for a reigning Incomparable."

"She never said that surely."

"Something very like. And that paper-skull parent of hers allowed as how if I married her posthaste by Special License, she would be more than happy to turn a blind eye to you."

"Now that was truly encroaching."

"I've sent the lot of them packing, Jo," he said quietly.

The change in his manner was jarring. She looked up and caught the warmth in his dark eyes, and forced herself to turn away. "Yes, well, I hope you did so for you rather than for me."

"Am I that far beyond the pale, Jo?"

"There was a time when I longed for you to choose

me over your mother, Dree, but you were too blind to see it."

"I was away too much that year—and she was widowed within months of the wedding. With both of you in black gloves for my father, there was little sense in taking you to London when I attended Parliament. Fool that I was, I had dreams of a political career."

"So you left me with her."

"I thought if she became better acquainted with you, she'd grow to like you."

"Well, she didn't. Pigs would fly before that happened. No, there was not a day that passed when she did not remind me how unworthy I was."

"I'm sorry, Jo—truly sorry."

"In any event, that is water under the bridge now, isn't it? I'm not eighteen anymore, and I don't believe that passion can sweep every obstacle out of its path. I learned from Gary that friendship in a marriage is far more steadying than the sort of passion we had, Dree."

"I suspect it takes both."

"With a dollop of trust thrown in for good measure, something you were exceedingly short on, I'm afraid." She turned back, meeting his gaze. "How could you let her spy on me? Knowing what she thought of me, how could you have listened to her?"

"I was only twenty-three, Jo."

"I was only eighteen, Dree, but if the world had accused you, I wouldn't have believed it."

"I don't want to dredge up old wounds," he said, his voice harsh. "God knows I've got as many as you have."

"At least you were not hounded from the country."

"I couldn't stand the whispers, the pity either, Jo. I bought myself a commission in the light dragoons because I wanted to be as far away from the Armitage as the war could take me. I went from Spain to Portugal and back again, winning and retreating, then winning the same ground twice, and it was hell. Ciudad Rodrigo. Badajoz. Salamanca. Vitoria. I was there, Jo—at all of them."

"But the scandal was of your own making. You chose to go, and that's very different from being forced to leave the country of your birth."

"I told you—I couldn't stand the pity."

"But you left Gary no choice, and he didn't deserve that."

"The two of you—"

"The two of us what, Dree?"

"It doesn't bear saying. It's over, anyway," he said, running his fingers through his hair distractedly. "Gary's dead, so it doesn't make any difference anymore."

"It does to me."

It was as though he looked at her across a gaping, bottomless abyss, and he felt helpless to bridge it. "It's been more than six years, Jo. For the sake of Justin, can we not cry friends at least?"

"I don't know. I'll always be grateful to you for saving his life."

"You don't have to run away with Barrasford. You cannot say you love him, because you are barely acquainted."

"There's quite a lot to admire in Johnny, actually. He reminds me a great deal of Gary."

"You give no quarter, do you?"

"Did you?" she countered.

"You could have answered the charges. You could have made me believe they weren't true."

"No. If you could think me capable of such baseness, there was nothing to answer. Some things when they break are irretrievably broken. But as you say, the truth still doesn't matter to you. Justin will get well, I will marry Johnny, and you'll be well rid of me again."

"For God's sake, Jo!" he all but shouted at her. "At least find someone you love!"

"I wed for love once, my lord, and the result was excessively painful. Now, if you will excuse me, I should like to change my gown. You have company to see off, and I daresay Mr. Blake will not let you downstairs like that."

"I'm a sad trial to him," he admitted. Then the oddity of their situation hit him, and he managed a faint smile. "You ought to recommend the poor fellow to Barrasford, for there's a master to make a valet proud."

"Yes, he does wear his clothes well," she agreed sweetly. "But if you mean to imply he's a man-milliner or something, I can assure you he is not."

"Oh, there's nothing wrong with Barrasford," he conceded graciously. "I quite count him a friend. In fact, he's got a lot to recommend him—man's a bruising rider, capital driver, and a veritable Corinthian."

"And quite handsome, too."

"Most of the ladies seem to agree with you, anyway."

"Dree, if you mean to imply he's in the petticoat line—"

"No, no—not anymore. The last opera dancer cured him, I think—cost him a bloody fortune to pension her off." He glanced at his watch again before returning it to his pocket. "I'll make your farewell to my mother."

"Dree—"

He rose from the bed, collected his shoes, and flashed her another smile. "I shouldn't worry about Johnny, Jo—he may be a paragon, but he's not such a high stickler that he won't understand about this. If you wish, I'll write to him for you."

"Thank you, but I believe I should prefer to do my

own explaining. Indeed, I shall do so immediately, as I should hate for him to hear of it from anyone else."

"Then I'll frank the letter. Just give it to Mrs. Johnson, and she'll see to it."

She waited until he was gone and then tried the door between the two chambers. Finding it satisfactorily locked, she changed quickly into a plain day dress Mrs. Johnson had found somewhere, then she sat down at a small writing desk to rummage for paper, pen, and ink. Writing to Lord Barrasford and explaining her presence at the Armitage was not going to be easy, but it had to be done, she told herself, sighing. She composed her thoughts for a minute and then penned a few brief sentences outlining Justin's accident and the injury he'd sustained.

Debating for a moment on whether to tell him that Adrian's mother was leaving to protest her presence, she decided it would be better to be wholly honest. She finished with a promise to keep him apprised of the situation daily. Scarcely a loverlike epistle, she reflected wryly as she reread it, but then the circumstances were exceedingly awkward for her. Behind her Justin stirred restlessly and whimpered. She blotted the letter and put it away.

"'Tis all right, dearest," she said as she crossed the room. "I'll ring for breakfast, and after we eat, you may have some more medicine to ease your leg." She pulled the bedside cord and sat down on the edge of the mattress to smooth his hair. "Would you like a drink?"

He shook his head. His eyes were dull with pain, but he was trying to be manly. "Mama—" Struggling to prop himself higher on the pillows, he turned his face to where the imprint of Adrian's head remained. "Papa was here with me—I know he was."

"Justin—" She hesitated, uncertain whether to contradict him.

"I know he was, Mama," he persisted. "I talked to him and he answered me—I know he was here. I felt him, Mama."

"That was the duke, dearest."

"No—it was Papa." His voice quavered in intensity. "He told me he loved me."

"I see. Er—did he say anything else?"

"I don't know—I think so." He strained to remember, and his eyes brightened. "I was so sleepy, Mama, but he told me when he was little, and when he knew you and the duke . . . I went to sleep."

"Well, perhaps it was a dream, my love." She tried to keep her voice light, but inwardly she was angry that Adrian had raised false hopes in a little boy. "Here take a sip of water."

"It wasn't a dream—I felt him. He was holding me just like he used to when I was scared." He sipped obediently, then he fell back against the pillows. "I hope he comes back, Mama."

At a loss, Joanna was grateful for the interruption of Mrs. Johnson coming in with the breakfast tray. The housekeeper set it on a nearby table and bustled about the room setting it to rights. Pulling open the curtains, she announced cheerily, "'Tis a lovely morning, Your— my lady." Recovering quickly from the lapse in address, she added, "I think the rain's finally ended."

"I hope so."

"His Grace has sent to Haven for things for you and the boy, and it looks like the ford will be passable." Moving back to the tray, she lifted the warming cover to expose a platter of sausages, coddled eggs, and muffins. Deftly spreading a linen napkin over Justin's chest, she tucked it in the coverlet. "There—it wouldn't do to have a bed full of crumbs, would it, young master?"

He eyed the briskly efficient woman warily. "I want my mama to feed me."

"Ho, now—'tisn't your arm that's broken, is it? No, you let your mama eat her own breakfast, and if you need help, I'll cut for you." Without waiting for a protest, she began dividing up a sausage. "There."

"I'm not hungry."

"Here now—open up. See this ship?" Mrs. Johnson held up a bite of the meat. "It needs a harbor, doesn't it? That's the fellow," she encouraged as he took the sausage. "I remember when Nurse used to do that with your papa."

"You knew my papa?"

Mrs. Johnson looked up quickly and caught the warning in Joanna's eyes. "Ah . . . yes. That is, I knew all of them—your papa, your mama, and the duke—when they were as small as you are."

Joanna's food lost its taste in her mouth. The sooner she discussed the matter with Adrian the better, she decided grimly. It simply would not do for someone to come out and tell Justin that Gary was not his father. She couldn't and wouldn't stand idly by and let anyone destroy his memory of Gary. Setting aside her own plate, she told the housekeeper, "I'll finish that—thank you."

"Oh, my lady, I did not mean—"

"I know you did not, but I can take care of him."

Nonplussed, the rotund little woman bobbed a curtsy and hastened from the room. Joanna watched her and sighed. It was going to be difficult living even for a few weeks in a household where everyone surmised the relationship between the master of the house and the young earl. The sooner he recovered and they were safely in Ireland, the better it would be for everyone.

There was a commotion in the front hall below, but

Joanna paid no attention to it. If Helen wished to make a noisy departure, it was none of her affair, anyway, although she did take a small measure of satisfaction at the notion. Edging a bit of coddled egg onto a small section of muffin, she turned back to her son.

"Just a little bit more, dearest," she coaxed. "And then you shall have some more laudanum."

"I don't like it."

"I know you do not, but it makes you feel better, doesn't it?"

"It makes me sleepy." He eyed the offending bottle with disgust. "It tastes truly horrid, Mama."

"I know, but maybe by tomorrow you will not have to take it so often."

Just then, the door burst open, and a small boy barreled into the room to bounce on the bed. Justin winced in pain and gave his brother a shove away from his leg. "Robin, get off me on the instant!"

"Robert Sherwood, present yourself properly to your mama, if you will," Lady Anne spoke crisply from the doorway. "And do not be getting on the bed—your brother must not be disturbed like that. His leg pains him enough without your climbing over it."

"Maman!"

"Yes—thankfully, the ford is passable this morning." The dowager countess swept into the room with a twinkle in her eyes. "I have come to play propriety for you, my dear. And knowing just how the case must be with you, I have already written Lord Barrasford to apprise him of the situation."

"I wrote this morning, too, but I've not got it sent off yet."

"Well, he knows that I am here so I should not worry, my love." Turning her attention to Justin, Anne smiled affectionately. "Quite done up, are you, young man? 'Twas a rare fright you gave us, I can tell you."

"I fell in a hole, Grandmama."

"So I have been told." Grasping Robin firmly, Anne pulled him off the bed. "Your brother would not go to sleep until word came that you had been found." Leaning to plant a fond kiss on Justin's forehead, she frowned. "He's quite warm, Jo."

"I know—Dr. Goode is to be here this morning, and I mean to ask him about it. The wound was open and in the water, Maman."

"'Tis a wonder you were able to get him out—Roxbury wrote 'twas an abandoned well. Quite a deep one, I understand."

"Dree went down after him."

"Roxbury went down into a well? Surely not! Odd that he failed to mention that, isn't it?"

"It was quite dangerous really—the rocks kept coming loose and I was certain they'd both be buried in rubble. But we dared not wait for help, else the water would have risen too high, and Justin would most likely have drowned."

"Well, I have often thought there was more to Adrian Delacourt than we gave him credit for," Anne murmured judiciously. "And I have certainly never thought him a coward. Indeed, I have it on the authority of Veronica Wychwood that he distinguished himself rather well at Salamanca—got some sort of medal for it, too. I believe the Regent pinned it on him while we were out of the country."

"Oh?"

Justin struggled to sit up. "Mama will not credit it, Grandmama, but I saw Papa—I know I did. He was here just last night."

Anne rumpled his dark hair sympathetically. "'Twas a dream, my dear."

"No, it wasn't!" he contradicted hotly. "I know it wasn't—I touched him! He told me he loved me!" His face contorted with sudden pain, and he fell back against the bank of pillows.

"Of course he did," she agreed. "I daresay it must've been the laudanum—you are giving him some, aren't you, Jo?"

"Yes, but—" Joanna cast a meaningful look at Justin. "Well, I'll tell you about it later." She removed the stopper of the laudanum bottle and measured out the drops into a glass. Adding a couple of inches of water from the pitcher, she stirred. "Now, my dear," she addressed her elder son, "it's time you swallowed this and made the best of it. "

He drank it almost willingly, screwing up his face when it was down. "Yechh. Robin, I hope they never make you drink any of this."

The younger boy, who'd hung back while his brother spoke with his grandmother, reached to touch Justin's leg through the coverlet. "Does it hurt very bad?"

"Like the very devil," Justin muttered through clenched teeth. "Only time it doesn't, I'm asleep."

"But you have been very brave," Anne murmured gently as she sat beside him and stroked his hair back from his face. "I am quite proud of you, my love." Leaning forward, she kissed him again. "You must try to sleep now, and when you wake, I have brought some things for us to do together."

His hands slid around her neck for a moment. "I am glad you are here, Grandmama."

Tears sparkled in Anne's eyes. "I am so glad I am also, dearest. I couldn't bear it if you were sick without me to care for you."

Always careful to avoid jealousy between her sons, Joanna lifted Robin into her arms and carried him to the window. "See the garden below, love? 'Tis quite the best in the county, and perhaps the duke will allow us to walk there when Justin is asleep. There is a small maze beyond the taller hedge that Papa, Dree, and I played in when we were your age. I can quite remember getting lost and having them laugh at me."

"I don't want to get lost," he told her as he eyed the garden doubtfully.

"Well, I should expect to explore it with you," she promised.

"Mama, who's Dree?" he asked suddenly.

"The duke who lives here."

"You had better rest while you can, my dear," Anne reminded her from the bed.

"I am fine—I slept most of the night. Dree—" She caught herself and her face reddened at what her mother-in-law would think if she knew he'd stayed in the chamber all night.

"Nonetheless, you must conserve your strength for what I can only suppose will be a trying time for all of us. I left Miss Finchley below to see to the disposal of our baggage, but I am certain she would take Robin to the garden for you."

"No!" Robin twisted in Joanna's arms. "I want Mama!"

"You brought Miss Finchley, too?" Joanna asked incredulously. "Roxbury will think he's been invaded."

"It was his express wish, my love. 'Bring the other boy and his nurse when you come'—'tis exactly what he wrote to me. But I brought Miss Finchley instead, thinking she would be more useful in keeping Justin's mind busy while he mends." Anne rose, smoothing her skirt down over her petticoat. "I kissed Helen good-bye for you, my dear—she and the Benningtons were leaving as I came in," she added with a serene smile. "So you can quite see that you need the presence of all of us to suppress the gossip."

"It must be very difficult for you, Maman," Joanna murmured, "to be here after all that happened between

Dree and Gary, but I am ever so grateful you have come."

"Nonsense," Anne declared dismissively. "I can still remember Adrian Delacourt as he was before that unfortunate business. Besides, I blame Gary somewhat for not speaking up. But it was a long time ago, Joanna—suppose we bend our minds now to getting Justin well. 'Twill be difficult to go on as though nothing has happened, but I think we must," she added crisply. "For Justin's sake."

Joanna nodded. "For Justin's sake. But it will be difficult—so very difficult. Sometimes the memories here are just so great I cannot put everything aside."

"Mama, could we go down now?" Robin tugged at a lock of Joanna's hair insistently. "Could we? I don't want to stay with Finch, I don't—not just now."

"If you are not going to lie down, you would just as well go, I suppose," Anne told her. "And Justin will be perfectly fine in my care, as well you know. But do see if Miss Finchley is settled in a chamber, will you? I should hate to think she is merely wandering about somewhere in this great barn, and I cannot think Roxbury will bother to note her. Not that he is unkind, of course.

"He is rather distracted just now, Maman."

"I should expect he is," Anne murmured. "It cannot be easy for him, considering there are no rules for entertaining one's divorced wife. Indeed, I should think it quite awkward at times for both of you."

"It is. Very—for me at least." Looking away, Joanna sighed. "He still does not believe that Gary and I were innocent. He sent Helen away, but in his heart of hearts, he still believes her lies. Maybe he doesn't wish to, but I know he does."

Dr. Goode came, examined Justin's leg, and shook his head pessimistically. "There are signs of infection, I'm afraid. I'd like to cup him to reduce the inflammation in that leg."

"No!" Adrian's voice was harsh, almost angry. "We'll foment the leg with poultices to draw off the infection, but I'll hang before I let you bleed him. I saw too much of that in the war, and believe me, it is a useless, barbaric practice. I saw men die from being bled."

"Dree—"

"No—am I made clear on that head, sir?" he demanded of the doctor.

"Perfectly, Your Grace, but I must protest," Goode expostulated indignantly. "He is a boy—not a horse."

"Really, Dree—"

"No."

"My lord, but you must reconsider! The infection causes an imbalance in the blood between the legs. If we are to save the one with the break, we must bleed him. The humors—"

"Hang the humors! I know what I saw with my own eyes! Jo, listen to me—Justin's too weak already to lose any blood. Surely you can see that, can you not?"

"Yes, but surely Dr. Goode—" While she agreed with him, she feared offending the only physician for miles.

"Well, he would not do anything to harm Justin, I am sure."

"Joanna, I am for Adrian in this." Anne looked up from where she sat on the other side of the bed. "Bleeding may be efficacious in some instances, but I think Justin's too small to benefit from it."

"See—even your mother-in-law agrees with me."

"Dree, he's my son," Joanna reminded him.

"You cannot want him weakened further. Listen to me—have you ever seen anyone made stronger by a cupping? No—you have not," he answered for her. "Jo, his fever is rising even as we speak—let us not do anything to lessen his chances of recovery."

Unwilling to alienate both the Duke of Roxbury and the dowager Countess of Carew, the doctor capitulated. "As you wish, my lord. I can prescribe a poultice, but it must be applied diligently. As for the fever, it will not break for any length of time as long as the infection remains. Usually in cases such as these, there will be sweats followed by even higher fevers until the crisis is reached, then God willing, his temperature will gradually come down. Each time it breaks after the crisis, it will not rise as high as before."

"But he *will* be all right, won't he?" Joanna asked anxiously.

"Dear lady, that rests in the hands of a higher power than mine. Now, as I was about to say, I have something I've found useful in controlling fevers in most cases. I fear, however, that it is rather unpleasant to the taste, and you may have some difficulty administering it."

"It cannot be worse than the laudanum," Jo murmured.

"It doesn't matter—I'll get it down him," Adrian promised her.

"Good." Turning his attention back to his young patient, the physician patted Justin reassuringly. "You're a lucky little boy to be alive—you know that, don't you? But we've a ways to go yet before you are well. You've sustained a nasty break in that leg of yours, and that dirty water has set a poison to work on it." As the child's fever-bright eyes widened, he nodded. "Aye, and we've got to get rid of it."

"How?" Justin croaked.

"Got to wash it out of you. And you do that by drinking, young man—I want you to drink as much as that stomach of yours can hold, you understand. Aye, and take the medicine your mama gives you. It's not pleasant, but it'll work if you can keep it down." As Justin shook his head mulishly, Goode told him bracingly, "Here now —you're a big lad, aren't you? I'm relying on you to help me get you well."

"Yes, sir," came the grudging reply.

"And don't be complaining when they are putting hot poultices on your leg—you understand? That will help draw the poison out, too."

"Yes, sir."

"Good lad," Goode murmured approvingly. Looking up at Joanna and Adrian, he advised, "Do not let him throw his covers off on those occasions when he sweats, else he'll risk an inflammation of the lungs also." Reaching for his worn leather bag, he rummaged in it, then drew out a vial of powder. "Now, who's tending to dosing him?"

"I will," Adrian spoke up. "His mother is already worn to a nub."

"Then give him less than one-half a small spoon of this in a little water and see that he drinks all of it. Usually it will bring a fever down in less than an hour, but it will not keep it down. It's not a cure, of course, but hopefully it will make him more comfortable, Your Grace." Looking to Joanna, he warned her, "He'll sweat prodigiously each time his fever breaks, and he must be kept dry, my lady. I want the sheets changed with his clothes."

"All right."

"How often is he to take the medicine?" Adrian wanted to know.

"No more than every four or five hours unless he appears convulsive. In that case, use it immediately and repeat the dosage in an hour if the fever does not break."

"Convulsive?" Fear gripped Joanna in the pit of her stomach.

"Dr. Goode, may we be private with you ere you leave?" Adrian asked quietly.

"Of course. And then I need to speak with your cook about preparing the poultice, which you are to apply as hot as the boy can stand it every three hours for half an hour at a time. It is not quite like fomenting a horse, you understand. I'll expect the purulence to drain, and I'll warn you right now that when it does, the discharge will be most unpleasant—vile even. I'm not sure Lady Carew—"

"I'll take care of it," Adrian said, cutting him off. "I've seen gangrene, and it cannot be worse than that."

"Very well, then if Lady Anne will stay with the boy—"

"Of course I will. Go on, both of you, and when you are done with Dr. Goode, you'd best get what rest you can. And don't be looking at me like that, dearest," Anne told Joanna, "for I am quite capable of applying the poultice myself. Let me stay with him during the day, for I expect he will need you far more at night."

"I'd rather not leave him, Maman."

"And what good will you be to him if you are down yourself?" the countess countered. "Now—go on," she said firmly.

They followed Dr. Goode into the hall, where Adrian stopped him. "What do you really think?" he asked, searching the man's face. "His mother and I would have the truth, so you can give us the worst of it."

The physician hesitated, then looked to Joanna. "I'm not sure if her ladyship . . ." His voice trailed off significantly.

"I am neither squeamish nor fainthearted, sir," she declared.

Goode looked from one to the other of them, then he drew in his breath and exhaled it heavily. Finally, he addressed Adrian. "I think, Your Grace, that it will be a wonder if he keeps his leg."

"If he keeps his leg!" Jo's hands flew to her face. "Oh, no!"

"'Twas a dirty wound, my lady. It already shows some festering and the fever indicates that the infection is spreading. We'll just have to make him as comfortable as we can and hope for the best."

"Dree—the cupping—"

"It won't help, Jo."

"Doctor—?"

"Well, I—"

"Tell her the truth."

"Your Grace, I've never lied about anything like this in my life," Goode responded stiffly.

"You wished to cup him before," Joanna said hollowly.

"Aye, but His Grace—"

"Jo, you haven't seen what I've seen. If bleeding a man could stop the spread of infection in a limb, nobody in my company would have died of gangrene. I never saw the surgeon cup anyone who kept a limb or even lived."

"But he's just a little boy, Dree."

As she struggled for composure, Adrian's hand grasped hers. "I won't let anyone cut off his leg—not if there's a chance he can keep it and live," he promised.

"But I don't want to bleed him—I don't want him too weak to fight."

She bit her lower lip to still its trembling before she could bring herself to ask, "How long will it be before we know, sir?"

"Not long—a few days at most. Once the fever is high, the crisis usually follows within a day or so." Feeling intensely sorry for her, the physician told her, "The important thing is to diligently pursue the course of action you have chosen. The poultices must be applied as directed without fail."

"All right. Is there anything else you would have us do?"

"Pray."

"That goes without saying, sir."

"Well, then I shall confer with the cook before I take myself off," Goode decided. "The rest I leave to you. You will, of course, send for me if the need arises. Otherwise, I shall call again tomorrow."

As soon as the man left, Adrian took Joanna outside to the walled garden. "You may cry now, Jo, if you wish, but when you are done, we have to plan how best to take care of him. I suggest that we divide the day and night into four-hour portions. With you, the countess, and myself watching him in turn, we ought to manage that."

She shook her head. "I won't leave him—he needs me."

"He needs you well, Jo."

"'Tis so unfair, Dree! He's had too much to bear." Her face contorted as she fought back tears. "He's lost Gary, and now—oh, what if he loses his leg? How will he go on?"

"I pray it does not come to that, but if it does, you'll have to be strong. I'd rather have a one-legged son than no son at all."

"You do not think he could die?" As the awful words

came out, she swallowed hard. "I'm sorry, but I cannot help it. I must think . . . I must gather my wits, mustn't I?"

"Yes."

"I couldn't bear it if he died—I couldn't. You cannot know—"

"Don't say it—don't even think such a thing," he cut in, stopping her. "We're going to keep that leg packed in poultices until it ceases draining, and then the trick, my dear, will lie in keeping a little boy off his feet for weeks on end." Reaching out, he lifted her chin with his knuckle. "We're not going to let him lose that leg if there's any way on this earth to save it."

There was such conviction in his voice, such intensity in those dark eyes, that she almost believed him. Less than a month ago he'd not even known he had a son, and now he was telling her that he'd fight beside her to save him. He'd already done it once when he'd gone down that well shaft. Looking into his eyes, she was overwhelmed by the gratitude she felt just now.

"Thank you, Dree," she managed.

His hand cupped her chin, tipping her head back until her upturned face was but inches from his. His fingers were strong and warm and reassuring. She could feel his breath when he spoke.

"I did not discover my son to let him die, Jo," he said softly. "I just wish I'd been there from the first."

A lump formed in her throat, making speech impossible. She nodded as tears welled anew, wetting her lashes. Her throat ached with what she couldn't say.

"For his sake, I am asking that we set aside our differences," he continued quietly. "We need to bend ourselves together to the task of making him whole and well again. Even if you cannot stomach me as a husband, you must let me share the burden of a parent until this is done." He paused and searched her face for some sign that she agreed. "Look at me—tell me that you can put our past bitterness behind us for now."

The lump threatened to choke her. "I—I don't know," she managed to answer finally. "But I'll try."

He dropped his hand and sighed. "I have not the right to ask you for anything, I know."

The ache in her throat spread downward, tightening her chest painfully. "You put me in your debt when you went down that well, but—" Unable to put her years of bitterness into words, she paused.

"But you cannot forget what I did to you," he finished for her.

"No."

"Neither can I. The pain is still there when I look back, and sometimes I hate you for it, but I tell myself that you were not wholly to blame, that we were too young to wed, that maybe Gary—"

"Please—I'd not speak of that, not now."

"I wish I knew . . . I wish I had the reason still . . . I wish I could understand somehow why . . ."

"And what would it serve now?" she cried out painfully. "Would it change what happened? Would it bring Gary back to us now? Would my father suddenly decide to call me daughter again?"

"Jo—"

"Dree, I lost everything I held dear six years ago—my family, my friends—and most of all, you. I would have died had it not been for Gareth Sherwood. And then there was Justin. He was my constant reminder of what could have and should have been! But Gary loved him in spite of it, and so did I." Unable to hold back the flood of tears any longer, she turned away from him. "No, do not speak to me of pain, Dree! I lost you, I lost Gary, and now I may lose Justin—and I cannot bear it! I can't lose anything more!"

"Jo . . . Jo . . ."

He came up behind her, slid his arms around her waist, and rocked her gently against his body. Sobbing, she turned in his arms and buried her head in his shoulder. He rubbed along her spine with one hand and smoothed her hair against her shoulder with the other.

"Don't, Jo—don't do this to yourself," he murmured over and over.

"But I c-cannot h-help it!"

Finally, when it seemed that there could be nothing more to pour out, she shuddered against him and was quiet. He continued rubbing her back until she put both her hands between them and pushed him away. "I'm sorry—I am overset merely," she managed in understatement, "but I am all right now." Rubbing at her wet cheeks with the back of her hand, she flashed the briefest of smiles. "Silly of me, isn't it—feeling sorry for myself when my only concern should be Justin. I'm not usually given to an excess of sensibilities, you know."

"I know." He drew out his handkerchief and handed it to her. "Blow your nose, Jo. You cannot go back in there and let him see you blue-deviled. You're going to have to buck up and put your best face on. And so am I."

"I'm going to try."

"Shall we walk a bit until you have collected yourself, or do you think you are able to see him now?"

"I am all right—really."

"Come on, then."

He reached to take her hand and lead her back into the house. Outside the bedchamber door, he paused and half turned to face her. "I want to help you through this, Jo. I want us to cry friends until it's over."

"Just promise me you won't interfere with his memories of Gary." She tried to force a smile and couldn't. "I want him to remember how much his papa loved him. Gary deserves that much at least."

It was a bitter reminder of just how much he'd missed, of how much he'd lost. Of the fact that he couldn't claim his own son.

"I want you to promise it, Dree."

"I owe Gary that, I guess," he answered finally. "It couldn't have been easy for him to rear a mirrored image of me. I don't think I could have done it had things been the other way around. I would have felt cheated, I think. But then I suppose he was willing to accept anything to have you."

"You still don't understand, do you? It wasn't that way at all." Before he could say anything more, she turned the doorknob and slipped inside.

He stood there, staring after her.

"If I did not know better, Roxbury, I should say you ate something disagreeable," Anne Sherwood observed mildly, coming out of the sickroom.

"How is he?"

"Fretful and hot. Quite frankly, I am terribly worried."

"So am I." He glanced at the closed door. " 'Pride, the never failing vice of fools,' " he said softly.

"Are you speaking of Joanna or yourself?"

"Myself."

"Well, that is a beginning at least, isn't it? Though I suspect there was more than enough of that vice to go around."

"Why did he marry her? She said he knew Justin wasn't his."

There was a strained silence for a moment, then she sighed. "I expect Joanna could better answer that, don't you? As far as I am concerned, all three of you behaved rather rashly in the matter. Now, if you will pardon me, I'd best see about that poultice."

As she walked away, Joanna's words echoed in his ears. *I lost everything I held dear six years ago—my family, my friends—and most of all, you . . . most of all, you.*

The day was warm, the air blowing through the tall casement windows redolent with the fragrance of summer flowers. And yet a three-day pall hung over the house as hushed words were whispered in halls and crannies that the young Earl of Carew's leg was going from bad to worse despite the best efforts of Dr. Goode. Robin, restive from waiting while everyone hovered over his ailing brother, threw down his colored chalk and scattered the scraps of drawing paper mutinously.

"I don't want to draw anymore, Finch," he complained.

It had been a trial to keep him busy and out of the way, but Charlotte Finchley felt a genuine sympathy for him. "Well, I suppose we could take a walk outside," she offered.

"I want to go to Ireland and ride a pony."

"And you will. But first Justin must get well."

"Is he going to die, Finch?"

"Of course not—or at least I don't think so," she murmured, hastily amending her denial.

"My papa did."

"Yes, but your papa's boat turned over in the water during a bad storm. People don't usually die from broken legs." Seeking to turn the subject, she took his hand

and led him to the window. "Look at all those flowers, Robin—would you like to pick some for your mother?"

"I'd rather look at 'Bury's horses."

"All right." Just then, she heard a carriage coming up the long serpentine drive. Her gaze followed it as it made the last curve, then she gasped in recognition. "Oh, dear—'tis Lord Barrasford," she said faintly. Unconsciously, she touched her hair with her hands, patting it into place. "Poor Lady Carew," she murmured. "There's just too much on her plate right now for this. Well, I'd best warn her, in any event."

"Barryford's here?" Brightening, he clutched her hand more tightly. "Did he bring my pony? He said I could have a cart and pony, Finch."

"And so you shall when you get to Ireland."

"But I want it *now*," he insisted, trotting beside her.

In the hallway, they nearly collided with the dowager countess coming from the sickroom. "Oh, my lady, Barrasford's here, and I cannot think Lady Carew—"

"Justin's worse, Miss Finchley." Anne looked back, toward the bedchamber door. "Joanna's not left his bedside since yesterday morning."

"Grandmama, Barryford's taking me to Ireland!" Robin reminded her.

As he said it, a footman opened the foyer door to admit Joanna's betrothed and a soberly dressed man. Charlotte Finchley shook her head. "How very awkward to be sure, my lady. I cannot think he will wish to sit with Lady Carew and Roxbury in the sickroom."

"No, of course not," Anne agreed. "My dear, I'm afraid we must rely on you and Robin to distract—that is, to *entertain* Lord Barrasford while Justin is so ill."

"Me?" the younger woman gasped. "Oh, dear ma'am, I'm not at all sure—"

"Nonsense," Anne declared dismissively. "When one must, one rises to the occasion. I'm sure he'd rather visit with you than hover over Justin's bed. And I understand there is some acquaintance between you, is there not?"

"Well, yes, but he and Lady Carew—"

"Are betrothed," Anne finished for her. "And what is that to say to anything? He does wish to know Robin, and as my grandson's governess, it can scarce be considered improper for you to be in his company." Then, perceiving another possible reason for the young woman's reluctance, she said more gently, "From my rather limited observation of the fellow, he doesn't seem to be the sort of man to look down upon you for something you could not help."

"I cannot stand pity—anything but that."

"My dear, you are what you were born, and no one can take that away from you. There is no shame in earning your bread. Indeed, the shame would have been if you'd decided to do it less respectably. Now, I shall quite rely upon you to see that Lord Barrasford and Roxbury do not tread on each other's toes under these already trying circumstances—do I make myself plain on that head?"

"I shall do what I can to help," Charlotte Finchley promised.

A footman was leading Johnny and his companion up the stairs, and with no place to hide, the governess wiped her hands on the skirt of her plain green gown. But Barrasford looked directly to the dowager countess.

"I came as quickly as I could, Lady Anne. The boy's all right, isn't he?" But the older woman's face gave him his answer. "I see. Then perhaps it will not be taken amiss that I have brought Dr. Bascombe with me—you are acquainted with him, are you not?"

"By reputation." Anne extended her hand to the physician. "A pleasure, sir. Given that Goode does not seem to be able to do anything for my grandson, I can assure you that your services will be most welcome."

"I made inquiries over the whole of London, and the consensus definitely favored Dr. Bascombe," Johnny assured her. "And Joanna? How is she?"

"As well as might be expected, I suppose. Haggard with worry. I don't think she's slept above an hour in the last two days," Anne answered.

"Did you bring my pony?" Robin asked, tugging at Barrasford's coat.

"No, but he's waiting for you." Reaching out, Johnny ruffled the red-gold hair. "But I did think to bring you something I've hopes you'll like," he said, reaching beneath his coat to draw out a brown paper-wrapped package. Despite the perfect cut of his breeches, he dropped to his haunches and untied the package. "Go on—look inside," he urged the little boy.

"Sojers!" Robin exclaimed. "Finch—Grandmama, look! Barryford brought me sojers!"

"Soldiers, my love," Anne corrected him.

Charlotte Finchley bent over them, examining the carved figures. "Why, there must be a dozen grenadiers, Robin. And look, you've at least that many foot guards," she noted enthusiastically. "And see this one? 'Tis a Gordon Highlander. What do you say to his lordship?"

"Thank you, sir," Robin remembered.

"After I see your mama, we'll set them up in battle lines," Johnny promised. "I'll show you how we fought at Vitoria." Straightening up, he looked to Anne again. "I'd like to see Joanna. I've come to support her through this."

"Yes, of course."

"But we was going to play!" Robin protested.

Johnny ruffled his hair again. "And we will, but first

I need to see your mama. And I haven't seen Justin yet
either."

"He can't play, but he'll get better."

"Of course he will, and when he does, we'll all play
with your soldiers. We'll beat the Frogs together."

"He means the French army," Miss Finchley explained. "Remembering the dowager's request, she
turned to Barrasford. "I'd promised to take him outside, but if you'd prefer to come up to the nursery, I'm
sure we can fix up a place to deploy those soldiers."

"Nonsense," Anne said. "It is far too lovely a day to
spend inside, and I am certain there are any number of
suitable places to place an army among the walks. And
I'm sure Barrasford would enjoy your company there
as well as in the nursery."

"Yes, do come," he said quickly. "I've not much experience with three-year-old boys."

"I'm nearly four," Robin told him. "Next Christmas
I'll be four."

"Oh, that makes a great deal of difference," Johnny
declared, smiling.

"Yes, well, if you would see Joanna and Justin, you'd
best follow me to the sickroom." Looking up at Dr. Bascombe, she added, "If you do not mind, I'd have you
accompany us. I think the sooner we have your opinion of the matter, the better."

"I'll do what I can, my lady."

"Yes, well, that is all any of us can do, isn't it? But I
can tell you, sir, that my grandson is one very sick little
boy." She waited until Miss Finchley had Robin beyond
hearing, then confided, "I'm terribly worried that he
will not recover, and should that happen, I fear for my
daughter-in-law's very sanity. She has borne so much,
sir, that I am sure I do not know how she manages to
go on."

"Poor Jo. And it cannot help things any that she is in

Roxbury's house instead of her own," Johnny murmured.

"Roxbury has been all that is kind, my lord. Indeed, his devotion to Justin has been rather astounding." She paused at the door to Adrian's bedchamber, then she squared her shoulders. "I pray you will not be too shocked when you see Joanna."

Despite the brightness of the day, the room lay darkened behind heavy brocaded draperies, and the main source of light was a brace of flickering candles placed on a table near the bed. Johnny's gaze swept the room until he saw her. She sat in deep shadows, leaning forward in her chair to rest her head on the brocade coverlet. One of her arms was outstretched, and her hand rested on the small, bundled figure huddled in the center of the big bed.

"Jo?"

She stirred, then sat up, surprised by the sound of his voice. As the candlelight flitted across her, he was stunned. Her pale hair was a mass of tangles that framed her taut, drawn face, and her blue eyes seemed to have sunk into dark, swollen circles.

"My God, Jo."

"He's burning up, Johnny," she said hollowly. "He's burning up, and I can do naught but watch."

He moved closer to the bed, then he reached to touch the boy's hot, red face. "How long has this been going on?"

"Two days, but it's getting worse. I give him the medicine, but it seems as though every time his fever breaks, it just comes back higher within the hour." She looked up at him, her expression haunted. "I don't know what to do, Johnny—I just don't know what to do."

"You need to get some rest."

"I can't leave him like this," she said, her voice dropping to a whisper. "I've got to be here."

"I brought a doctor with me from London. His name is Bascombe, and I expect Roxbury will know of him, for he was much noted during the war for his treatment of the more dangerous wounds. Truth to tell, Ponsonby wouldn't be alive today were it not for Bascombe." Johnny laid his hand on her head, smoothing her hair. "Oh, I know there is a difference in circumstance, of course, but I thought dirty well water couldn't be any worse than some of the things a wounded man lies in on a battlefield."

"Bascombe's a good man."

It was then that he realized that Adrian Delacourt sat on the other side of the bed. The duke stood up and passed a weary hand over the dark stubble on his cheeks. He was obviously in as sad a case as Joanna.

"May I look at the boy?" the physician asked gently.

"Yes, of course. Dr. Goode's been attending him," Joanna told him.

"It would be a consult."

"Consult, hell," Adrian snapped. "If Barrasford hasn't engaged you, I will. I'm tired of waiting for Goode to kill him."

"Dree!"

"I'm just glad to see this man, that's all," he muttered. "I've sent to Knighton, but there's been no word from that quarter yet. I expect Bascombe's better for this, anyway."

"Thank you, Your Grace," the doctor murmured deferentially.

For a brief moment, Adrian looked at Joanna, then he turned to Johnny. "You'd best get her out of here while he does this. It's a damned ugly sight."

"I'm not going anywhere, Dree."

"Can you smell the wound, my lord? Do you see any putrefaction?" Bascombe asked him.

"No. It's the damned fever. You heard her—he's burning up with it," he answered wearily. His eyes met Bascombe's. "I'll pay anything you ask if he recovers. Right now, I'd give my last pence to rid him of this fever."

"Recovery, my lord, is in God's hands—not mine. I am but a mortal physician and surgeon. And it would be unconscionable of me to extort more than my usual fees from you."

Joanna closed her eyes. "Please don't take his leg," she whispered.

"I told you to get her out of here, Johnny."

"No—I'm not going anywhere!" Ducking away from Barrasford, Joanna clasped her son's hand. Leaning over him, she crooned, "Mama's here, Justin." Her free hand stroked the thick, dark hair. "Mama loves you more than anything. You are Mama's sweet little boy."

Johnny looked away as Bascombe unwrapped the splints, then exposed the swollen leg. For what seemed like an age, the physician moved his hands over the ugly, discolored break, pressing the place where the bone had come out. Sitting back finally, he observed, "It was set correctly, and the bone itself seems to be healing. Aside from a little seepage, there's not much corruption around the wound."

"Then why is he so ill?"

"The infection has spread to the blood."

"But the poultices drew off the pus, sir—I mean, how could that be?" Joanna asked helplessly.

"Blood moves, my lady." Leaning over Justin again, he held a candle close as he lifted the boy's eyelids, then he shook his head. "Does he respond when you talk to him?"

"Yes, but when his fever is high, he is confused. When it breaks, he is not."

"Then it does not appear that the brain itself is involved as of yet. I have to count that as a good sign at least." Straightening, he told them, "I shall have to conduct a more thorough examination, of course, but I can tell you this is a very sick little boy."

"But can you do anything?"

"I hope so, my lady—I devoutly hope so. It is my experience that some fever is not necessarily a bad thing, but these high fevers can be quite dangerous of themselves."

"Would cupping help? Dr. Goode has been pressing us to bleed him, but Dree—Roxbury, that is—is set against it."

"Jo, it will just weaken him further."

"Quite right, Your Grace," Bascombe agreed. "While cupping is efficacious under some circumstances, the low volume of blood in a small body makes it rather unproductive, particularly in the reduction of a fever. What he needs is more liquid in him, not less."

"I told you, Jo." Turning to the physician, Adrian asked, "How do you see this going, sir?"

"How long has he run this high fever?"

"He was feverish day before yesterday," Joanna answered.

"But it wasn't until yesterday that it reached such heights," Adrian reminded her. "Until then, we could get it down with the medicine for a little while at least. Now when it breaks, it returns almost immediately."

"I see. Has he suffered any convulsions yet?"

"No. He just doesn't know where he is, and he does not recognize me. He thinks I am—he thinks I am his late father."

"I see." Looking from the duke to the sick child, the physician tried to hide his surprise.

"My husband was Gareth Sherwood, Earl of Carew," Joanna interposed hastily. "But that is of no moment now, sir. It soothes Justin to think Gary is with him now."

"I must consider it a good sign that there have been no convulsions." Bascombe chose his words carefully, trying not to alarm them further. "Usually in these cases, there is a crescendo of sorts, whereby the fevers increase both in intensity and duration until the patient reaches the crisis that ultimately determines the outcome. At that point, the body either begins to triumph over the infection, or it loses the battle." Laying a hand on Justin's forehead, he said, "I must think his crisis will come within the next day or so. Until then, it is imperative that we reduce the intensity of this fever without eliminating it. Otherwise, the brain will be involved, and after that, a full recovery cannot be achieved."

"I don't understand," Johnny said.

"A fever of the brain is usually fatal, my lord, and even when the patient survives it, there is a severe loss of faculty. In those cases, it would have been kinder had the patient not survived."

"No!"

"As I said, my lady, I must count it a good sign that he has not convulsed. Now, as soon as my bag is fetched, I should like to proceed with my examination. And I should like to conduct it alone."

"Oh, but—"

"My lady," Bascombe said patiently, "even if he recovers, your son will get worse before he gets better. He will require the utmost care in his nursing, and without rest, you cannot provide it."

"I could not sleep if I tried, sir."

"Perhaps not, but I am ordering you to your bed for the next four hours at the very least." Looking to Anne, he added, "I will give you a recipe for a tisane I wish prepared for her. She is to drink all of it, then she is to lie down. A cold compress applied to her eyes will reduce the swelling."

"I'll see it done, sir."

"I cannot leave my son," Joanna protested.

"For God's sake, Jo!" Adrian snapped. "Listen to the man!"

Bascombe turned his attention to him. "As for you, Your Grace, you look as though you are in desperate need of rest also. If you are to have a clear head when he reaches his crisis, you must get some sleep also. A few drops of laudanum—"

"I don't need any damned opium." Realizing how ungrateful he must sound, Adrian wearily passed his hands over his hot, dry eyes. "I'm sorry—I should have just said I've an aversion to the stuff. I don't like anything that clouds my mind, particularly at a time like this."

"In any event, Your Grace, I don't wish to see you back here for four to six hours. As fevers tend to worsen at night, he will need your attention more then than now."

Seeing that Joanna still didn't want to go, Johnny spoke up. "I've not much experience with sickness, but I am more than glad to sit with Justin while you both get some sleep."

"He doesn't know you," Adrian said harshly. "No, I'll stay."

Anne laid a hand on his arm. "No, you'll all go on. I'll sit with my grandson, and if the need arises, I'll send for you." Noting the set of his jaw, she said gently, "I love him, too, you know." Looking past Roxbury to Barrasford, she reminded him, "You've a little boy waiting to play at war with you, I believe. As he has been sadly neglected during all this, any help you can give Miss Finchley with Robin will be truly appreciated. Even though he knows Justin is quite ill, it is difficult for a three-year-old child to understand why everyone is more concerned with his older brother. And it will give you a chance to become better acquainted with him."

"I'll do anything you want me to do, Jo," he told Joanna. "If you wish, I can come back up when I am done with the younger boy."

"No." Nearly too tired to think, she looked up at him. "I'm sure she is right. Robin has the greater need of you." Managing a smile, she added, "I am glad you are here, Johnny."

"I couldn't stay away." Circling her shoulder with his arm, he brushed a light kiss against her cheek. "I'm sorry you are going through this, my dear. I wish I could do more to help."

"Keeping Robin entertained is more than enough," she assured him. "It's not an easy task, believe me. Poor Finch must be at her wit's end."

"I don't know—she seems quite competent in that quarter."

"Yes, but it has all fallen on the poor girl's shoulders," Anne said smoothly.

"I'll do what I can," he promised. To Jo, he said, "Try to sleep," as he kissed her forehead. Releasing her, he nodded to Adrian. "Your servant, Roxbury."

"You are staying to dine, aren't you?" Anne called after him.

"If I am needed," he answered.

As Barrasford left the room, Adrian muttered, "The house is at sixes and sevens already."

"Yes," the dowager countess agreed mildly. "But I do think Miss Finchley will appreciate his company—where Robin is concerned, of course. Now, Joanna dearest, you will go to my bedchamber where 'tis quiet, and you will lie down for those four hours."

"Maman—"

"Bess will bring your tisane. Now, go on—if you get down, we are truly in the basket. And the same with Roxbury. If he does not go, I shall push him out the door," the five-foot woman declared.

"Go on, Jo," Adrian urged her. "I expect we've another long night ahead of us." Moving to the window, he watched Johnny emerge from the house and cross the lawn to where Robin and the governess waited. As much as he liked Johnny, he found himself wishing the man at Jericho. Aloud, he observed, "You know, your Miss Finchley is rather pretty, isn't she? I mean, if she had the means to fix herself up, she'd be quite fetching."

"Odd, isn't it?" Anne murmured behind him. "I was thinking precisely the same thing when I sent her down to entertain Lord Barrasford." As he turned around, she added innocently, "Well, someone must keep him occupied, don't you think?"

The ornate clock on the bedside table ticked away the hours, hours that Joanna had ceased to count. Every fiber of her being cried out from fatigue, but she'd long since passed the time when she could sleep. Through tired eyes she studied the small, restless body of her son as he thrashed fitfully in Adrian's great bed. One of the candles sputtered, then went out, leaving the room in an eerie semidarkness, but she did not even note it.

Her lips moved silently, fervently in prayer, beseeching, promising everything, anything in exchange for one small boy's life. The case was desperate now, the crisis near, Bascombe had told them. The fever still racked Justin's body and clouded his mind, and the London physician now feared it had finally reached his brain, making it a far more dangerous enemy than the gangrene they'd once feared. As the brain swelled, it would almost certainly kill her son.

Leaning forward, she rested her head on the edge of the mattress. Her weary mind couldn't even pray anymore, for the thoughts were too jumbled, too incoherent for even God to understand. But she could not and would not give up. Not as long as there was even one breath left in Justin's body.

She felt a hand on her shoulder, and she looked up to see Adrian standing behind her. He looked as tired as she felt, but his grip was strong and comforting as his fingers massaged her sore muscles, easing the aching bones beneath. She leaned back for a moment, closing her eyes and savoring the relief while he began working the knotted muscles of her neck and shoulders.

"I didn't hear you come in," she said simply.

"I didn't wish to disturb your prayers."

It no longer seemed odd that he should be here. In the days since Justin's condition had worsened, there had sprung up between them a sharing, a common ground, a battle jointly fought for their child's life. And it had become a situation that the entire Armitage household took for granted—there were no whisperings of scandal above or below the stairs—from the lowliest groom to the housekeeper there was only an aggregate shaking of heads over the tragedy that had befallen "the poor little master." Doors to His Grace's bedchamber were left open now to admit servants, who went silently about the business of tending to their duke and the wife he'd once discarded. Only an occasional hushed inquiry or observation broke the silence everyone seemed to share.

"Any change?"

"For the worse perhaps. Do you think we ought to wake Dr. Bascombe?" she asked as Justin suddenly cried out and clutched at the air. "I'm afraid as hot as he is, he'll go into convulsions."

Rather than answering, Adrian moved to lean over the bed and catch the boy's hands. Murmuring soothing words, he sat down and pulled Justin against him, where the child huddled, shaking and incoherent. With an effort, the dark eyes flew open and tried to focus. "Papa?" he whispered through fever-parched lips. "Papa, take me home."

Joanna had long since given up protesting the pretense. It was obvious that her son drew comfort from it, and it was obvious from his fevered rantings that he believed Adrian to be Gary. Later, when he began to recover, she'd put a stop to that, but not now.

"Get me some water, Jo," Adrian ordered curtly. "And a cloth." Turning back to Justin, he adjusted the small body against his shoulder, bracing him, while he murmured, "Papa's here . . . Papa's here, little one." His hand stroked the thick, waving hair. It was as though he held a hot brick. "Jo, when did you last give him his fever medicine?"

"I don't know—less than an hour ago, I think. I forgot to look at the clock."

"Papa—Papa!" the boy cried, thrashing wildly against Adrian.

"Shhhhh. When did he drink last?"

"When he took the medicine, though he didn't much wish to. I had to keep at him to get all of it down."

"Papa!" Suddenly Justin's body arched violently, then went rigid.

"Get me more water and a cloth, then pull the bell cord, and for God's sake, hurry!" Laying the boy on the bed, Adrian forced his body flat, then held his twitching limbs down with his own. "Where the hell is Bascombe?"

"He ought to be coming—I pulled the bell cord myself," she said, running for the door.

"The water, Jo!"

She came back to pick up the pitcher. Her hands shook as she poured its contents into the shallow basin. She found a clean, folded cloth, then handed both to him.

"Hold him down, will you?" he ordered curtly. Scooping the water from the basin with his bare hands, he splashed it over Justin's body, soaking his nightshirt. Reaching across the child, he picked up the paper he'd left on the stand earlier, and he began fanning vigorously with it. "Got to cool him down," he muttered.

"It's as though he's on fire." Dipping the cloth into the basin with one hand, he awkwardly turned Justin's head to the side with the other. "I've got to get some water into him, but I don't want him to strangle on it."

Joanna moved to the other side of the bed to help by lifting her son's head slightly, while Adrian pried his clenched jaws open and forced a corner of the dripping cloth into his mouth. "You've got to drink, Justin—you've got to try to drink. Come on, try—for Papa, try," he urged. The boy gagged and fought him, flailing wildly, turning his head away. Fighting tears, Joanna stroked his hair, whispering, "Just a little, Justin—just a little. Do what Papa asks." This time, when Adrian got the wet towel into his mouth, Justin sucked feebly. Water trickled from the corners of his mouth, then he began swallowing it.

Adrian repeated the process over and over until Justin finally pushed his hand away. Laying the boy back against the pillows, he looked up at Joanna. "He's calmer now, so I think we've done some good." Dipping the cloth into the water again, he wrung it out and wiped Justin's forehead. "If I thought he could swallow it, I'd try to get some more of the powder down him. Maybe if he got enough of it, this fever would break. But I don't think he could drink it from a cup."

"I told you—I gave him some last hour."

"Maybe you didn't give him enough."

She picked up the vial and held it up to a candle. "There's some left. Perhaps if we did not try to make him drink it, if we just put it on his tongue . . ."

He shook his head. "It's too bitter. I don't know how you've managed to get as much as you have down him."

"He fights me every time, but right now, I don't think he'd even know what it was. I think he's too confused to know anything, Dree."

Looking down on his son, he felt desperate, but he couldn't let her know how afraid he was. They had so little time—Bascombe had predicted the crisis at any time now. Even as he watched, Justin's arms and legs tremored again, then his whole body was racked with violent spasms.

"Dree!"

"Give me the medicine and go for Bascombe yourself," he said as calmly as he could.

"He's convulsing!"

"The medicine, Jo!" Reaching to take the vial from her, he all but shouted, "Go on, get Bascombe—now, Jo, now!"

Joanna watched with alarm as her son's eyes rolled when Adrian lifted him. She stumbled blindly into the hall and shouted, "Dr. Bascombe! Dr. Bascombe! Please, dear God, won't somebody help us!"

Doors opened above in the servants' quarters and feet stampeded in the hall as everyone seemed to take up the call. "Dr. Bascombe! Come quickly—it's the young master!" Mrs. Johnson, disheveled from sleep and heedless of her nightrail, pounded on the physician's door.

"There, there now, madam," Blake soothed as Joanna leaned against the doorjamb and wept openly. "Mrs. Johnson's rousing him."

"My son is dying, Blake—I know it." She'd finally put her worst fear into words. "My son is dying, and I can do nothing to stop it! I'm accursed, Blake—everything I love is taken from me!"

Alarmed by the outburst, the valet caught her and shook her. "Now, now, you cannot know it—the doctor's coming, my lady."

She seemed to crumple in his arms, her face contorted hideously in the faint lantern light, and she sagged against him, weeping into the shoulder of his hastily wrapped robe.

"Joanna, whatever—?" Lady Anne emerged from a chamber down the hall and ran barefoot to them. One glimpse of her daughter-in-law told the tale. "Oh, my dear—no!"

Blake hastily pushed the weeping Joanna into the countess's arms and joined Mrs. Johnson in rousing Dr. Bascombe. The good doctor, still befuddled from a sound sleep, finally opened the door. "Here now! What's the bother?" he demanded testily as he tried to focus on all the people gathered in the hallway.

"It's Justin," Anne told him succinctly. "I fear he is worse."

Adrian didn't even hear the commotion. He pried Justin's jaws open and emptied the bitter powder directly into his mouth. The boy retched almost by reflex, then fought wildly, flailing and jerking his arms. Dipping the cloth into the water again, Adrian tried to get it into his mouth again, but Justin's head twisted and bobbed, making the task nearly impossible. Even as he imprisoned Justin's flailing arms against him with a tight embrace, he ordered sternly, "Drink for Papa—you've got to swallow for Papa! Can you hear me, Justin? You've got to get this down!"

As he entered the room, Bascombe saw that the boy convulsed. All business now, he shouted his own orders to the staff that hovered behind him. "Get me a tub of water! Make it cold water!" To Adrian, he barked out, "Hold him down—don't let him harm himself any more than necessary, my lord!"

"If I hold him any tighter, he's going to break something," Adrian muttered back. In desperation, he lay down beside his son, imprisoning the small body with his arms. "You are all right, Justin—you are all right," he told the child over and over. "I'm not going to let you go."

It seemed that the small boy had the strength of a

man as he thrashed wildly, mindlessly, against Adrian. "Papa! Papa!" he screamed out. "Mamaaaaaa!"

Joanna ran back into the room and scrambled onto the other side of the bed. "Mama's here, love," she managed, her voice breaking.

"Hold him, Jo!" Adrian ordered. "Don't let him hurt himself!"

She rolled against her son, wrapping her legs around his and pressing him between her and Adrian. The bed rocked with his violent thrashing. "Justin!" she pressed his head against her breast. "Try to lie still—try to lie still for Mama!"

"The water's ready, Your Grace," Blake announced from behind the bathing screen.

"Water?"

"We've got to plunge him into it, my lord," Bascombe explained. "We've got to stop the convulsions, else he is lost."

"He'll take a chill!"

"It's the only way left to us to bring that fever down, my lord."

Adrian rolled off the bed, scooped up the bucking boy, and thrust him, splints, nightshirt and all, into the cold water. As he ducked Justin's head underwater, the boy grasped wildly for the side of the tub, then he came up screaming, "Papa! Papa!"

"Papa's here," Joanna murmured from behind Adrian. "Papa's holding your hand, dearest."

Adrian gripped the small hand and held on. "That's the ticket—just sit still and let the water cool you down." Slowly, the violent tremors subsided, and the boy began to shake from the chill. "I just hope to God he doesn't get an inflammation of his lungs from this," he told Bascombe.

"Just now, Your Grace, that is the least of my concerns. But you've done just as you ought, for the water's got to take the heat from his body."

Joanna, her eyes brimming with tears, began dipping the cool water over Justin, letting it run down over his head. He sputtered and floundered in the tub, trying to duck away from her. His eyes flew open, and he tried to focus them. "Papa?" He looked in bewilderment at Adrian, who still held his hand. "Where's my papa?"

"He'll be back," Adrian promised him.

"But he was here!"

Joanna and Adrian exchanged helpless glances and then she dropped down closer to her son. "Papa had to leave, dearest, but you must not worry—he was here when you needed him, after all."

Turning to Blake, Bascombe noted, "The convulsions have passed for now—we'd best get him out and dried off, Mr. Blake."

"Let me do that for Your Grace," Blake offered. "'Tis unseemly for you to do this."

"Nonsense," Adrian retorted. "He is, after all, my—" He stopped short, unable to finish the sentence. "Well, I don't mind it, and I'm already more than half-soaked."

"Let me help you, Dree," Joanna cut in quickly to smooth the awkwardness of the situation. "Mrs. Johnson, if you will but see to clean linens on the bed, we'll have him ready to get back in it in a trice."

Together she and Adrian dried Justin, put him into a fresh nightshirt, and tucked him between clean sheets. He was feverish still, but by no means as hot as he had been. For a long moment, they stood there watching as he drifted back to a calmer sleep.

"He's better now, Jo," he said finally. The relief he felt was so overwhelming he wanted to shout it.

"Yes—yes, he is," she agreed softly. Looking up through tear-drenched lashes, she managed a smile. "Thank you."

"Well," Bascombe said, obviously relieved himself, "I'd say he's better—at least for the time being." Leaning over Justin, he felt the boy's forehead with the back of his hand, then he nodded. "At least the fever's manageable for now."

"I gave him some of Goode's powder just before you came in," Adrian admitted.

"And I'd given him some of it an hour earlier," Joanna added. "I hope we haven't overdosed him."

"Overdosing him is the least thing to consider right now," Bascombe told them. "Too much could affect his hearing, or so some of my colleagues believe, but the alternative is unthinkable. No, one cannot deny its efficacy when properly used—stuff comes from the bark of a tree grown in the Andes Mountains. One of the few useful things the Spaniards have given us, I'd have to say. Now, if the apothecaries could just take the bitter taste out of it, we'd all be prescribing it for everything from the ague to pneumonia. As it is, I've found the taste a fair cure for hypochondria in bored females," he admitted, smiling slightly. "Yes, well, now that he is peaceful for the time being at least, I should like to go back to bed. You are, of course, to waken me if this happens again, Lady Carew."

"You needn't worry on that head, I assure you," she said, betraying a trace of asperity. "I was frightened half out of my wits and so was Roxbury."

"You look haggard, the both of you," Anne told them. "I know you won't go far, but you ought to at least walk a bit. I'll stay, and if there's any change, particularly for the worse, I'll send for you. You both need air after this."

"No." Joanna shook her head. "I want to be with him."

"So do I," Adrian agreed grimly.

"As I have already said, the nights are always the

worst," Dr. Bascombe observed to the dowager countess, "so perhaps it is better if his mother stays. I suspect
the crisis is imminent, if it is not just past. Perhaps you
would rather sit with him in the morning," he offered
not unkindly.

If it is not just past. The words penetrated Joanna's
mind, giving her a surge of hope. She looked up to see
if Adrian had heard them. He had. Their eyes met, betraying mutual gratitude. "Thank you, Dree," she whispered again. It seemed as though she had something
else to thank him for every day now.

"Well, it does not appear efficacious that all of us
should be standing here in the middle of the night, does
it?" Anne managed through her own mist of tears.
Planting a soft kiss on Joanna's cheek, she murmured,
"Wake me if you need me, my love."

"I do not believe there's anything more to be done
just now, Your Grace," Bascombe declared. "But as I
told Lady Carew, I shall be at your call."

"Yes, of course."

After everyone else had filed out, Adrian sank into
the wing chair and leaned back, drained by the intensity
of what had just passed. Closing his eyes, he told her,
"You really should lie down for an hour or two, Jo. If
you cannot rest on the day couch, you can take my
bed."

"As if I could sleep anywhere," she retorted. Instead,
she pulled up a chair next to his and sat.

For a long time, both were quiet, each lost in his own
thoughts. On the bed, Justin had settled into a deep,
even sleep. The clock ticked away, measuring the night
with its steady cadence. Finally, after a time, Adrian
roused himself to ask quietly, "Why did he love Gary
so?"

She gave a start at the suddenness of the question and

then appeared to consider the answer. "Because Gary loved him best," she admitted quietly.

"I don't understand."

She sighed. "He was born so soon after the scandal, Dree, and the resemblance between you, even from the beginning, was so striking that he could have doubled for you. At first, I could scarce bear to look at him, but Gary, thankfully, did not harbor such bitterness." She looked over at the bed for a long moment. "Perhaps God punishes me now for what I did not want."

"Nonsense, Jo. You fairly dote on the boy."

"Now. But sometimes I wonder if he did not somehow know that at first Gary wanted him more than I did."

A sense of desolation washed over him. He owed Gareth Sherwood so much, but he'd never have the chance to repay him. Without thinking, he wondered aloud, "Did he think Justin was his, perhaps? Before he was born, I mean. Could he have thought so before he saw him?"

"He knew he could not be," she answered almost absently. "No, he loved Justin because he loved you."

"And you."

"Yes."

"But surely he wanted Robin to be his heir."

"He did not care about that. His only regret was that we could not bring Justin back to England because of the resemblance to you. 'Duke's Double,' he used to call him when we were alone."

He fell silent again, troubled anew by guilt and doubt. There was so much he still wanted to know, but the newfound peace between them was too fragile to risk destroying it by opening old wounds. They shared a charity with each other now, a charity born of a singular interest, and he wanted that to last, even at the expense of his peace of mind.

At a loss for anything further to say on the subject, he
rose and reached to touch Justin's forehead. He did not
know whether it was because he wanted so much for it
to be so, or whether it was real, but he could swear the
boy's skin was not nearly so hot beneath his palm. The
breathing was easier, less labored, that was certain.

"Jo—"

When she didn't answer, he looked back to where she
sat, her expression distant, as though her thoughts were
elsewhere. She had to be as weary as he was, he decided. In the five days she'd been at the Armitage, she'd
had almost no sleep, and he realized with a start that
she looked thinner, more haggard than he'd ever seen
her, even at the trials. And yet she was still incredibly
beautiful. Beyond his own fatigue, he felt tired, so very
tired of struggling within himself, of denying what he
wanted. Tonight, at twenty-nine, he felt incredibly old.
Walking over to the day couch, he picked up the shawl.

"At least one of us should get some sleep, I suppose,"
he said, lying down and stretching out his tall frame.
His feet hung incongruously over the end, and the
shawl did not begin to cover him.

"You might just go to bed."

"And you might just not wake me. This way, I'll hear
if you need me."

"He seems better, don't you think, Dree?"

"Maybe," he answered cautiously.

She moved to the wing chair and prepared for her
lonely vigil. Behind her, she could hear him shifting his
body uncomfortably on the couch, and then she could
tell that he finally slept. He did not snore precisely, but
neither did he sleep noiselessly. The sound of the clock
was magnified with the steady, heavy breathing of ex-
haustion.

She tried not to think of him, to concentrate instead
on her son, but it was an impossible task. If Justin sur-

vived, it would be in no small measure because of Adrian's efforts. He had given unstintingly of his own physical and emotional resources, scarce sleeping, always ready to assist her in caring for Justin. When she thought about it, she had to marvel over the change she had seen in him.

Had anyone ever said that Adrian Delacourt would give himself over to the nursing of a child, his son or no, she would not have believed it possible. But he had. He had destroyed her life once, and yet he had been willing to risk his own to rescue the son they'd made between them. Unwillingly she let her thoughts wander back to memories so painful to recall that she'd kept them locked away in some dark corner of her mind during her long exile.

When Helen had first accused her, Gary had insisted that Adrian was an honorable man, that he would listen to the truth. But she'd been too heartsick to believe it then, too distraught to fight. If Dree believed her capable of betraying him, then she had nothing to tell him. She wasn't going to beg for the trust that should have been hers, she'd told Gary. And yet now that she was older, perhaps a little wiser, she had to wonder if things could have been resolved differently, if she could have spared herself and Gary those years of exile. Even now, when she thought of him, she felt guilty for what she'd cost him. She'd loved him like a brother, like a dear friend, and he'd deserved far more than that. The worst of it, she had to concede, was that she'd been the grand passion of Gareth Sherwood's life.

Now, with the space of six years between her and that awful time, she had to wonder if she should have fought back. But would Adrian have believed her? Would he even believe her now? No, the pain he'd inflicted on her was still too great, and nothing could change that. He'd believed Helen's lies.

And yet there was some small voice in that dark corner that made her blame herself. Had she let her wounded pride rule her? By keeping silent, did she bear at least some of the responsibility for what had happened to Adrian, Gary, and herself? No, she never should have had to answer those charges. If Adrian had loved her, he wouldn't have believed them, no matter what Helen had told him.

Resolutely she leaned over to feel Justin's head, and she gave a start. It was moist beneath her fingertips. As exultation washed through her, he stirred sleepily, then opened clear, dark eyes. "Mama?"

"Oh, dearest!" she cried as she enveloped him against her breast.

"My mouth's dry, Mama," he complained into her chest.

Her pulses racing with excitement, her hands shaking, she poured a cup of water and helped him sit. "Drink slowly, my love," she reminded even as he drained the cup. As she laid him back against the pillows, it came to her that the age of miracles had indeed not passed. "Let me cover you up, lest you take a chill," she said, fussing happily over him.

"Mama?" He lay back weakly, but his mind was obviously clear. "Where's Papa?"

She hesitated, unwilling to open that subject just yet. "Papa is in heaven, Justin," she answered finally.

"But he was here when I needed him." It wasn't a question, but rather a statement of fact.

"Yes, dearest, he was."

Too weak to pursue the matter, he closed his eyes. "I'm glad."

She sat on the edge of the bed, holding his hand for a long time. When at last she was certain that he slept comfortably and that his fever was not coming back up, she stood up. The room was strangely rosy, illuminated now by the rising sun. She went to shake Adrian awake.

Too tired to fathom what she was saying, he merely rolled over and tried to reposition himself on the narrow couch. Not to be denied the sharing of her news, she shook him more insistently.

"Dree!"

"Unnnhhhh . . ."

"Dree!"

"Wh-what?" he murmured sleepily, sitting up.

"He's better."

"Huh?"

"Justin's better, Dree! The fever broke, and he's had a drink."

It sank in slowly. He caught her arm. "You're sure?"

Nodding her head, she smiled through a mist of tears. "He's going to live—I know it. He's not running a fever, Dree. It's not coming back up."

He was awake now. Setting her aside, he lurched toward the bed to touch his son's wet forehead. "We did it, Dree!" she announced gleefully as she caught his elbow. "We did it! Oh, God, thank you, Dree." Overwhelmed by what she felt, she whispered huskily, "I could not have stood this by myself."

"He's not fully mended yet, Jo," he murmured softly, "but I think maybe the crisis has passed." He turned to envelop her in his arms, holding her as tightly as if she were life itself. Burying his face in her fragrant hair, he savored that bittersweet moment of triumph. He was, he realized, hopelessly in love with her. Still. Again. And the hell of it was that she was betrothed to Johnny Barrasford.

Somewhere in the house, a clock struck the hour of four. Adrian lay wide-awake, staring into the blackness, contemplating the terrible muddle he'd made of his life. While still elated about Justin's chances for recovery, he realized that once the boy recovered, he'd have to accept the fact that his role in the boy's life would be a small one, more like that of a godfather than a father. Maybe not even that, for Barrasford would have some say in the matter, and once he got Jo and the boys to Ireland, it was unlikely that he'd want Adrian hovering at his door.

Joanna. God, what a fool he'd been in that quarter, he reflected bitterly. He'd lost the only woman he'd ever loved, ever would love, for that matter, not once but twice. First to Gareth Sherwood and now to Johnny Barrasford. Wounded pride and youthful arrogance had led him to do the unpardonable, and he would have to pay the price for his precipitous divorce for the rest of his life. He needed to face that, and he needed to accept it, but he didn't want to.

He'd cost her everything, she'd said. There'd been a time when he'd wanted it that way, when he'd wanted to punish her and Gary all the way to perdition. When he'd been almost glad to hear that some fool had brandished a pistol in Gary's face, threatening to kill him for committing the crime of adultery. As if full half the *ton* hadn't been guilty of the same thing on a far grander scale, as if most of the gossip hadn't speculated on who was conducting an *affaire de l'amour* with whom or who had fathered some titled lady's latest brat. He'd not wanted to be played for a fool back then, but in perhaps the cruelest jest of fate, he'd done it to himself. He, not Gary, had fathered Justin by his own wife.

He wasn't even sure there'd been an affair anymore. Gary had tried to deny it at the time, of course, but Joanna had said nothing. He could still close his eyes and see the look on her face when he'd accused her, only now that look accused him. He couldn't even fault Gary for his halfhearted attempt to defend her, for Gary had always loved Joanna, and Adrian's charges against her had only driven her into his arms.

What fools these mortals be. The bard had the right of that. He was at least a dozen ways a fool, all right. He'd moved heaven and earth and even Parliament to shed his supposedly wayward wife, and now he'd do anything he could to get her back. But he was six years too late.

The summer night was hot, the room stifling, and his thoughts gave him no peace. Unable to stand it anymore, he flung back the covers, got up, and threw on enough clothes to decently get himself downstairs. What he needed more than anything was to get out of this room. Everywhere he looked, there lurked enough memories to make his body ache for her. If he couldn't sleep, he might as well retreat to his study and obliterate that ache with a good bottle of wine. He hadn't had a drink since Justin's accident, he reminded himself.

The silence was overwhelming, eerie almost, as he let himself out of the bedchamber into the dark hall. The candle he carried flickered from the faint breeze that blew in from the open window by the grand staircase. Barefooted, he padded noiselessly down the steps, across the marble-floored foyer, into the small bookroom, his private retreat off the Armitage's much-vaunted library. For four hundred years, his ancestors had collected the written treasures of a kingdom, but now most of those books rested in locked cases, too priceless to be read. It was a waste, but Delacourt pride had kept them there.

He lit a brace of candles from the one he'd carried down, then he poured himself a large glass of Madeira and sat down to contemplate the portrait of Richard de la Court, the noble ancestor who'd founded his line here. Hawk-nosed Richard stared haughtily down, his dark eyes piercing anyone who viewed him. Dressed in full armor with his plumed helmet tucked in the crook of his arm, Richard had a fierce aspect to him. Adrian lifted his glass to the old warrior, then he downed the Madeira.

"Dree, what are you doing up at this hour?"

He looked up. Joanna stood in the shadows just beyond the open door, an apparition in her white lawn nightrail. Light from the candle stub played upon her lovely face.

"I could ask the same of you."

"I was too exhilarated to sleep."

"How is Justin?"

She stepped inside. "He has a fever again, but it is not nearly so high. Dr. Bascombe has hopes that we saw the worst tonight."

"I'm glad."

"I can never thank you enough for what you did for him," she said quietly. "I just seem to keep repeating it, but it's true. I know he wouldn't be alive were it not for you."

"I don't want gratitude," he declared flatly. "He's my son, Jo. The Sherwood name . . . taking him to Ireland . . . nothing can change that. Even if I never see him once he is recovered, he's still mine." He took a deep drink of his Madeira before he looked up again. "For me, watching him struggle to live was like being there for his birth. It made me wish I'd been there from the beginning."

"Dree—"

"You know if you'd told me—"

"What would you have done?—waited until he was born to divorce me? And what if he'd looked like me rather than you?" she asked wearily. "I don't want to discuss this anymore. You cannot sweep the water back across the bridge."

"No." He eyed her for a long moment, then said, "You are not entirely without blame yourself. You let me believe you and Gary were lovers."

"No, I didn't let you believe anything. Your mother did that. It was you who did not believe in me. Or in Gary, for that matter. You didn't ask, you know—you accused. I deserved better than that, Dree." She glanced at the empty glass in his hand, then at the bottle. "I'd best be getting back upstairs, I expect. I just came down to warm myself some milk, but the stove is cold. I decided not to light it."

"You should have wakened a maid for that."

Her eyebrow lifted. "At this hour? The poor girl would love me for that, wouldn't she? But then I don't suppose a man of your consequence thinks of such things, does he?" Moving closer, she smiled faintly. "Unlike you, I was reared in a ramshackle household where the maids were turned off regularly so my father could avoid paying them. Being an 'impecunious baron,' as your mother was wont to call him, he wasn't nearly as high in the instep as you. We learned to do things for ourselves."

"I remember he was never home. I used to think you were an orphan," he recalled.

"I suppose I might as well have been. He was always selling something, then going off to London in hopes of parlaying the money into a fortune in some gaming hall or other. He always lost, you know."

"He won enough to give you a Season."

"No, that was my Aunt Ephingham. She came to visit once, told him I should make his fortune, and persuaded him to give permission for her to take me to London. I don't suppose you remember my come-out dress?"

"It was white tissue gauze over a white satin slip—it had tiny pink flowers embroidered on the skirt. And you carried some posy from an admirer."

"I'm astounded," she admitted. "In any event, it was remade from my aunt's second daughter Sophie's gown. The posy we bought ourselves at a stall in St. James. But never having heard of Madame Cecile, I thought I was quite grand, anyway."

"You were, Jo. I remember every minute of that night. I danced four country dances with you, didn't I?"

"Scandalously. And you cast my aunt in transports. While we were outside taking the air in her garden, she had everyone believing you meant to come up to scratch that very night."

"As I recall it, I did."

"Yes. I was never so giddy in all my life," she admitted. "I was in alt for weeks."

"So was I."

"Yes, well—" she said, recovering. "That was a very long time ago, and I don't know how it happened to come up tonight."

"Memories. We've got quite a lot of them. We had a year together, and I remember—"

"It doesn't signify now, anyway, does it?" she said quickly, interrupting him. "We've had two entirely separate lives since that night, and the bridge between those lives is gone. I suspect we're just being maudlin because Justin is better." She sucked in her breath, then let it go. "Yes—well, I daresay I'd best be getting back upstairs," she said again.

"Don't go, Jo. We cried friends through this, didn't we?" he reminded her.

"It was more like a truce, Dree." Still, she made no move to go. "We had Justin to think of."

"Here—let me pour you some of this," he offered. "It'll help you sleep, I promise you." Holding up the bottle, he declared, "The best Madeira ever made." Rising, he went to get her a glass from the Elizabethan sideboard. On his way back, he opened the latticed doors to the small private garden, and the warm breeze carried the fragrance of the flowers inside. "I thought it rather stuffy in here," he explained, filling the glass. "Go on—taste it."

She took a sip, then nodded. "It's quite good." Drawing another deep breath, she savored it. "It's a lovely night, isn't it? Now that Justin seems so much better, I don't even feel tired anymore."

"It feels a bit warm to me. But since all's right with the world just now, I won't complain." Looking over the rim of his glass, he said, "I don't think I would have known how to console you if he hadn't survived. You've lost too much in this life."

"I'd rather not think about it now."

"You know, I remember the first time Gary and I saw you. Your governess was looking furtively this way and that, afraid she'd be caught out, and you were tripping blythely along behind her with your dress pulled up to keep it out of the water. We had you marked for a shameless little hoyden."

"And you were the bully, as I recall," she countered. "No matter what we played, you were the leader, even though you and Gary were of an age."

"I was always bigger."

"It was a good place to grow up, wasn't it?" she said suddenly. "We had such good times when we were children—or at least I did. I'd forgotten so much until I started showing Justin where we played. That's when he got lost, you know." Her mouth twisted wryly. "You were terribly angry that day."

"Furious. I almost didn't stop when I heard the boy. And then when I saw him—my God, Jo, there are no words to describe my thoughts." Seeing that she'd drunk almost half of her Madeira, he leaned forward to fill the glass again. "It was a shock."

"Yes, I expect so." Abruptly changing the subject, she looked up at the portrait. "You have to wonder what he was like, don't you?"

Feeling rather mellow now, Adrian leaned back in his chair to study the picture. "I expect he had a lot of blood on his hands. Back then, kings rewarded loyalty on the battlefield. And considering that he was nearly landless when he began what must've been a stellar military career, he had to have been rather ruthless, I'd think. Whatever he did, it gained him the heiress who brought him part of this land."

"Maybe he was somewhat like William the Marshal, whose honor was never called into question by anyone."

"England's greatest knight?" He eyed Richard de la Court again, then shook his head. "No, I think ruthless describes him far better. Look at those eyes."

"Actually, they remind me of yours."

"I rest my case."

As they sipped the strong wine, they fell into a contemplative silence, each lost in his own thoughts for a time. In the semidarkness, he studied her, thinking how very beautiful she was, how he'd never seen any female to compare with her. She had her hair down, and the breeze lifted the damp tendrils that framed her face. His gaze dropped lower to the fine lace that edged the neck of her nightgown and followed it down, noting the top buttons were undone, revealing the pale skin, the crevice dipping between her breasts. The rush of desire overwhelmed him, drying his mouth, making his pulse race. Tearing his eyes away, he rose and walked to the open doors. A hundred stars dotted the ink-black sky.

She could feel the tenseness between them, and she knew she ought to leave. Instead, she set down her glass and followed him. "It is an incredibly lovely night for England, isn't it?" she observed softly. "It reminds me somewhat of Capri."

"I was thinking of your come-out." He took a deep breath, then exhaled it. He could feel her nightgown billow, brushing at his legs. He closed his eyes, trying to master his lust. But it was as though even the wind whispered to him, reminding him of how it had been to love her, and every fiber of his being was on fire with the memory of her touch.

She looked up at him as the breeze ruffled his thick hair, and she was struck again by how handsome he was. He had the profile of a Greek god and a body to match. As she studied him, he opened his eyes. "I remember everything, Jo," he said, his voice hoarse with his desire. "Do you remember how it felt when I loved you?"

She had to close her eyes to hide from him. "Yes," she whispered. "How could I ever forget?"

"God, Jo, I want to feel that again. More than anything, I want to feel that again."

She heard him move closer, felt the heat of his body

touching hers, and she wanted to know every inch of that body again. But some small voice of sanity reminded her it was wrong. "I can't, Dree," she cried, breaking from his embrace. Backing away from him, she whispered, "Don't do this to me, please," then she turned and ran into the garden, where she crossed her arms over her breasts. Her eyes seemed enormous in her pale face.

He caught up to her and grasped her elbows. "Don't do this to you?—no, don't do this to me," he said, his voice rising. "'Twas you who came down in naught but that thin gown," he reminded her. "'Twas you who gave life to my memory, Jo."

"But I can't—"

Her words died in the crush of his arms, in the hunger of his kiss, and she was drowning in her own desire. Forgetting all else, she yielded to the force of his passion, and they were wrapped in breathless embrace. His mouth was hot, searing hers, as his hands eagerly moved over her body, tracing fire. A flood of pent-up need washed the last vestiges of resistance away as she answered every kiss, every touch with her own. She wanted everything he could do to her tonight. As his lips left hers to trail fiery kisses from her ear to the hollow beneath her throat, her small cry of protest dissolved into a yielding moan. "Let me love you again," he whispered hoarsely, lowering her into the soft bed of moss.

They were a tangle of arms and legs, but as his lips sought hers again, the thought that she was an utter fool died as it was formed, and suddenly nothing beyond the man above her mattered anymore. Her hands grasped his shoulders, pulling him to her, demanding more. His hand slid over the thin nightdress, gathering it up, exposing the bare skin beneath as her twisting body eagerly urged him on. His fingers touched her hot thighs, then slipped between them, finding the wetness there. She answered him by unfastening his buttons, releasing him. And as his mouth found hers, she guided his manhood inside her.

Beneath him, she writhed and bucked shamelessly as he drove himself mindlessly into her. Her nails dug through his shirt into his back as she strained against him, seeking all he had to give her. Caught in his own primordial rhythm, he barely heard her crescendo of moans, the piercing cry as he felt himself explode in release deep within her. And then he was floating, panting to catch his breath as he collapsed over her. It felt as though her body had carried him home. Sated now, he smoothed her wet hair away from her temples.

"God, how I have missed you," he whispered huskily against her ear.

She lay silent beneath him, her eyes closed, listening to the rapid beat of his heart, to his labored breath. The damp, musty fragrance of the moss mingled with that of a hundred flowers as she came back to earth. As the intensity of physical union faded, she realized what she'd done.

Sensing the change in her, he rolled off of her to stare up at the star-filled sky. Her silence cut into him like a knife.

"You're sorry, aren't you?" he asked finally.

Mortified now, she pulled her gown down and sat up, her back to him. "I suppose I behaved like the whore you thought me. The widow who cannot do without, so to speak," she said, her voice low.

"You were my wife, Jo."

"That was a long time ago, Dree." Pulling herself up by a low branch, she stood over him, rubbing her arms as though she was chilled. "I'd best go in."

He felt empty, bleak. "You were tired unto death—it was the Madeira."

"No." Feeling the trickle of his seed going down her thigh, she turned away from him. "Wine is a weak man's excuse—it cannot make one do something if he doesn't want to," she told him miserably. Smoothing her gown, she tried to regain a measure of dignity as she started inside. "It was foolish to think we could be friends again, Dree," she said, turning back to look at him from the safety of the door.

"Jo—"

"Please do not make anything of this. It was lust— nothing more." Before he could think of any further words of comfort, she fled upstairs.

Before he went down to breakfast, Adrian stopped to look in on Justin. As he entered the room, Anne looked up, smiling. "Dr. Bascombe was just here, and he told Joanna there is no question that the crisis has passed. I gather it will take some time for Justin to regain his strength, but I am so grateful I cannot think whether to laugh or cry."

Immensely relieved, he looked to the sleeping boy, then he asked abruptly, "Where's Jo?"

"Outside, I believe. She seems overset, but I daresay it could be the letdown from Justin's ordeal, don't you think?""

"I don't know. I don't know much of anything anymore."

"Surely both of you cannot have gotten up in the same mood," she said, eyeing him shrewdly. "Having won the battle, you both seem to have been afflicted with a bout of the blue devils."

"I don't know what it is—a lack of sleep, perhaps," he lied.

"Yes, well, at least you will not have Barrasford to contend with for a few days as he has gone home to pack. He's leaving tomorrow for someplace called Baxter Greys."

"Oh?"

"His godfather died, I believe. The news seems to

have upset Miss Finchley, too," she observed mildly. "I collect her whole family knew him rather well, you know, and I believe her sister is married to Barrasford's godfather's cousin. Quite a small world, isn't it?" When he said nothing, she observed, "I think it would be a good thing if the poor girl attended the funeral, too, don't you? She is more than a trifle homesick, and both of her sisters still live in that little village."

"She'd have to take a maid with her. I suppose we could spare Bess for a few days."

"And if Joanna does not mind it, I can send to Haven for a mourning dress for the funeral—and for some suitable traveling clothes also. I'm sure she won't begrudge them to Miss Finchley."

He eyed the dowager countess shrewdly for a long moment. "You really wish Miss Finchley to go, don't you?"

"It isn't that I wish it precisely, but I do think we owe it to her," she answered, smiling slyly. "After all, she *has* been so very kind and helpful with Robin in these trying times that I am sure I don't know what we would have done without her. Indeed, but she and Barrasford have kept him quite busy with those toy soldiers. And I do think that since Justin appears to be improving, I could entertain Robin myself."

"What does Jo think?"

"I haven't broached the matter yet, nor have I asked Barrasford if he would take the girl up, but I mean to do both, I think. I was just wondering what you thought of the notion."

"She's in Joanna's employ, not mine."

"I collect you must have quarreled," she said mildly.

"Lady Anne—"

"Well, I suppose one interfering mama is enough for one lifetime, isn't it?"

"Yes."

"She hasn't eaten a thing this morning—not so much as a cup of chocolate."

"Miss Finchley or Jo?"

"Joanna. She said she did not feel much like breakfast."

He moved closer to the bed to look at Justin. When he reached out to touch the boy's forehead, he found it warm. "He's still got some fever," he said, frowning.

"You will recall Bascombe warned us of that." Coming up behind him, Anne murmured, "You've surprised me greatly, Roxbury. I own I'd never thought you would come to love him like this. I thought perhaps it was your vanity that made you send Mr. Thorne to see Joanna."

"At the time, I expect it was. But now I have so many regrets on that head," he admitted. "I wish I'd been there from the beginning."

"Yes, I expect you do."

"Gary really loved him, didn't he?" he murmured. "At first, part of me did not believe that, you know. But I do now, and I'm glad for it. Believe me, it is no easy thing growing up as nothing more than a necessary inconvenience," he acknowledged. "I doubt I had a thousand pleasant words with my own father in the first twenty-four years of my life."

"He was Gareth's firstborn son, Adrian. He doted on him from the first time he held him."

There was an awkward silence between them, then he said abruptly, "If you wish to let Miss Finchley go, I'll help you with the other boy."

"That 'other boy,' as you call him, is Robin—Robert, actually. And I think you'll find him an engaging little fellow once you get to know him. Alas, once he is in Ireland, you won't have much opportunity to do so, I fear."

It was another reminder that Joanna intended to

marry Johnny. "I don't see how I can help that," he said wearily. "I can't very well hold them hostage here."

"No, of course not. But I want what's best for my grandsons, Adrian—both of them. And Joanna, too, of course. Now, while you are about it, I wish you would see that Joanna eats something," she said as he reached for the doorknob. "I worry a great deal about her, too. She is, after all, the daughter I never had. I was a widow at three and twenty, you know, else I should have had a houseful of children myself."

"You should have married again."

"Alas, but there was only one great love in my life, and I fear it is the same with Joanna, if she could ever bring herself to admit it. But she won't, of course. In her own way, she is as stubborn as you are."

"Wait—" As she half turned back to face him, he said, "If you wish to send Miss Finchley off in style to visit her relations, you'd best see that she does something with that hair. Tell Bess to cut it for her."

"I shall. And as she is not actually in mourning herself, I think perhaps something green for traveling. With hazel eyes, green is quite becoming, you know. But we are wasting time discussing Miss Finchley, aren't we? If I were you, I should look to Joanna."

He found her in the walled garden, sitting on a stone bench not fifteen feet from the bed of moss, looking utterly haunted. If she heard him close the gate, she gave no sign. He stood there, studying her fine profile for a long moment.

"What are you going to tell Barrasford?" he asked finally.

"I don't know. How does one tell someone he was mistaken in her character?" she countered dully. "That I am the whore everybody thinks me?"

"Jo—"

"No, don't come any closer. My head throbs like a drum this morning."

"You don't have to tell him anything. It isn't like you are supposed to be a virgin."

"Please don't."

"The *ton* is full of free-favored women, and none of them pay a price for it."

"Coming from you, that's rich, Dree."

"He doesn't have to know. You aren't even wed yet, so you cannot be accused of playing him false." Sitting down beside her, he leaned forward to place his elbows on his knees. "I shouldn't have given you the wine. The fault was mine, not yours."

"Until last night, there'd been no•one since Gary," she said low.

He could almost feel her misery. "You don't love him, do you? Barrasford, I mean." When she didn't answer him immediately, he pressed her. "If you can say you do, Jo, I'll wish you happy and leave it at that."

"He is incredibly kind. Like Gary, he wished to stand up for me when no one else would."

"Is that enough for you?" he asked harshly.

"It has to be. I cannot cry off—I just cannot."

"I see." He'd had his answer, and it wasn't to his liking. She was still going to marry Johnny. "Your mother-in-law says you haven't breakfasted yet, and neither have I."

"I'm not hungry."

"Come on, let's go in and eat something. We just had too much wine last night, that's all. It wouldn't have happened otherwise."

"I wish I could believe that, Dree. It would make facing Johnny so much easier if I had something to blame besides myself."

He drew in a deep breath, then exhaled it heavily. "Blame me."

"No."

"For what 'tis worth to say it, I won't take advantage of you again." Rising, he held out his hand. "I know what you said last night, but I'm asking you to cry friends again, Jo—at least until Justin is recovered enough to leave the Armitage. Come on—we've more important things to do than feel sorry for ourselves. We've got a son who's still a long way from well."

"Oh, dear ma'am, but I couldn't!" Charlotte Finchley protested. "I mean, the children—"

"You are not to worry on that head," Anne reassured her. "I am perfectly capable of entertaining my grandsons for two or three days."

"Yes, but—" The younger woman drew a deep breath, then exhaled it before admitting, "I've no wish to go home a poor relation, my lady. And I cannot think Lord Barrasford is wishful of being burdened with me, even for so short a time."

"He does not mind at all," Anne declared dismissively. "Indeed, when I asked it of him, he assured me it would be no trouble to take you and Bess up with him as he is going there, anyway."

"But—"

"And you need not worry about looking like a poor relation either, my dear, for Joanna has dresses to spare. Indeed, Bess has laid out several for you to try on."

"But why—?"

"Well, for one thing, your devotion to Justin and to Robin has not gone unnoted, and I must say we are most grateful for it. I am sure we could not have managed without you. Bess," she said, gesturing for the maid, "you will help Miss Finchley choose suitable clothes for her trip to Baxter Greys." To Charlotte, she added, "While the black gloves may be de rigueur while you are there, you can most certainly wear color in your gowns. I think perhaps something green—Bess, Lady Carew's green traveling dress, if you please—the one with the black braid frogs. It has quite a dashing shako hat that matches it. But of course, you will need to crop those curls, else it will perch atop them like a monkey's cap, and short hair is all the rage, anyway. We'll just frame the face a bit, don't you think?"

"Aye, my lady."

"But I don't—dear ma'am, what is Lord Barrasford to think?" Charlotte asked anxiously. "I would not for the world have him think I've rigged myself up to cast lures at him. He's certainly going to know I cannot afford such luxury for myself."

"If you wish, I will make it plain that we wish to see you visit your family in a style fitting your birth, not your circumstances. Indeed, but I know not what we would have done without you here, my dear."

"I would not for the world have him think the wrong thing."

"Your scruples are admirable, but unnecessary in this instance," Anne assured her. "Unlike Lord Rivington, Lord Barrasford is a gentleman in every sense of the word."

"You know about Lord Rivington?" Charlotte asked, horrified.

"Well, I surmised from Lady Rivington's recommendation that there must have been a problem—oh, no— not with you, my dear. Let us just say Joanna and I have a passing acquaintance with his lordship, enough to know how awkward it must have been for you to live in his house."

"Dear ma'am, I could not turn around without encountering him. It was a most uncomfortable situation, believe me. And before that I was employed by Lady Miltower, whose husband was very nearly as difficult as Lord Rivington. You cannot know what a joy it is to teach in a household where there is no gentleman forever pinching or clinching at one. I'd begun to despair of ever finding a position like this."

"It is the bane of being both pretty and at an employer's mercy," Anne murmured sympathetically.

"Well, I am just hopeful of being asked to accompany the boys to Ireland," Charlotte confessed. "I do so enjoy them."

"I have every hope that you will be going to Ireland, my dear. But it is much more to the point now to see that you are ready to leave for Baxter Greys when Lord Barrasford arrives to take you up. A gentleman, even a good one, does not like to be kept waiting."

"Yes, of course. Dear ma'am, I can never repay you or Lady Carew for such kindness."

"Ah, but you already have. Now—the green traveling dress—and the navy twilled silk, of course. The grey muslin will do for the funeral, I think, and the bronze carriage dress for the journey back. That leaves the blue figured muslin—and the peach sprigged one—for day dresses."

"Will she be dressing for dinner, ma'am?" Bess wanted to know.

"My sisters live rather modestly," Charlotte answered.

"Yes, but just in case you are invited somewhere, I think perhaps the green gauze," Anne suggested judiciously.

"But I shall have need of a whole trunk."

"One should always contrive to look one's best, my dear."

"But everyone will know I cannot afford—"

"Hush. Let them think you have come into a competence."

"I shudder at what they are more like to think."

"These are not the gowns of a Cyprian, if that is your meaning. Indeed, but they are all quite modest when one considers the current mode. No, indulge an old woman, my child, and I think you will be most pleased with the result."

"I hope so—I devoutly hope so," Charlotte told her. "I would not for the world give Lord Barrasford a bad impression of me."

"Well, I shall leave you and Bess to get you ready. I collect Lord Barrasford means to leave shortly after nuncheon in order to make Harby by nightfall. I forget what it is that Harby is noted for, but I daresay I shall recall it later."

"Maid Marian was said to be born there," Charlotte said, smiling.

"Was she now? How very interesting, to be sure." Rising from her chair by the window, Anne glided toward the door, where she stopped to look back. "My dear, I hope you know you have earned this for your devotion to my grandsons. I just wish the circumstances of your going home could have been happier. But at least you will arrive in style, and you will no doubt have a pleasant coze with your sisters."

"Thank you, ma'am."

"No, it is I who must thank you, my dear. Oh, I almost forgot—since I am quite sure that Lord Barrasford is too much the gentleman to let you pay your way, I have taken the liberty of giving him thirty pounds for your expenses."

"Thirty pounds!"

"If that should not prove to be enough, I hope you will tell me when you return."

"My lady, I do not know what to say—that is—"

"Nonsense. Do try to have as pleasant a time as possible, my dear. I'm sure you will be the envy of half of that little village."

As the image of Lord Barrasford crossed her mind, Charlotte did not doubt it. But it would be a bittersweet triumph, for a man like Barrasford, even if he were free to do so, would never look twice at a mere governess. Nor could she allow him to, for he was betrothed to her employer. No, even if she were an heiress, she couldn't compete with the beautiful Joanna for anyone's affections.

The carriage barreled down the narrow, rutted road, jostling the three occupants, who endured the rough ride in silence. Johnny looked across at the two women.

"It will get better once we reach the post road," he offered.

"Oh, I do not mind this," Charlotte assured him. "Indeed, but I am just glad enough of the chance to go home again."

"You look quite fine, you know."

"I beg your pardon?"

"That hat becomes you."

"Oh. Well, thank you, my lord," she answered, smiling shyly.

"You ought to smile more often."

"I shall take that under advisement."

"No, really—I'd not noticed that small dimple before."

"I'm afraid it's always been there."

The feeble attempt at conversation failed and silence descended once more. For a time, Johnny looked out the window at the gentle hills, thinking it was a devil of a time for him to be leaving Joanna at the Armitage. "I don't suppose you've heard how much longer it will be before the boy can be moved?" he said finally.

"I beg—oh, you mean Justin?"

"Yes."

"No, I haven't heard, but I should think another few

weeks—because of the splint, I mean. I believe the doctor wishes him able to get around a bit on it before he will be allowed to travel."

"Oh."

"At least he is much better."

"Yes. I'd just like to see him go back to Haven." Sighing, he admitted, "As long as he's snug at the Armitage, he's not going to like me. With Roxbury hovering near him, I've not got much of a chance."

"Well, when he returns to Haven, I'm sure that will change, my lord. Indeed, how could he not like you? I mean, I find you much more approachable than the duke, and I'm sure the boys will, too. Truth to tell, I think Roxbury too—" She paused, searching for the right word.

"Too what?" he asked eagerly.

"Well, I was going to say overbearing, but that's not quite right, I suppose."

"Arrogant?" he supplied.

"Not arrogant precisely."

"Disagreeable?"

"No. Indeed, he's been nothing but kind, but—well, I don't know how to say it. I suppose it is an assurance born of always getting what one wants. I expect it comes from his being a duke, don't you?"

He smiled. "Not being one, I'm scarce an authority on that, Miss Finchley."

"Oh, I did not mean—that is, I assure you I did not mean to imply—" Coloring, she finally managed rather lamely, "Lord Barrasford, such was not my thought in the least. Indeed, I find you much more preferable to Roxbury." Then, realizing how that must sound, she attempted to remedy the situation. "If I may try to make myself plain, my lord, I meant that if I were Lady Carew, I should count myself much more fortunate to have you than Roxbury—and I am sure she does."

"Thank you."

She looked at her folded hands. "I don't see how she could help feeling that way. He behaved rather abominably to her, didn't he?"

"Very."

"One should never hurt the person one claims to love."

"The romantic Miss Finchley," he murmured.

"If you are laughing at me, I wish you would not. Just because I shall never wed does not mean that I am to have no opinion on the subject surely."

"You are scarce on the shelf, my dear."

"I am four and twenty, my lord, without so much as a feather of expectation, and I am an utter realist about the matter. I accepted the situation with as much grace as I could muster when I discovered my stepfather had squandered Mama's money." Daring to look up at him, she nodded. "And as I quite like children, I have chosen to educate someone else's."

"I'm terribly sorry."

"The last thing I want is anyone's pity, my lord." Her chin came up with surprising defiance. "I am not so weak that I cannot take care of myself."

"No, of course not. It just seems unfortunate that a woman of your breeding must do so." Aware that he was probably making matters worse, he turned the subject back to Joanna and her sons. "What does Justin think of Roxbury?"

"Justin has been too ill to think, my lord. However, I am sure that as he gets better, he cannot help but know it was Roxbury who helped nurse him through his illness."

"Oh."

"Though I do count it somewhat devious that he allowed Justin to believe that he was Carew when the boy was too ill to know otherwise. I'm quite sure that did not please Lady Carew."

"I shouldn't think so."

"And now that Justin is getting well, the duke is trying to make himself agreeable to Robin. Though he is not nearly as popular as you in that quarter, my lord," she reassured him. "Robin has certainly enjoyed those soldiers you brought him—and I must admit, so have I. However, if it were up to me, I should have more of the Gordon Highlanders. You see, one of my mother's grandmothers was a Gordon—of the less prosperous ones, of course, but a Gordon nonetheless."

"Does that make you a relation of Byron's?" he asked, teasing her.

"Distantly, I expect." She stared out the window for a moment, then confessed rather ruefully, "While I cannot condone the licentious life he has led, I must admit I've enjoyed his work."

"Really?"

"I laughed until my sides ached at his satire, 'English Bards and Scots Reviewers.' I don't suppose you happened to read it, did you?"

"No. *Childe Harold's Pilgrimage* was enough for me."

"You didn't like it?"

"I liked it, but then so did everyone else in the world, it would seem. Unlike most of them, however, I didn't think it a biography of Byron."

"I think he just cultivates the image of a dark, tortured soul," she agreed. Intrigued by this brief glimpse into Barrasford's mind, she murmured, "You like poetry, then? Do you have a particular favorite?"

"Thomas Gray. I think his 'Elegy Written in a Country Churchyard' one of the finest pieces committed to the English language."

"How very odd—I do, too, you know. 'The boast of heraldry, the pomp of pow'r. And all that beauty, all that wealth e'er gave, Awaits alike the inevitable hour . . .'"

"'The paths of glory lead but to the grave,'" he said softly, finishing the verse for her.

"When I feel put upon, when I cannot help feeling envious of those whose wealth and titles provide them so much, I find a certain comfort in those words. In the end, the lowest and the highest must share that common fate."

"Inevitably, Miss Finchley. And spoken as a vicar's daughter, I might add."

"Well, if ye was to ask me, I don't want to hear nothing about death," Bess spoke up. "Be bad enough when it gets here without a body sittin' around waitin' for it." Having made that declaration, she added, "And there ain't no doubt in my mind but as the duke's ever' bit as interested in Lady Carew as he is in that boy. Written right on his face, it is."

"Bess—" The warning in Charlotte Finchley's voice was unmistakable.

"Blind if he don't know it," the unrepentant maid said. "Oh, I ain't saying she's interested or anything like that—seems plain enough to me that she ain't. Least not yet."

"Bess, we've both done enough gossiping for today," Charlotte told her severely. "And I'm sure Lord Barrasford has no wish to hear us speculate on such things."

At that, Johnny leaned back against the squabs and momentarily closed his eyes. No, Miss Finchley was wrong about that, he admitted silently to himself. He wanted more than anything to know about Joanna and Roxbury, but it was scarce the sort of thing he could ask about without making a cake of himself.

"Way I see it, His Grace ain't resting until he gets her back," Bess declared.

"That is quite enough." Without thinking, Charlotte

leaned across the seat to touch Johnny's hand. "You must not listen to her, my lord. Circumstances have forced a degree of civility between the duke and Lady Carew, that is all, and any gossip otherwise is undeserved."

He looked down at her hand, its slender fingers neatly covered in black silk. The small, delicate hands of a gentlewoman, he thought. His gaze traveled upward, taking in the demure cut of her green carriage dress, the neat row of black braid frogs going up the bodice, the stand-up military collar, the rich auburn curls that framed the delicate oval face beneath the smart green and black shako hat, and it struck him that she was far too lovely to be a mere governess, that there was no justice in a world that could let that happen to the Reverend Finchley's eldest daughter.

"Is something the matter, my lord?" she asked, peering at him with those large, expressive hazel eyes.

"No." Sitting up, he looked out the carriage window. "I was just thinking that no one in Baxter Greys will recognize you. You don't look much like that wild-haired hoyden I used to see when I visited there."

"There is nothing to say that you must stay cooped up here, particularly not now that Justin is so much better," Anne assured Joanna. "And I would remind you that you do have another son, my love. And with Miss Finchley visiting her relations at Baxter Greys, Robin has the greater need of you."

"But Justin is so restless," Joanna protested.

"As he should be. Really, my dear, but if you persist in coddling him beyond what is necessary, you will spoil him beyond bearing." The older woman crossed the room to where the convalescent Justin sat up in bed, one leg crossed, the other lying straight in its splints. "I have brought cards, dearest," she addressed him, "so that we may while away some time while your mama gets some air."

Despite the mutinous set of his jaw, she sank down on the bed and began to divide the cards. Her eyes twinkled as he reluctantly took up the hand she dealt. "You may go first, my love." As if by afterthought, she spoke over her shoulder to Joanna. "I believe you will find Robin in Roxbury's company somewhere near the stables."

Joanna sighed. She knew she was being managed shamelessly, but she could not dispute the truth of Anne's argument. Justin was infinitely better, for his fever no longer came up at night. He was so much improved, in fact, that Dr. Bascombe had returned to London. Now Justin's pain had been replaced for the most part with boredom. And since that morning when they'd last cried friends, Adrian had been a true gentleman. He no longer even baited her about marrying Johnny.

"Very well, Maman, but I think it incumbent to warn you that he gets out of reason cross when he loses."

"I am not inexperienced in the care and entertainment of young boys, my dear," Anne reminded her firmly. "Out. And do try to get some air, for you are become positively peaked."

Outfaced, Joanna had little choice but to take the older woman's advice. Crossing through to the rose chamber, where she'd removed herself once her son's recovery was assured, she caught her reflection in the dressing-table mirror. She did in truth look a trifle haggard, she had to admit, despite the fact that she now had her own bedchamber and she was getting sufficient sleep. Adrian himself had chosen to move to a guest chamber down the hall, and to her surprise, not even Blake had seemed to think it odd.

She debated momentarily whether she ought to reply to Johnny's last letter, and decided against it. He'd written that since his godfather had left some business for him to attend and Miss Finchley was enjoying her visit with her sisters immensely, he did not expect to be back before the end of the week. Deciding she had no news worth reporting, she hastily dragged a brush through her hair, then she set off to find her younger son.

She did not have far to look, for rather than being in the stables, he and Adrian were trotting toward the house even as she came outside. Robin broke away when he saw her and barreled toward her.

"Mama! 'Bury's taking me fishing!"

"Oh." She shot a questioning glance at the man behind him. "I didn't know you fished anymore."

"It's been a while," he admitted. "But the water's down, and I thought we might catch something just above the ford. Besides, we've already beaten the French three times today."

His face was flushed, probably from chasing after Robin, and his dark hair was rumpled, but the smile he flashed was utterly disarming. She dropped her eyes from his face to where his white cotton shirt stood open at the neck to reveal the dark hair underneath. "That sounds very nice," she managed even as her pulse pounded with an awareness of him.

"Come with us," he asked suddenly. "We'll make a picnic of it." Seeing that she hesitated, he mistook the reason. "Justin's fine. If you keep hovering over him, you'll make a man-milliner out of him." Realizing what he'd just said, he quickly attempted amends. "My apologies, Jo—I should not have said that—you cannot be faulted for being a good mother."

"Please, Mama—say you'll come." Robin's small hand caught at hers and tugged. "Grandmama can stay with 'Tin."

She had to smile at the way he shortened names to a workable length ever since he'd been born. Justin had been 'Tin from the beginning, and now Adrian, whom the countess had insisted was Roxbury, became simply 'Bury to him. She squeezed his hand. "How very odd, but that's exactly what your Grandmama said also, Robin."

"You'll come?" he persisted eagerly.

"Well—I am not at all a fisherman, you know," she admitted as her eyes met Adrian's once again. "But, yes, I'll come." Her heart gave a lurch at his answering grin, a grin that reminded her so much of the boy she'd once known.

"What a whisker, Jo. As I recall, the time was when Gary and I quit taking you with us because you always came back with more than we did. Your mother, Robin, was a capital angler."

"Well, I recall no such thing, my lord, for I never liked having to remove the poor creatures from my hook."

"Yes, but you always kept us busy baiting your hook and taking off your fish. Admit it. Truth to tell, that's probably why we never caught anything ourselves."

"I admit nothing," she answered airily. "Do not believe him for an instant, Robin. He's telling Banbury Tales on Mama."

Her words gave him pause, and the grin faded from his face. Those were the very words she'd used that last day in London. "I admit nothing," she'd said. And he couldn't say he'd gotten much more out of her since.

Robin looked from his mother to the duke and back again. Even at his young age, he could sense the change in mood between them. And his own sunny disposition could not abide it. He dropped her hand and bounded toward Adrian like a puppy eager to please. "Please, 'Bury, can we go now? Finch won't care—she won't."

"Miss Finchley is not here, anyway," Joanna reminded him.

There was so much of Gary in the child that Adrian almost could not bear it. Only the eyes that implored in the small face gave any reminder of Joanna. It crossed his mind that the two people he'd loved the most had made this child. Robin's hand clutched at his thigh.

"'Bury, I want to fish. I want to catch one this big," he said, holding his hands a good two feet apart.

"Then, by all means, let's go." Adrian swung the little boy up and set him on his shoulders. Robin squealed with delight and grasped the thick, black hair for balance. "Ouch! Hold my neck, urchin, else I'll drop you, and then where will you be?"

"I'll have a cracked head."

"Exactly."

Their departure was watched silently from an upper window by Anne, who felt considerable satisfaction. For the first time in her life, she was trying to play matchmaker, and with considerable success, she told herself. While Roxbury was far from perfect, he'd certainly shown himself worthy of her grandchildren, and unlike Barrasford, he wouldn't be taking them away from their home. She just hoped the dresses she'd sent with Charlotte Finchley were having their desired effect, because if Joanna would not cry off, then Barrasford would have to do it for her.

"There must be something interesting outside," a maid observed. Coming up behind Anne, she looked for herself. "They've got fishing poles with them, my lady."

"Fishing poles!" Justin howled. "'Tis not fair!"

"Hush, love," the dowager countess murmured soothingly. "How can you complain when you positively have me in dun territory?"

"Fustian, Grandmama. You're letting me win," he complained.

Anne's delicate eyebrow rose. "Letting you win? I am not! I assure you that you are a Captain Sharp compared to me, young man."

"But—"

"But you find an old woman's company tiresome, do you not?" she sympathized.

"No, but I wish I was with the duke instead of sitting here with my leg tied up."

"Do you like the duke?" Anne asked casually.

"Oh, yes!" He eyed her suspiciously. "Don't you?"

"Very much so—I always did, you know."

"He and my papa were friends, weren't they? He said they were."

"He and your mama and your papa were dear friends, love."

He appeared to consider this and then shook his head. "Sometimes I think so, and sometimes I don't."

"Yes, well, it gets terribly confusing sometimes, but I think they still like each other." She tied a string around the cards and set them on a table nearby. "But I suspect you are tired of being a gamester, aren't you?"

"Yes. I hate sitting in bed."

"I suppose I could find us some oiled cloth, and we could practice your watercolors."

"I don't want to paint either!"

"Nonsense. You must do something, after all, Justin. You will paint your mama a pretty picture, and then I will read to you. And if you are very good and do not complain excessively, I believe I can persuade the duke that you should be carried belowstairs for a while."

"Would you?" Brightening, Justin grinned. "Oh, Grandmama, I'd be ever so grateful!"

"Then do not complain," she reminded him. "Now I'd best get your paints. I'm sure Miss Finchley left them somewhere."

"No."

"Justin, you know your mother cannot abide a liar."

He capitulated gracelessly. "They're in the box by the duke's wardrobe," he said finally.

Gathering up the oiled cloth, Anne passed by the window table just as a carriage was coming up the drive. Her eyes narrowed as she tried to make out the family crest on the black-and-gold paneled door. "Oh, dear—not now surely," she said unhappily. As the coach rolled to a halt, a coachman jumped down to open the door. She stood transfixed as the gentleman stepped down, then turned back to help the young woman. His hands did not linger on her waist, Anne noted with disappointment.

"Who is it?" Justin wished to know.

"Miss Finchley and Lord Barrasford."

"Thought they was visiting dead people."

"Well, they are back. And I daresay Miss Finchley will be exceedingly glad to see you."

"I don't care if he gives me enough horses to fill the duke's whole stable. He can turn Robin up sweet, but not me. I don't want to go to Ireland, and I won't. I want to stay with the duke, Grandmama."

Curious that Lord Barrasford had cut short his visit after sending a note otherwise, Anne quickly summoned a maid to finish setting up the bed for Justin's paints, then she excused herself, telling the boy she'd be back momentarily.

They were coming into the foyer as she made her way downstairs. "Is aught amiss, my lord?" she asked. "We were not expecting you just yet."

"All's well, but I thought perhaps we ought to get back after all. I've been rather worried about Joanna. I wouldn't wish her to think I didn't want to be here to support her. And Miss Finchley graciously agreed that perhaps it was time to come back."

"I see."

"I brought my portmanteau and valet," he added significantly. "I thought perhaps to stay until Justin is well enough to go home."

"Yes, of course. I'm sure Roxbury will not mind," she managed, knowing perfectly well that Adrian would wish his rival at perdition. It crossed her mind that perhaps she ought to send him a note of warning, then she dismissed the notion.

"How is the boy?"

"Doing much better, really. A bit restive though, for he is still not allowed to put any weight at all on his leg.

Last night, Roxbury carried him downstairs to sit outside for an hour, but I cannot say that improved things at all. Now he would like to be anywhere but his bed."

"I'd like to see him."

"Yes, of course—do go on up, my lord. If he's a trifle testy, I hope you will forgive him."

"I'd find it understandable."

As he trudged up the stairs behind them, Anne turned her attention to Charlotte Finchley. Dressed in the gray lustring with a bonnet to match, the girl actually looked quite fetching.

"I hope you had a cozy coze with your sisters, my dear," she murmured.

"Oh, it was wonderful," Charlotte assured her. "I cannot begin to thank you for arranging the journey for me. Aside from the funeral, which was quite naturally a somber occasion, everything else was utterly enjoyable." Smiling, she explained, "Between wearing Lady Carew's clothes and arriving in Lord Barrasford's grand carriage, I cut quite a dash at Baxter Greys. Oh, my lady, but you have no notion!" she declared, her eyes shining. "Barrasford was everything that was kind, taking me about to see everyone, drinking tea with every elderly female in the village—I cannot even begin to tell you how enjoyable it was."

"I'm glad you found it so, my dear."

"You find me repaired and ready to take over Justin again. From what you've said, I collect he's in sore need of entertaining." The governess's smile faded. "Barrasford really wishes for a friendly discourse with the boys, you know."

"It may be a false hope. Justin still balks at the thought of going to Ireland. And he and Roxbury are, I fear, two peas from the same pod. Once they make up their minds, they are quite passionate about it."

Glancing up the grand staircase, Charlotte shook her

head sadly. "He is too good a man to disappoint, my lady."

"We are agreed in that, my dear. But the greater disappointment can sometimes lie in what we think we want instead of what we truly need. I suspect Barrasford's broken heart will mend, and rather quickly, too. But I daresay he will have need of a staunch friend."

"Yes."

"Then we are understood." Standing back, Anne regarded the governess almost soberly for a long moment, then she nodded. "Yes, you do look as fine as five pence today, dear."

With her skirt tucked decorously about her knees, Joanna sat on the paisley shawl Adrian had brought and watched as he baited Robin's hook and threw it in. They were down the bank some fifty or more feet, where the lowered water level had left a smooth, brown expanse of ground that gently disappeared into the river shallows. The leaves above her rustled in the soft breeze, creating a peacefulness broken only by the occasional cries of birds.

Even as Adrian threaded a reluctant worm on his own hook, Robin began dancing excitedly beside him. "'Bury—'Bury, look!" In his eagerness, he dropped his pole to clutch at Adrian's arm, and the pole, its line securely anchored in a fish's mouth, bobbed crazily for a moment before floating toward deeper water. "My fishing pole!" Robin squealed in consternation as he waded into the shallow water, trying to catch it.

"No, you don't, young man." Adrian grasped him from behind and firmly planted him on the bank. "You could get in over your head in places."

"But my pole!" the child wailed.

Heedless of his boots or pantaloons, Adrian went after it. "Stay there," he warned as the water topped his boots and reached his thighs. He could see it plainly where it had caught beneath partially exposed tree roots on the other side.

"Dree, be careful! The water's swift in the shallows!" Joanna yelled.

Ignoring her, he crossed over, carried some twenty feet downstream by the current against his legs. The bank was steeper on the other side where the water had eaten away soil loosely held by a brace of trees. Roots, vines, and underbrush dangled and tangled from above. He caught a low-lying branch, tested his weight against it, and pulled himself up to walk above the river until he was directly over the still-bobbing fishing pole. Sliding back down into the water, he disentangled the line and possessed the pole. To his surprise, the line slackened and then tautened sharply—Robin's fish was still on the hook. A boyish grin spread over his face, and the battle was joined.

"We've still got him!" he shouted back in triumph. "And he's a big one!"

Afraid that Robin would run into the water to see, Joanna abandoned the shawl and ran pell-mell toward him. He turned as she reached him, chortling, "Mama, 'Bury's got my fish! He's got my fish!" As Adrian crossed back, Robin danced and skipped down the flat edge to meet him. "Capital, 'Bury! Can I see him?"

Adrian emerged, his pantaloons bagging from the river water, his once clean shirt wet and dirty, with his grin still intact. He stopped long enough for the child to inspect the fish and exclaim over it, then he walked upstream with the fish in one hand and Robin firmly attached to the other. He held up his catch in front of Joanna. "If I'd known there were fish this big still down here, I wouldn't have given up fishing."

Her eyes strayed from the fish to where his shirt plastered wetly against his chest and arms, and the old, still-familiar thrill went through her as she saw the outline of masculine muscles beneath. Tearing herself away from thoughts that threatened her composure, she looked down. "I think you've ruined your clothes, my lord."

He'd not mistaken the look, and he knew it. Keeping his voice light despite the rush he felt, he ruffled Robin's bright curls. "I know. Since you came back with your urchins, I've ruined more clothes than I care to count. Weston ought to pay you a portion of his bill, my dear."

"Blake will not be amused," she reminded him.

"Can I hold him?" Robin demanded with a tug on Adrian's arm. "Can I, 'Bury—can I?"

"He's your fish. Tell you what—you go get the basket and you can put him in it."

The child trotted on sturdy legs to where Joanna'd left the shawl, the fish basket, and the food hamper. Adrian shaded his eyes with his free hand to watch him. "He's very like Gary, isn't he? He has that enthusiasm for everything."

"Very like him." She turned to watch Robin for a moment. "As I've said before, neither of my sons got much from me. I think I told you that Gary used to call Justin 'Duke's Double' when he was a babe, but it was a term of affection. Then when Justin was old enough to wonder about it, he stopped. You always were 'Duke' to Gary, even when we were small. Now Justin calls you that also."

A lump formed in Adrian's throat, constricting it. "Gary would be quite proud of this one, I think," he managed quietly.

"Gary was quite proud of both of them."

"I miss him, you know."

She looked up, a bitter retort on her lips, but bit it back at the pain she saw in his dark eyes. A sense of shared loss stole over her for a moment. "So do I, Dree. He was very good to me."

"You loved him." It was a statement of fact rather than accusation.

She drew in her breath and exhaled slowly. "I think I loved him much as you did, Dree. He was such a good person, it would have been difficult not to have loved him, don't you think? But he was never my grand passion, and he knew it."

Her answer, though he'd heard much the same before, raised the nagging doubts again. There was still so much he wanted to know, so much he was afraid to ask about her and Gary. "I loved him like a brother, Jo."

"Yes," she agreed simply.

"'Bury!" Robin was breathless from running with the fish basket. "Now can I hold him?"

"He's cold and wet," Joanna warned him.

Adrian looked down at the dangling fish, now almost limp from being out of the water. "I think we'd better get him back into the river before he dies. Here— give me the basket and I'll give you the fish."

The exchange made, Adrian opened the woven cage and held it out. The boy plopped the fish in and waited expectantly. Dropping to his knee, Adrian removed the hook embedded in the fish's mouth. "There now." Nearly level with the child, he grinned. "Come on, Robin—let's put this fellow in the water and get back to fishing. And after a while, your mama will set out the food."

Joanna went back to her shawl, sat down, and leaned back against a tree to watch. The old pain, while by no means gone, was eased somewhat in that they could at least touch on Gary, could still share in some small way something of what they had lost. And she did have much to be grateful for, she reminded herself—Justin was alive, after all. She just wished that somehow things could be different, that they could go back to happier times. Then she caught herself. Nothing could be worth the pain that had followed those times.

Despite a small boy's shrieks of delight and a man's shouts of encouragement, she found herself once again daydreaming, remembering long-forgotten days when she'd been that hopeless hoyden trailing after two often grubby boys. She'd had such a happy, unconventional childhood growing up, for her father had never bothered much about her, a circumstance she'd learned not to regret. Sometimes, she had to wonder if her governess had not married Adrian's tutor what would have happened to her. Given her father's improvident ways, she probably would have married a plain mister, or possibly she would have had a life like Charlotte Finchley's. Instead, she'd been Roxbury's duchess and Carew's countess. She'd known a passion so intense it had consumed itself in just over one year. And she'd known Gary's far gentler love. And now she was haunted by that one brief, furious encounter when she'd let herself forget the pain, when she'd given herself to Adrian that night. And once again, she was caught up in the old familiar yearning.

"Wake up, sleepyhead!" Adrian was shaking her awake, forcing her to open her eyes slowly to the bright sun. She must've dozed, she decided, as she became aware that Robin held a full basket of fish, a basket so heavy he could barely carry it.

"Look, Mama! Me'n 'Bury got 'em!"

"Actually, I think I baited more hooks than anything," Adrian admitted modestly. "My dear, your younger son has the makings of a bang-up fisherman."

"Dree, I absolutely refuse to eat my nuncheon while being stared at by a string of fish," she told him severely.

"I'll put 'em back, 'Bury," Robin offered.

"No, infant, you will not. I'll do it while you and your mama lay out something for us to eat."

"You know, Mama," Robin announced as he sat cross-legged on the corner of the shawl, "I like 'Bury—I like him even better'n Barryford."

"Barrasford, dearest," she corrected.

"I don't ever want to leave here."

"Pray do not tell the duke that."

"Oh, I already have," he answered happily. "Me'n him's agreed on it—he wants us to stay with him. He likes us, Mama."

"So does Lord Barrasford."

"But I don't want to go to Ireland anymore—I want to live *here*."

"I am afraid that is impossible, Robin." She cut him a slab of cheese and laid it on a napkin with a piece of fruit. "We are going to live with Lord Barrasford in Ireland. You like Lord Barrasford—remember?"

"But I don't want to leave Grandmama neither."

"She will come to visit us."

His bright blue eyes were serious as he tried to understand. "Don't you like 'Bury?"

"That has nothing to do with anything, my love. I am betrothed to Lord Barrasford, and as such, I am obliged to marry him."

"Can't you say you don't want to?"

"No, I cannot."

He digested that, then decided, "Well, maybe he'd like to live here, too. He likes 'Bury, don't he?"

"Doesn't he, dearest," she corrected him. "Robin, we cannot be the duke's guests forever," she tried to explain patiently. "Indeed, in another week or so, or whenever Justin can be moved, we shall be returning to Haven. Here—eat your bread and cheese."

"But 'Bury said—"

"I don't care what he said. He doesn't have the ordering of your life," she countered irritably. "*I* do."

"Well, I see you did not wait for me," Adrian observed as he dropped down beside them. "I'm famished, Jo."

"You can have mine. I seem to have lost my appetite."

He eyed her curiously for a moment, his concern evident. "You are not feeling ill, are you? I mean, you seemed fine a little while ago."

"Of course I am not ill," she retorted. "I am overset, if you must know."

"About what?" he asked bluntly.

"I cannot discuss it just now." She glanced significantly to Robin. "This is scarce the place."

"I see. Then perhaps we should take tea in the library when we get back, and you can tell me then."

"There's not much to tell." She picked up an apple and began munching on it. Between bites, she fixed her gaze on the river and asked, "How long do you think it will be before Justin can travel?"

"Weeks."

"Surely not. I'd like to get him home to Haven as soon as possible."

"I expect Goode could tell you. Since Bascombe's gone back to London, he's almost in charity with us."

"I mean to ask him tomorrow."

He made a mental note to speak to Goode first, for he had no intention of letting her leave just yet. In those long, harrowing nights when they'd fought for Justin's life, he'd admitted to himself that he loved her as much as he wanted her, that he'd forgive her anything to get her back. And since he'd had her that night in the garden, he'd thought of little else. Even now, if he closed his eyes, he could taste her mouth, he could feel her body beneath his. And he knew if he let her go back to

Haven, she'd wed Johnny Barrasford out of obligation, not love.

"As you wish, my dear."

His complacence in the matter irritated her even more. "I am not 'your dear,' my lord."

"My lord?" His eyebrow shot up. "What in the devil has gotten into you, Jo?"

"Do not swear at me."

"All right—what in the deuce has gotten into you, then?"

"I cannot discuss it just now, I told you."

"I fail to see why not," he pointed out reasonably. "Unless I am very much mistaken, Robin is asleep. While you've been carping at me, he seems to have crawled over there and dozed off."

She turned her attention to the corner of the shawl and found that her son, used as he was to taking naps, had succumbed to the habit. He lay curled up contentedly beside the remnants of his nuncheon, his bright curls spilling over a still-chubby arm. His small chest rose and fell rhythmically in sleep. When she turned back, Adrian had stretched out full length on his side next to her, his head propped on his elbow. His dark eyes betrayed a hint of devilish amusement.

"Well?"

"Well, what?"

"I believe you were going to tell me what it is that made you suddenly out-of-season cross, Jo."

"I am not out-of-season cross, as you choose to call it," she snapped.

"No? Then you can outperform Mrs. Siddons, my dear, for you've certainly made me believe it. Come on, Jo—what is it that I've done now?"

He was far too near for her peace of mind. His damp, clinging shirt and his rumpled hair, rather than detracting from his appearance, gave him a certain reckless appeal. It wasn't fair what he could do to her when he looked at her like that. "You cannot turn me up sweet through my son," she gritted out finally.

"He's Gary's son too, Jo—how could I help loving him?"

"You did not have to make him want to live here! You know very well that I cannot—that I won't!"

"Ah," he said, sighing. "I see—you are all starched up because the boy likes me."

"Yes! You know very well that we are going to Ireland, so why must you try to throw a spoke in the wheel? Why are you doing this to me?"

Instead of appearing contrite, he flashed a grin designed to disarm. "Before you get higher on the ropes, Jo, perhaps you would care to hear how it came about?"

"I do not care—I won't have it."

Ignoring her, he continued, "He said he'd like to live here, and I said I'd like to have him—is that so terrible of me? I'd count it a privilege to rear Gary's son, you know." His dark eyes were warm, appealing as they searched her face. "You know, I'd do no less for his son than he did for mine. I owe him that, Jo, but even if I didn't, I know I could love both boys. I don't want to let you go again." His hand absently stroked her gown where it lay against her thigh.

She sat stock-still, her hands clenched tightly to control her reaction to the nearness of him. His touch, slight as it was, sent a wave of desire that threatened to engulf her. She closed her eyes to hide from him and exhaled slowly. "No."

"You cannot deny that what we had once is still between us—you cannot. You cannot forget what happened the other night any more than I can."

"It was the Madeira—you said that yourself."

"Not for me. For me, it was you."

"Dree, we cannot go back to when we were both young and moon-mad. The other night was hunger, nothing more. I can't love you again—I can't," she said desperately. "The accusations—the divorce—they destroyed what we once had."

"That is a patent falsehood, Jo. I think I forgave you the first time I saw Justin." He leaned closer and trailed his fingers down her arm, tracing fire. "I still want you as much as ever."

Angrily she pulled away and lurched to her feet. Heedless of the sleeping child, she flared indignantly, "'Tis overgenerous of you, my lord! Your forgiveness is unsought. I deserve more than that—I deserve belief!"

"Jo—"

"No! Hear me out, for 'tis my only word on the subject. I was a good and faithful wife to you, Adrian Delacourt! I gave you no cause to doubt it—but you believed your mother's spiteful lies, you let her twist the innocent acts of friendship into a sick tale of adultery! You divorced me! You ruined me! And now you would forgive me? I think not, Your Grace! Forgiveness is not nearly good enough!"

"I love you, Jo."

"If you loved me, you would have believed in me!" she retorted hotly.

Her cheeks were flushed from the outburst, and her bosom heaved indignantly. As she stood above him, Adrian wanted to pull her back down beside him, to stroke away the anger, to soothe the raw pain, and to begin anew, but it was impossible. Instead, he watched helplessly as she shook Robin awake.

"'Tis time to go back, my love," she told the child. "Grandmama is probably heartily sick of Justin by now."

He sat up sleepily, rubbing his eyes in bewilderment.

Deprived of his nap, he burst into tears. "My fish! I want my fish!"

Adrian pulled himself up by the tree behind him. "I'll get the fish," he told Joanna in defeat. "You pack the hamper."

When he returned with the fish basket and the poles she was standing beneath the spreading tree with the hamper on her arm and Robin on her hip. "Can you carry the hamper?" she asked finally. "He's too tired to walk, and I cannot manage both."

"I'll carry him and the hamper," he offered, "if you'll take the fish.!"

"I think I'd rather have the food basket," she answered as he took Robin and hoisted him up on his shoulder like a sack of grain. The little boy settled against him, cradling his head between Adrian's neck and shoulder and holding on with a chubby arm. Despite her anger, Joanna could not help seeing the incongruity of the Duke of Roxbury laden with poles, fish basket, and grubby child. "The fish stink, Dree," she told him.

"So do I—river water does not have much to recommend it when it dries," he admitted ruefully, "but he does not seem to mind it."

"Only because he is asleep."

The long walk back was strained as each tried to sort out his conflicting emotions. For Joanna, there was almost a sense of relief. It had taken her more than six years to tell him what had wounded her the most. The scandal, the divorce even, paled in significance against his willingness to believe she could have done such a thing, and he obviously believed it still. Beside her, Adrian trudged silently, deeply torn by the overwhelming loss he felt. In the days she'd been once again at the Armitage, he'd allowed himself to hope, to think that there was some way of reliving the love of his youth. He knew now she was what he wanted more than anything, desired more than anything, loved beyond everything. He wanted to believe that she felt it, too. No, he *knew* she did. But he'd botched the matter again.

He'd meant what he said about Robin. He could and would love the engaging little boy—there was so much of Gary about him. He wanted desperately to close the circle again with Joanna, his son, and Gary's son. He had to find a way to do it.

He did not look up until he reached the drive, and then he stopped short in disbelief. For a long second he stared at the carriage pulled up before the portico, and then he muttered succinctly, "Damn!"

She stopped, roused from her own troubled thoughts, and looked ahead. With a dispirited lack of enthusiasm, she sighed. "Johnny's back."

The object of this observation watched from the library window as they came down the drive. Taking in the sight of the duke in his muddy clothes, the child on his shoulder, and Joanna walking casually beside him, the three of them much like a picture of bucolic amity, if not bliss, he felt a sense of unease. Looking up, he'd already noted the rehung portrait of Joanna as it faced Adrian's. And certainly comments Bess and Charlotte Finchley had made during the journey to Baxter Greys had done little to reassure him. It was as though every sentence about Joanna had to include Roxbury.

As they drew up in front of the house, Joanna stopped to reach for Robin so that Adrian could take the fish and the poles around to the back. The scene was so domestic to Johnny's eyes that he had to look away. Behind him, Charlotte said quietly, "I'd best be getting Robin—I know you will be wishful of being private with Lady Carew."

Joanna absently dressed for dinner, making no complaint even when Bess had to work particularly hard to remove a stubborn tangle from her hair. A lingering uneasiness, a sense of impending loss perhaps, stole over her as she stared into an empty grate.

"'Tis such lovely hair ye have, mum," the maid observed as she twisted the thick wheat-blond mass into a rope and knotted it at the nape of Joanna's neck. Standing back to admire her handiwork, she nodded appreciatively. "Ye're prettier'n any picture, Your Grace. 'Tis no wonder—" She caught herself guiltily when Joanna's shoulders stiffened. "Oh, I . . . that is . . ." Her voice trailed off lamely at her mistress's haunted expression. "Oh, my lady," she almost wailed, "'tis sorry I am—I did not mean—it's just with yer picture hangin' down there again, well, I begun to think of ye as the duchess."

"It's all right," Joanna assured her, despite her own jangled nerves. "Everything is so mixed up right now."

"'Twas that Mary!" Bess burst out suddenly. "Martha and Blake and me was talkin' of it—it wasn't right! His Grace gone to Lunnon and th' duchess payin' th' greedy fool t' spy on ye!"

"I said it is all right, Bess—it is over. I'm afraid the water's been over that bridge a long time."

"But if we'd ha' known it—if we'd ha' been there,

she'd not ha' dared to tell him th' lies! But 'twas Lunnon, ye know, and done afore we knew it! It ain't right, my lady—it ain't right. And th' poor earl—him as was His Grace's friend from short coats—well, we knowed it wasn't so! Why, he would've cut off 'is arms ere he'd a hurt His Grace! Oh, that woman—that evil, evil woman—now how could a body do summat like that to her own flesh and blood, I ask ye?"

The unexpected and uncharacteristic outburst from a servant who knew her place moved Joanna deeply. "Thank you, Bess, but you must not dwell on this," she managed to whisper as her throat tightened and tears welled until she couldn't stand it anymore. "Oh, Bess— I am the most miserable of females!"

Alarmed at what her own outburst had caused, the maid reached to pat her mistress awkwardly. "'Tis me accursed tongue, my lady—should ha' never spoke a thing about it. There now—ye don't want to ruin yer pretty face a-crying," she coaxed helplessly. "Not with that handsome lord ye'll be a-marryin' awaiting downstairs for ye."

Barrasford. Joanna sniffed back her tears and tried to collect herself, but the thought of Johnny Barrasford only seemed to make things worse. In that brief interview after she'd returned from fishing, he'd been somehow different, more subdued, more reflective— and more distracted. Not that he was not all kindness itself, of course, she admitted, but something seemed to be subtly changing between them. Perhaps it was nothing more than mere imagination on her part, her own sense of guilt even, because she felt so little enthusiasm for their approaching marriage. Still, for the first time since their betrothal, Johnny'd barely kissed her. He'd been on the road since Baxter Greys, she reminded herself. And certainly she'd been out in the heat herself.

She just had to face the situation with Johnny. She

could not draw back, would not even consider doing so, for she'd been the one to throw herself at his head. She'd needed his support against Adrian, against the world, too, and she'd gotten it. No, she could not in conscience cry off. Nor could she tell him about that night when four glasses of Madeira had made her weak. But the nagging fear that she could have conceived made it imperative that she find the means to delay the marriage until after her courses came. She could not saddle Johnny with Adrian's child.

"Are ye all right, mum?" Bess queried curiously. "I'm sorry to have overset ye so."

"Oh—yes, of course." Joanna forced a smile. "I am just a trifle fatigued, I fear, but I am all right." She rose quickly before the mirror and surveyed her reflection briefly. "That will be fine, Bess—indeed, I thank you for making me presentable." Smoothing the soft rose silk of her skirt over her hips, she turned back. "I believe I shall see Justin before I go down."

She let herself through the connecting door and pasted a smile on her face for her son. As she came past the bathing screen, she drew up short, her breath caught somewhere between her chest and her throat. Adrian was there, still stocking-footed and in his shirt-sleeves, sitting on the bed and absorbed in unwrapping small objects. He looked up suddenly and grinned boyishly. "I think I've ordered the rest of the British army to complete the set Johnny bought the boys," he said, holding up a brightly painted wooden piece. "Indeed, we were just about to set up the lines for Salamanca." She drew closer, her heart thumping painfully at the sight of the two of them sitting there, their dark heads bent over a collection of wooden toys laid out on the coverlet. Justin had them divided evenly by their uniforms. "Look, Mama! Duke's got me a whole set of Queen's Dragoons! With Robin's set, we've got the whole battlefield covered." He twisted sideways away from his still-splinted leg. "Blake!"

"Here, young master," the valet protested affectionately, "'tis not deaf I am."

"Have you seen Finch and my brother?" Justin demanded.

"I believe they are still in the nursery."

Justin's face fell. "I wanted to show my brother my soldiers afore supper," he muttered. "I wanted him to bring his down."

"I shall see if he can be found."

"And bring Miss Finchley, too," Justin called after him. "She'll think they are capital!"

"Now that they are unwrapped, you'll need to line them up into separate camps," Adrian advised as he slid off the bed. "And if you fold the covers just so, you can make a battle line. Then you may bring your cannon up like this." He demonstrated by placing some older carved guns off to the side. "You must be careful, of course, to see that your firing position does not endanger your own men. That can be truly disastrous. I know, because I saw it happen."

"I remember that piece, Dree—that is from that set Papa gave you when you were still in short coats," Joanna murmured behind his shoulder.

"The artillery did not come, so he'll have to use those." He turned around, his tall frame scarcely a foot from hers. The fresh, tingly smell of Hungary water floated down from him and mingled with the scent of her lavender soap. He was far too near for her peace of mind, and her nerves were still too unsettled. She stepped back, her hands crossed defensively over her chest. It was a gesture not lost on him. He moved away while observing casually, "I collect Johnny means to stay a few days."

"Until Justin is ready to return to Haven."

"I don't want to go back to Haven!" came the petulant retort from the child on the bed. "And I don't want to go to Ireland neither!"

"Justin!" Adrian reproved sharply. "You will not speak so to your mother while you are in this house."

"But I—"

"Justin—" There was a low, warning note this time. "I'll not brook any disrespect to her here—or anywhere else, for that matter."

"I—I am sorry, Mama."

"That is more to my liking, Justin. You must remember not to be impolite to ladies, and particularly not to your mama." Adrian's eyes met Joanna's for a moment. "Not even when you are vexed, I fear, my dear fellow, and you will be vexed often, I can promise you."

"I did not ask Johnny to come back, Dree."

"I have no quarrel with his being here again—none at all. You may surround me with whatever menagerie you see fit, Jo, but I can scarce imagine the comments that will go around the neighborhood this time."

"He cannot like it either," she admitted, "but he feels he ought to support me, particularly now that Justin is better."

"Does he now?" The black eyebrow rose and the corner of his mouth twitched with a suppressed smile. "Aye—I'll wager he does."

"What is that supposed to mean?"

"Perhaps he's jealous."

"Well, he needn't be." She caught herself guiltily and looked away. "I've no intent of drinking any Madeira with you again—ever. And while I suppose I ought to have told him, I just couldn't bring myself to do it, so he doesn't know about—about my foolish behavior."

"He doesn't need to. I'm sure he cannot help remembering what we once were—I know I couldn't if I were in his shoes. I saw him admiring your picture, by the by. No, I think your being here has made him jealous."

She started to refute the notion and stopped even before her mouth opened. There was something quite strained about Johnny since he'd returned from Baxter Greys. "Well, I shall have to make certain he does not misunderstand, shan't I?" she managed lightly. The slightly rosy light of evening haloed Adrian against the window, outlining his shoulders and softening the shadows of his face, reminding her once again of just how very handsome and masculine he was. His thick dark hair lay in a perfect Brutus while his still open-necked shirt revealed bare skin.

"You'd best finish dressing for dinner, don't you think, Dree?" she reminded him as she tore her eyes away.

"Yes." He looked down to where his shirtsleeves were still unbuttoned, the studs hanging in the buttonholes. Deftly he looped the hole over one of them and then held out the other hand. "Get this for me, Jo, will you? Blake's not here at the moment, and I've always had a devil of a time with these."

"Oh, uh . . . .yes, of course." She reached gingerly to pull the cuff across his wrist.

"I'm not going to eat you alive."

"No, of course not."

Her fingers shook as she worked the stud into the buttonhole. His hand was warm and vital and his pulse beat steadily beneath her fingertips, sending a tremor between them. She looked up and caught the hunger in his eyes. Dropping her gaze, she quickly fastened them.

"Ah—I thought I'd come to see how the boy does before dinner."

They spun around at the sound of Johnny Barrasford's voice. Joanna's face flamed for a moment, as

much from the thoughts that had been going through
her mind as from the look on his face. She dropped
Adrian's hand as though it had been a hot poker.

"He's much, much better, thank you."

Justin, who had been totally absorbed in lining up
his troops to advantage before Robin arrived, looked
up. For once, his delight in the toys obscured his mis-
trust of Barrasford. "Robin and me are going to play
soldiers!" he chirped excitedly. "See—here are the
Queen's Dragoons! And Robin's going to bring down
the set you gave him. We'll have a whole army, sir!"

"Let me take a look," Johnny offered as he bent over
to see them. "Oh, this is a capital set, isn't it? Here—if
we roll this back, I think I can show you what it was
like at Salamanca."

"You were a soldier?"

"Briefly. Nothing like Roxbury, of course, but I was
there." The gray eyes twinkled for a moment as he
sized up the pieces. "We'll have to move these men
over this way and bring these down here. And your artillery needs to be positioned on higher ground—just
so. There."

As Adrian and Joanna watched, Barrasford sank
down on the bed and began moving the pieces around
to suit him. Just then, Robin burst in, pulling Miss
Finchley after him. "I say, 'Tin! Blake said you had
more soldiers! Just look at all of 'em, Finch!"

"Why, you do have an army," she said, appropriately
admiring the set. "Why, look at all those cannons."

"Can't fight a war without 'em," Justin told her importantly. "Sit down, Finch, and you and Robin can
fight me and Lord Barrasford."

"Well, I—"

"Please, Finch—please," Robin pleaded.

"Miss Finchley's brother was a soldier," Barrasford

told them, and then frowned. "I am sorry, my dear—I did not mean to distress you."

"Oh, no! That is, it was all so very long ago," the governess assured him as she pulled up a chair beside the bed.

"If you'll excuse me, Jo, I think I'll finish getting dressed," Adrian murmured to Joanna. Leaning closer, he whispered even lower, "Buck up—he didn't think anything of it."

Dinner had been a quiet, subdued affair characterized by pleasant but mundane conversation, the bulk of which had been carried by the dowager countess and Miss Finchley. Adrian, Joanna, and Johnny Barrasford had, for the most part, merely reacted to whatever was said to them. And, for once, the governess had risen admirably to the task of carrying on the social discourse, showing a wit and liveliness heretofore unsuspected. The dowager countess, presiding opposite Adrian, eyed Miss Finchley with renewed hope.

After the covers had been removed, Joanna declined the customary tête-à-tête by expressing fatigue, Miss Finchley reluctantly remembered needlework that simply would not wait, and Lady Anne decided to personally supervise the tucking up of her grandsons. Finding themselves thus alone, Adrian and Johnny withdrew to the library for the obligatory glass of port. Settling into a chair by the darkened window, Barrasford looked from one end of the room to the other as he took the first few sips of wine. His eyes took in the portrait of Joanna again, thinking she was without doubt one of the most beautiful women he'd ever met.

"Lawrence's work, isn't it?" he asked with a gesture toward the picture.

"Yes," Adrian acknowledged. "I commissioned both

of them when she was eighteen, just after she accepted my suit. It was a long time ago, I'm afraid, but it still does her justice, doesn't it?"

"An excellent likeness." Barrasford shifted in his chair and nodded toward the other one. "He did not do nearly as well with you, you know."

"Oh—in what way?"

"I can't really say, but there's something not just right about it. He got Joanna just as she is. He even captured that certain vulnerability that intensifies her beauty. But he missed you by ever so little. I don't know," he mused, "but perhaps there is a trifle too much arrogance in those black eyes, in that little half smile."

"You think so?" Adrian appeared to study the offending portrait. "I always rather liked it, I'm afraid. I thought it rather flattering to me."

"No. Pour me another glass, Roxbury," Barrasford ordered as he leaned forward and held out his goblet. "You know, I've a fair mind to get disguised tonight." He waited while Adrian poured, and then he swirled the liquid around, staring as intently into it as if he were a fortune-teller reading tea leaves. "'Tis plain as a pikestaff that she loves you," he said finally.

"No." Adrian shook his head and stared morosely into his own wine. "I destroyed her, Johnny—she cannot forgive me that. Believe me, I tried to cut you out at every corner. I tried my damnedest to win her back."

"Roxbury, you are a bloody fool," Barrasford murmured under his breath.

"What?"

"I said you are a bloody fool."

"You're foxed, Johnny."

"I wish I were." Without warning, he lurched to his feet and reached for the decanter. "Sorry to leave you so soon, old chap, but I think I'd rather just take this up to my chamber, if you do not mind. Dreadful manners,

I know, but I am really not feeling particularly social just now."

"Johnny—"

"No—leave me be, Roxbury, and I'll come about."

Adrian watched helplessly as Barrasford left him, and then he rose to get another bottle from a cabinet. Returning to his chair, he poured himself another glass and stared up at the companion portraits, first his and then hers. Now the faint arrogance of his own smile seemed to mock him from across the room, while Joanna's eyes looked down on him with an innocent seductiveness that was unbearable. Johnny was right about that: Lawrence had captured Joanna just as she had been as a young girl. He raised his glass to her, a toast to the most beautiful woman in the world. He was a bloody fool and he knew it, but there didn't seem to be any way to make amends for that. With the exception of that night in the garden when she'd been disguised with his Madeira, she'd rebuffed all of his attempts to rekindle any love for him.

A faint tap sounded at the door, jarring him back to the present. His first inclination was to ignore it, but then curiosity got the better of him. Glass in hand, he rose to open the heavy dark-paneled door. To his surprise, Anne Sherwood swept past him into the room.

"Do not stand there like a gaping ninny, Roxbury," she told him crisply, "and pray put away that glass. I cannot abide drunkards, you know." Incredibly, she was smiling despite the tone of her voice. She waited for him to close the door, and then she held out a box. "I think Gary would want you to have these, Adrian— indeed, I know he would, else he'd not saved them."

"What is in it?"

"Some things Gary saved. Open it," she urged.

He moved back to where his chair was drawn up by a brace of candles and sat down. Removing the lid of the small enameled box, he took a deep breath and looked inside. There, nestled in the folds of a piece of blue velvet, lay two items—a gold watch case and a locket. He didn't have to ask about the locket—it was the one in the portrait, but his hands shook as he reached in to retrieve the watch case. His dark eyes questioned Anne's.

"I don't understand."

"Gary's dead. There's no bringing him back to any of us."

He nodded and exhaled slowly as he turned the gold watch case in the palm of his hand. With his thumbnail he pried open the hinge and looked inside to discover a familiar wheat-colored curl tied in a thin gold thread, all neatly flattened into place behind a glass. Across from the lock was the plain face of the clock, its hours marked with tiny diamonds. Wordlessly he closed it and turned it over to read, "To Adrian, on the occasion of our first year together. May it forever stand as a symbol of my love for you. JMD." JMD—Joanna Milford Delacourt. He felt as though he'd been planted a facer squarely between the eyes.

Aware that she watched him intently, he managed to say, "It was to be mine. My God, I never knew."

"After the divorce, she wanted it destroyed, but Gary couldn't bring himself to do it," Anne told him simply. "And while I cannot think she would wish me to show it to you now, I think this stupid quarrel has lasted far too long."

"Then it wasn't for Gary." His voice dropped to a near whisper.

"No. She sent to London to have it made. She had Gary bring it back to her when he came home. It was to have been a grand surprise for you."

"And the locket?" he dared to ask. "He kept the locket, too?"

Anne nodded. "She didn't know that either. She told him you gave it to her as a symbol of your love, and it wasn't worth anything to her anymore. He retrieved it from where she'd thrown it away. He wanted to send them both to you, to let you know how wrong you'd been."

"Why didn't he?"

"I suspect there were two reasons, really. She didn't want any further discourse with you, she said. 'If he needs proof of my character, there's nothing more I'd say to him,' was the way she phrased it, I think."

"And the other?"

"Your accusations drove her into his arms."

He closed his eyes and could see again the way she'd stood there, white-faced and disbelieving, while his mother gloated. She'd started to speak, but the duchess had cut in, accusing her viciously, and he'd let it happen. Joanna had turned to him finally and told him, "You cannot believe in me, can you, Dree?" and when he could not answer, she'd fled the room. He'd wanted to go after her even then, but his pride would not let him. When he'd calmed down enough to speak with her, he'd been told she was gone, that she'd left the house with nothing more than the clothes on her back.

She'd run to Gary then. No, that was wrong—she'd run to her father first and been turned away, told to go back to her husband. Then it was that she'd gone to Gary. He could still remember exactly how Gary'd looked, as incredulous as Joanna even, when he'd sought Adrian out. He'd called him the greatest fool on earth, and he'd been right. Adrian squeezed his eyes tighter and felt anew the pain of hearing that they'd fled to Italy and married. His hand closed over the watch as though to crush it.

"How they must have suffered for my folly," he spoke finally.

"Nonsense," Anne dismissed flatly. "Make no mistake about it, Roxbury—as much as he cared for you, my son loved Joanna more. If you can but admit it, you gave him the greatest gift of his life when you divorced her."

"Why are you telling me this?" he demanded harshly, his eyes suddenly intent on her.

"Because I love her and my grandsons—both of them—and I would see all of you happy if I could. Gary forgave you, you know, and I would that Joanna could also." Her blue eyes met his steadily. "Oh, Barrasford's a kind, compassionate man, I know, but it would not be the same. Justin and Robin would be in Ireland and neither would know his patrimony." Her mouth drew into a wry smile and she nodded. "Aye— Robin is too little to remember Gary for long, and Justin cannot but know one day that he is yours. I'd think it best to see both of them reared here, knowing that you could love them. I think Gary would wish that."

"She must surely hate me."

"Hate is a strange word, Adrian—it connotes such depth of feeling that one cannot but wonder how close it is to love. I've seen what passes between you when you are together, and I think you have it wrong." She hesitated, uncertain whether to press him further. When he merely sat there, his shoulders slumped, his elbows propped on his knees, she sighed. "Well, I have done it, and now I find myself unbearably tired. I pray you think on all I have said and that you do not judge yourself or Joanna or Gary too harshly. That, I think, you ought to reserve for the viper who bore you."

"I could never make up for the pain. No, she's far better off to take Johnny," he decided finally.

"Adrian Delacourt, of all I have ever known of you, I'd never thought you were weak-spirited," Anne declared with feeling. "Weak-brained perhaps, but never weak-spirited. Well, I've had my say, at any event, and I leave you to think on it."

It was a long time after she left before he could bring himself to seek his own chamber. Instead, he sat and brooded, staring unseeing across the empty room and listening again to echoed thoughts of six years past. The candles flickered and guttered while he pondered it all—Joanna, Gary, Barrasford, his son, Gary's son, and his own mother. The wine decanter was still full when he finally roused himself from his own condemnations and climbed the stairs to his bed. Blake was there, hovering solicitously with news of just how Master Justin had played until bedtime with his soldiers. Adrian sprawled in a chair while the valet removed his shoes.

"Tell me," he asked casually, "do you remember Mary Cummings?"

"Humph! Aye—saucy bit of baggage, she was—always looking to catch your eye," Blake sniffed. "And when she couldn't, then she decided to fill her purse with gold."

"I don't suppose anyone knows what happened to her after—after she testified during the trials."

"She came into a competence," Blake replied pointedly, "and opened a millinery shop at Paxton Grove."

"Paxton Grove," Adrian repeated blankly.

"Yes, I believe Her Grace your mother had some connections there. Distant relations, wasn't it?"

"Yes. Some cousins."

"No doubt they helped her go into trade," the man observed slyly. "Two hundred fifty pounds in her pockets when she left here, I was told."

As the carriage made its way through the narrow, cobbled streets, Adrian searched the shop signs until he found the one he'd hoped for. The tall, red-framed windows displayed an assortment of hats, while the sign above them proclaimed CUMMINGS MILLINERY, in large gold and black letters, with the notation "The finest in hats and Parisian corsets" beneath it. Over the doorway between the windows in bold script was "Mary Cummings, Proprietress." He tapped the ceiling of the coach with his walking stick, ordering his driver to stop.

At almost the same moment, a young woman unlocked the door from within, opening the shop for the day's business. Stepping outside, she briskly swept the small stoop, then she saw the Roxbury coat of arms on the carriage door, and she hastily retreated. She was fumbling with the key when Adrian pushed his way inside the dimly lit store.

The woman gasped as her hands flew to her face, then she backed away from him. "Your Grace," she managed feebly.

"There was a time when you were not nearly so reluctant to encounter me," he reminded her. "There was a time when you seemed to be on every stair waiting for me."

"What—what on earth are ye doing here?" she asked, her eyes as round as dark saucers.

"I could ask the same of you," he said brutally. "You never earned enough money to buy yourself a business."

"I had me an inheritance."

"That is a lie. You got the money from my mother, didn't you?"

"I—I don't know what you mean." Eyeing him warily, she moved behind a wooden counter laden with chipstraw hats. As he followed her along the other side of the counter, she passed her tongue nervously over her lips. "You got no right coming here accusing an honest woman."

"I want the truth, Mary—and I want it *now*."

"Here now, me lord, but I ain't got nothing to say." Judging the distance between them, she bolted from behind the counter for the door.

"Not so fast, my dear," he murmured, catching her by an arm. Spinning her around to face him, he saw the fear in her face. "I ought to beat it out of you, you little witch." As she cringed, he fought the urge to strike her. Finally, he gave her a small push against the wall, where she shrank into a corner. "What did she pay you?" he demanded, advancing on her. "Damn you— answer me!"

"I got nothing t' say."

"No, by God, you're going to tell me the whole, or you are going to jail for perjuring yourself." As the color drained from her face, he nodded. "Three times you testified against my wife, didn't you? And it was all lies, wasn't it?"

"No—no, my lord, I never lied!"

"You lied, Mary, and you are lying now. I swear to God I've never hit a woman in my life, but if you don't answer me, I'll do so now!"

"No!"

"Then tell me—tell me how you lied, Mary—tell me what she told you to say."

"I can't, sir—I can't!" she cried.

"You never saw my wife in Gareth Sherwood's arms, did you?" Reaching out, he caught her shoulder and shook her. "Damn you—answer me!"

"She'll take me shop away!" As he released her, she crumpled into a heap at his feet, sniveling. "She'll send me to jail—she said if I was to tell, I'd go to jail."

"And if you don't, you damned sure will! Do you know what it's like in Newgate, Mary?" he asked, his voice soft now. "Do you want to find out?"

"No! It wasn't me, m'lord—it was her—I just said what she told me t' say."

"But it was all lies, wasn't it?"

Mary Cummings rolled into a ball and wept piteously. "Ye can't send me t' jail—I can't go to jail."

"How much did she give you to besmirch my wife's name?" Reaching down, he caught her arm and forced her to stand. "How much, Mary? If I have to stand here until hell freezes, I'm not leaving until I know the truth. You can tell me now, or you can go to jail for perjuring yourself three times over, so the choice is yours." When she still didn't answer, he demanded again, "How much was it? Tell me, and I'll let you go."

"More'n I could ever make on me own," the woman answered piteously.

"How much?"

"Nigh t' three hundred pounds—'twas s'posed to be twice that, but when 'twas done, the old duchess said it wasn't worth any more, that if I was to complain, she'd see me charged with stealing what she'd already given me. She told me if I wasn't to leave, she'd put me in jail."

"So you lied under oath when you said my wife betrayed me."

"It wasn't all lies, my lord. The earl visited her at the Armitage."

"He never slept with her, Mary. He was as honorable a man as ever walked this earth, and you know it. You twisted everything that was said between them, didn't you?" When she wouldn't look at him, he asked her, "How could you do this to a woman who never said an unkind word to you? How could you do this to me? Do you have any idea the sort of pain you've caused?"

"The old duchess paid me a king's ransom," she whispered. "How was I t' turn it down?"

"A king's ransom? Hardly that. My mother spent more than that on one ball gown."

"'Twas more'n ten years wage t' me. It was enough for me to open me this shop. And I didn't know why I was supposed to lie, Your Grace—I didn't know I'd be tellin' it in court, and then when I was wantin' t' tell the truth, she said she'd see me hanged or worse. I was afraid to tell anybody then." Not daring to look at him, she hung her head. "It was supposed to turn ye against the young mistress, that was all. It wasn't just the money, Your Grace."

"I don't understand."

"Ye wasn't looking twice at me with her in the house."

"She was my wife." His jaw worked as he tried to master his temper. "All right," he said finally, "I won't press charges if you will tell me the whole. I want to know everything, Mary. I don't want you to spare me anything."

It was well past noon when Joanna came down the sweeping staircase to find John Barrasford waiting for her. He looked up, taking in her neatly knotted hair, the fine, straight features of her face, those lovely eyes, creamy neck and shoulders, the rose-sprigged muslin gown that clung to firm breasts before falling straight from the high-banded waist. It was as though he meant to fix her forever in his mind. It was not until she reached the bottom step that she noted the portmanteau and trunk sitting by the door.

"I wonder if I might be private with you for a moment, my dear?" he inquired soberly, his hand on the blue saloon door. When she nodded, he stepped back to let her pass, and then he followed, shutting the door behind them.

"Is anything amiss, Johnny?" Her heart thumped painfully as she asked. He was dressed for traveling, his masculine frame correctly covered in dove-gray coat, striped waistcoat, and black superfine trousers. His hat and cane lay on the table just within the door. There was a hint of sadness in his gray eyes, but the smile he gave her was warm.

"Naught's amiss that cannot be remedied by plain speaking, I think." He moved to the window facing the garden and looked out into the profusion of summer flowers. "You know, Joanna, I've often envied Roxbury for this place," he mused aloud for her benefit, "and now it seems that I must envy him for you."

"I beg your pardon?" She started guiltily and her eyes widened.

He turned back and met her eyes for a moment. "I think you must face the fact that you still love him, my dear," he told her quietly. "I know I have."

"But you cannot know that—Johnny, I am not even sure of that myself!" she burst out when she found her voice. "And he does not love me! If he did, he wouldn't speak of forgiveness. He'd be asking for it."

"Oh, my dear," he sympathized, "you may think you hate him, that you have merely reached some social discourse because of the boy, but even a blind fool would know otherwise."

"Johnny—"

"No. Hear me out, Joanna, for I've thought of naught else since I came and saw you together."

"When we came back from fishing? Johnny, we had quarreled!"

"No, it wasn't that, my dear—it is what passes between you every time you meet. There is that feeling that sets the two of you apart from everyone else in the room."

"Johnny—" She groped for words to refute him and found none. Finally she simply asked, "Is it your wish to cry off then?"

"No, my dear, but I believe that in your heart you do."

"I cannot love him," she whispered desperately. "I cannot—not after everything that has happened between us."

"Joanna." He moved closer and placed his hands on her shoulders. "I would wed you in a minute—will, if you still wish it—but I cannot think I can make you happy." He took in her stricken expression and his arms closed around her. She burst into tears against his shoulder. He stood for several minutes holding her, rubbing along her spine with the palm of his hand, soothing her until the tears subsided. Then he gently set her back and reached for his handkerchief. "No need to be in such a taking on my account, my dear," he reassured her, "for I'll come about—and so will you."

She turned away, her thoughts disordered and shattered. "But it is so impossible, Johnny. And what of Justin? Justin could never understand how it was—why he—? I cannot destroy his memory of Gary—I cannot. He's Gary's heir, not Adrian's."

"Justin's a little boy, Joanna, and will learn what he is taught. In time, you can tell him what happened, and by then he will accept it. Until then, why tell him anything? Let him love both of them. It won't matter."

"Won't matter? Johnny, Gareth Sherwood gave his name, his love—everything to Justin. I cannot take that away from either of them."

"That's not for me to say, my dear." He came up behind her, and his hands closed on her shoulders once again. "I wish you loved me, you know, but I understand." He squeezed her and released her. "Godspeed, Joanna."

"Godspeed, Johnny," she echoed hollowly.

Joanna stood rooted to the floor, unable to follow him. Outside, she heard his baggage collected, the closing of the front door, and a quick staccato of footsteps following him outside. Sinking into a chair, she realized she felt more grateful relief than anything. John Barrasford, gentleman that he was, had done what she should have done more than a week ago.

As his carriage drew up to the steps, Charlotte Finchley caught up to him. "My lord!" she called out. As he turned around, she hesitated, then she forced a small, crooked smile. "You must not blame Lady Carew, my lord," she said gently. "One cannot help where one loves, you know."

Her hazel eyes were large, luminous in her pale face, and wisps of damp hair clung to her forehead and temples. It crossed his mind that she was a pretty girl. "No, I suppose not," he answered, sighing. "I think I've known for some time."

"But it isn't easy to let go of one's dream, is it? Believe me, I quite understand that, my lord."

"No. She was what I wanted in a wife."

"She's so very beautiful."

"It was more than that. The Marriage Mart is filled with empty-headed beauties more interested in clothes and expensive fripperies than in the things that ought to matter. Joanna, on the other hand, has a genuine love for her children." He looked up, frowning into the sun. "I wanted to settle down, to rear my heirs in the bucolic tranquility of my Irish estates. I've done everything else, lived my salad days as fast as anyone, and I was ready for a wife and family."

"I know, my lord."

"I wanted someone capable of caring, someone capable of loving me and our children. I don't care if she's rich or poor, or if she isn't an Incomparable. Maybe that's why I admired Joanna so much—her wealth and her beauty did not hide an empty head or an empty heart. God, how I envy Roxbury for his damnable luck."

"You have your share of female admirers."

"And how many of them want to live in the country, surrounded by horses and children?" he countered.

Realizing that once he left now, she'd probably never see him again, Charlotte Finchley gambled her heart, her pride, and her life. "I would," she declared baldly. As he turned incredulous eyes to her, she fought the urge to run. "I should like it excessively." Biting her lower lip to still its quivering, she managed to nod. "My lord, I have loved you full half of my life."

"My God."

"As I said, one cannot help where one loves."

"How could that be? I mean, you scarce knew me when you were at Baxter Greys."

She could feel the hot tears welling in her eyes. "You were so kind to all of us—you were a Corinthian, and yet you were so kind." Knowing that she'd gambled and lost, she wiped her eyes with the back of her hand as she turned to go back inside. "Godspeed, my lord," she said, her throat aching.

"Miss Finchley—Charlotte—" She felt his hands on her shoulders, turning her back to him. "I had no idea," he admitted in understatement.

"I quite understand that I have made an utter fool of myself," she whispered. "Please forgive me."

He lifted her chin with his knuckle, forcing her to look into those incredibly beautiful grey eyes, giving her nowhere to hide from him. "I could certainly do a great deal worse," he said softly.

"Please do not be funning with me," she managed miserably.

"I want a house full of children, Charlotte."

"Now I know you are laughing at me."

"I assure you I am not." Bending his head to hers, he brushed his lips against hers. "Before we rush headlong into this, I want you to know what you'd be getting."

Her eyes widened and her heart gave a lurch in her chest. "You—you aren't laughing at me?"

"No. I'm deeply touched, Charlotte."

"I see."

"I want more than a schoolgirl tendresse, I hope you understand that."

It was as though he'd thrown cold water in her face. "Yes, of course—foolish me."

"And you've got a right to more than some notion of Galahad you've formed in your mind. We've got to know each other—we've got to trust each other."

"Yes."

"But more than anything else, we've got to love each other." As she opened her mouth to speak, he stilled her with a finger to her lips. "I mean that, Charlotte. Let us write to each other in hopes of discovering that love, my dear, and if we find it, we'll have the grandest wedding Baxter Greys has ever witnessed. If not, we'll cry friends forever."

"All right."

He enveloped her in a crushing embrace, kissing her thoroughly, leaving her utterly breathless. When he finally released her, she had to hold onto his arms to steady herself.

"I've got to go, but I will write. And once things are settled here, I'll be back to visit. Until then, God keep you, Charlotte."

"And you, my lord."

Smiling through an excess of tears, she managed to wave his carriage out of sight, then she turned and walked to the back of the house, where she took the servants' stairs up to her room. Alone, she hugged herself, unwilling to share her newfound love with anyone just yet.

Having had her own good cry, Joanna wiped her eyes with Johnny Barrasford's handkerchief, then pocketed it. It was as though another chapter of her life had ended.

"Mama?"

Robin's voice was tentative, curious even, as he peered around the open door. Joanna nodded and dropped to her knees as he scurried toward her. "Well, Master Robin—" She managed to smile. "Would you care to sail a paper boat in the fountain? Or shall we feed Roxbury's geese for him?"

"Feed the geese!"

"Maybe Miss Finchley would like to come with us, do you think? Or is she with Justin?"

"Finch's practicing letters with 'Tin, Mama."

"Well, then I suppose it will have to be just you and me, won't it? Go ask Cook for some bread crumbs and I shall change into better shoes."

She found Justin and his governess absorbed in their work while Anne busily plied her needle by an open window. Her mother-in-law, taking in her red-rimmed eyes, rose silently and followed her into the rose bedchamber.

"Joanna, my dear child, is everything all right?"

"Yes." Joanna threw open the wardrobe doors and searched on the shelf for her walking shoes. "Barrasford's gone, Maman," she murmured as she bent to pick them up. "It is decided that we shall not suit."

"You quarreled?"

"No. Johnny's far too much the gentleman for that, Maman. It is but that he believes I still love Dree."

"My dear—"

"The fault was mine," Joanna went on, "because 'tis true. I feel like such a heartless jade, fairly flinging myself at his head to keep Justin, Maman. But he did not task me with that at all."

"He'll come about," Anne reassured her.

"So he said."

"He's three-and-thirty, Joanna, and ready to settle down. I should not be surprised in the least if we were to hear from him again, and soon, for unless I mistake the matter, he feels a certain compassion for Charlotte."

"Miss Finchley? Really?"

"Miss Finchley," Anne repeated emphatically. "And why not, I ask you? They are not unknown to each other, and certainly her lack of fortune will not weigh with him. And she does like children."

"Miss Finchley would not even dream—"

"She's a female, Joanna—she would. So I would not be repining on Lord Barrasford's broken heart, my love, for ten to one, it will not be broken long."

"You seem pleased."

"I am—I never thought for a moment that you and Barrasford would suit."

Joanna sat on a low bench and fastened her shoes. "You haven't seen Dree today, have you?" she asked suddenly.

"I breakfasted with Roxbury before he left for someplace called Paxton Grove."

"Paxton Grove?"

"That's all he said on the subject, but I shouldn't think he'd be gone long, would you? I mean, there cannot be much business to attend to in something called Paxton Grove." Anne eyed the sturdy shoes with distaste. "Surely you do not mean to wear those here."

"Robin and I are going to feed the geese in the park."

"Well, I daresay one ought to be comfortable, of course, but—"

"Mama, can 'Bury come too?" Robin danced into the room carrying a sack of dried bread. "He just rode in— can he?"

"Well, I . . ." She looked up from her seat on the bench and her breath caught in her chest at the sight of him. He bent to pick up the small boy, hugging him affectionately before passing him to Anne.

"Not so quickly, infant. You go with your grandmama, and we'll be down directly. The geese won't starve, I promise, and I need to speak to Jo."

"Actually, Roxbury, I'll take him on to the park,"

Anne volunteered. "I haven't fed geese since you and Gary were grubby little boys yourselves."

"I want 'Bury!" the child protested.

"Of course you do," Anne murmured as she possessed his arms firmly and propelled him toward the door. "And I daresay that he'll be along to feed his share of the birds." She stopped just long enough to close the door carefully.

Joanna sat very still, her heart pounding as he came nearer. Her mouth was dry when he stopped in front of her, his body blocking everything else from view. Her fingers gripped the edges of the bench.

"Can you ever forgive me, Jo?" he asked quietly.

Her eyes widened in stunned disbelief.

"I've been to see Mary Cummings today, and now I know the whole. I know what happened—I know what my mother did to you—what I did to you—and I wish I could make up for everything." He moved closer still, until his leg touched her knee. "I'd give anything I have to be able to go back those years and do it differently, Jo." His hand touched her hair tentatively, resting lightly on her crown. "I've been such a fool—such a proud, bloody fool."

She closed her eyes and swallowed hard to fight the lump that formed in her throat. "Please, Dree—"

"I've no right to expect anything, I know," he went on, "but I love you, Jo. I've always loved you, and I always will." His fingers closed on her chin, forcing it up. "Can you ever forgive me?" he asked again as he released her.

Her lashes were wet, her throat unbearably tight, so tight she couldn't speak. Instead, she nodded and leaned forward to slide her arms tightly around his waist. it was as though the years of bitterness faded as she touched him. For a long time, she merely rested her cheek against the hard, flat plain of his belly and held on. His hands crept to smooth and stroke the shining crown of her head.

"I want to marry you again, Jo," he said finally. "I want to take you to London and shout to the *ton* that you have been wronged, that you were the innocent one. We may not have a friend in the world when we start, but I'll do my damnedest to see you are received everywhere."

"It doesn't matter," was the muffled reply.

"Doesn't matter!" he choked out. Pulling her up roughly against him, he closed his arms around her shoulders. "Of course it matters! You are the Duchess of Roxbury, Jo—my duchess!" He stopped suddenly and looked down. "You are going to marry me again, aren't you?"

"Oh, Dree . . ." She had to bite her lower lip to still the trembling, but she managed to smile mistily. "You know I am."

His lips met hers, tenderly at first, tentatively savoring the taste of her, and then it was summer in London, the Season glorious with the promise of youth, the music seductive, and the breeze fragrant as they explored again the wonder of each other. It was a long time before he raised his head.

"I'll send Sims over to fetch the vicar from Greenlea. If you do not mind it, I'd like to be married here today."

"Today? But my hair—"

"I stopped by the bishop's on the way home and obtained a Special License."

"But today? Dree—"

"I want to share your life and your bed from this moment on. What do you say?"

"Oh, yes—yes. But, Dree, whatever will we tell Justin?"

"Whatever you wish, Jo. If you want, I'll say nothing until he's older and can understand somewhat. He's

Gary's heir now, and somehow that doesn't seem right because of Robin, but if that's the way you wish it, I'll accept that." An unholy light crept into his dark eyes. "I don't expect to have any dearth of heirs here, you know."

"As warlike as Robin is, he'll probably prefer a military career to a title, anyway," she murmured, raising her lips to his again. "Kiss me, Dree." As his arms tightened around her shoulders once more, she felt as though her heart had come home.